Toscanelli's Ray is a brave and wonderfully ambitious book, a meditation on memory, identity and history. It is both a love song to the city of Florence, its ancient beauty and tangled history, and a clear-eyed examination of the cracks and fissures that the new millennium has thrust upon it. In the course of a single day, Wilde-Menozzi's remarkable characters (including a long-dead Etruscan woman) circle, engage, damage and heal each other in ways that never cease to surprise. This is a novel of big ideas, one that raises provocative questions about immigration, difference and culture—even our notion of time itself, and simultaneously it is a novel full of the stuff of life—passion, guilt, betrayal, politics, and marriage. A stunning accomplishment, and Wilde-Menozzi's generous heart and lucid intelligence illuminate each page.

☀ Kathleen Cambor, *The Book of Mercy*

Wallis Wilde-Menozzi's stunning novel digs deep to unearth the new Italian mosaic: the Americans and Florentines are still here, alongside the Etruscans, but so are the Nigerians, and the Eastern Europeans. Can Florence rise again to spark a new renaissance? Her intricately woven narratives, tough and elegant, illuminate the afterlife of the humanist dream as only the best fiction can.

☀ Askold Melnyczuk, *The House of Windows*

Toscanelli's Ray is an epic tale set in Florence with its ancient glory, its new graffiti, its bourgeoise, expatriates and illegal immigrants. Through rich mosaic-like fragments we glimpse the utter strangeness of our own lives in the twenty-first century. Voices from the global south, lives lived at the edge, in penury, without papers force a new reckoning of what Europe might be. Wallis Wilde-Menozzi's language is iridescent, her grasp of the complexity of human time so sure, her sense of intimacy unerring.

☀ Meena Alexander, *Fault Lines*

Modern fiction often adopts Dante's populous weaving of human destinies: Melville's whaler deck, or Woolf's dining table in *Mrs Dalloway*. Happily this novel renews the contract. Farina, the Nigerian child at its focus, is also the flour whose name crosses from Latin into Italian and English. Of course she comes to matter intensely, but so does the annua solar event in the Duomo which makes this writer's global Florence int our Chichen Itza, Chaco Canyon, or Montségur: a shrine to alignmen amid spinning flow, at one moment and one angle visible. "The solutic the song, the prayer was the child. Farina. The light that needed to extended."

☀ John Peck, *Contradance*

TOSCANELLI'S RAY

Also by Wallis Wilde-Menozzi

Mother Tongue, An American Life in Italy (memoir)

The Other Side of the Tiber, Reflections on Time in Italy (nonfiction)

L'oceano è dentro di noi (essays)

Heron Songs (poetry)

Toscanelli's Ray

Wallis Wilde-Menozzi

Cadmus Editions
San Francisco

Toscanelli's Ray copyright © 2013 by Wallis Wilde-Menozzi

Cover photograph and details, page 1 and page 201
copyright © 2013 by Franco & Francesco Furoncoli
Photographs within text and back cover
  copyright © 2013 David Battistella

Printed in the United States

Chapter Two appeared as "Brunelleschi's Dome,"
Notre Dame Review, No. 32, Summer/Fall 2011

Part of Chapter Three appeared as "Sitting at Rivoire Café,"
Hawaii Pacific Review, Fall 2012

The ten lines of Montagu Slater's libretto for Benjamin Britain's opera, *Peter Grimes*, have been reproduced by permission of Boosey & Hawkes Music Publishers, Ltd., © COPYRIGHT 1945 BY BOOSEY & HAWKES MUSIC PUBLISHERS LTD.

First Edition / Spring 2013

Cadmus Editions
Post Office Box 126
Belvedere Tiburon
California 94920
http://www.cadmuseditions.com
email: jeffcadmus@aol.com

Library of Congress Cataloging-in-Publication Data

Wilde-Menozzi, Wallis.
  Toscanelli's ray / Wallis Wilde-Menozzi. -- First edition.
    pages cm
  Includes bibliographical references.
  ISBN 978-0-932274-74-8
  1. Summer solstice--Fiction. 2. Santa Maria del Fiore (Cathedral : Florence, Italy)--Fiction. 3. Florence (Italy)--Fiction. 4. Interpersonal relations--Fiction. 5. Social psychology--Fiction. 6. Psychological fiction. I. Title.
  PS3563.E54T67 2013
  813'.54--dc23
                    2012049272

                10 9 8 7 6 5 4 3 2 1

If I shall touch that workman's arm with some ethereal light;
    if I shall spread a rainbow over his disastrous set of sun;
    then against all mortal critics bear me out in it,
    thou just Spirit of Equality, which has spread
    one royal mantle of humanity over all my kind.

—Herman Melville, *Moby Dick*

Go right on and listen as you go.

—Dante Alighieri, *Purgatory*, Canto 5, line 45

There would seem to be nothing more obvious,
    more tangible and palpable, than the present moment.
And yet it eludes us completely.

—Milan Kundera, *The Art of the Novel*

Already waiting in the clearing
the single image of light.
The day that you see this
is the day you will become it.

—Sun Bu-er 1124 CE

TO CLARE

CHAPTERS

THE MOON, MATERNAL, a luminous spectacle itself, is holding its milky light over the cathedral. Rising like a hill proclaiming earth and weight, the dome, with its own bright moon, looks like a massive tope, full of mysteries. Moonlight stays on its eight long marble ribs turning them whiter than they are. The strong light smoothly etches each red tile and catches in between the herringbone lines also flooded by electric spotlights. How steadily and freely it comes, the reflected light. This evening on the Via Riccasoli, the shop windows curving round Santa Maria del Fiore are almost as bright as they are in the day. Yet the bright flow of light also pushes shadows. Lifts them. Uncovers what might have hoped to hide. There in full view, near the north chapel, not far from the sculpted Madonna in the almond shell, sprawls a beggar. Another one.

Passed out. And look at his feet. Blackened by filth and city life, his nails curve like talons. His heels underneath split with dry, deep cracks.

Eyesore. Criminal. Sufferer. Refugee.

All night long, unless the police pull him in, people passing the Duomo will find words and cast them in his direction as they cross his path in the moonlight. Next to his beer bottle is an identity card. Look, he is wearing a cloak. It is made of bark. Bark, like cloth from a tree. The identity card is torn. Grimy. As grimy as he is. *Firenze.* It can't be his. Florence, it says.

TWO

I NEVER TIRE OF LOOKING at Brunelleschi's dome.
Its rough red-tile hump inches up near the window and
inhabits the sitting room, like the back of a rhino. Its massive red curve almost rubs off on the floor. Even on the
darkest days, when the street below is pressed by motorcycles
and garbage trucks, slick rain and rabid shouts, its glow reaches
the window like a sun made by man. Luck abounded to offer
up this apartment temporarily in a city of life-long contracts.
Florentines know that Americans find Italy cheap and will be
content even with a dark atmospheric hole. Yet I pay very little
for this noisy jewel belonging to a *principessa*. And the view is
Brunelleschi's dome at the end of the street. As unlikely as it
seems, I found the address on a hand-printed card on a board
at the university.

As a visitor it's natural to try to snatch some of the city's
sublimity for the hard landing back at home. Just place
Florence's frisson of beauty and strength in the eyes of a man
used to the greens and grays of a recent suburb of Des Moines.
For whom red-tile means imitation Victorian state university
architecture. You probably can understand how the luck of
landing in this apartment endows me with a specialness. Since
May, the dome has been my own possession. An immeasurable

upgrade. A cultural waking dream. Every hour of the day and night its planetary glow leans into the room and unloads a sense of belonging.

Fifteen years ago, I used to feel at home in the national Florentine archives; it's true the original storage in the Uffizi didn't even have electric lights. Fear of fire. The idea of moving all these records came with the '66 flood and the ruin it brought. Then it took twenty years to make it happen. The workers are a little faster now but I feel uprooted and not because the building is new or even that I am middle-aged. Something intrinsic is missing. The director is harder to find, but he's still dapper in linen and citing Foucault as the way to understand these documents. The familiar oak tables are gone, but what's changed is the atmosphere. It's a rat race to keep a chair.

For a historian like me, changes are work for my mind. It's ironic to hear bitterness about a struggle with fiscal issues we academics faced back in the seventies. Italians pretend they have never heard of budgets. Some of my gripes are with the two young Canadian researchers. They have checked out a rarely cited *foglio* on slavery in fourteenth century Florence and kept it from me for more than two weeks. One or the other— he has braces on his teeth and she awful tobacco stained fingers—is always there when the door opens. We are competing for the same plague records. They succeed because no one holds them to the rules. But I suspect this is symptom rather than cause. License is widespread. People here seem aggressive and confused.

Tonight, sitting in the dark, bathed by the intruding glow of Brunelleschi's triumph, swirling the ice in my whiskey, my feet up, it's still more than possible to feel my problems shrink. Not so long ago I read that the only manmade feature of the earth visible from the moon was the spine of baked bricks from the many defensive walls of China. I was surprised then to find that Florence's dome didn't reach as far as the astronauts' vision.

Imagine later discovering that the story of the Great Wall's visibility was a *montatura*, as they say here in Florence. The story was invented, appealing, but not true. I don't know why the press didn't check it out at the time. But the story seized the popular imagination. And that is the link with Brunelleschi's dome. Nothing built by human beings can be seen from the moon. The dome's eternity, all the learning and struggle and triumph of its standing, doesn't extend even that far. My wife, Janet, might subscribe to that. Especially now that I have taken a three-month sabbatical, leaving her and our daughter, Melissa, who is at a delicate age. Don't get me wrong. Janet values history, but she would add, most life has not been told, starting from the reality of the family, which she never slights. Yet Brunelleschi's massive project changed Florence and the world. With each buckled ring upwards he gave a new shape to the unknown. This touches me deeply.

The nothing-counts yawn looking down from the moon doesn't hold. When Brunelleschi and Ghiberti were at each other's throats, competing for the dome's design, undermining each other, the whole of Florence pulsed with the atmosphere that competition brings. And that probably is what's changed. I realize that I had not experienced that heat before as I toiled in the archives, expecting privilege, expecting to be nearly alone in my task. Fifteen years ago as an American scholar, I was barely troubled by others, who didn't have my funds. Now the *Archivio* is packed with threadbare academics from eastern Europe and lots of western ones with grants large enough to curry the director's favor. And we Americans are no one's darlings. But that, in itself, is not reason to be so uncertain. I'm beginning to fear that I am looking for the wrong documents. And that I can't admit. The number of foreigners, not tourists, makes me wonder whether right before my eyes I am really seeing a shift as profound as what became ever so slowly the Dark Ages. Whether underneath the restlessness of Florentines are deep fault-lines started by the collapse of the Soviet Union. Whether I, too, am hoping for research stories that have been surpassed. Art history is in and economic history is out. But the loss of a point of view goes far deeper.

Tomorrow, I'll have been here two months. At noon, Toscanelli's great gnomon, once a dream of unity for the Catholic Church, will be used. Brunelleschi's dome is the place. The ray, after five-hundred years, will be late in striking the floor because the axis of the earth's tilt has moved. The meridian itself is a relic. The bronze meridian and marble disc in the floor are covered by chairs, so I've only seen it in books. Yet Toscanelli's derelict science is still a source of wonder and research. I've heard that the ray coming out of darkness, having pierced the lantern's small hole, dropping through the gnomon's lip, is applauded every year. Surpassed but undefeated by other measurements. I feel as if I need its blessing. After all, the measurement announces summer. Late suppers in restaurants. Sunflowers doing head-turning exercises in the fields. But change as well. And light as learning. Spheres' intrinsic orders. It's not overcast tonight. Tomorrow, who knows? The ray might not be visible. But I'm curious, hopeful. I have another month in Florence. Time enough to re-enter the race for the plague statistics, if I can settle down.

Bufo Bufo would be the name in an encyclopedia. The species name for Italy's common toad. And it is a nice name in itself. Bufo in Italian, with just one more f, can mean funny or silly. But this toad has been named by Susan Notingham, the woman whose garden he lives in, above Florence, in the vegetable part beyond the endives and radicchio, near the tomato plants, catching with his hurling tongue that unwinds and then winds like a yo-yo, the flies he reels in. This toad is called Virgil, although he has no name for himself, nor name for his ten vaguely webbed toes, nor for his orange knobs carried like two trunks, which hold unused poisons. Unused, at least until now, they wait for instincts to transform into sudden weapons that might see him through terror. Virgil is awake and his entire body is distantly tingling. The hand-sized toad knows the beat like a sleepwalker. Skin time, changing skin time, dull, tugging toil time. He's done the travail twice. Without moving his soft white belly, he absorbs the unsettling urgent message telling him to rise. The navy blue sky studded with silver stars is not yet nearing light. Cool air rises from the clods, pointed and graded by Signor Luzi, Susan Notingham's gardener. The black diamonds of Virgil's pupils photograph the moon-driven shadows shortening. A southerly wind bows the silhouettes of the cypresses here and then scatters them there.

A few hours ago, before pulling the shutters closed in the living room, Susan Notingham leaned on her elbows out of the window and marveled audibly at the almost full moon. On the olive groves it shone a bright path, a gorgeous silver cloak netting the terraces. The terraces and then that ring of darkness and then below the lights of Florence winking and thick with color like any modern city. It was a pity to close the window, but now even in summer she pulled the wooden shutters tight and snapped the iron bars through the locks. It was paralyzing to be frightened, but ever since she had entered the garden and found an unshaven man sleeping under a tree in full daylight, she realized the immigrants were coming closer, however much she wanted to feel sympathetic. It was surprise she felt and sympathy when the supine man rose from his sleep, raised his arms like a huge kestrel, and screamed, poor devil, before jumping over the stone wall and dropping eight feet into the next yard. Stumbling, he was gone. But the sympathy faded when she thought about the tall, emaciated man, with baggy pants, who probably meant to enter the house. The years were over when the wiry woman felt absolutely safe in the villa with cars slowing underneath her window, shifting gears, climbing up the isolated road.

Her daughter, Marina, still not home, Susan, in a silk robe that gave comfort by its being wrapped closely around her, hands plunged into her pockets, entered the study and felt her own breathing. Her neck ached from the last session. The room, like the slow to brighten light bulbs, was always an extra duty at night, and strange in the dark, an office off-limits. The large standing sandbox and some metal shelves crammed with objects, the hub of her work and center of her office, otherwise furnished with imposing bookshelves and leaded glass, those odd professional notes and the spare sandbox behind the couch always made the room look like the half nursery, half laboratory that it was. A place between day and night. A space between illness and health. Repentance and salvation. Pain and giving it a shape.

On the desk the picture of Marina shaking a head of infant curls caught her eye. It was Marina who insisted the early family be displayed. The complexity nagging around her daughter's upbringing was like living with a trick knee. For Susan it was her never knowing how much weight to put on Marina. How far with yes, how far with no. Photo after photo of Luigi and she holding Marina, beach pail and sailor hat, she and Luigi watching Marina bent over the black and white keys. Grouped in silver frames like an archipelago of smiles, young faces, before the divorce gave them more definition. Luigi with hair covering his ears, Susan with locks to her waist. Who were those two young bodies sharing a child? By now they should have been lying flat in a drawer.

The digital clock's red numbers jumped. The tasteless plastic box, used to alert patients of the session's end, purposefully stood guard between Freud's collected works and Jung's. This hour of no-child-but-a-young-woman-who-was-probably-in-bed-with-Carlo was one that Susan accepted, but it unsettled her and made her wish for someone in the leather chair facing her, a partner for consolation, not a lover, not Vaclav examining desire's three manifestations, no, just normal domestic understanding—a back rub, a glass of red wine—to restore the late evening without a telephone call to the less dramatic perspective of a daughter's thoughtlessness, a shrug.

The official reason the trim red-haired woman stood rubbing her own shoulders in the large room—the low energy light bulb now fully heated and shining on the two red leather chairs—was to put the sandbox back in order. One rule was never to leave the last patient's story in full view to sit overnight. Restoring the sandbox was not like doing dishes or bed-making. It was of an order like putting operating instruments away. The scene had been photographed, filed. Here was a battleground, here body and soul struggled to stammer through wordless sand. Signora Picci's heavy mud tunnels still humped like military bunkers in the box. Let's let the energy go, Susan said as she raked the lumps into soft ripples. She had half a mind to open the window. So much suspicion and despair lay trapped in the tunnels of the Signora's idea about marriage. So little vision of her emerging feet.

The aluminum sides of the box painted blue showed chips and dents in the muted light. Little desert, she said. Ocean, she said. Patience. Even years of it. The light made the whole tray look worn out and shadows fell behind each little ridge. The sand needed sieving. The last day's objects needed to be soaked in Lysol and left to dry. The elephant, for example, was inexplicably muddy, but not just the elephant. The pipe-stem palm trees looked wilted. Before tomorrow afternoon, all the figures, the Noah's arc of animals, the flora and fauna, the royal couples, all the players in the dramas of her patients should be sorted by category. Snakes with snakes. Birds with birds. Car light intruded and slowly dragged across the wall. Hoping the light might be Marina returning, as the discs floated away leaving the bookshelves in their muted shadows, Susan knew there was nothing left for her to fuss with. Although she could pull the Persephone statue from among the knit chimps.

At this same hour. A conundrum that drove the Florentine mathematician and astrologer Toscanelli to take up the maddening problem of Easter around the world in the fifteenth century, a problem that will be remembered in Brunelleschi's dome at noon tomorrow, at this same hour, Luigi Dell' Istante has just taken off his long socks, rolling them like skinny inner tubes down his legs, and decided to go to bed. He was Susan's husband for twelve years and, in those years, and the fourteen years since he has made an international name in forestry, but the years have been lived as if he is a moth flying against a screen. Luigi's life has never been one he could recognize as his own. Rocking on the edge of the mattress, he punches the button that dials Maria Grazia's number again. She was his curly brown-haired student and now she is waiting for a child. He wants to hear her voice, which can be more than soothing, her succulent tones can reach into his pockets, whisper in his ears, hum his whole body into an energetic healthy anticipation. Of something. Of him. Of them. Her voice can drown out the vast and steady creeping uneasiness that surrounds him. Only now it is a shrew's voice, a file that wears him down, a laser beam with aims and ends that are not his. It is indignant, surprised. Pushy, it pushes him until his heart begins to pound. Luigi looks at his cordless phone. He will call, although he feels the tip tap of defeat on his shoulders. His feet twitch as if they are wondering when to begin pacing. The shift. The shift is what nearly fells him, making it a mistake to open the telephone channel.

I called to say goodnight. He is looking at himself in the mirror, studying the two dark pouches under his eyes.

What do you want me to say?

Something sweet. Now he has noticed an ashen quality under his high cheekbones. The whole face is withering.

Like what?

That you would like me there in bed. The tall man hesitated, staring now at fear in his eyes, shifting like dull wolves as he felt her silence as sarcasm. He thought of how he might appeal. He smiled, tried pulling his lips up, vaguely nodding to the indisputably fifty-year-old face in front of him. He thought of a phrase, 'white thighs' but the words caught like a stale joke. An awkwardness already prepared itself for her merited dismissal.

Don't bother, the voice said. It dipped as if it were hurt. You know every day is a cross for me. Not just the marks on the calendar but a real cross. As her voice began to slip out from under her, Maria Grazia pushed the 'off' button, and sat down in the broad horsehair chair, where the magazine still lay open. Her brown eyes looked sadly at the phone. It was so unexpected the emptiness she had been handed. I hate phones, she said, biting a nail, as she returned to the open page. Pears dipped in chocolate. Sounded delicious. As did the wheels of sliced oranges soaked in maraschino. Maria Grazia wished the spectacles would cheer her up, as the pages one after another led her towards beautiful tables laden with colored fruits even built into marzipan towers to look like Giotto's. The magazine was not her idea. It was her mother's not very subtle way of suggesting a wedding. Maria Grazia didn't really care about that. She hadn't fully realized until she was carrying the child, that she would feel so serious about its thrilling flutter, so pulled to its challenging potential life, even when she was in the lab preparing gels. The wedding wasn't the issue. It was Luigi's unwillingness to be a father to her child.

Maria Grazia felt the child quiver like a brave guppy. A noble Argonaut in the salty brine of her new body. The crackers she carried in her backpack for waves of nausea. Her swollen breasts. Rationally she knew the symptoms were temporary, but the fluid shifting inside endowed her with a sense of being in an ocean. Of swimming with no shore in sight. Maybe that was natural. The pain and disruption of the changes, the inability to settle and enjoy the mounting eruption, came from his unpredictable shallowness. The baby was not a parthenogenic creature. He had a father, who was scared to death. Who had seemed connected to her but even more to his own obdurate and untrivial concerns. Who sought her opinion about sampling designs for the cypresses. Who used to make love in strong, ardent strokes, kissing beautifully, groaning and swaying as lonely became private and then a shared word that he let melt.

So why more and why rush on in this Florence? The rushing, that's nearly television. It's a bad habit, the inability to stop and linger, to live without making some basic connections. Italian TV, especially since the commercial channels were given an illegal way to come into existence, they have changed Florentines a lot. The new channels bought lots of films from America, and gave up a rhythm of dullness and familiarity as place. The government channels used to show so often a Totò film where the angular starving man stuffs stolen spaghetti into his pockets, into his hair, letting it hang from his mouth that the rite could be seen as a form of Mass. Hunger. Poverty was an everyday theme. Its slaps were everyone's life. Poverty was one of the keys to the nation. Now on TV, one hour focused on Luigi and Susan and Marina and Maria Grazia would be soap opera. About wealth. That's what people watch. The story would be about Maria Grazia, and whether she would marry in a filmy white gown with a reception like those in the food magazines. Then four minutes of commercials and then local news. 'Dallas' has influenced the news, juicing it up with human-interest stories. One minute and ten seconds on that woman whose purse has just been snatched. Then the pathos of a fire started by an old pensioner abandoned by family and living alone. Then two minutes on a new Arab rock group. And then maybe, squeezed in on an opinion show following a brawling raucous chest-thumping program on soccer and large patches of publicity, a documentary on prostitution. Or even Nigeria and its oil. And now, of course in this minute, no bombs, just how Bosnia is faring. And then back to Florence, with its parking problems, and tax evasion problems. And then commercials. And the judges. The judges. It's a new rhythm and young people like it.

Centuries ago when Dante told his story about Florence, a sense of good and evil, within a person but also from above, defined life in the city. No one was immune. In his spiral of hell, all classes from all walks of life from emperors to Cardinals to poor Paolo and Francesca are held in place by moral measure. Now in Florence, where in Dante's time the civil war created centuries of confusion, the climate of confusion is ideology's sudden collapse and the long practice of corruption made naked by judges suddenly challenging it. The new climate is creating something new in politics. Something is forming but who is listening? Even the Pope can be switched off and then soccer or those girls in brief panties and bras come on. Publicity is stronger in some ways than the news. People who had nothing or little for so long can buy the envy they've felt forever. They can roam by changing channels. They can try to make themselves into the person who fits in the Ferrari or the girl who meets boy by answering her *telefonino*. But the news that once seemed outside of an ordinary life, when one had time to believe a life was real and even to long that the news events made by others were closer, those days are gone in Florence.

In the Cafe Giubbe Rosse, where Luigi and GianFranco, his friend, used to spend long hours of their adolescence, in the rear room, the walls are papered with manifestos and photos of Italian intellectuals like Montale in the troubled years before Stalin and Churchill and Roosevelt finally divided the world up from short lists in their pockets and the women in Italy still couldn't vote. Those times have evaporated in the speed of television. The cafe is a shell of nostalgia: the bar with newspapers hanging on hooks. They hang with current headlines, but they are a picture of the past. Luigi Dell'Istante's mother Giada often talked about casting a ballot for DeGaspari, when the soldiers at the polling places stood, nervously, as if they were on guard for war. The young shaved faces were old enough to feel fear remembering the ache of no supper, and the running pop of machine guns, and the stink of charred beams and rubble burnt by bombs falling from the sky. They stood at attention hoping there would be no attempt on that historic day to re-ignite an undeclared civil war. But in this Florence, who even votes? For poverty? Some of the men and some of the women, but not the young. They vote for success. For the bald man who made it. In this television city, it's not the past exactly that needs renewal. It's the present that needs enlarging. There's amnesia in Florence in 1994 and an ominous silence.

Prostitution in 1994 must be our next image. Prostitution is by no means new. People still unthinkingly call it the oldest profession. And it is shockingly old. But now it is back with a twist that is even more shocking and older. Slavery. Thousands of immigrant women are indentured to get papers and sold as slaves. Only a few weeks ago, Susan got very upset by the indifference. She was talking with a friend, Marge Brunstom, an English teacher, comfortable and sincerely separated from the life around her, who brought it up as a danger to herself. They were sitting in the Cafe Rivoire, facing the broad wonderful space where a copy of Michelangelo's marble David was placed to brood and Marge Brunstom said,

Those women bring in violence. They pass on AIDS. And they could break their bonds, as far as I can tell. I think they should be all shipped back. Rope them and put them on boats.

Susan was surprised by the detachment and nonchalance, the two of them sitting in the piazza, so surprised that as her emotions rose and her face reddened, she pushed her lemon slice down so hard with her spoon that her tea spilled.

Did you burn yourself?

Susan didn't ever feel close to Marge, and now with that straw sunhat making her look more colonial than ever, she couldn't keep herself still. Her temper flared and she even raised her voice so that an old couple at the next table looked away, as Marge blotted with napkins.

Their fault? What do we know about prostitutes? It's the Italian men if anything. Or even the Italian women, the wives who let it go on. But that's not what I meant to say. We project our shadows, don't we, upon others? Isn't the world we see inside of us?

Marge opened her eyes wide. Susan, I didn't expect to get into a fight. Shadows. I find that jargon.

What do we know about danger and poverty? It scares us. The harder a life is, Marge, the harder it is to get away.

Really, Susan, you never get beyond being intense. You wouldn't want one living next door would you?

In a room not far from the freeway near the exit Florence North, where the Michelucci cathedral rises, so dingy now, covered by years of car exhaust, where it was once a soaring wing of futuristic statement, on a street where laundry flaps from balconies in heavily loaded lines that recall Italian neo-realist cinema, the late forties and the whole of the fifties, when Italy was trying to recover from the war, on the way out of starving, but no-where near comfortable, when heating and indoor toilets were being added to the outside of buildings, now, a young child with brown skin, a girl of a little more than three and one-half years, is sleeping. If you say the color of maple syrup or the color of a deer or the color of Gauguin's women or the color of a monk's robe, you are already setting up a way of seeing Farina, for that is her name. But it is not her context. A brown child the slightly washed color of dust in Port Harcourt, the color of dust lightening mud brown feet, is her color. It is not surprising that this delicate child with deep-set eyes and thin legs and arms is an echo of color from that Nigerian city. That is the city her mother, Milli, left from, when she paid Madame Bette to come to Europe to be a hairdresser. A hairdresser. Oh yes, that was what she agreed to. Europe. Italy. Curling. Cornrows. Wink. Wink. Bathtubs with gold faucets. That was what she agreed to when she paid to be sold.

Farina is sleeping in the corner, on a small canvas cot. She doesn't even suck her thumb. Her mother Milli hasn't come home, although no one knows that she's been held by the police, and is in the Questura, her head bobbing off to sleep as she sits on a bench, with a female guard nearby writing at a desk. She is nodding off next to an Afghanistani, who has been caught with a knife and two grams of heroin. He smells bad and is shoeless, his soles like cracked hooves, and Milli has moved down to the other end of the bench. Irene, Milli's friend, another prostitute, more independent than Milli, a gypsy, strange to say it but she, too, took her chances and became an ex-gypsy from Romania, is sleeping on a cot near Farina. Nylons hung on strings are an eerie screen of limp legs dangling. The shadows are shorter than the stockings and they give an oppressive complication to a room that is mostly bare. As bare as a convent, the simple cots and the wooden table, and Igor, an Albanian who never stops smoking, there with a green lamp lit, is sitting next to the phone. Matrushka, a tall Russian with a wild head of blond hair, throws her belt with its silver buckle full of plastic opals crashing to the floor. She's been mauled and short-changed. Her fury is nothing new. The clatter makes Farina turn in her sleep. Her face seen up close is damp from the heat of the June night trapped by the shut windows. Small beads across her cheeks. Over her upper lip. Asleep, her oval face seems distended, wise, there is no other word for a serenity that makes the child's features look old and deliberate, the broad mouth with pearly baby teeth puckered almost in a smile.

At this same hour. That was the dream of Toscanelli's science. Placing a meridian line on the floor of the cathedral, using the most exact measurements and letting it be struck by a ray, which would then announce the summer solstice. *At this same hour.* In Port Harcourt, where Milli's son and her father live, near the equator, there is only one hour of difference; being west of Florence it is earlier. In Minneapolis, where Charlotte, Susan's widowed mother lives, it is seven hours earlier. But this story hums and moves in Florence.

In this hour it is still night in Florence. Slightly muggier night in Port Harcourt. Before supper in Minneapolis. But there is one sun over the earth and it is this sun that inspired so much thinking about time. It is this sun that was one possibility for telling time, along with the moon, until mechanical time comes in, and today when the sun rises in Florence, sending its longest rays out into the terraced fields and taps Virgil telling him the day to change his skin has arrived, when the sun will have skittered on the second floor of casa Michelangelo and eventually climbed and fallen through the lantern in Brunelleschi's dome and, still moving, lands in the north chapel of the Duomo on the meridian, officially it will be summer.

Early sunlight will slant across the river statue in the first room of Michelangelo's house, the first room off the stairs. It will pool and glide on the statue's belly and then be moved on by the earth's spinning, as if light were water. The River god is the only model of Michelangelo's that is known to exist. Michelangelo didn't call the River god the Arno, but why not? The Arno runs through Florence, so why not call the strong brownish god-body made of sticks and mud the Arno? The dark night Arno that is floating with the images of globed lamps on the streets and the bridges, the strong channel dividing the city, the Arno that will weave the rays of today's sun when it rises. The one ray that will pass through a small hole in the Duomo after one in the afternoon will be off the mark put in the floor in 1510 to receive it. Off and yet this ray will strike the floor and its light will dance like a struck match. The ray will have to travel still to Port Harcourt and on and on to Minneapolis but unheralded and not telling the same time. The hour that the Catholic Church wanted to regularize all over the earth so that Easter could be celebrated in the same moment cannot be, ever, the same. Time in Florence is its own.

And this is all. And the story is being told in English. If it were being told in Italian, it would have to start with Dante. He told Florence as a real place seen from inside the soul's need, the voice of witness, and the endless spiraling love of God. And Vasari told Florence from the point of view of genius and its sufficiency. But this Florence in English is no longer being told by men with voices like Henry James who knew that darkness was a metaphor in Italy, who observed that Italians were full of inner tunnels where they faked and turned. It is not being measured by the social scales of Edith Wharton. The story like the ray has shifted, because the angle of the earth's axis has shifted and the idea of unity has shifted. The sun and the moon no longer define it. What is a day or a Florentine when Luigi can fly to Vancouver to explore a birch tree-tribe with DNA script and go through the sunrise coming up twice, while Farina, who has no papers for any city or country sometimes lives the whole day inside the closed room without seeing the sun. Once the Greeks refined their tragedies until Iphegenia could cry, 'look the sun is setting', and the line was timed to be said as the ball of fire sank in the red and enflamed sky.

Now television gives that sensation of realism, without the

awe of order. The face of Calvi, the Italian banker hung and found under Blackfriars Bridge in London, or the dark bruised face of Moro, head of the Italian Christian Democrats, spilling out of the trunk, dead, these terrifying images come at not quite the same minute but almost the same as when they happened. But these instant stories are not theatre. Not at all. And the stories are not built from unities but facts that have been ripped from contexts, trimmed, edited, and yet insisting on their place in reality. The story of Susan and Milli and Marina is a story, like the ray in the cathedral that no longer hits the circle at the right time. But this experience can never be television or publicity. It is not a product trying to elicit envy. Perhaps empathy. Consciousness. Realities' overlaps. That is the story's zone and resolution, an awareness, like a piece of music, to return to. About a specific place.

When a phone rings, think of what that means in Florence. A phone is not a heartstring. Nor is it emotion. But it can carry those things immediately like a hot flame. However the phone now won't necessarily have a cord, whereas even ten years ago, many Florentines waited for party lines, or stood in booths with sacks of metal slugs, hoping for a switchboard operator to connect them for a few minutes to another city. So expensive then when your money came from five olive trees and a string of vines, Susan's neighbor, Signora Caffo, after she put in the coins, fifty, clink, clink, clink, found herself speechless when she heard her sister's voice, shouting from Calabria. Often she just banged the receiver down, standing there on a country road, in the booth below the hill near Susan's house. Trembling, she was awestruck by a dry voice that sounded like sheep and rocks and oregano, not like her sister, Vesta, who once shared a bed.

Luigi Dell'Istante turned out the light and under the linen sheet he feels its scratching weight covering him like a shroud. Before he can review the latest reminder of the friction that is spreading, even down the corridors of the institute where he can feel gossip waiting on the lips of congregating students, Maria Grazia having allies in many of the other researchers, he falls asleep.

The dream starts in the umbrella factory, not the shop on the Corso that got built in the early seventies, but where Grandpa Umberto used to stand with the women with peddle sewing machines. There are muddy paths. Out behind the slanted windows, open, with the flies, Luigi peeks into the dark shed with carcasses, the smell overwhelming of ammonia and rot. His mother, it seems like his mother, the hump, but he can only see her from the back. She is white-haired and old, now lurching toward him to tell him to stay out of the shed. It's a surprise how she knew they were not doing their homework. Gian Franco went pale and then tried to take the blame. Giada doesn't even see him and speaks in an aggrieved voice. How many times has she told Luigi San Casciano is not his place. And when he reaches out to touch her, she won't turn her face to him. A growing sense of fear, and he pushes her a bit and before she can turn, his own breasts swell up into two ripe and obscene tits, pink and hairy; they start to drip and then just gush and flow. His mother turns as if she wants to hide with shame, like Eve in the garden. No, Luigi cries, swinging his arm as if to strike her hard across the face. His heart pounding, a shallow darkness fills his eyes. The pillow is wet. He's glad for it. In the dark, the mirror holds an opaque smoky light. Luigi touches his breast. Now he is fully aware, the crisp crumpled cloth is dry under his fingers. His uneasiness is only that of being awake in a shadowy room papered in calla lilies.

Once his parents slept in the room. Laid one beside the other within the bed's long wooden boards carved from Egyptian cedars still beautifully carrying crosses of Malta. Not that he had slept there after the divorce, Giada, his mother did. It was easy moving back to the house after his and Susan's divorce. Much easier than staring at the crystal chandelier flicking glints on the ceiling now. His mother left him alone. She let him assume the position at the head of the table, let him remove his father's books on Roman Law and Fascist Law and put them under the roof. She let him have his friends in and asked for permission, his permission, when her friends still came for readings behind the glass doors. It seemed easy to settle into the known memories of each room, and the gray hair and growing frailty hardly seemed real, even after she died. But with his mother's death, Diniza, the maid, announced she too would leave. That changed the house, from one minute to the next, withdrew ordinary, healthy song like the canary, Tela, who went with her. Her small, modest room, with her single bed and reading lamp, in someway now was the most difficult to open up, lifting the shutters, looking down into the central court. Entering the kitchen was hard, too. Diniza's solid face so often red-cheeked, perhaps from blushing, quiet, nodding as she dried a pan, as if she understood every secret and sadness in the house; her murmuring complicity was missing. That was the vague sensation he experienced as he padded down the long halls or sat in his study. Missing. Looking. He was looking for a silent nod. Perhaps Giada's. But perhaps Diniza's. Her steady eyes so long ago had told him Susan was the right girl. Now in these slightly weird years of looking for the nods and not finding them, his changing of things stopped. Not repairs. He kept up with those. Light bulbs. Washers. It was the bulky cupboards, starting from the three filled with women's shoes. He left untouched, as Diniza had, the four rooms, where Tina, his mother's sister and her kids stayed, when she came from Buenos Aires for months on end. The glass doors where his mother had held her feminist meetings—where eight or nine women in décolleté dresses drew on mother-of-pearl cigarette holders and puffed madly while proposing articles about emancipation, he seldom pushed them open. Such excitement about women working in rice fields. Teachers who arrived at their posts by mule. Mariella Rinaldo did write novels, and one of her romances about the fated Faladina was announced in that very room. All middle-class Italian matrons held their breath when headstrong Faladina left her husband and children to dance in Melbourne. And they knew it; they knew her reach for hope would end tragically. And it did, when she broke her leg and then, in Aldo Borini's film, underlining her sin of female independence, she died penniless in an alley, in a cold, heartless country, her face wet with tears.

The rooms seemed like flushed, crowded store-windows that never changed. The apartment on the fifth floor, with its groaning terrace of camellias and roses and lemons, which looked down on the Arno and caught its evening light and the orange accent of the dome, had an unhealthy stillness to it. Luigi wondered sometimes if he shouldn't return to the room he had had when Giada was still living, leave his parents' bed, with its ample perimeters and take over the south facing room and re-do the Venetian stucco. Once Cesare, his father, and Giada, his mother, lay on the very spot, on the very sheets, he was lying on now. Not tucked in. Smoothed under sheets and entering separately.

It had always been difficult for Luigi to withstand his father's rectitude. That assumption of obedience that had his employees rise in his presence. The forced nod of respect as he gave them pay envelopes in his own hand. Casalini's smirk, Rodolfo's eyes registering regret. His father wouldn't have allowed himself to get caught by a smooth back. By a wide mouth. By independence. Cesare would never have allowed himself hungrily to touch another woman. Not a researcher in his lab. The way Cesare touched Giada on the shoulder was like patting a stubborn horse. Luigi reminded himself that Maria

Grazia was old enough to consent when he first put his hand on her firm breast. He didn't pick a minor. She placed his hand on the other one. Maria Grazia had caught his eye when she took notes while other girls never stopped laughing, but he hadn't approached her then, even when he gave her the best grade, the grade she deserved.

Luigi sat up and leaned on an elbow. Then, hunching, he slid back onto the pillow after turning it over. Suddenly it seemed as if the bodies of his father and mother were lying side by side, nearly under him in the bed. Cesare, like a reticent soldier retired to this very room quite early after dinner and, sitting on the couch, from a decanter or the silver shaker, with his mother often laughing in the living room with her women friends, he poured himself a drink. A few or many. She never mentioned that he passed out. Never said that he didn't make it to the bed. But Luigi when he was young, sometimes walking down the long hall, heard her urging him to lean on her for those few steps. Those sounds, so unexplained, were some of many set sounds that never worked into the story of day. His father's wolfish breathing was absolutely gone, when by seven-thirty, Cesare, was up, pale, unspeaking of the night. He was perfectly scented and straight as he lathered cream on his face with a marvelous shell handled brush and, in deliberate strokes, revealed his regular, determined chin.

Luigi stretched to reach for the bedside light. The room's silence was helpful. The walls lit clarified what was real and what was an intruding dream. It was disquieting seeing the dream Gian Franco in the dark alley behind the shop. Although he'd seen the current, harried version with his arms full of tax records near Ponte Vecchio last Friday. Strange how exhilarating cigarette smoke was forty years ago. The beginning gate to sex. Even Susan smoked when they met. She inhaled crookedly in a way that never fit her proper mouth. Luigi rolled over and pulled the sheet up over his head. The liquor cabinet had been moved by Giada, very soon after Cesare died. It was too far away to pad down the halls. More disturbing was his feeling of reluctance to reach over to the bedside table for the exquisite study of adaptation of Norwegian pines to light. The Norwegian sampling study went on over twenty years. It would be as good as studies got. Resting on the table next to the bed like a crystal of excellence, the study of the trees depressed him. The laws of stoicism and wit in the dark, lonely forest were powerful, how the steel needles shortened, searching, feeling and adjusting just to have light. The thought of the edgeless black days of a Norwegian winter, and the straight trees set to figure out and match that frozen, sunless world, their determination to survive, chilled him.

Luigi is not alone in being haunted by family. Susan has a whole shelf in her study on mothers and daughters. She has published two papers, which were received rather well, on women in the Bible who move out of their families. And below the Andronicus Icon of the Consolers of Mothers, she has a shelf of padded packets, which are tapes from her mother. They have been coming for two years and after the first three or four monologues Susan decided not to open them any more. But she can't throw their scotch-taped bulk away, any more than she can throw pictures away. Letters, yes. But the act of tearing a photo seems a mutilation. She doesn't like the tapes closed and doesn't like them open. She has mentioned to Charlotte that Marina would rather have her take a plane over, but Charlotte has not responded to that complaint. Only once she came before Marina went to middle school. So her mother, who has outlived her father Leonard by thirty-three years, is a resistant presence in her life. By remaining unopened, the tapes bother Susan at her core. She thinks of her life as one of opening things, addressing them. Her work is dedicated to that. But this night, before she gave up on Marina, nearly all the doors within her sight caught her attention and distracted her with a sense that she had closed them.

And then there is the extraordinary woman who never leaves Susan's mind. She is a real skeleton in Susan's garden. Over a year ago, when Susan took the pole of an apple sapling to put it down (since the gardener had to take his woman friend to the doctor), she leaned on her shovel and it kept on going. For more than a meter. So that her shoulder almost slipped from the force. And then solidity. Then a clunk. A clunk. Just as it happened in Lascaux, where the two French boys nearly fell into the caves with the dusty ochre signs of horses and leopards, paws and spots and red dashes, Susan's shovel went down and kept on going. And in the first hour her hands brushed the dried mud from a horse's bronze bit. That was how it started. But the underground probe has stopped. It is illegal to dig, to disturb the past that belongs to the Italian government, to upset the dead who might have been murdered, to take grave goods that might be sold. So underneath the ground in her garden, with samples made here and there, systematically and then passionately, Susan knows there is a buried woman. A buried woman. Imagine. And she wears a bronze ring holding an amber disk. And there is a bronze horse bit. The woman was someone. And Susan keeps questioning her. That is a story made of land and sky and the un-deciphered speech of history.

Susan almost stopped digging when she came across a papoose. Yellowed linen strips and moving shredded leather straps. A child, wrapped in sad careful linen. She touched heartache and a sense of violating what must not be disturbed. But she didn't stop then. The uncompleted task is a constant in her mind, a more or less permanent door: a buried woman, a live woman who rode a horse, a woman who wants to be uncovered. A mother who lost a child. The woman is an obsession for Susan Notingham. The bones, the story, seem like a puzzle given to her, left in the garden, her garden, her sandbox.

Charlotte Notingham fussed with the tape cassette she snapped into the machine. Her short fingers were swollen and it irritated her pushing and missing. But nothing about that sign of age could erase the fact that she and Don had actually gone three exits down the freeway, with she driving. It was nothing Charlotte could make fit with the puzzle of the past, except that it was she, the woman liberated at last, pumping the outsized gas pedal, and accelerating up in the high cab with the foam dice dangling. Truck of the Year 1990. This was she, Charlotte Notingham. The sentence with the pronoun in its place made her think of her mother's schoolteacher's voice. Not her, she would say, her is an adjective. This was her book. No, Charlotte thought smiling, revisiting her mother, no, books were you. This is my thing. This is danger and weight. The open road. My trembling hands can just about turn eighty tons onto the asphalt and straighten out the cab.

Something about making the tapes gave Charlotte hope as she stared out of her fifteenth story window. She could see that the stadium lights were just going on. Strange to watch them. On in daylight. The Catholics were good at parish activities. The ballpark was used quite often and it kept members coming. It depressed her, really, having a distant view of the ballpark. Not that the lights and cheers were intrusive. There were trees in between and a few roads. But she hadn't anything quite like this old folks home in her background. It was Mr. Veril taking off his shirt in the elevator, not clear how his thin chest got covered in bruises, that was the toughness of this place. Charlotte closed her eyes, and when she opened them, there was Leonard's early choice before her. She had gone along with the idea of modern. But really, the worn out white carpet looked cold. What was Swedish design but the bare lines of the Upsala landscape of green pines?

It had been Bernice, a woman on floor six, who suggested making tapes. They were pretty boring as far as Charlotte was concerned, but Bernice swore by them. Who knows why her children liked to hear her talk about the apples she baked, the Stephen King books she read? But why not try? So Charlotte bought a pack of eight cassettes and then another. Not that Susan or Marina reciprocated. But by now she liked the production and the sense of doing something. If Susan didn't care, she thought, at least Bernice gave her a pat on the back for the effort. The trouble perhaps lay in the lure of the microphone itself. Charlotte loved the effects of microphones. She loved hearing her own voice. Keeping it. And erasing it. It was marvelous, if after playing back and hearing the rather surprising hesitations, the deepness of her voice, its unlilting lunge, how she could actually erase her words and start over. Wouldn't that be wonderful, Charlotte thought, if families worked that way? Wouldn't it just be wonderful to take words back. Anyway, nothing on the little spools was about the truck driving. Bill would be appalled if he knew his mother at seventy-five were going out with a man who delivered beer and stopped in taverns. Susan might not mind, always the non-conformist, always extending the possible, but Charlotte minded. Don wasn't someone you could bring home, although she'd met him in front of the First Presbyterian Church. Charlotte sighed before pressing the 'on' button. She sat down and kicked off her shoes. The chunky heels on her black pumps disappointed her. Heels were dangerous and an effort but when you have nice legs, she thought, stretching them and wiggling her toes, when so much has been taken away, when most women are saggy and have blue veins blotting their legs, why not wear heels if you can take the pain?

The machine spun. This is mother speaking, Charlotte said. Then she paused. If she said Charlotte she wondered what it would feel like. Gray-headed permanent, more wrinkles than a bulldog. When she thought Charlotte she thought prom queen, heads turning as she walked down Chester place. The machine ran on. Her thumb didn't work. She finally snapped it down. To go back. All the way to the beginning was just a few seconds. Again. This is mother speaking. Glide. Glide. I'm getting ready to read. I just turned off the TV. I don't know if you see the news there. I don't know how things work in Italy, you never really tell me. Every once in a while we see your Pope. She stopped the machine. She shook her head. It was hard to know how Susan got so taken in by a country with a Pope. She started it again. What kind of voice to use she thought. She could hear it dragging. It was depressing like a leg with a limp. Here we are watching reruns of the Gulf bombs. It's amazing what they can do now in wars. And seeing Schwarzkopf again, he's marvelous, really. If your father was alive, I'm not sure what he would think. He was so much more conservative than I. He would have found the changes in our world astounding. Even the freeways weren't circling Minneapolis when he died. And now we can fight wars, technologically, without any, well not any, but just about none of our boys being lost. Oh I know it's terrible for those who die. No one in our family ever served in a war. And maybe you didn't agree with the bombing. Down went the button. Charlotte felt disappointed. She liked it when her talks took her back to some memory of the kids when they were little, when Leonard used to take photos of them all. In front of American sites with philanthropist's names. Carnegie Hall. Stanford University. Success stories. Charlotte suddenly felt wooly about meeting Don out on the freeway tomorrow morning. He would have slept in his truck, but would have washed, combed his thin hair, and would be wearing a tie, just for her. It was strange how someone with a red neck and a beer belly was not frightening to her.

There are no eight-lane freeways in Harcourt. The road to Bori would be dusty and broken, hot and long. Ramada's fancy sport shoes that he had found in the Harcourt market made him feel as if he were walking on rubber waves. His big white shoes were like a car. Fancy. They made his feet sweat maybe because they were too big. But he hadn't paid his week's wage just for fanciness but use. He might need them in a war. A large smear of oil had dropped down onto the tongue and laces of one. The garage was always greasy like that.

Ramada wondered how far his grandfather would react, raising his caterpillar eyebrows when he would finally be back facing him. He wouldn't believe his grandson when he would say, I was in a school. I was. He'd frown, shrug, too tired to protest. Aki's eyes would wait, rest in Ramada's eyes, just long enough to say he knew Ramada was a good youth. Then he'd shake his head. Where's your mother? Why did she run off to Italy? I'm too old, with six children of my own in the house, two wives, to be worrying about you.

Ramada, even when he couldn't talk Tiku, his friend, into skipping school to listen to Ken Saro-Wiwa's supporters, decided to go to Bori anyway, since Tiku might never follow the path of a rebel.

You don't get oil under control, Tiku had said, by guns. They were sitting down by the port. The yellow tankers were anchored out beyond the harbor. Ramada watched the police boat motor by.

Saro-Wiwa doesn't use guns, Ramada offered, hoping it might be true.

They all do. My parents say he's no good.

Well, said Ramada, faced with the thought of his stubborn friend, with his clean shirt and his father who worked in the post office, how do you stop things?

My grandma says you study until you get a job as an engineer.

Ramada wrinkled up his face in disgust and admiration. He smiled, showing a gap. How you going to do that, when you don't like math? And you don't have books?

You'll become like them, Tiku said, seriously, as a scrawny

cat scurried over his feet and disappeared into the tangle of mangrove root.

You're just scared, Ramada said, feeling his head spin. I can't change just by going to a meeting. Why you go tell me that to scare me? he said, putting an arm on his friend's narrow, book-bent shoulder. And he looked away, and then tossed a stone, not far, into the water.

Ramada had heard his grandfather and his graying friends mention Ken Saro-Wiwa, often, in quiet voices. Beer and mumble. Danger. Danger. Saro-Wiwa was true stuff. Keep it from the boy's ears. Saro-Wiwa lost his place on television because he grew too strong. Ken Saro-Wiwa was a god. But keep the boy from MOSOP. As if he couldn't read the declaration of Ogoni rights with his own eyes. As if his garage mates hadn't talked ever since Saro-Wiwa's arrest.

No eight-lane freeways in the River states. How different from Florence where Milli, his mother, lifts her skirt on the side of the freeway, although her son doesn't even know in which picture book city she works. He knows Italy is somewhere that let his own heart grow a little shut. Ramada, Milli's fourteen-year-old son, had been walking since early evening and was now limping on in the dark. Now he is alone, although in the afternoon there were plenty of Fords and Rovers and even some Mercedes, lots of pickup trucks customized with graffiti, flowers and baby Jesuses and capital letters HONK HEAR that had been brightly patched. Now it is dark.

Ramada doesn't mind walking. It's the only way, when one doesn't have *nairas* and he is more than used to moving in the hum and chatter, the go man and explosion of human voices, the slow to fast pace and ripe and sharp smells among the cows and goats, the warmth of dung and the spicy burn of eucalyptus, and the peddlers and women and children, holding up plastic pails, new, new, from the last plank market. Generally he liked the wide encircling noise of human voices. And backfiring trucks were his bread and butter. But soldiers were a problem for him on these roads. Always. And especially now. After dark. The soldiers with their open hands, their rifles and their brown uniforms. Their open hands, asking for a few *nairas*. They made him nervous. Always. Their wide fat jeeps and the way they jumped their rifles from their shoulders to a straight aim in one swing made him flinch. There were always roadblocks and the soldiers' open hands. Not all had open hands, but just those who wanted to make things hard or impossible to pass. They were rough. And now more than ever since the strike was on.

Ramada never thinks he stands out in a flow of erect walkers, when there are many balancing bright colored baskets, many limping or carrying babies on their hips. He knows he is handsome, though, tall, erect, with blue jeans that hug his hips. But now when there are shadows and not many voices, it's a different thing. As he pushes on, his head swims with thoughts of the meeting he is aiming for and the stir it will cause at home. The garage, Sky Survival System, will not look for him until tomorrow and will then let Aki know he's skipped work. He knows that routine like he knows that a stepped-on asp will strike. They will wander down to the corrugated roof, with his grandfather on the porch, and ask if he's still in bed. And Aki will bark back, not having slept for one minute, eyes wide open, waiting on the porch.

Ramada reviews the day coming to a close. His hot blisters urge him to sit without scanning for danger. The meeting he is heading to, with its talk of resistance, its talk of not letting the Ogoni people die, is broad future. Maybe his. Maybe his people's. The meeting joins him to becoming a man. Getting control of the oil flooding the brains and houses and bank accounts of government officials excites him so much he nearly speaks to the dark. To the jacarandas. To their shadows. Walking in the flow of people from Port Harcourt going out of the city, and the villagers going towards Harcourt for things they can't find, Ramada had felt like shouting to them: *Don't you under-stand? Don't you see the officials getting the oil, with their mile-high flames, scorching the villages and killing the rivers and streams, that it's time to get the oil under Ogoni control?* On this road he has already passed the refinery, its barbed wire fences and snarling dogs, but its flame is still there on the horizon, a skyscraper of flame, hellishly bright. He doesn't look back and doesn't feel grateful for the eerie glow it shoots into the otherwise tempered dark. And the smell of sulfur stinks, and the black ash dropping, dropping stings.

Boom. Boom. Boom. Those are the firecrackers that shattered announcing the coming solstice day over the Arno that flows. The Arno that floods. Rocking, gleaming water. The river Arno that Susan sends her patients to sometimes; Swing your arms and look ahead. The river, which the Mugnone runs into, where Milli and Farina have a space under a foot bridge. Different hours when Milli is off-duty. There under the bridge where she has fought off two other immigrants to keep her box with its folded plaid blanket and newspapers to sit on. The Mugnone is where Farina was born, yes born, on the grass with Irene helping Milli to get her out. There are rivers in these lives. The Niger and its delta that Europeans thought they could take over, the River Bonny that Ramada knew. The Mississippi near Charlotte's home, named by the French, long after Native Americans swept its length and breadth in dugouts not much different from those carved from logs used by tribes in Nigeria. There are real and historical rivers in these lives. Brown waters, powerful rushing waters, forgotten and forgetful waters, wet floods and crystal trickle and today the Arno is just coming out of the dark. The Arno is the river in our story. Its flow and time. The swifts are beginning to circle up and down it and swoop with jackknife skill, screeching and quivering, flipping and skimming the air of its insects.

Susan is laughing as she swings her arms. It was terrifying at six o'clock, that ring. Who wouldn't feel dread but once the booming voice kept apologizing and saying, Marge Brunstom said you were a sport, honestly. And it was made clear it was just an hour and the emergency was not Marina, or even an emergency, except that the prostitute was being held and it was good to have a translator. Poor women. And Marge had said that Susan was a peach, understanding, one who could empathize and see that it was a matter of life and death. Life and death? Susan said, now fully awake and shaking her head of red hair as she put her feet on the carpet tinted with sun. Life and death. You know, the woman had laughed, these women are slaves. They can be killed. Sometimes just one sentence can be the one. Susan wondered if she dared ask why the excited voice was unable to keep her translation commitment. Measles. My granddaughter gave them to me. And so there it was, although years ago conventions would have made it impossible for a stranger to ask for a favor at six in the morning. But basically, Susan thought, basically the breaking down of borders was good. Not all good. But what did they mean if most of those conventions kept social classes apart? Yet there was such upheaval and speed. Like the sign she nearly hit yesterday coming home. It had been thrown down on the road. The Coro radio marker. It commemorated eight deaths of partisans hiding in the woods, operating a short wave radio, hoping to outwit the Germans. And something, or someone wanted it down, as Robert Frost observed so long ago. There was a lot of confusion about borders right now, a lot of confusion about interpreting values in Florence. Was it drugs? Was it people resisting history? Wanting to say they hated facts?

It's going to be hot, Susan thought, already imagining how difficult parking would be. It will only be an hour, the voice had said. Having decided to walk before going, not breaking up her routine before seeing patients in the afternoon, as she climbed the hill past the tiny church Susan decided not to go back to the house and leave a note. What would she say to Marina? Welcome back stranger. You should have called, dear daughter. The words were traps on all sides. As she got into her car, she could hear the peacock raising his voice. Poor fellow, she thought. The peacock had flapped over the fence again, leaving Signora Caffo. A pest. Almost asking to be killed. And then laughter overtook her. She threw her head back and couldn't stop the hysterical giggle shaking her shoulders. The ridiculous plight of the hen-pecked bird. There were borders, and the peacock, too, was confused. He'd lost his compass. Arvon. Susan found it strange that the old peasants chose such an odd name. She thought maybe Signora Caffo got a deaf version from one of those door-to-door women, selling brushes and creams. Or maybe she got the English river wrong. Florentines often got things in English slightly off. They called a garage a box.

Signora Caffo was up and already missing the rhythm of toss and peck, of bright eye and coxcomb. She was missing her peacock, Arvon, but it was no surprise. She couldn't bear to tie him. She had been tied as a child, tied by her father. And she had pulled her daughter's hands away from a belt when she wanted to tie her retarded son. She didn't like ropes and belts. Didn't like cages and couldn't understand why, though, God made creatures like Arvon who couldn't settle and couldn't find what they wanted; why a peacock with fine feathers and room to roam would choose to be a hen. That's all you could call Arvon, a hen. He wanted to mother chicks. She wished she could find it amusing, but it hurt.

Signor Caffo had learned to ride with his wife's taciturn disappointment, just nodding when the scene came up nearly each morning when they went out to feed the two sheep. Months back, he had hoped. Sometimes, he said, creatures can change.

But looking at their setter, Marta, slumped on the steps, growing gray, panting with her tongue out, he didn't believe that. He didn't believe it about politics, either, in spite of all the parties' new names. The corruption was like manure that plants needed to grow.

Too bad, he said, quietly, letting his wife express her surprise and disappointment seeing the coop empty, as if grave robbers had come in the night. Too bad, he said, turning his head towards the latticed pine, where Arvon used to sit, a peacock king, with a hanging robe of iridescent feathers. The emptiness troubled him, too, to tell the truth.

Why does he think he's a hen? Signora Caffo asked, thinking of similar mornings when she awoke as a child with hunger banging her stomach, and then hunger consuming her while she was pregnant and then, even after the depleting war, when bread or chestnuts soaked in milk might be nearly a feast. How can he lose his head when he has food, shelter, admiration? Not even a Christian can ask for more.

THREE

MILLI SPIT INTO the pitted sink. Her mouth was dry and cottony. It had lived these hours closed and thirsty. The policeman who had forced her into the car, left no time, then, even to get the rubber taste of sex out of her mouth. The faucet dripped miserably. Without her wristwatch, Milli felt lost, but it was morning, that's for certain. She'd ask for a drink of water. No use trying to get one's head under that torture machine. The drops wet her palms and Milli spread them and put her hands to her face. Letting the stingy trickle cool her cheeks and fore-head, she wanted more to gush out. It would be nice to drown, but the drops of water, and the no towels, so you had no choice but to wipe your hands on your polyester dress made it not the finest hotel she'd ever seen, and even worse, she was facing questions. Milli lifted up the hem of her black dress, bunched it above her hips, spread her legs, putting her feet on the two porcelain platforms and crouched, on wobbly high heels, while the pee trickled into a hole that hadn't been disinfected. Hot and stuffy, there was no window to gaze out of.

The tall, lithe woman looked up at the low ceiling, its bloat-ed cracks ominously close. She'd seen lots of worse places, but better ones too. Once those tattered rooms with blue and orange

Ogoni cloth covering the divans seemed dirty but now no longer. At least air moved in, moist or sharp with dust, and mixed with the inside palmy smells of women and men and utaka frying in garlic. Those rooms were clean when you thought about how Italians shut things up. Like this toilet. They didn't like air. Closed windows, even in the front seats of cars. But the way her life was going since before midnight nothing would get her back into any air unless she answered their questions in a smart way. What was smart when no one wanted to listen? Milli, even when someone listened, didn't like having to measure whether a mind was going straight or turning. The policemen last night, her pussy ready for bed, grabbed her, but she had bent her head like a keen scoop lifting the two men up, and they knew she would do whatever they wanted, even strange things she always refused, if they would let her go, give her back her beige handbag and let her disappear beyond the shoulder of the freeway. But neither man, not even the fat one whose eyes brightened, made gestures towards her power. They were dead set and firm. What was smart to offer when they had her papers, with a fake birth date, and a fake name? Milli didn't like her identity card and many women told her not to have one. Common wisdom said it was a way of stepping into prison. Even though her fear around the card was not its information but its weight taken off the body of a dead woman. Looking at the small black name as she signed a paper in front of Igor for another debt, Milli wondered what had changed. It was the dead woman that made the card bad: her untimely spirit lost in a strange land. But Milli Mugabe had been her own name now for a long time. And what Mugabe sounded like when it belonged to the dead woman could only be forgotten. The picture with those eyes drooping in shame, that was her own picture glued in and stamped, no longer Widu but worn over until its falseness maybe looked true. They, those organized people with pens and low voices that could flare up and press; they were good at seeing false names. They could help but they wanted things for their help. Milli didn't like the knocking. Why didn't that skimpy police-woman, who had looked at her all night long as if she wasn't a human being who needed to buy food, who didn't need to make money to feed her child, why was she rushing her now?

Are you ready? the guard shouted through the door.

Milli rolled her eyes and lifted her hands, trying to smooth down her skirt. She didn't answer as a fly buzzed down near the hole. She pulled the handle and the water rushed over the toilet embedded in the floor and the last drops of pee dripped down her leg. She had no purse. She had paper in her purse, and towelettes, and handcream and a lovely spray of mist. Lipstick, cream to make herself decent. Milli was used to eyes observing her as tall and striking. They wanted to strip her down. This hole, where there was no soap, no dignity, where no one knew her, why knock so hard? The knocking was like her heart, pounding, and her palms growing wet when she had just dried them.

The toilet was a place of detention. But she was alone in its smelly solitude and cracked cement. The walls protected her. When she stepped out, they were hoping she would grovel in front of their laws. Milli wondered how long it would take, what was waiting on the other side of the door. They didn't let her brush her teeth, her hair. The best clients, they knew how to get past disgust and find some reality in washing, putting themselves back together and letting her do that too. The ones who even took her home and let her walk away on high heels, near-ly free of torn covers, the ones who wanted sex, not guilt and punishment. Every night, last night was no exception, there was always someone who wanted sex like no man in Nigeria would dream of, wanted just to watch and to touch himself. In the chipped mirror Milli's stiff sprayed hair looked worn out. Imagine no window to breathe, but a mirror to make you see what a forlorn and dusty worm you are. Milli traced the lost look of a woman with no sleep and wondered how she could hide it without her little cheek and lip brushes and paints. Her hair without a comb. She shook her long fingers shiny with red polish. She looked distracted when she wanted to look balanced, as if she believed her name and everything her name would tell. She tugged one of the straps of her black dress and set it straight on her shoulder. Now stay there, she said.

Milli had never been brought in before, never been forced to rub her fingers in ink and leave their mazes on paper in the five years she had been in Italy. She wondered what it meant, being caught. Whether it meant the end of living in a hidden world, the end of a money machine and getting back to Harcourt. The bottom end of the line, where Italian women wouldn't do it on the street and in the bushes any more, and so Nigerians could. She didn't know if the night spent in police headquarters meant that her protection, when she had killed a chicken with a knife, and eaten its still jumping heart, and crawled on her hands and knees promising to obey the madam, and then running away finally, running with Farina still in her womb, she didn't know if that broken promise had turned on her, now that she was caught. If her protection was gone. Everyone believed a little in voodoo.

The knock had turned into a shouting order. The door itself jumped. Milli looked at her bare palms. She had no phone. She had no way to call back. Igor would not help anyway. It would be Irene. And Farina. Farina would need her. Milli felt her body, weak from hunger, tighten the tendons of steel in her neck. She was not only locked in the toilet with its bare bulb and terrible stink, she was locked to stand near the freeway, Florence north. She was locked into a debt that was two years short of being paid. The weights she had put on her back since she rode from Harcourt to Benin on that long start into slavery were far beyond her ability to organize them. Farina. She couldn't apologize for Farina; she couldn't do anything but expect Irene to help the child this morning. Milli closed her eyes. It's better in the dark, she thought. Better not to see anything. She fanned her face with her fingers. Stars. But then the dark looked too dark, the smell of urine became too strong, and she flipped the lock on the door, hoping for air.

Susan had two minutes to spare as the guard at the Questura searched her bag. His gun was in a handsome leather case more elegant than most handbags. A lot had changed since Susan had last been to the Questura. Looking around, she saw a glass reception booth that was probably bullet proof. Such an odd mixture of social planning, the building had been. The marble plaque impressed her: the first hospital for children, eight-hundred years ago, then the first hospital for the insane, then an armory for the Fascists. The last time she had been in the Questura, she had climbed the marble stairs. Now there was an elevator, carved from some unused space. Susan shut her bag. She had pencils and a notebook in case they were needed. She felt an unidentifiable sense of anticipation as the guard gestured patiently to go forward. Susan had faced young policemen on the other side of protest barriers on the Via Nazionale. Even recently. Most massed together with a spirit of nervousness, and the horses often responded to the excitement by pulling and stamping, but some of the police had waved their approval for Bosnia and peace. Most were older men. This one staring past her, under his ceremonial helmet with red plumes, was young. His male authority and handsome macho pride were as obvious as the flirty plumes.

Susan walked through the door just after Milli passed in front of her, with a middle-aged guard holding her arm. There was no smiling to be done, because Susan saw her back, her long legs, rather than her face. The tall woman was on show. Susan was

41

always grateful to see a person at a distance, when she had time to focus on the messages in gestures and bodies. Such remove and such tension. A bold walk that clattered on the marble and yet broke its illusion by carelessness that whispered, don't look for me in these steps. Who knows, she thought, what other attributes are there. Now the guard, who looked weary herself, had stopped in front of the clerk, a young perfumed woman with a bright short skirt and a low red blouse smothered by gold chains. Benedetta Livi nodded efficiently and showed Milli her identification card, asking for confirmation. The clerk didn't like being in the musty room, with streaked windows, didn't like Giudice Pingello's request that they put in extra time just to move through a growing load of cases, but secretly she admired him and his message that the law mattered. Her earrings and her fitted top, her mascara were the latest tight and glittering look, but in her heart she knew Giudice Pingello had significance that went beyond form, and that he was fighting a lonely battle in the Questura, trying to organize the flow of poverty and criminality, desperation, political legitimacy that now was replacing what used to be Italian petty crime. Her father didn't like her working for the Questura. He thought she might even catch a disease. Leprosy, he insisted. TB. I'm sure they don't wash their hands. Benadetta Livi didn't believe her father. She thought he was blind about the future.

Buon giorno. Buon giorno. This was Roberto Pingello entering the room, hanging up his jacket on a hook, and he would have rolled up his sleeves but he couldn't push decorum that far. He was already breaking the rules by running his own plenary court outside the normal hours. He nodded at his clerk and meant to smile appreciatively at her promptness, but he disapproved of her skin-tight outfit. And so he frowned. Rubbing his bald head, he already felt the push he would make this morning. The prostitute sitting down, just one of two or three who fell in their net every day and wriggled away, looked

mute. But he had to hope she would be different. Most prostitutes understood so much more than their tight lips would
reveal. That wasn't true for a lot of the immigrants, or maybe
it was. The new waves of Arabs and Africans had no awareness
of where they were, certainly no memories of Florence and
its civilization. The law held no dignity for them, no honor.
Maybe it mattered when there was an amnesty, but mostly the
law was perceived as barbed wire and spikes. And what could
the Questura do, except send them back onto the streets, where
slowly the city was changing its appearance, substituting what
thirty years ago were southern widows dressed in black with
women with chadors, ill dressed *contadini* with bare footed
beggars. The recent petty crimes, the homelessness, the complete lack of understanding of where they were, there were still
many hollow-eyed people who passed through his office whom
he wished to rescue. Rescue would be too much. But they had a
right to be heard. It couldn't be forfeited. And sometimes in the
exchange of defense and accusations, a clue to how important
and possible it was to be heard was revealed. But day to day,
his interrogation was like giving them the rough slap a baby received being born—and hoping that its shock would confirm
what they knew—you are somewhere else and cannot go on as
you are on your own. The law exists.

Benadetta Livi copied Susan's identity card.

Yes, a substitute. Psychotherapist. I had no idea you performed such a service, even providing translation.

We found a small European fund, Roberto Pingello said,
proudly interjecting. But it's hard to find Arabic translators,
and sometimes, it's a question of speaking dialect only. Not
only New York copes with over one hundred languages. He
looked at his watch and ran his finger down the list of people
to be brought in. Six of the names were unpronounceable.
Signora, he said, gesturing to Susan, even though she probably
understands Italian, I would like you to convey my remarks to

Signora Mugabe in English. Sometimes it helps and to translate hers to me.

Your age?
Twenty-nine.
Pingello had seen a lot who had aged worse. She was frail in some way; her thinness said I am not that strong. But the way she bobbed her head there was cockiness that would probably mean she had no intention of helping herself.

Milli scowled at him. Pingello scowled back. And then he leaned back in his chair. It was too early to press hard. She was looking bored, disinterested. Pingello decided to call her to attention.

Signora Mugabe. It says you are married. Where is your husband?

Susan took the words and dutifully spun them into English.

Milli had heard from many of the prostitutes that it was important to move out as far as possible from the truth. But to remember what one had said, in case they made you back up. And for the husbands it was important to say they were still in Nigeria.

Port Harcourt, she said, lowering her eyes and wishing she did not have to stand in the open. But he's dead. That was true. Meniki was dead. Ramada's father had died in a fishing accident, in a family of fishermen, he had died. The thought of putting that far-off death into words in the room with large windows stopped Milli. What she had just said had come up like a bit of vomit. She would have liked to wipe her mouth. She should stay away from the truth. The truth stabbed and pushed, and then blinded like a mirror. Meniki's bloated face appeared in her mind, the men having brought her to the river, laid him in the grass that bent around his bruised body, obliterated and bloated by the water his body had filled up with. Those swollen vacant eyes pulled like bulbs from the earth, but they were his eyes, in a face that had been twisted into a horrifying runny mask that had puffed and pulled his mouth. Milli covered her eyes and didn't want to believe what the men were insisting were only minutes when the waves passed over him after he hit his head. They were already calling Nardela, the goddess, while Milli was trying to absorb what evil had entered the boat and tipped it, and tied his arms, which could swim for miles, on the same day that the sun had come through the window to wake him before he left her side in bed.

Do you have children?

Milli turned toward the woman who was translating. Imagine having red hair that looked like a clown's. Tell him I have three.

Three?

They are all in Harcourt with my mother. Twins. Milli bit her lip, hesitated, since either boy or girl would be the truth. She didn't want any trail, for the buzzards and vultures that circled. She'd seen that even with her husband, while the face could be brought back to his nose, and his calm words, as she was still staggering and screaming, how they were wrapping him in canvas to keep the black buzzards that were right there at the river, their humped backs and wings dark in the gnarl of the trees. Twins, she repeated, deciding the judge didn't need to know the sex. And an older child.

Susan watched Milli suck on her thumb. It was easy to understand and was a kind of sign. Susan appreciated the silences for what they were. She was feeling impatience overtake her. Where was the judge going? She wasn't certain where she would take it, but certainly the young woman was not going to answer any questions. Underneath the thin pose she was putting up, what was there? Not much calculation. Exhaustion. Pride but not the right kind. Susan hated that conclusion, and wondered if anything could change the young woman's distress, the way she was wringing her hands. Words just couldn't reach her. That was the strength of sandplay. Imagine if they would just let her sit in silence in front of a box feeling the reassuring smoothness of the grains of sand. Making her own connections with a body image and her memories of pain. While touching a floor of earth.

Now Signora Mugabe we are going to play a tape. I'm not going to ask you how you earn a living. I think we know from the men who brought you in. Also you know, Pingello said dryly, that prostitution is against the law. I think you know that. And I think you know the law even says you mustn't practice your work in the city of residence. He nodded towards Susan. She trotted the English words forward.

Milli felt the words come down on her like pebbles falling on her head and rolling down her back. He was so sure of himself with his little gold pen. She sighed loudly.

I don't have to do this work you know, Pingello said, catching her eye as he rocked in his chair, stopping for a moment. He thought better of his anger as he saw Benadetta Livi bite her lip. It was useless to want gratitude from a woman who probably saw ten men a day, and had a debt, and maybe even was sending money home. Signora Mugabe, I am here to remind you that you are breaking the law. But we can help you. I want to tell you that. I am more interested in knowing if you are a slave.

Do you know that? He waited for Susan's version and knew Milli would not lift her eyes or respond. That moment, which he lived eight or ten times a week, that dead stone wall, where he had every temptation to simply assert his power and have them taken out, where the government's law would then release them at most within twenty-four hours. But his passion had not died, not even under these conditions, the stubborn fire of so many years ago that had made him believe in the law's part in building a just city.

We are going to play a tape. It is talking about Nigerian women being sold. If you can tell us anything, it will help you.

Milli shook her head. Tell him I don't know anything about Nigerian women.

Pingello slammed down his fist. Why do you say that? Why? Don't you know more than two hundred of your women, you deceived women, have been murdered? Tossed in ditches up and down Italy. Don't you know anything?

How did you get from Port Harcourt?

Milli looked out the window and steadied herself with a hand on the back of a chair. She wasn't going to open her mouth, that dry space growing tighter with worry as he spoke, and tell him about the trip, even the final piece through Amsterdam, in March, in the train compartment with two other Nigerians from Benin, and the broken heating, her legs so cold, even crossed, they trembled, being told then that once they got to Turin, the debt was insurmountable. It was a cage, a trap like so many things in her life. She had known from the minute she had heard how she could earn money rolling hair up and teasing it out, that Italy was a trap, most talk being the opposite of the words—most talk being like straightening hair—fixing it the crimps seem straight but with a little rain the hair pulls right back into curl. Underneath all those fixings, hair remains what it is. And everyone knows. That money in Italy, those gold bathtubs, that doesn't come from washing hair. Too many had not come back to Harcourt, at all, or they had, but with too much silence about their years. Milli knew the invitation was a trap and believed the opposite—like the songs that burn your heart and get your hips swinging so like water and then how the drops of baptism water come back into memory and make a terrible confusion. And now she was facing the police.

Signora Mugabe, will you listen and tell me if you recognize the tape?

Traps hung on set to spring shut. The same way her mother put up a cross that made them Christian and Nardela into an idol, and how her father's second wife kept the carved wooden goddess under the bed and after her mother died, put it right where the cross had been, and said, Touch it, touch it.

Do you have the money? Forty-five million lire.

That was one of the opposites, one of the many opposites, looking over her shoulder to see if her mother's ghost was around. And if her mother's pungent hair and interrogating face had been there, made contact, if she had been able to stand by Milli when her heart convulsed with sorrow, Milli knew she would never have kissed the goddess, never forsaken Christ. Milli had different voices inside and one told her what she wanted to hear, and another said, don't, don't, don't be tempted. She knew brains were like the universe itself. Fire and lightening. Snakes and parrots. Such promises and then just giving in.

The room in the police station looked broken down to her, with its dusty closed windows, looking as dusty as those poorer rooms in Harcourt, full of drunk war veterans, petty thieves and low level clerks. And now she was tired of the faces in front of her. She'd had a long night and it was time to go home to set out with Farina, to sit under the bridge and nod with exhaustion. Milli watched the woman with the red hair and realized her eyes were resting on her face. Milli almost wanted to pinch those eyes. Pinch them away with their comfortable resting on her.

Signora Mugabe. We are going to play the tape again.

Susan couldn't believe her ears. The tape was scratchy and vague. It said: do you have any money? And then it said: forty-five million lire. They had listened to it twice and it only produced a glazed over expression in the prostitute's eyes.

Pingello raised his finger to cue the clerk.

Giudice Pingello, Susan said, don't you think we have already heard that tape enough times? What if we move on into unmapped relations? Let her think.

Maybe Susan had meant to say that. Her certainty surprised her, though, that she had blurted out and in such an indignant tone. As if she were running things. After the shock, and Signorina Livi's gasp, Pingello exploded, making his glasses slip on his nose as he wagged his entire head. What could she do once his fury exploded, the way he cursed and slammed his fist down, putting the dusty room growing warm into a crisis? Susan's hand flew to her lips. Pingello shouted, Go on. His shaking hand struck the air as if to wipe the atmosphere clean of her stupidity and arrogance, her clumsy meddling: an American woman interrupting the intricate give and take made him boil. Unmapped relations? Let her think? Feeling his hand tremble, Pingello removed it, placed it inside the other one to keep it still. There, there, he glared at Susan. There, there. She'd seen that glare forever in Florence—an open distain for women using power. Yet she understood perfectly how she had stepped out of bounds. It might have been a small offense if he had not been the person he was. But he was the person she was dealing with.

Milli, watching the two faces redden, wondered if the questioning was over.

Do you have the money? the tape intoned.

Giudice, Susan gasped. She dared not speak.

Either translate it or leave the room. We are here to restore some hope to human lives.

Susan was even more surprised hearing that honorable sentence. She thought of leaving, but rejected that childish move. The clerk's eyes were on the floor. The click of the keys suspended. Susan didn't like being forced to comply but realized she must, hoping that the room would fall back into an official rhythm. It was strangely necessary, that appearance and rhythm. Just by looking at the young woman's disbelief Susan could see that more incomprehension had been introduced.

I don't know anything about the money, Milli said, twisting her neck a bit and rocking on her heels. The keys started clicking again.

That's all, Pingello said, standing up, visibly impatient, while he brushed the wrinkles out of his pants. All, he said, as if he were washing his hands of a betrayal. He motioned Signorina Livi over, purposely ignoring Susan as she stood to rise. His eyes looked past her to the door, where a man with matted long hair was coming in. The judge told the young clerk to open the windows as Milli turned to leave. More. Open them more. The disturbance in the room flitted like a fly from the prostitute, to the judge, to the Afghanistan man limping in, wearing a cloak that seemed to be made of bark.

Milli's arm was taken by the guard. Let me give you your things. Milli put on her wristwatch, and then she asked, My identity card? The woman went back into the room to take it from the clerk.

It felt like her actions were clattering down the stairs. Susan had never figured out how to walk without leaving that crashing sound on marble in Florence. She rushed past the guard without bothering to smile. What an unexpected outcome for an act of charity—being banished after having blown up a process that might have helped. The further she walked along on the hot crowded street the more her incredulity grew. The motorbikes with their large plastic windshields formed nearly solid barriers along the already narrow walk. So much of Florence seemed to be doing battle. Susan was already settling, returning to the cool shade and peace of her villa, so far away from the city. But it didn't sit well that wish to escape. It didn't sit well that she had offered nothing, no wisdom, no insight to the young woman from Nigeria. And that she had caused a fight. How she regretted the jabbing irritation that leapt out this morning. The judge was not effective, but that shooting voice belonged to her. Her impatience had created, not just today but more often than she would like to see, friction. She and the judge weren't that far apart. The problem was, until only a few minutes ago, she believed that she was an effective player.

Susan waited at the stoplight, and a convertible with four young men sitting on the folded roof, stopped, too, with a boom box casting vibrations that fell like a lasso on the thick crowd of tourists. Yesterday in front of the Duomo, as Susan headed toward the river, she had come across a group of white-gowned Muslims, each with his head down on a colored mat. Facing east they blocked nearly the entire space between the golden replica of Ghiberti's doors of paradise and the Cathedral steps. At noon, under the dome of sky, they were praying to Allah in such a determined way. She had gone the other direction, around the four sides of the back of the Baptistery, but it was surprising. Today there seemed to be police on mounted horses, high profile sleek Arabian ones, keeping the pathway open. Susan didn't dare hope to see Marina in the hoards around her, but she saw two or three striking faces that might have been her daughter. Each of them was surrounded by friends. Each seemed to be caught up in laughter. Why that should make her feel relief was anyone's guess. Marina was like a stranger, closed against her in this moment. And Susan's encounter with the judge. Here was someone actually trying, and he didn't have the right tools. And she had forced him to feel what she knew well: that virtue is often not sufficient.

The summer light was already quite fierce, heat was pressing, so warm that even between her soles and the inside of her shoes there was a sticky contact. As Susan reached the car, she saw the prostitute or someone like her slipping into the crowd near the market. A tall woman wearing a black dress. One impulse was to push along and run after her. But facing the woman what could she say? Seeing those wide frightened brown eyes, what could she say? I'll give you free hours to get in touch with your life through the sand? Admitting that incongruity to herself, Sister Morena's brown face appeared in Susan's mind.

From New Delhi, she was part of an order in the city that asked no questions whatsoever. Her open face was not a radiant one. But her seriousness was untroubled; her words were often striking, bringing a very small smile to her lips. We are drops in the ocean. But drops that count. The Little Sisters were used to slums, squatters, and had no qualms about what help meant.

Susan scanned the human flow, both tourist and citizen pouring into the market, advancing on the stalls loaded with t-shirts and bags and violet and green and yellow scarves filled out by the wind. How stupid she had been not to have stayed to catch the prostitute after she left the room. How absurd it was to have been so isolated by her own imagined drama. It was too late now to turn into that milling crowd, flicking with flags and officious tour leaders, and have the luck to find the young woman who bristled with diffidence and distain.

Farina rubbed her eyes and looked around the darkened room. She couldn't see Milli, who usually was stretched out, long and uncurled, on a cot next to her. Irene was at the sink, her back to the little girl. Farina didn't like the morning already—with its empty space—but she knew what to do without speaking. Down her little feet went on the cool floor with dirt rubbing on her soft skin. She eased her seat back on the cot and brushed her feet off. Down they went again and without looking around, she took a small aluminum pot near her bed and went to a corner, and sat on it facing the wall. She rather expected the hand that then touched her neck. Irene's long red fingernails were like bright feathers that didn't poke. The fingers were good in a way, touching her skin, and invading in another, reminding her that her mother was nowhere to be seen.

The two didn't talk. Irene did talk around the others, and willingly listened to the night tales and woes of white women who were under Igor, the women, who with the Albanians' supremacy had pushed the Nigerians out. The Russians and

Albanians were the victors in the latest shift to control work procured by subterranean deals. But she and Farina didn't talk. Farina was an apparition in the room with eight prostitutes and the coldly calculating Igor, surveying the room, procuring the protection needed to keep them in business. Farina, that lapse on Milli's part, that had sent her away from her Nigerian sisters in Turin, the Nigerian madonna with a child born on the banks of the Mugnone river, with Irene cutting the cord, was like a remonstrance among the eight women, who dressed and undressed in the armour of hooks and lace, and tight straps and stays that left marks and gouged into pockets of fat disciplining it upwards or inwards, whose tight clothes were thrown like whirlwinds over lines. Farina was a small unfussing bundle of intense watching who no one really bothered with, but whose two or three fevers and measles brought thoughtless cruelty out of most mouths as they chalked and greased their lips round and round making their lips red targets that would soon be used with cleverness and agility.

Igor was strangely indifferent to Farina, as if he had a memory of children in his own Albanian village, Valona, near the coast. Or maybe a sister or a cousin who lived in his mind, although was never mentioned. Igor threatened Milli but an understanding about some small hope in life made it difficult for him to turn her out. His tolerance was a matter of degree. He was always waiting for a lapse, to hold her culpable, and this morning, with Milli still not back, he found himself reviewing the options. He bent his head and watched the child from the corner of his eye. Farina was a parody, with her old lady way of folding her sheets with such concentration. The child's quiet got on his nerves. It bothered him, as if she was a spirit, who might bring bad luck with her observing eyes, watching all the unkindness that stamped and smoked in the room. His instincts prickled when he thought of the little girl with the squash nose. He wasn't afraid of her, but her shadow seemed as if it were gathering up all the ruin and judging it. Sometimes he gave her something that might have come into his hands at a bar—a small chocolate wrapped in green-foil. But the damn child was too wizened to even smile seeing a treat lifted towards her.

Sometimes Irene disliked, no, felt oppressed by the purposefulness of the child, her watchful intelligent face, measuring and thinking. Sometimes her proud straight head irritated her and reminded her of her own steps, so watchful of others, when she had been a girl in her gypsy tribe. Farina was so funny for being so young. She conveyed an air so much older than her mother, Milli, who hadn't come home; who hadn't called; who had bad days when she wouldn't wake up and would sulk or explode with laughter, excited by dreams that she couldn't make work out. Smiling, that was nearly out of the question with Farina, but Irene knew the child was, even with her short little leg and how she ran, limping even with her little disguises of waiting and watching, a child who was quite balanced, able to extract from herself a way to deal with the strange terror unleashed by the blurting restless women, their bickering and shouting, around her.

Irene found herself staring at Igor. There was a look in his eye, maybe disagreement, disapproval. Matrushka had her head upside down and was brushing her hair into a wild exciting bush. He perhaps was waiting to talk to her about business, not that he ever asked much except when the next payment would be made. It was difficult to understand how he made himself valuable, with his constant reminders of debt and the limits of patience. The whole scheme rode on fear and inertia. Keeping them scared. She'd told Milli and Milli'd agreed. But he did sometimes anticipate a crisis and even used delicacy if one had been beaten up or burned with a cigarette. And sometimes, like all of them, Igor simply made a nostalgic remark about a blue sky, or a church bell that made them feel he remembered poverty, remembered that he, too, could occasionally reach the ground they all remembered and denied. And while no one expected sensitivity, or a feeling as genteel as feeling sorry, there was a sensation, sometimes after a collapse, when Diana, for example, knocked Jean to the floor, in the violent tumble, Jean kicking Diana down until they both wrestled and twisted each other's arms over a pair of nylons that Igor, too, hoped the room would come to an end as a place of desperation. Sometimes his lined hard face showed weariness at being part of their exile, all of them crammed into a life for hiding the dispossessed. Not that he would ever even consider pulling up the shutters to let the light occur as a splendid reminder of a different world. Strips of light, bars of it squeezed through narrow gaps, was all he permitted.

Irene didn't trust the sudden alertness in his eyes, as she followed his gaze straight to Farina. His attention was too excited, too hungry, too willing to pounce on weak prey. Of all the deals he forced on them on hand-printed lists of their debts and his need for compensation for the showers they took, for the lights they kept on, for the telephone he used himself, he had never brought up until recently what Farina cost him. Irene could see that he was looking at the little girl and the still young, strong-bodied woman didn't know how she understood without words, but it was as if she could hear Igor talking in his mind. Igor was weighing up Farina's costs and deciding that he might sell her. He was watching her small hands pull up her little white pants, and drop the flowered dress over her head, tugging it. He was thinking, and Irene could hardly believe it, but in his look there was a new greed, a dull expansion of his territory.

Matrushka shouted at Igor. Where's the hot water?

Ask Lola and Irene. They used it up.

Irene nodded at the puffing head reappearing through the tight hole. We're going out, she said, not wishing to get pulled in and hoping to step out of the door before Milli's absence became a topic Igor would ask her to comment on. Good or bad news, she would try to reach Milli herself. Farina's hand reached up and held firm. She knew she couldn't ask about her mother, although her eyes returned to the empty cot. She looked at the table with the knife and the two yellow apples resting there.

I paid for those, Irene said, taking one in her palm. Farina, you eat it for breakfast. And seeing the query in her face, Irene picked up the knife quickly and peeled it, handing it back wet and sticky. The patience in the child's owlish face with large cheeks struck Irene deeply. Farina, if ever a child could be, was a blessing. And that she could read was nearly a magic power, given that Milli had never taken the time to even find her a second book. Farina's gift of reading was a sign to be noticed, a consideration, an omen to others, like the way queens were chosen in earlier times.

That's when he said it. While Farina chewed her pieces of apple. There's a market for kids.

He hadn't heard the alarm, and now with the sheets tangled near his neck, Luigi was awake, late, and filled with a haunting sense of remorse as he entered the bathroom to take a quick shower. The white fluffy towels were, as always, too white to use. Seeing the small bank of them along the wall, he wondered why he still went along with that feminine scheme. Pulling one down and then another, he stood on them, and ground his feet on the soft mound. He liked standing naked and shook his shoulders a few times. The folds around his belly he pulled in. Seeing the black marks his feet left, he grinned. He wished he could hand them to Diniza. The discrete sturdy Diniza had never seen him naked, he thought. Unambiguous. In her faded crisp blouses and skirts, there was always her touch and not a touch of sex. An air of balance, perhaps a nurse, but never the air of a servant. She would have taken the towels with a look of surprise, wondering and yet almost knowing why he had wiped his feet on such white towels.

Luigi stopped at the sink. Diniza resigned so unconditionally after his mother's things had been sorted out. It made no sense and was certainly not a lack of affection. If anything, there was a complicity that might have become a natural relationship if the two of them lived on in a new way alone. Luigi scratched his full head of hair and could almost see Diniza's melancholy face, its brow a series of moving reactions. Her opaque light skin, the way the war made her lose her studies as a medical student, meant she was far closer in age to Luigi than to his mother, when she came to them, deeply quiet and very thin, having walked away from a German camp near Salo'. Until this very moment Luigi had never asked himself what happened to her in those ten days she was walking before the British found her. Whatever happened she never spoke of them. But the escape seemed not to have given her faith in herself or the world, but a measured view, a habit of holding her tongue, while she appraised the smallest things, seeing where she might place them in the puzzle of life, which she believed always revealed a picture.

Taking off his watch to step into the shower, Luigi's eyes stopped on the diamond space enclosing the date. It was useless to pretend. His mother, Giada, died five years ago, on this very day, a few hours from now. It was his choice, he reminded himself, not to make a show at the grave. It didn't mean he didn't honor her, although honor wasn't all that close a synonym for memory. Good God, if that were so, even the way the white towels were still Giada's arrangement, defying most human behavior, would mean his mother was the most honored woman on earth.

Luigi shook his body under the warm drops as he stepped in further. Memory was in fashion these days. It was as fashionable as truth was unfashionable. Luigi liked that thought as he caught water in the cup of his hands and slapped it over his face. He never turned the water on full blast. It wasted the tributaries of the Arno. Memory pained him, really, because he simply couldn't escape it anywhere: at work, with his friend Gian Franco, with his ex-wife. Their versions of memory were such subjective renderings. The stories the Communists and Fascists continued to tell were like the size of the fish that grew; how the Partisans delivered Italy, how the Fascists never were. And the muck was there on all sides, so piety only led to counter piety. And their versions of memory didn't interest him. Luigi didn't want to muck in the muck. Luigi heard his own voice. He was shouting under the dripping flow. All around invented constructions were passed off as memory. The reality getting through was no more than the trickle of pouring drops. The rest was lip service. Susan's view expanded memory until it was the only explanation for behavior. She saw it as freeing, but for Luigi, it was the worst kind of fatalism, like the Greek stories. Most of ecology spoke against that very concept. What seemed like laws were under pressure from adaptations and mutations. And yet, the dream last night was surely a memory trying to grab his attention. Luigi pushed the soap against the hairy bushes under his arms. There had been no way to exterminate it.

The dream told him, not as he wished to put it, but, in the end, the dream amounted to what he thought: his mother was displeased with him and she wanted to turn him into someone like herself. Giada wanted to call him up to her grave for remembrance, love, and that guilt-producing thought, which had moved in and out of Luigi's mind, had mercilessly persisted beyond his efforts to repress it for weeks. The unfaced conflict had overtaken him during a lecture when the students' talking had peaked as he was trying to make them focus on stomata—millions of jaws opening to let out a chemical that we all need—

he saw his mother's elegant pained face trying to get his attention when he often interrupted her mid-sentence, turning his back on her and that rude habit pertained to his teenage years. The irony of his stale guilt struck him speechless. When Maria Grazia complained about his indifference, even coldness, when she issued her angry torrent that came hurling from her young incredulous mouth as she fussed with hair that was pulled back tight and said 'Never' to an abortion—whose face did he see, but Giada's. It shocked him to feel Maria Grazia's pressing fury, her fingers pulling and gripping his shirt and seeing his mother, silent and calm, mocking the determined young woman and blaming him. One or the other or both of the women locked up his innards and twisted them. Even though he was a scientist, clear about what he believed about Catholics and the afterlife, what he thought about buying bunches of bright flowers, which were really sops to guilt, his conscience's campaign was not to be quelled. He couldn't shake off the sense of culpability knowing that he had not visited her grave, not just this past year but for five years. It was as if he had passed some unforgivable limit. He had not gone back ever, once they carried her down the gravel path to that pompous family tomb. And the dream said it.

Giada had cared so much about honoring the dead. It was a mystery and even morbid, although she insisted it gave her something to do, riding out into the country, tending her family's tomb. The fact is, Luigi thought, rubbing in the cold shampoo, it wasn't a tomb, but a cult. And her addition had been particularly heavy. No one thought she would be so willful, and yet those stone carvers were there for more than a week, chiseling out a proclamation with claims, which, surely, his grandfather, Umberto, and his father, Cesare, had no interest in lying under. 'Lo I am with you always, even until the end of the earth'. And when he had met Gian Franco near the bridge, last week, when he had not been thinking about her anniversary, that sensation of Giada came over him again. In the panic of seeing an old friend's face as a blank, in that second of admission of not belonging to any relationship but a false one, a shadowy chilliness overtook him. He felt his mother's calm elegance gluing them together. His mother was such a part of the growing up the two had shared. Her shadow, Luigi reasoned, turning off first the knob for 'hot' and then for 'cold,' is why Gian Franco was in the dream. And why Diniza circled in his mind. Unless the dream was about another kind of deadness, he thought, enjoying the warm air as it started to dry his hairy body.

The last meeting had been like many. He and Gian Franco had hugged, having bumped into each other, and then like boxers in a clinch, leaned on each other, and then standing up again, with the flow of people passing around them, half-heartedly rushed with laughter to fill up an unpleasant undefined sensation. Luigi had had the distinct feeling of nostalgia—the privilege of seeing someone who had been in their house going all the way back to putting kidney beans in piles to do sums, and yet, once he put aside that elegiac building ground, the uncountable hours and many years since spent in bars and the occasional meetings at the country club only confirmed a long loneliness. Gian Franco never even acknowledged how difficult Luigi's life might have been all the years on his own. Instead, it was assumed by Gian Franco, as they sat down, and appreciatively remembered Matilda Gaslini and then Carla Rodone, that Luigi was free and lucky not to be burdened by a wife. Always men knew how to talk about a period of youth where supposedly there had been pure male life. That was the level they clung to like climbers hooked to the same rope. Part of Luigi didn't mind that easy drop to the past, but mostly it seemed like fright, like a waste of time. And meeting Gian Franco on the Ponte Vecchio, although he would have needed to talk about Maria Grazia, she was the last topic that would have come out of his mouth. Maybe there was shame constricting his throat, because of the child. But it was repulsion that constrained him, a perception that Gian Franco would sully the topic, would joke, and would not imagine that he and not Luigi had become the unpresentable character one could not bring home.

The conversation had been the usual mixture of moves that led in a circle, where jumping in meant getting farther from shore. Gian Franco shook his head. Let's face it, we wasted a lot of time pretending more compassion than was called for. And what do we have to show for it? He waved his packet of tax papers in the air. Ingratitude. High postures of principles and calling it corruption.

There had been beers. First raising his finger for two. Then before he knew it, his glass was empty and the waiter had returned.

Luigi knew his old schoolmate, knew perhaps he was better than his awful words. But only perhaps.

Are you worried? he had asked.

If I'm worried all of Florence should be worried. They are going after some of the big socialists, and we are way back behind the lines. You know what I mean. We're small fish. And the tax office. You must know, as well as I do, the ones who take bribes.

Luigi disliked the leveling, the way Gian Franco's words assumed a brotherhood, assumed complicity. The way he spoke he seemed to want to destroy the frail confidence that was left. His words seemed colored by their amber drinks.

Once he and Gian Franco envisioned political roles. Luigi could imagine that Gian might be in some sort of trouble. The doctors in private practice had endless ways to avoid taxes. And some of these schemes led all the way across Europe, some of them extended to hospitals, some made inroads into the universities, real estate, soccer.

And then the topic changed to tennis and Gian Franco's special privileges.

What do you think of the new proposal? And don't give me the pious answers of twenty years ago. The tennis club had recently elected Gian Franco president after he announced there would be no membership for Arabs or any of the new Russians with their bags of cash. Gian Franco lifted his tortoise shell glasses off his nose and poked Luigi's chest. Not hard at first, but then the edges of the frame began to hurt. The immigrants are too much. We are forming a committee to see if there can't be a sweep along the river. And I like the new direction, where we might even cut the country in two.

It was not a surprise, but hearing how far they had drifted apart, Gian Franco reversing himself totally from the years when they talked about revolution behind his grandfather's factory, Luigi could not find a chord of trust. He couldn't find—hearing Gian Franco with his dyed hair pronounce that he might support men who opposed any ideal that he and Gian Franco had once stood for—any base on which to make a new promise to his friend, not that Gian Franco was asking.

By the time Luigi had dried his feet, spreading his toes to avoid any lurking moisture, and tugged on his long elegant socks, Luigi realized he was nearly hopelessly late for his appointment with a student. His students. Now, there was a field of battle and unrecognized valor. Honor. Such a ridiculous fantasy—his father's and Marcus Aurelius's obsession. And yet, it drove him, too. Obviously since its dry ambiguities and obligations had given him such a miserable night. And lateness. It was his father who forced his workers to push stiff cards into a punch clock.

When the noodling sound came, Maria Grazia vaguely expected it to be Luigi. Then the sigh filled her, the sigh that appeared like a shadow when he got close. She was helpless to supplement the relationship by answering the number on her phone. The signal that he had tried to get in touch gratified her. That was the risk. If she pushed 'on' and his voice was distracted, even if she could rationalize it with his being in traffic, she would meet that irritating feeling that he was still fumbling with the problem, unaware of her existence. Disinterested in the child. Maria Grazia rubbed her belly and tilted her head. Don't listen to me, little one, she said, pensively, rubbing with both hands. How she wondered about that quickening that caused tension anytime she had to think about Luigi. Only by hearing the ring and not letting more in, could she relax and feel safely the connection that he and she were unsure of.

As she rubbed her burgeoning stomach, the child inside trilled his stumps as he turned and swayed. He moved like a tongue, searching for a mouth. He knew nothing of a father or mother, nothing of sadness. He could barely hear the watery surges around him. They were vibrations rolling him, shaking him. On his growing spins, which were a potentiating expression of capacity, he apotheosized like a current or a leaf rustled by wind. Going in and out as far as the walls of her placenta, bumping and then trembling free from the curved limits around him, the voyager on his tether half slithered, half swam, not resting or fearing for his life. His young body obeyed without obeying.

Unable to do anything more courageous, and unwilling to show up in the lab, Maria Grazia hauled the heaviness of her limbs, the sleepy lazy feeling of heat and summer, down the stairs to her bike. In the hours before the heat became oppressive she would pedal over to her mother's, who, unless she had mounted her Bianchi bicycle and was volunteering one of her two mornings at the Centro Sociale, a Liberty style building that had been a busy active cell of the now dissolved Communist party and was struggling to pay its rent. Like the anxious men and women sitting in rows, some with nearly masked locked faces, many unable to start up a conversation, but dropped off while families were at work, the transition as it was called, the transition into whatever Italy was to become, seemed palpable in the confusion and sense of loss in the room. The manifestos in the halls with Occheto declaring *avanti* from the 1980s and Castro as a young man, and even Gramsci with his glasses, had no replacements since the Berlin wall fell. They were tattered now and the united crowds pictured had become mouthwatering images. The social mornings, looking after old people, were a new function and perhaps would not be funded much longer by the Party coffers. Signora Ester, Maria Grazia's mother, volunteered for many reasons, but the one she enjoyed most (it remained marvelously simple) boiled down to the cards that were dealt at ten o'clock in the morning. However, today was not one of Ester's days at the center and she was at home in her kitchen, planning to roast peppers, and then to peddle down to the Duomo at noon to attend the solstice ceremony at the cathedral—Lorenzo Melandri was an old friend—to watch the ray announce summer for another year, when her daughter, not winded from the ride nor the climb to her parents' terraced apartment above Santa Maria Novella, came in.

The room flooded by terrace light crossing the salotto and hall and finding its way across the table where her mother was slicing green and red and yellow boat-like shapes in heaps of gayness suddenly felt painful to Maria Gracia. The stability and healthy naturalness which nearly made her yawn when she lived at home seemed so safe that, for a minute, she might have curled up like a cat and let the sun put her to sleep in its comforting depth. Instead, her mother's face, with that split second of wariness, of expecting Maria Grazia's visit to have a purpose underneath, prodded the young woman into covering up her doubts and not making excuses for herself.

Politics was always a free ride. Her parents were solid Communist members who had even tithed when Togliatti requested it; they had started separating when Hungary fell to the Russian tanks and slowly they rolled over as the party rose strongly for a while and then changed names. They said they were on the Left like an Englishman might say of driving. They knew the road and would never ask for the steering wheel to be moved or the system reversed. Comfortable. They were comfortable with an idea that poverty should be eliminated in part by social pact. If they had dug, contrasts abounded between the family members. But more or less, because they saw themselves as standing on the Left, and that was a commitment and virtue, there was an easy commonness about assumptions. Maria Grazia actually had a lot to quarrel with, but not at the level at which their chats about politics took place. Politics could be safe, because they basically held to the same side. Discussions of this sort tended toward ritual, tribe, strengthened belonging. Others might have fallen on music or food, but the Bobanellis found a lot of common twigs and mortar in this sense of a nest. Maria Grazia could grow tired of not moving closer and speaking about problems of the family itself. But all of them, her father, her mother, her brother Ivan could swing into that undisputed land. So this kind of banter about current events was something the two women could do, without thinking or feeling, if need be.

The beautiful flushed woman pecked her mother on the cheek and said without even greeting her, Have you seen the new figures on the Socialists' Swiss accounts? Not millions but billions stolen.

Her mother looked up from the slash of yellow skin that she held so confidently between her fingers and the knife and decided to smile and settle for a talk about politics instead of the reason for the visit. How are you? she asked. It was early. She didn't need to give any sign of searching for ways to heat up her daughter's life. She didn't like the way Maria Grazia seemed anxious, didn't like what seemed to be humiliation in her fine intelligent eyes. But she didn't need to know, she told herself, mixing the colors in the pile as if it were a children's game.

The Swiss may be covering the Vatican as well as the track of Socialist money running right across Europe.

Don't you think they're separate things? Ester asked, knowing that her daughter was prone to secrecy and conspiracy ideas, prone to believing that the entire system had to be reformed. She wanted her daughter to sit down, but she was old enough to pull out her own chair.

Instead, if the north of Italy decides to break off, all this tearing apart at one moment could really be dangerous.

It won't happen, said Maria Grazia, pulling hard on a crust of bread she had sliced for herself. Without asking, she slathered on some marmalade.

Sit down, if you are going to eat. Ester, whose knuckles were worker's hands, in spite of all the chalk she had held, the pencils and pens she had used to correct Italian, appreciated her daughter's attention and liked having her, the warmth, if the not the precise topic of conversation, as she worked around the kitchen. She decided to give her little speech. It was only words, and words directed to her daughter, who knew them by heart, and underneath nearly accepted the same thing. But it was hot and it comforted her to assert that Italy would not split in two, would not find a racist solution that would undo all the effort of the last century in its not totally blind crawl upwards.

I believe people are not that stupid. Life has gotten so much easier. They forget but there were no cars, no refrigerators, no central heating. There was, really, hardly any food. University was a luxury. I think unless memory is of no use, people will not forget and they will know that we are a country that cannot break in two. If it ever comes to a vote, they will remember. It's young people who might not remember.

Maria Grazia tired quickly of her mother's slow logic. She never constructed proofs, but asserted her faith by single examples. The split in the country was not the same as the corruption. How funny these games were played with straight happy faces. She chewed another piece of bread, yanking the crust with her white teeth, not convinced but not interested either in testing her mother's skills or showing off her own darker readings of the groups challenging and disrupting Italy's transition.

The bread helped with her twinges of nausea. The queasiness sent constant communication and reminders of the growing life that she would have to address. She looked at the only two significant wrinkles in her mother's face, deep V's in her forehead, like Van Gogh's blackbirds. Her mother, a middle-school teacher, had been beaten by her own mother, a woman with eleven children and from the stories told, half crazy and poisoned with hallucinations from the impossibly heavy farm life she'd led. She'd never spoken with Ester after her headstrong daughter ran away with Maria Grazia's father at age eighteen. They were miracles of sorts, her parents. Her father, a doctor and willing to let his wife go to school. Her father had never made a career in medicine but had served, as a labor union member arguing for doctors and her mother had never objected. There was harmony of sorts.

Sitting at the table, Maria Grazia felt love as solid as it was, worn as were the cupboards and the cutting board where years of bread had been sawed off. What to do with the love that both of them felt and yet held no answer for what Maria Grazia needed to decide. What to do with her family's love when what Luigi offered was so measured and tight, so unbending and frightened.

Maria Grazia felt her mother's gaze. Resting on her, it probed and then said (because Maria had seen the look often), I shouldn't open my mouth, as she let the words burst.

Any news?

No, Maria Grazia said, wanting to say something helpful, but feeling sour.

Don't worry. He'll come round.

That made Maria Grazia bolt. She reminded herself to keep her mouth shut, but she couldn't.

It's my business. It's painful. It's nothing to talk about. And she would have said—but her pride was too strong—I'm scared and I'm furious. I want a father for this little moving thing. She would have also said, because her mother was a friend, I don't want a child for myself. I am uncertain of all this weight. I have good research that will be impeded, but I never thought so shallowly as a feminist as to say diapers will keep me from doing it. I don't see a child as generated by a female alone. Whatever happens I will react. I am your daughter. But I don't want you and dad to look after my child while I measure my reagents. I want Luigi to be with me. I don't want to be alone or brushed off or heroic. I want a man's body around me. I want pleasure and not just sacrifice raising a child. What did you give me if not some sense that marriage is possible? What did you and dad give a stab to if not some solid basis to stand together, inside a house and outside in society?

Nothing could answer the growing sorrow she felt. Of course she could handle the child alone but it was a whole different life. And the child would be scarred from the beginning. Compromised. If Luigi did not really want him.

Her mother cut open a red pepper. Blight inside blackened the red walls.

That's the second time in a week that Boromeo has sold me things gone bad on the inside. I'm sure he doesn't mean to, but he'll have to speak to his importer. These have probably been on a boat for weeks, once they left Chile.

FOUR

THE GAWKY PLASTIC sheet was so brittle that the act of removing the long covering took determination. All of winter's melting and spring's pollen had adhered since that awful February day when the bones of two fingers had poofed into dust. The ring, she supposed, was still near the remaining frail knuckles, where she re-placed it and its yellow bead, and then returned muddy soil lightly and more soil, as she always did, erasing, in the end, her stolen hours' work. But as the withery frail hand settled under the bumpy backfill, the heap smoothed, her decision was final when she said to herself, I mustn't keep doing this. Before burying the yellow knob in the ring, Susan had drawn the amber like everything else. Put its characteristics in the book with her other notations. The small incisions on the bronze jumped like two fives crossing each other at right angles. The so-called phoenix was, in fact, an Etruscan symbol. The rising bird dominated the first dream of her first patient: a warrior falcon in flames flying from Signor Dominici's smoke-filled house. Deep in the brain's organization, deep in the stories of what the earth was about, the image of rebirth stuck and re-arose. Rebirth in life. Then in death.

When Susan found an identical ring in Gordon's book on

Etruscan jewelry, the page seemed like the other glass clinking in a toast. The bronze ring with two loops probably joined the woman buried in her yard with a specific people. That day, the same one Susan decided not to return the morning after to dig further, the ring identification gave her the impetus to name the human figure lying stripped like a leaf's veins in the earth. She'd tried many in the months she'd fiddled with patches of soil gripping the Etruscan. Maddalena. Queen Bora. Persephone. But Teresa sounded and felt right as she searched the vision she had extrapolated of the short, stocky woman. When Susan reached for continuity, thought of women on wheels, St. Teresa, holding the leather reins came to mind. The brilliant mystic pulled by donkeys, riding her rickety tumbrel over the hills surrounding Avila, creating her place in a world that had plans to crush her—St. Teresa's roots merged with the woman buried in the yard and what was a slow, almost imperceptible ascension into self-sufficiency through faith.

The next three pages of Gordon's book confirmed the phoenix as a sign of belonging, like wearing a cross. But the cloudy amber was an anomaly. Suggesting trade. Or travel. Being converted or captured near Chiusi, sacked tomb number 24 was identified as possibly holding a female chariot, because of its size, and the posts of two gold earrings. The wheeled chariot appeared later in female burials in Mongolia and was not necessarily linked with battle. The sensation of correspondence between the book and the body in the earth was close to the process of working with symbols and sand: Susan loved the inferences, the working out from clues.

But when the bones vaporized, crumbled into little dice, the secret mission collapsed. The fingers weren't the only things her puttering had destroyed. Nature was at work and surely opening the grave she had speeded funguses along. She'd seen lots of ravaged metal in conservation books. Daggers' thin consumptive edges compared with gnawed holes in tattered vessels.

Loss. Loss. And what had she done with the rims—gorgeous wide pounded curves attacked by white flaking patches corroding them—but buried them? Susan revisits the beautiful wheels in the shaded details of her drawings of indentations where hammers struck. In the hole, instead, she eased the rims' dissolving blue-green powder deeper into the soil.

Nothing justified her illegal digging. She knew about fascination. Curiosity, mystery, a sense of possession. All true, but not sufficient. Italian law insisted that touching antiquities was a crime against history. A phrase applied in tribunals to torturers, to the mass graves in Bosnia, yet, its somber authority extended to what she had been lamely disturbing. Even early knowledge about women's lives. And so she stopped. When the fingers broke, she had drawn a line. That exercise of indeterminate value that was like re-channeling the Arno. She drew a line, as she and Vaclav had done, knowing of each other's existence, returning on the phone, in reconsidered meetings, but breaking the encounters off. I can't. I can't. Had she said that? Or had he? After seven years of meeting as if their bodies together would become their permanent and unprecedented life. They had set up borders.

The analogy with Vaclav was right, because forgetting him, denying the past as well as his life in Prague, now, was pretending. Keeping him buried. A ruse. Seeing him in newspapers, unreal and yet, an effort every bit as great as those alcoholics who must vow never to touch a drink. But not entirely. Sometimes Susan wonders how she survived. Marina and even Luigi lived the benefits of a generosity and cheerfulness that she felt she owed them because of her lapse. And Vaclav, in that light, appears with an awfulness that borders on looking at a noble collie lost and stuffed so many years ago. Lover is completely the wrong word in that light. In that brutal light she sees herself as a young mother, as a guilt ridden Midwesterner and therapist who even for a few weeks broke those rules and then entered into the deeper water where rules between people break. She sees herself as an emigrant who was lonely and immature, who used her American skills in organization to become an intern in management, who kept ledgers calculating moves and losses, emotional supplies, and wore herself out with what she really wanted. Vaclav's wife was in London but Susan had none of that space. She had the intrusions of patients, and Luigi, and Marina, and no extra help, no fashionable evenings discussing the responsibilities of artists and the best way to live that concern. She had passion that spun off in the end into guilt and rage and longing. When Vaclav left for London for the last time, and she walked through the insignificant electric doors at the airport in Florence, Susan fled as if she might have really been caught by them, crushed if she hadn't run.

Now, coming back into the yard, something odd had snapped without any explanation in the hot day itself. She could not bear her own forgetting. Her own swept up life. The excavation, which was a fantasy and yet held a real skeleton, could not remain untouched in the soil. Maybe the last straw had been that blue Porsche behind her, pushing her all the way up the hill, adding to that feeling of intolerance for being pushed. Maybe it was how she lost track of the prostitute's questioning because Pingello chose to read her wrong. The chance that lay in that tomb—that woman who might have even consulted books made from leaves of gold—Susan understood that she was about to join the line of chariot drivers originating in Teresa. She had battled on and something new was happening. A choking darkness, a discouragement, it was unbelievable how her throat felt clear. Something significant was clearing away.

The parking space below the lilacs was empty. Empty as a crib. Susan couldn't resist noting the thoughtlessness on Marina's part. But Marina was not the problem. For the first time her daughter was looking forward instead of tilling a past of minor losses. Marina was watching her life open and if Carlo and his engineering straightness weren't right, at age nineteen it didn't matter. She was in love now and learning what that intense mixture was about. The business she felt about the divorce was something she would have to uncover from her own slow discoveries. Susan's sober blouse clung to her back, wet from the long ride. She put down the large padded envelope she had pulled from the red cast iron mailbox. The strong handwriting had not a wobble in it and had hardly changed since Susan was a girl. Inside was her mother's sealed distant voice that might as well be from an unexcavated tomb but was not, and why was that? As she had turned the small mailbox key to close it again, Susan knew it was she who was a slow bomb ticking. She was the one on fire.

The sensation of lifting, lifting startled her. The excavation would soon come to an end. The unresolved problem of Teresa was nearly over. Her horrible indulgence over. The word flew like a bomber from the padded envelope she put down near the hole. Indulgence was a word her mother, Charlotte, might have used. It knew nothing of professions, choices. Indulgence never integrated with the world. No, that isn't right. It did touch a self. Charlotte used to say every so often, just indulge me. And she might emerge happily balancing a blunt tower of new shoeboxes. At least the excavation was not that. Teresa was a passionate discovery. She was what the world was about: memory, the present, working to uncover connections.

The first cicada rasps throbbed and sawed. The dirty planks were easy enough to push aside. This morning the burial would come to an end. The admission felt so good Susan wondered if it were really true. The garden was lovely and at its height. The terraced walls bobbed with tumbling jasmine, and hibiscus, that, like the hiss in their name, hosted tongues, dragon bursts of seductive purples and whites and peach, pulsing and glowing with wonderful tumescence. The yard, which she and Signor Luzi had labored over, swayed with scents and shadows chasing light. Except for the cypress that Luigi had advised her not to cut, the yard was a dominion under her control. Yet the garden disturbed her. A feeble feeling less than jealousy, less than greed, troubled her pleasure. Accepting the villa from Luigi, in the name of Marina, never sat right.

Susan likes the idea that ridding himself of the villa was convenient for her ex-husband. That he gave it away because he didn't want to uncover the peephole on his great grandparents' slaughter-house money from Argentina. That the villa, with its questionable thirties beginning and then the marriage lapse, bothered Luigi. Embarrassed him. And the house relieved his conscience about his daughter. That version of Luigi's deed means her living in the villa can't fell Susan's pride. But around the edges, she knows he has often been willing, more than disinterested, when, without any questions, he provides whatever she or Marina asks. That is the indifferent-to-money husband she never understood when he would pay the cleaning woman twice what she was owed. The wealthy Luigi whose redistributing Communism had fascinated her when she and he were chanting for North Viet Nam. But this morning even the motive for the villa's ownership has lost its attraction. Maybe she can toss the question into the hole. What was holding her inside the high-beamed rooms except a life and objects that she was not? For how long had she wanted to leave for a life she postponed in Marina's name?

The light breeze jostled her, cooled Susan down. Relief freed her body, letting her breath draw in as she imagined Teresa's skull and her feet and the blue-green barrel of a chariot assume reality in the light of a normal day. The horses in her sampled anatomy, the porous foreleg and what seemed to be brown fragments of two enormous pelvises, argued for two. Teresa had driven them, presumably standing in the bronze cab, their bells chinking. And then they were stilled. Their necks slit? What brought those two horses to be buried?

The hole was deeply cracked along the north walled surface and altogether, absurdly large. Two lizards trickled out of a crack and zoomed on flying feet. It was impossible that her gardener Signor Luzi hadn't noticed the maw for what it was. Impossible. He'd argued at the beginning, tried to snoop, but then he gave up. It was obvious from where Susan stood, from any angle he surveyed it, he must have perceived the excavation. Just the depth of the arid hole would make anyone think as much. Hers was the blind denial. Luzi's dry Tuscan silence was raw and voluntary. And what about Marina, through her smart eyes? When she lay in the hammock, the plastic covering was directly in her line of vision. She probably would be surprised to know that her mother did illegal things. But maybe not. Maybe that was only what Susan wished to think. That Marina had never perceived a dramatic stealthy side in the rather steady mother of patients, jam-making, and loud American peace songs with whom she shared the house.

These were the few minutes when there were no shadows on the villa, only slabs of sun. For the first time, looking down into the large hole, Susan felt the raw wealth lapped over by the dirt and perceived her risk. Signor Luzi's loyalty shone like one of those broad, white patches of light on the house. The black-eyed Tuscan peasant had known—in a way that was unusual for the taciturn but often sly Florentine peasants—what he didn't need. He didn't need to turn her in for money.

Susan kicked a plank back further and listened. Arvon's harsh cry. The peacock's blood curdling, nagging scream. The hens riled clucking. Another fierce fight beyond the hedge. Turning her head, she stopped short of going. It was useless to put herself in between. The garden, for all its summer ripeness, was never a magazine picture of serenity. The questions around the buried ancient woman were today's issues. Foremost, if the word got out, the doorbell would start ringing. Susan wondered if she and Teresa were ready to be reached by the popping flashbulbs and crowd of official diggers who might, in the end, pry the ancient body from the earth, carry her off, putting her in an ambulance. It was more than likely. If there was a chariot, they would name the skeleton, too, and put her on television, finding an angle for whatever remained of her sunken face. Her grimace would be flashed across the world and she would be called a queen. They would weigh her, look at her teeth, and figure out the type of flax wrapping her dead baby. And list her grave on a map with two stars linking her to the growing special Etruscan finds from Viterbo to Naples. Terra-cotta caskets with couples embracing in death. Wall paintings with leopards. And now, bronze wheels.

A sharp sting filled Susan's eyes. Taking the ancient woman out and bringing her into the light, discrepancy would disintegrate the image. Nevermind the stories she had told herself. No, it would be the drama of watching a life lifted from its sacred space. It would be difficult to witness the body detached from another time. That underground glory and connection would be gouged out of the land. Its removal and exit would chop up and cut off a very old link, even to the brilliant sky. It was her fault that this Etruscan, who—wherever or however the woman had died—was now exposed in present day Florence. Teresa, the ancient traveler buried and settled among her things, was about to be pulled into a world of blue Porches and slave traffic. And terrorist bombs in the Uffizi.

Susan had three hours in her possession. Three hours when she could be her own patient. The trowels were out in the greenhouse, lined up with their stiff red handles. Albina would come in the afternoon. The determined melancholy woman was doing well in a mysteriously difficult life. Giving up her ear practice, no longer being able to bear looking at people's reddened eardrums, touching their faces, suiting them up for hearing aids once a set of iron rods had come untied on the freeway and pushed through the back seat window, killing her son instantly, she'd finally found sculpting as a way to stay sane. She'd changed houses, and while her husband let her go back and forth between them, she had moved to a village for its space and peace.

Yes. She had chosen to fire metal and bend it into long piercing arrows. But finally she realized that the shape she had chosen slew her son. So she chose broader surfaces and more flexible metal that could take the marks of being pounded and beaten. She needed to leave signs of memory, as if they were fists pounding walls or rain that had entered the soil. She thought, then, she had created and expressed a world that would speak for others. She identified her sculptures by numbers, No. 6, No. 403, followed by The Disappeared.

Yes, yes. There were ways to extract meaning.

Susan likes Albina. Albina's eyes have translated her sorrow into depth, dark waters waiting. Peace. Her eyes, if you look at them, also allude to the anvils she beats and the mask she wears to shield her eyes and prevent her eyelashes from being singed off in the welding. But the fire used for bending pieces is a working hill fire that roars on, often breaking up the night. And now her neighbors are complaining about the smoke. Threatening her with summons. Tormenting one who was offering healing. And her husband wants her to move back.

Yes. We are each dealt a shape and some are so difficult to bear. Susan had not one patient at the moment who was seeing her just to explore an opening in life. They were all particularly burdened and tried. And being nearly late June, no clients would be added now.

Susan looked down into the hole. If she changed her clothes, she was prepared to fit herself back in that claustrophobic space. On her way toward the house, coming down the steps, rustling filled a silence that had returned. The still-fresh battle between Arvon and the angry hen had whirled chicken feathers, rooster plumes and blue-black peacock medallions as far as the bushes. The rustling was apart, a soft rummaging.

Virgil, Susan sighed, as she bent down, feeling her knees ache. The slow hopping amphibian was hooded over. The jacket of dead skin bound his body by covering his eyes. The deft motions of his two front legs, and the back ones that were rolling the skin forward, while the front ones, with their talons, received it, tugged it, pulled it over his bulging eyes, over his black nostrils, blind-folded him as he tried to stuff it into his mouth. There was no fairy tale she knew that had recounted this detail: skin used as nourishment, being devoured and eliminated. Certain aborigines honored the placenta, but that didn't involve being blind for a while, and unable to move. The danger of the blind passage was part of the realization her patients finally made, when all was still unsettled. The unknowing walk in the dark. Virgil, Susan said again.

Virgil couldn't stop. Engulfed by the savage middle of his task, if his energy kept up, the grinding bone-wearing effort would end and he could plop into the beautiful idleness of rest. But now he was still in the fight and must keep at the condition, which was his and would release his limbs. The tender state of bruise and shock. His quaking. The first hours of the soft new white robes of his belly. His front talons worked like weavers' hands gathering up the old hanging skin. Shirring, wrinkling it, stuffing the ghostly circles closer to his jaws.

She hadn't turned her phone off. Milli fingered her coin purse, the lipstick bulge, and as she reached the empty corners of her bag, felt so angry she might have thrown the large pouch against the wall, or even let it crash into the store window of flying, suspended summer silk blouses. So she spit and kept walking with her head high. They kept it. So the police stole too. Or the last client did. Stole her phone and cut off her way to calling Irene. And why was that man shouting at her? Raising his hands? The unknown, she thought, hot and head filled with pounding humiliation, the unknown was a constant. She spit again. There was no way to guess what would go right or wrong, from the moment you put on your shoes in the morning and the child had a sore throat. That was true all the way into the night, bending into each car, lying down in the grass looking for the motives in a pressing face. To be taken by the unknown. Like a veil. Like a hand. Like a snatch. That was true in Harcourt, when the water came up and became Meniki's death, or bad moves by soldiers holding up rifles asking for bribes, but different, different, the muscles in the unknown where one was not an immigrant, a stranger who stuck out like a seductive, wilting black flower.

The decision to stop in the cafe came quickly to Milli. Weakness coming from hunger. She had no reason to rush to the apartment only to suffer under a barrage of blows. You would have to be stupid, she thought, to add more trouble to an already endless succession of disasters. And Irene, she sincerely believed, wouldn't mind watching Farina. By now, even if she had wings, it was too late, anyway, to cross the city. Board the bus. Weary.

It wasn't the first time Milli had sat down at Rivoire's, although she had refused many occasions when clients, often in a crisis, wanted to show her off, positioning her near the fence, out under the yellow flapping awnings, wanting to wiggle their pink tongues at her, starting with their mouths full of those black little fish eggs considered such fascinating food.

Only on my own, thank you, Milli said sitting down and easing off her shoes with delicate skill.

The chair was warm and comfortable, body hugging for a tired back. Looking out across the square, the crowds' endless movement seemed sluggish, unlike Harcourt where people swirled from one stall to the next, chattering, and balancing loads on heavy bikes, old and young swirled like a hundred pieces of excitement and judgment, picking up this and putting down that, children hopping, students buzzing with politics and the old ladies with prices. Radios and voices. Whereas the crowds before her eyes were stuck in dull clumps, each clump slow, wadded up, and being driven by one little tourist driver with a handkerchief whip.

Florence, which Milli rarely thinks about, never sitting down with Florence in mind, jumped out at her. In spite of the blue sky with its silver fish clouds, the square reminds her how unsettled and sick and tired her life is and now with police. The square is one big mystery, a big, cold mystery, since she is a stranger and can see it with the eyes of a person who has lived outside Italy and has read books. Milli saw a photo of the statue of David before she ever left Harcourt. She had seen him and remembered how beautiful she had found his muscled thighs, his sex. She'd seen him in a schoolbook in Father Mark's study and admired the sculptor whom the priest had said was a genius. Milli had never thought white or colonizer. She never doubted then for a minute when he said, tapping her on the head, seeing her interest, that David was the highest expression of art.

The waiter dropped a plastic menu on her table without stopping for an explanation.

Milli knew that kind of poison dart. That way certain men who weren't men had of being imps, of making a point of your differentness, your work.

Her armpits smelled and she was sorry about that. But she was going to have something to drink. Something for the bad night that had passed, for her cold sweat, for her liberation. When he came back she would charm him, why not?

She looked across the piazza bobbing with tourists. They were all excited, and she felt worn out, drifting like someone who was far from home. What could they see, she thought, with their rapt faces? What could they see in David's forehead? Worry and more worry. The wrinkles showed the size of the giant. She had not noticed at first, but slowly, one time or another, she had stopped to look at each of the statues in the large piazza *Signoria*. Maybe she had thought of showing Farina, and that was when she had noticed the woman cutting a man's head off with a sword. That was nothing to show a little girl. And so she walked on. And what were the statues? A woman covering her face, a dead man under her, and her mother tearing at her dress. Blindfolded. A soldier with a club. Another gruesome murder, with a man holding up a woman's head and standing on her body. Standing with his winged foot on a body that looked like real dead flesh. And letting her head, crawling with snakes, swing. Snakes. Then another statue of a young girl, twisting and tearing out of the grappling arms of two men, pushing with her helpless plump feet to get away from being raped. Then two more muscled soldiers with spiked clubs. It had surprised Milli because she hadn't realized that the men she saw at night, in cars, the half who sought pleasure or the half who hardly ever did, and the men and women who were carved in marble, however intelligent or brilliant the sculptures might be, were all pictures of unhappiness, of violence, of sex. She had never imagined when she first said—Farina, Look— that she didn't want her child to see such acts. It took her brain in different moments when she was passing through the arches and around the fountain to realize in every niche of the piazza that horror was present no matter how people went on that this was art. They remembered horror more than beauty.

Milli had seen Nigerian art. That, too, Father Mark had shown in a book in his study. One book showed round women, with clay bellies holding children and those were older than anything in the square. They were women gods at the very beginning and while the priest said they were not important, I mean primitive, heathen, he said, not done in the time of Christ, he said that they were what Africans, at one time, thought was art. They made art about fertility. He said, Nigerians were God's little children, made things like children. Father Mark didn't teach much art, and the book, which might have been big and thick, but Milli didn't know anymore, had been an absolutely radiant book in comparison with the few worn, curved school books with broken backs with numbers in them, and the text with pictures of Nigerian crops, and the stories of Noah's ark and the flood and the slaughter of innocents. It had to have been in his thick book she had seen a clay woman, a black woman but the clay was red, who had tribal incisions like cat whiskers on her face. That woman statue was like no face she had ever seen. She was lofty. Knowing. Different than Nardela's crude wooden face. Or Christ's sad one. She was at peace.

Are you ready? the waiter asked.

Milli shook her head. I like studying the menu, she said, pertly.

Be my guest, he said, unevenly, and moved away.

Milli didn't want to sit much longer. The waiter had managed to get under her skin. He made her feel so far away that she thought something she rarely thought. How did I get here? How did I leave the port and Ramada and get to a place where I am a stranger? There must be some misunderstanding. I am baptized and this work is just something I do to pass the time of day and my daughter Farina, how will she ever fit here? And then she thought she might order a whole bottle of wine and sink away from memories that were making her feel so bad. Sometimes she did buy a carton, but not here, rather in one of the small shops with the smell of laundry soap and a cat who slept on a pile of doormats, and then, under the bridge, once Farina would sleep, she would let the wine grip her and warm up her body and make her poverty not seem so similar to a chain tying her to Florence. But a bottle of wine in Rivoire's would cost what a man paid to divert himself, forgetting his pain, talking afterwards, arguing about costs, while she tried to do her work well.

No thanks, she said, putting the menu down. A cold glass of beer was more than enough. It would make her just a little bit dizzy and then she would go, ready for the dark light inside the room, the curious questions about where she was, the way Farina would hang on her arm until it ached. For Igor's anger, and perhaps for Irene's breakdown in tolerance, Milli didn't want to anticipate that. It would be like facing two terrible and different lawyers complaining about her crimes. She'd already faced a harping judge telling her about his city's wish to help. And Igor could hit hard when he let go.

Luigi glancing into the assistant's room didn't see Maria Grazia. It was satisfying most mornings to look in and find her, glasses stuck in the weeds of curls on her head, her purposeful and friendly young body covered by a lab coat, looking up and warmly summarizing the evening before. It quieted him as much as filled him with purpose. His own feelings of being moved, comfortable, protective had been so strong and seemed so serious that any issues of inappropriateness appeared conquerable. But now he felt annoyed that she was not at her desk being professional. The shallow new feeling was not unexpected but was unwanted. Unwelcome. He wished for the warmer infusion of feelings that they were linked. But no one was sitting at her desk or standing, hands on her hips, at the sunny window. Only the fresh water aquariums bubbled. The other technicians hadn't reached their desks. There were no colored cotton sweaters limp on the hooks. Piero, his student, wasn't in. Science held no life for them. Held none of the mystique that sent people into the jungle or out to take risks at the top of trees. No one stayed up nights babying runs of electrophoresis, hot to see if a pattern was there. Luigi knew if he poked around in the sleepy stillness of his lab he would be repaid by uncovering unpleasant signs of negligence, like tardy orders for enzymes. The unmourned-for hour in the morning when no one was at his or her station. It was an hour that fascinated him and, yet, in this light it made him feel his isolation. Who was he? A poor imitation of his father, exaggerating, writing a role for himself in which he solemnly raised his hand as the only one and swore: I pledge to dedicate my life on the high altar of looking for truth.

Instead, the inactivity irritated him. The bureaucratic filing cabinets, the turned off computers with their beige hoods made him feel grouchy and ogreish. His lab, in spite of his dreams, had produced almost nothing. It counted things, kept records, like a reasonably prosperous insurance office. But no one imagined the toughness required to make inroads even into understanding the delicate patterns of breeding in forests. And when he thought of solutions for activating his lab, they sounded like betrayals of his early beliefs, sounded rough like the new language Gian Franco used. They said, fire people and open up competition. They were words that put him in a charlatan group he despised, the slick pair doing genetic engineering down hall, narrow-minded researchers who were like gold rushers following the latest talk. Luigi couldn't see the words except as television concepts that were fast and unexamined. They were words that had appeared and had been kidnapped, like the American heiress that Susan used to point out who was brainwashed by her captors into being a social rebel. Patty Hearst. The climate of transformation slightly resembled that. Brutal change that had kidnapped people who had only a shallow understanding of the responsibility they held for the future of Florence.

There was an uncapped pen on her desk. Once he would have known what to write. Maria Grazia's crystal prism. He picked it up, hoping the sunlight would break into its seven rainbow colors. Instead he contented himself with its sharp cool edges in his palm. Next to that she had a cheap calendar with reproductions by Guttuso, the Communist painter. So adamant, the whole recent history of Italy. So contentious. The black heavy scrawls drawing workers and the expressionistic reminders of sweat and injustice. Sentimentalizing violence. They were such a damaging oneric language for Italy. Once Luigi could have asked her about them, even explored why she liked them. Her answer would have interested him, would have tugged at his vast memories of his grandfather's and father's tormented relationships to workers. And his own evolution in social re-distribution. But now if the words 'unjust worker conditions' would come out of her mouth, they would make him feel a vague fear as if he was almost physically touching the intractable conviction that ran through her. She was sure, the way Guttuso, the Communist painter, was sure, by using a very broad brush. And swirling dramatic, threatening suggestions of blood. By marking every face with hunger or greed. The painter blurred each picture of a life with sentimental swashes of man lives by bread alone. Luigi sighed. Maria Grazia was such a fiery person, he thought as he rubbed his cheek slowly. He could distantly feel her marvelously smooth skin with its touch of salt. Maria Grazia was probably too young for him. A tragic mistake that was no one's fault.

Piero, the student Luigi had rushed in for, was tapping him on the shoulder. He was one of the few students ever to volunteer for climbing to the top of cypress to bag their most recent seed. That was to his credit. But then he fell onto the side of the Church. A St. Francis type. A kid who liked to listen to trees.

Excuse me, *Professore.*

Luigi cut him short.

If his ponderousness were not such a blinder, Piero was a good kid. Perhaps the tall humorless boy reminded him of himself. Serious. Gloomy. Luigi felt uncomfortable in the presence of a boy whose sneakers smelled. Why was it, even now, that he, a man over fifty was unable to feel joy or to wring it from narrow findings, the fallibility of his workers, and the promise of a baby who had somehow slipped past the basic knowledge of two biologists?

Professore, Piero said, smiling. I think it would be very interesting to measure the water systems in cypress. I think they are what we should face next.

A strange encouraging chill unexpectedly reached his skin. This is what Luigi had been thinking about for months. Had someone actually heard him? Standing in the hall seemed inappropriate to Luigi. But Piero didn't want to move. He spoke with a modulated soft excitement for all to hear.

I think the secondary water systems in trees are overlooked—the fact that we see roots as the pumps, but it is not that way at all. That is a myth. Water rises in trees in response to the sky, in response to the atmosphere. There's suction.

Luigi nodded, perplexed by the tone of voice. Really, what he was saying was hardly news.

The stomata in the leaves. The little gates, open and close, releasing oxygen, but also responding to temperature. The gates take as well as release.

What have you read? Luigi asked pointedly. He could see Piero's eyelids fluttering. In a matter of minutes he might reach the song of the universe and its spheres.

Tompkins and Blake; Surinam and Mesham. I think the attentiveness of trees has always been perceived, and now it's time for molecular biology to reinforce this intuition. The leaves have an intake too.

Luigi studied Piero's face. It was soft around all the edges, but quite open in this moment, his eyes brown almonds peering through smudged wire glasses. What had happened to make him be so bold?

The phone in Luigi's pocket beeped and squealed. Pulling it

out neither Maria Grazia nor Marina's number appeared in the small box. But the voice was clear enough. It was Gian Franco's.

Her anniversary?

She was like a mother to me in many ways.

I could, Luigi said, although it was the last thing he intended. His heart began to thump more slowly. A rhythm of sadness and shame.

Five years is a milestone, the plastic surgeon said. I feel like a wretch. When I think of how she did my math. Gave me a sense of the importance of taking up work one loved. Her meals, Luigi.

Diniza's meals. At least that for the record. My mother never cooked.

Hypocrite, Luigi thought, as he tumbled into the rushing event. Gian Franco's words had a terrible effect. Here was a man who was remembering the way he sat at the table with Giada doing sums, remembering the tea she poured for him and now, in his life, which was hardly one of rectitude, he was clamoring to return to that source of certitude for a nostalgic sense that he was the same man. He was willing with his dyed hair and shabby politics to stand at her grave. Luigi turned hot with rivalrous resistance. His body, uncomfortably trapped by a tie and tight collar button, began to sweat underneath.

What time are you going?

It was crazy that his friend had decided to call. Flowers, yes, but only for the living. Gian Franco, on the other end of the phone, surely never imagined that Luigi had not visited his mother's grave, not once, not even a single time walked to the tomb. He was her only son. Her husband was dead. The plastic surgeon wouldn't believe the lapse if he knew. But if he did suspect, Luigi knew that Gian Franco would smile, not broadly, but by nodding his head in that complicit habit that infected Florence. Nodding, barely concealing a malign glee, as one more citizen was drawn into the circle of compromise. You signed that contract with a second copy with different numbers? You heard from your neighbor that the bomb set in the Uffizi was agreed upon by whom? Those tables in the university, the bids will be adjusted far above what they cost. That nod was a mission in the city not to let anyone get away. It said: we know that you know how things are run and how human we all are. Luigi could see that nod of discovery reaching Gian Franco's consciousness and his rush to conclude that his friend, like he himself, had drifted so far from what they were once. Like Chianti. Once it was a fresh wine made from local grapes. And now it was specialized and oak-casked. And marketed. And the new wine was not authentic or sincere. But everyone nodded and said it was better. There it was, that perplexing nod, cynical, asleep. The wolfish nod said with confidence, a vague fast wink, we know, we know. But don't forget it's you as well as me, we are not good at all, except at deceit.

Luigi felt the silence growing dangerous on the other end of the line. He couldn't avoid saying yes. The grave and its call to honor were waiting. But he couldn't mouth the words. That didn't mean that their visits had to coincide. If he went quickly, perhaps he could leave before meeting Gian Franco there. Just lay the roses and go.

Ten-thirty?

Last night's dream had jumped its banks. His mother's predictive presence was rushing forward. And he was running to stay ahead of its churning flood.

Piero had stepped back and had his hands slumped in his pockets. Luigi didn't offer any opening because he was unwilling to mix worlds. His job was to make Piero mature in a professional way. Luigi didn't mean to be brusque. To offend. To appear as if Piero's idea had no worth. But he dismissed the boy with aggression. Dismissed his seriousness, his sudden excitement and naive surprise over the water systems in trees. It wasn't the science but his awkward private expectations. Facing

Piero was like looking at a young version of himself and he wanted to say, wake up before it is too late. Don't be swept away by obligations of any sort. No ideologies. No families. And seeing the boy's confusion, the swift hurt, Luigi almost wanted to give him a deliberate shove.

FIVE

U NDER THE LITTLE footbridge, nearing it, Irene could already see that the dark space hidden in shadows was empty. Squinting, perhaps she could make out a heap. Very small and that was probably Milli's plastic pouch. The plaid blanket, the newspapers crouched in shade. But no woman fast asleep.

Farina riding on Irene's arm frowned and tightened her grip on Irene's blouse.

Mamma? Where is she?

Coming, Irene said, wondering what to say next, she's coming, Irene said, sliding the child down her hip. The blanket smelled, and shaking it in the air, Irene noticed people staring down from the footbridge. How quickly eyes move, she thought, as the man in a suit and boy in a cap flicked them and then pointed with long fingers, seeming to be looking for schools of minnows in the water drudging by. Pretending not to be curious. Pretending the water was more interesting than rummaging through their homelessness. Irene had seen how the dry cement caves under the bridges were competed for. By border crossers without papers, hiding in a way that prostitutes did not. Some didn't even hide, couples asleep, papers over their heads and their children splayed over their dirty feet, all curled up in the shade behind trash bins. So a cave-like space to make the world pull back and the watchers go off on their surefooted way was a treasure.

The blanket still smelled. Swoosh for the damp. Swoosh away the grip of being closed in. On the bus the child had been good. Standing on her own feet and holding Irene's hand. She had walked from the bus stop, through the linen suits and brief cases and high heels clicking past her, down on the ground, nearly the only child not in a checked or ruffled stroller, she had kept up and only at the stoplights queried. She had made her funny little walk without objecting. Short leg. Long leg.

What?

Now seeing the space empty, Farina could wait no longer. Flying pieces of remembering her mother earlier, not finding her after the long walk, the way Irene had said she'd be there, worry swirled in and she didn't know what would come next. Farina opened her mouth and began to wail, loud, convinced sounds of having no more strength.

Stop, Irene insisted, alarmed and trying to help, as the little life next to her exploded. Stop. Farina squeezed her eyes tight and as the tears poured down, Irene slapped her. Not hard. Just an escaped gesture. A slip of frustration and anger at Milli. Where was the woman when this little child was growing upset?

Farina opened her eyes, rocking with tears. The salty drops dripped on her face and stopped in the creases of her neck. She took her fingers and made them into fists and wiped her eyes. While she felt even more flooded with sorrow, Farina saw the large face above her and knew she had not the words to explain how much she missed her mother, but also how this shady space under the bridge wasn't very nice, either. Farina knew she hadn't the words to explain to Irene that she wasn't crying because she wanted something. She was crying because of an enormous sadness that filled her up not like the crouching down she did when the women started fighting, shouting and raising their voices in green and violet shrieks. Farina knew she had no words that would cover the large feeling, the cloud of sadness, making her feel small, knowing that she couldn't find her mother, or help Irene, or even buy her a piece of white pizza with money.

The red eyes being rubbed, the child trying to stop her tears, Irene felt remorse, hot as the sun. She punched Milli's number again and there was no answer. Farina, don't, she snapped as the little girl moved down towards the stream. Don't. Farina looked back at her as if to say, why do you stop me. I just want to see the brown stones turning with water on top of them, leaves floating along. I don't want to sit on that blanket. The grass is soft.

There's broken glass. Do you hear me?

Irene put the phone away. They all had stories about the police. In Milan they were tougher. But the impotent seekers of prostitutes were worse, if one discovered his own seeds of rage blow up, as he pushed and shoved with naked limpness. There was not that much distance between helpless and killer.

Irene had been locked flat on the floor in a car on a lonely road near Prato. She had felt a knife. When the lonely road's gravel stopped in silence, the darkness changed. But knives didn't frighten her. She had known how to lift her head and look right at the edge of the steel. And shrink the man with scorn. It seemed like a tale, but her scorn had come without asking it to. It arose and spilled all over him like volcanic ashes. Sharpening steel or iron. The color of metal stains. The Rom knew iron and when her people had come into villages, to mend the pots, to grind the knives, to dance with knives between their teeth she had learned to play with flashing knives, to watch men with them, watch men flick them and arrange their skills. The short knife he held at the gate of her neck was a language she knew, and he had no idea, with his awkward threat, that she could speak knives and spit them out of her mouth. He and his heavy breathing. He didn't know even that the most effective moves were light, so light, blood stayed inside the slit. It shocked him when he wiped it off his cheek.

Farina was sitting still. Still as a wise woman. Amazing, Irene thought, that composure. She could remember her own mother growing so tired of her brothers and sisters, so strange that she didn't even treat them as if they were her kin. In the thick light-steeped forests, around the fire, in the camps, they were more like a little pack of wolves she sent away.

The back of the child was straight. What was she seeing in the river that made her sit at attention? Maybe it was just a wall cutting off the space where Milli usually sat. Maybe, with her looking forward, facing the brownish-stone wall that banked the river, she could forget about that fact.

Irene lit a cigarette, drew down the smooth release. A while ago, she would have enjoyed lying on the grass herself. Taking the sun and letting it warm her breasts. But the sun was harsh, like sand scraping at her skin. The city sky was not gray but veiled. Different from Bucharest, where the skies were sooty and made the eyes burn. But this sun, too, had changed. Was meaner. But not so bad. Irene held out her hands. This morning her nails should have been redone while the women, who came back, gave pictures of the night before. Irene didn't mind listening. Often the night was little more than a shrug. I did two of those. And three of these. Scorn was a game if nothing special had happened. While she dipped the brush into the red polish, Matrushka might decide she was going to spend the day looking for a man on her own. As the nail took the polish, the red carpet down the middle, the nudges on her toes, Stella might be talking, planning to go home. By now, whoever was there would be mentioning Milli and wondering if Irene had disappeared. It was different in many ways; the security had very little pity in it. Each woman kept to herself, or at most one other friend. But like the gypsy camps she had grown to dislike, the tribe that imposed silence, Igor's room contained the same curtained way of closing over danger. Keeping the dangers caged by living in evasive speeches. Knowing the ceremony of handing over money, each month, and still not being out of the hole, one still got caught like a woman in a spin, twirling and twirling, until the vertiginous dance was one's life.

One more try on the phone. Nothing. It signaled trouble, even if Irene didn't want to think that. The silence bothered her, because Milli in spite of her silences and absent ways, connected for Farina. Sometimes like an old cat, she could not pay much attention, but she hung onto the child, and had projects, when she wasn't too tired. She kept her washed and out of Igor's way. Sometimes too distracted to know, but the child was so solid Farina could take Milli by the hand and show her what the next move was. Even if it was only nudging her mother towards the pot for boiling water.

It wasn't pleasant sitting in the sun. The child, pretending she was on the edge of the world, didn't deserve the life she had. Irene had stories spilling from all sides. She needed to pick up some dry cleaning, two skirts where the grass stains smeared on the soft fabrics. She needed to get up from the banks of the Mugnone and escape from the uncertainty.

Water was fascinating. Watching Farina slide closer to the water on her rump, rowing with her legs. Probably she was looking at the ferns, the rush of current. She probably didn't see the condoms. The bloated paper cartons. Irene didn't dislike this position. She hated the Florentines looking down from the sidewalk, down from the bridge. But she, too, could turn her back. It was impossible sitting there not to remember that Farina had been born on the plain bank.

If there was a thing that had frightened Irene it was that night. And if Jesus had ever wondered where He was born, Irene could have told Him about the slope of the Mugnone where a black woman and a gypsy were alone on an October evening. Not that she hadn't heard the shouts of childbirth in the camps, in the forests near Bucharest, where she had grown up. She carried those forests, under her eyelids, in her ears, the humid, filtered light, the winds that sounded like cries from the universe. The damp fronds, the thickness of leaves where light couldn't reach. No one, not even Milli, knew what a forest could be. But that childbirth, where she had had responsibility, it made her think soap. It made her think boiled water. Hospital. There in the night, with Milli, her nails clawing the grass, and Irene, holding her hand over her mouth, feeling the wave lumbering, reminded her that she never had wanted children. But as the sun crept up, at dawn, as the black head slithered out slippery as soap, as she wielded a knife, struck the cord into a long rope and a short stump, it made her think. Now, looking at the proud curly head still lifted towards the river, it seemed to Irene that the little head had so much in it. I had that pride, the same straight back, but I would have used it to poke, to scorn. Farina's was a quieter thing, as if she possessed a set of golden scales. The head with the squash blossom nose, it was fine, brilliant, and in many ways easier to trust than Milli's.

They had never said much in the many, many times they browsed in the market, for tight skirts, for belts, long earrings. Never mentioned any plan. If anything the plans were set in futures and they nearly always divided even there. Milli, dreamy as ever, would say she was going home. Back to see Ramada, her son, although she had no letters from him. She knew he was growing up and was going to be a teacher. And Farina would go back to school, and Milli, with her savings would fix hair. That all came out excitedly. Short on detail. But high on certainty. And in the same conversation, Irene would stay. She didn't think she would necessarily stay with the other women. She would probably, though, stay with the job. Irene sometimes tried to imagine what brought the other women together. Like Candy who shot heroin through her ankles. She had heard Milli's story, never told the same way, except for the getting on the ship and changing ports, and a man named Wole.

But for Irene, it was hard to mark when she left. Probably it was the rushing Danube itself. The day she knew she would never get across to Yugoslavia, never get away from the tribe, unless at Timisora she jumped in to swim. Three days she walked to the edge, heard from people in villages that it was not being watched, and realized that once you got to a certain point— in excitement, in sex, even diarrhea in the body, it was hard to stop the body until whatever it was came to an end. She hoped her body was stronger or as strong as her wish to reach another country. Irene clapped her hands. They had never made a plan for Farina, seeing the apartment as such a prison that nothing would happen there. They lived in shadows that kept them blindfolded to the deep lapses that rested in the shadows.

But Milli had never been so late. Only twice since Irene had been with Igor had there been close calls, only twice, but Maryann had been beaten up so badly Igor took her in for stitches. One of those rare times, he showed confidence enough to walk her in with his papers. Her face was blue-black full moon swollen. They took the long tear down her cheek and left points, where the needle went in, where it exited. A closing without fantasy. But if Milli had turned off her phone, how could there be help across the city. If someone were beating her up?

Somewhere on the banks, Irene and Milli had actually buried the placenta. It was a blue-white girdle as tough as anything nature could weave. It's our first cradle, Milli had said. It's the boat that carries us from the other world. It's not garbage. It's not waste.

Irene had forgotten completely about that until now. The blood girdle. But that hardly changed the present. The child had lain down on the grass. More quiet, more serious than ever.

It was the word 'sell' that had really brought her to this place. Igor's word. And the fact that Milli had left no plan. Unplanned really this emotional rush to the bridge. But that's the way feelings were. This morning it was true, without Irene looking out for her, Igor could have taken her away. An absurd assumption of normal trust made Farina's life one in real danger. Milli never thought about those hard decisions. 'Sell' was not the finest word used for their bodies. It was a word Irene liked to keep in a wallet and not really think about it. But 'sell a child,' you had to think. Maybe she could tell Farina a story. Tell her how she was born. Tell her about the large black horses she rode, even standing up on the slope of a stallion's back. The horse's dry pelt between her toes. Just a story and maybe then she would know what to do.

Irene, of course, had many memories. But none stronger and more devastating for the tribe, in that cold humiliating winter, than when they were freezing near the Bulgarian border, hunting for firewood, when finding firewood could get you jailed, when a child, a little girl with eyes like blue china, disappeared. The Bulgarian border guards were arguing, smoking cigarettes, with their rifles at their sides. Her people, of course, couldn't cross. It was freezing and the fire threw out no snapping flames. But her people were shouting back and forth to the soldiers hoping for a lead.

The camp was convulsed. A troubled group of women in shawls and long skirts muttered, apart from the men. Men in their poor boots and scavenged coats stood round another fire. Irene's mother's face was disfigured by mistrust. She brooded in silence all that day. Women had collected where she was stirring a kettle. Irene's mother's fingers, which had deep cuts and cracks from the cold, struck the air in signs of disagreement, but she never spoke. Irene still doesn't know if the horror of the child's disappearance was so great that she couldn't speak, or if she knew what really happened and couldn't tell for fear of betraying someone. But it seemed there had been a traitor.

Irene always marveled at the quickness of her people's hands. Fingers that moved like flames over the strings of a fiddle to, yes, catching knives, and how they could switch from bowing to a gypsy queen to stealing silver from a house. There was freedom in their hands, their horses, how they drank from others' fountains and carried their babies in slings. But also tyrannical loyalty, the ability to lie to keep the group together. Often the deeds were women's ideas and the costs decided by men.

It was that loyalty to silence, to keeping people in their places, which had had made Irene leave. Silence deeper than the forests, going back into blood itself that came up when she woke some days, after a nap, wondering where she was. And seeing the bars on the windows, hearing the drone of haggling over, the Italian television speaking, she knew why she had chosen to get away. Because even in the squalid room, one day she would buy her own life. And could leave the group and lead a life, not in caravans, not in parks where they pick-pocket and keep children out of schools. Having their fathers tell them whom to marry. Not to belong is why she swam those five hours. Waves hitting her, and she pushing them down.

That ability to run. Those words came out of her mouth the morning Farina was born. After she had cut the cord with a knife. After Milli had staggered down to the water, and washed the blood from between her legs. She was holding the baby, wrapped as tight as an almond in a shell, having been wiped, while the sun spilled into the water and Irene said, why don't you run? Just take her and go somewhere. I can help you.

And Milli put the baby down. Put her in the grass and although she was still dizzy and wet, half drugged by the lack of sleep, she leaned hard on Irene, and then almost twisted her arm.

Don't you get ideas about changing my life. You're my friend. You want to make me crazy? I got here. I got my plan.

The face in front of her was holding a little ball in her hands. Not more hopefully than a very cautious puppy.

The eyes were so much more balanced than cock-eyed Milli's. Irene wished she could ask the child what they should do. Probably Farina would know. But there were two things, really. Milli and if she was in trouble. And 'sell.' The word that had atom-bombed. Farina had turned her head when Igor said, 'market for children.' She knew it meant her. The rest it was hard to believe she could understand. Only women like them, who could see into dithering feverish lives of the men who paid them, only women like Irene knew that in a city like Florence, in a few hours, if sold, Farina would disappear and be devoured in its ruthlessness.

Catch.

Farina's eyes lit up and her hands flew as the ball whizzed past her.

Try harder.

Farina frowned.

Irene sent the ball up in a short skip that Farina caught between her hands and her skirt.

More, Farina, said, already thinking of telling Milli how she caught the ball. She could imagine her mother shaking her head, almost not listening.

She looked up wondering why the ball wasn't coming.

Irene pitched it straight so that Farina had to run down the hill.

Too far, she puffed.

You need to be faster.

Too far.

For another second Irene considered talking it over with Farina. She would listen.

And what would her speech be?

do you know that Igor might sell you, he might try

do you know what men can do to your fine little back the golden scale of your mind that private body between your

if I turn you over to some nuns who will sprinkle you with their magic words and get you papers

will you ever forgive me if I give you the feeling forever that you can be left

in my land in my language there is a story about a little girl who goes into the forest and is eaten by a bear, but she tells a sparrow

is that the story? Can we be strong?

Farina was waiting for the ball. She had begun to believe there would be a game. That Irene would not tire.

More, she said and started to run.

It surprised Irene that such thoughts were at the front door of her mind, pounding again. She didn't have or want the power to separate Milli from Farina and yet what could she do? It was ridiculous that she was waiting here under the bridge at ten o'clock without any word. It wasn't spite, or impatience, although she would have liked the morning to straighten up her things, wax her legs. It was, who knows. A sensation like scanning a client and in his eyes, not his pocket, finding out he has a gun. You just know by reading the body, the way a head jerks. Igor had switched the premises of the room. Farina couldn't go back. And the other thing was the child herself. A tiny life who had taught herself to read. Irene knew in a way she never expected, from these years, through measles, through not much affection but steady consciousness, a happiness that had come from Farina. Irene wanted to see the little face grow and grow and not in a shocking way. She wanted to see her intelligence not be flipped back and forth in hiding, but strut ahead, without people looking down on her.

Farina wanted to play ball or to go. She looked at Irene who was fussing with one of her long red nails.

One's broken, she said. We can't play ball.

Farina knew what it was like to slip her hand in between those nails. It was like being inside a cage of bright swords. She liked the sensation of swords and flames. Her mother's hands had short nails. They seemed like pink rabbits. Bleeding sometimes, Farina would ask, Momma hurt?

And what if Irene were to run with her herself? Could she get on a train, and slip into a city like Rome and move with Farina, move into the crooked streets, disappear in the ones where the Jews stayed at the time of Christ. Take the child and raise her. Hide with her and get her into school. Move into the market with a flint wheel. Become a knife sharpener. Yes, like a gypsy. Such wild thoughts amazed Irene. They were as dizzying as any dance her feet had ever taken part in. And why not a dog. And two pots of geraniums. And then writing to Milli telling her to come. Why not?

Since Irene had gotten on that first coal burning train, when her father stood silent and then hurled out his judgment for those villagers who were waiting to go into Bucharest to hear: Don't ever come back, she had had no home. It was as bad as if he had cut off her black hair, judging her, in the station, after he had picked the avid dark eyed Petti for her, a stupid young man with a business of sorting metal in the camp, dumb hands thinking money from nails, money from tin cans. That day she knew she would not see her father's rough sun burnt face again. As she pulled out, her heart pounding, he had seared her, burned through her skin and put that pride of entering a city or a village, swishing around it with skirts swinging and insinuating mystery and threat, that swaying with one's kind, inside her in a new way. Irene carried her once proud homelessness now as no group. The coal burning smoke pouring in the train windows, that pulling the windows up and coughing and choking anyway, leaving and not even knowing where she was going, that turbulence still boiled even in her dreams. The people staring at her in the carriage. The red cinders from the coal. She left. And then the five hours in the Danube. Her arms' long strokes, even when they ached, shoulders and neck, nearly wrung from exhaustion, those pawing frantic strokes knowing she could not go down were a part of her. Italy had open borders, holes in their fences. They had money and churches that would put you up. She could walk from Yugoslavia, put the shadows and cool hiding places of the forests around her. Once she crossed the water, she could get there.

Is it me or the chair creaking? That was Aki saying that. Gray headed Aki who the neighbors joked about. Not all of them but there were many who thought he should not have let Widu go.

Aki rocked slowly on the porch, pushing the colonial rocker with his bare feet on the cement. It was useless to look for the boy now that he hadn't come home last night. Not useless. Worse. To call the police when they had such fire in their government brains. To ask them to look for a boy who was interested in MOSOP was like turning him in. Asking them to arrest him. There were shootings on the road every day and the paper said Saro-Wiwa under arrest was still part of the problem.

Get up. Up. That was Sabula, whose hard practical heart was one reason, Widu, the young widow, left. Up, Sabula said sweeping around the blades of his chair with fastidious brisk moves. He should have told you, she said, puckering her cheeks and not letting go of her scold. No worry in her voice. No line of memory of the boys being shot. She didn't want any of that revolution talk in the house. Didn't want murder. Soldiers with boots kicking down the doors and shooting in the villages.

Don't let them come knocking on my door. No way. No way. Didn't they have enough trouble keeping an electric cord paid for in the house without bringing in worries of whose side are you on. Her skirt, tied up in a knot, made it tighter, but it was not time for that.

Aki shaded his eyes and went on rocking, even though she slapped him on the head. Move, she said, grunting a little. But he didn't even turn his unshaved chin in her direction. This is my house, he thought, and you think chickens are your house, and that rose bush you keep trying to water, and the shrine with cones and you aren't completely wrong.

But what is this shack, with its trickle of running water, if we don't have schools that are good, and my parents' land is worthless and the yams don't come up and the fish float dead in the mangroves from the oil spilling like disrespect, spilling like black blood.

Sabula almost tapped him on his head again. She knew what he was thinking. She could see his concern coming out of him like a shepherd, a deep cloak that he carried inside and put down for his children. She hadn't liked Ramada. Too quiet. Too much like a boy who slipped in behind you and had so many thoughts in his head that his head drooped. His eyes were heavy lidded, not from lies, but from seriousness. She liked faster people. She felt impatience with most of the children, with the mold, with the flies, with the soldiers, the police, the strikes, the shops that kept asking for more *nairas*. With Ramada's mother Widu gone forever in Italy he was hers to raise and they had no common language.

He should have told you where he was going.

Aki kept rocking. He wondered when Sabula would finish sweeping, the pretence of sweeping and take her obvious poking inside. The strike of the last few days had been murderous. Gunfire. Curfews. Tension all the way up to the colonial residences. Tough on her, he thought. Just getting water. Getting past the soldiers. It made her hysterical. Impatient. No wonder she insisted so stupidly that Ramada should have told them.

Aki reached into his pocket for a bill. Here, he said wearily, but with a smile, trying to offer her a nerve gift. Here. Sabula took it but didn't stop dragging her broom across the dust. He understood her nervousness. That was something he knew in her. Not in his first wife, Bene. And not in the beauty and patience of his third. But they were both Christians. And Sabula was gnawed on by uncertainties. By voodoo. But she was hard working. It was she who wanted a fence around the house. She who wanted to plant palms. She cleaned the drains. She hung out the clothes after she had scrubbed them with a brush. And politics to her were what ruined life, what made her plans of hard work a ruin.

Aki could almost understand what Ramada saw with his eyes. What he heard with his ears. Not just from the porch where he and Amos and Ben had picked up and put down so many days of the struggle. He had not wanted Ramada in the responsibilities. He looked at his parched wrinkled hands. They had a deep meaning to him. His hands had always been clear. The heart line long as the Niger and the head line straight as if God had drawn it with his own finger. But what could Ramada see in those hands. Nothing. At fourteen, the boy was too old to be taught. And what did he see around him? Probably at the garage, among the fist full of boys older than he, they made tradition sound good, making it sound like the old Ogoni and the honoring of the land. If only that were true. If only one could walk backwards and have Odumu take over the land, have the huge python wrap itself around Shell oil and twist it until it gave in to everything the Ogoni were asking. But MOSOP too was full of thugs. Joining up with a movement was a way to make a man feel he could be a man, strong, with the ability to work. But then it was hard to do.

Aki sighed and wished he could almost not blame the

boys who carried knives. Wished that Ramada was truly learning from the smart boys that the oil has made the Ogoni even smaller, made the men smaller, unable even to sing the old songs to the land. But probably Ramada had learned that smallness from him.

Dadila hopped down the steps followed by her mother's voice. I don't want that cat in here. You know it.

Aki nodded as she went skimming past as if the voice went over her head.

That's the thing, he thought. I can't really keep law in my own house. I can't make words mean the same thing. I couldn't stop his mother from going. I can't stop Sabula from keeping up rituals that don't make for order. She sets one example and dead Bene and Vola set another. And I preside over it all. Saying, but my words don't mean much, that I will take the law into my own hands in my house.

There was gunfire down the road. They were peppery shots and who knows if someone was bleeding. Aki wished he could use Sabula's approach and put on a mask, become a bear and growl and growl until the people facing him trembled in awe. But he was a Christian. And that order was what he had to try to see this morning. Anger choked him, caught him when he thought of his daughter getting on the boat, throwing away her life with each headstrong step up the gangplank. That blind walk into extinction into a white man's world choked him. Widu's trip. Not into the Christian world of mysticism and education. That tall daughter who left her son to him for today's mess. Aki felt disagreement and disapproval barking in his head and yet desperation, too, at having let Ramada slip away. Who was the shit he could blame? Who was the shit that brought all this chaos about? Who let in the white men who made strong men into weak ones?

The whole of the sky said there would be a storm blowing up and letting loose within minutes. He was still the patriarch of his not completely small family. He never forgot that. He was not one to let his family live mouth to mouth. That's why he'd given up farming in the first place. That's why he was a Christian. He did not beat women. He did seek medicine when it was necessary. His desperation, thinking about Ramada and what might have happened to him with the government crackdown just tapering off made him think of getting on his knees. That thought to bend, that thought of how the world proceeds, made him walk straight into the memory-battlefield of his daughter's abrupt leaving.

Love for Widu—how she looked like her mother, whose fulfillment was ruined by her daughter's leaving school—love and not judgment of her came upon him slowly. A new set of memories, not that Widu was not a fit mother, not that she was a superficial woman who had learned from Sabula to envy, but his daughter, whom he had nearly willed dead. Widu came back in his mind, quick-witted, laughing. He was not afraid of her closeness. The thought of her returning gave him an unexpected lift to his worry. He would ask where he could write to her. He would ask Father Mark, who must be tied up in these days of government turmoil, if he could get the sisters in Turin to give him some news. He would write to her and maybe she could reach Ramada before he became. What?

Aki didn't know. Some of the MOSOP boys were terrorists. Killers. But some were not that irresponsible. Some were just caught in the winds of events that grew too large for them to control. Anyway, Ramada needed to be brought back, shown how many people wear masks. And not just in the government. It was not up to boys, to youth to set Nigeria straight. It was up to the elders. Up to the men, like he himself, to speak up and get the constitution back.

His Lancia was a blast furnace. The university courtyard had no shade. Easing his way in, tugging his pants across the seat, he leaned through to the other door and opened it, while fumbling for the ignition and air conditioning. The burdensome phone came to his mind. He would take it out of his limp linen pocket. The phone. Luigi wasn't certain what the analogy was but probably it was sexual. Smooth. Rounded edges. All right for women, but for men to be pawing its small and finicky buttons, as if it had power, was just one more sign of the moment. He, too, had slipped into the circle of idiots. Idiots all over the city with their mouths open, yakking, and searching their phones for something to see. The phones were an autism taken to a new level where others—the unasked for bystanders to your banalities—simply didn't exist. The thin guts of relationships translated out loud in front of people who didn't know. Why Piero didn't step back when the phone rang was one example of the failed etiquette. But it was everywhere—not only the banality of TV but also now the level of telephone discourse in public. When the person standing next to you planned to come home. How the dentist had broken a filling. That the bank-o-mat was out of cash. The litany of relationship reduced to exchanges that would kill any romance. That's what he hated most. There was no poetry, no sharp observations. No purpose. No history. No civic sense. Time was the conversation but it seldom enveloped desire. Cell phones. And what was cell's connotation? Prisoner. Bee hive. Not Apollonian power. Not the unit certainly that biologists counted on. The cell phone passed on into circulation the shallowest moods, laments, words without will. He looked again at the black phallic item that wasn't a tool. Plastic dildo, acquired unconsciously by the thoughtless packs. His fingers gripped it, like a lonely adolescent. He'd taken it out to free his pocket and now here he was hesitating over to turn it off or leave it on.

Automatic behavior. And what could he say and to whom? For what? Solace? I had a bad night? My mother still makes me feel so guilty I am going up to meet her demands? I don't want the child I have fathered? Who could he call but Susan? Forget it.

Luigi pulled out of the courtyard, made a quick illegal right turn and headed for the Lung'Arno. The last thought he was certain of. He couldn't be a father again. It filled him, a biologist, with a rage that such a simple act as lying with Maria Grazia, following her into a room, stripping off her clothes, asking her if they were protected, could lead to such life determining consequences. As if he didn't know, as if he thought he could mock the eternal gods, the pregnancy was a slap in the face. Luigi felt revulsion for the fertility in sex and the injustice of that spasm. He, who loved nature's purposefulness, hated its pitiless free ride in the tangle of human attraction. Why couldn't he be immune from the whip? What had gone wrong?

For no particular reason, as he idled at the stoplight near via Machiavelli, Luigi felt rage for his Catholic education begin to swamp him. Don Boscolino's round unhealthy face wagged its chins and the overall structure of guilt like a patrimonial scaffolding around sex came on as a squalid castigator. By now the car was chilled to an air-conditioned frost with no trace of real weather. There was no way around it, Luigi thought, as he checked his mirror to pass, Maria Grazia would have to have the child herself. Forming the thought made him feel as if he would disappear. As if the white line on the road would suddenly cross and wrap around the car. In one phrase he felt grief. It was a terrible heavy sensation. That he would have to give her up. Impossible idea. An intimation of the loss blew like a soft wind still far off, but once he refused the child, she would cut him out. He could feel that the crack, her pain and anger, would leave him chilled, alone, dying again, without any greatness except as a distant idea of his undervalued mind. That in some sense was why he couldn't be a father. He needed someone to focus on him, someone who would not abandon him, would let him finally reveal his strength.

Imagining his colleague's scorn, not that they would have moral scruples, Luigi thought that he could survive. No one in the department would dare to say anything to him. Not to his face. He didn't have to go very far to see that the beaten down characters surviving through inertia and cowardice as much as something like tolerance, would not change his university life. Professionally they had to respect him for all the steady standards he brought in. No one could accuse him of molesting.

Luigi had some hope for resurrecting the work Piero did. Maybe Maria Grazia would be willing to work with him. He couldn't get her eyes out of his mind. Couldn't get that wonderful mouth with its vast repertoire out of his mind. Without warning, Luigi processed the body lying in the middle of the road, perhaps asleep or dead. He lifted his foot from the accelerator, and honked, honked and before he knew it the setter with white spots and feathery markings on its tail, rolled and started to rise. There was no time to react to the body and the sensation of a waving mirage rising from the tar. There was space to the shoulder and no traffic behind, so he swerved right and felt his front fender impact, knock down or toss the slow animal, and felt the left wheel rise up over the lump and then the back wheel elevate slightly and roll down so fast he could barely keep control of the wheel. I can't believe it. Luigi glanced up in the mirror, hardly focusing and because of his foot pressing harder and harder on the pedal, he could scarcely make out the still heap on the road. He felt certain that the head and torso had been flattened by the wheels. What a dumb, dumb dog, he said, surprised to be at a stoplight and felt himself fill with shame as he flicked on his right turning signal meaning he would not go back to witness the crushed brain. With frightening power and speed he had hung on and not even skidded but the wheels had crossed the body. It was a sickening feeling, but the Lancia had been easy to control.

God damn it, Luigi said, panting. I'm not going back, he said as all the junk in the backseat, a yellow raincoat, books on global warming, two plastic containers for water slid to the right as he turned right so fast two ladies at the corner jumped backwards. The car was now more terrible than when he entered it. Luigi was grateful to be alone as a feeling of bad luck and revenge poured through him. He prickled and burned. The dog was stupid. Sick. Probably already dead. Any dog lying in the road was not in his right mind. The villages speeding by with their laundry tickertape and their torturous turnings, where the buildings facing each other were buried in shade, were tough places to speed through.

I'm not going to be trapped, Luigi said, even though regret was beginning to sober him up. There are hundreds of stupid hunters who kill all the fucking birds and real hit-and-run drivers who knock off real heads and people who poison rats so why single out me? The feeling of the wheels conforming to the bump of the dog lodged in his hands. It was an awful thudding, like a trapped animal moving under a cloth hood. It shivered unpleasantly in his fingers and went up in a tremble to his elbows and onto his shoulders where its presence hovered with resistance and unease. The day had been relentless, driving him deeper and deeper into a hideous hell.

Luigi was grateful no women had been with him. That was good luck. At least in this terrible morning for this awful event no women had been witnesses. The thought made Luigi's head spin. Marina would have made him stop. She would have been sobbing emotionally from the moment the accident happened. No earlier. As soon as the ghostly animal tried to get up onto its feet, she would have been Miss Animal Rights. Papa, can't we help him? Can't we take him home? Maria Grazia would have insisted on vets and splints. Susan would have performed the first aid herself. Tied the old Girl Scout knots she learned in Minneapolis and his mother? Any and all of them would have taken off their blouses and made tourniquets if there had been no other means. Little Florence Nightingales. Women willing to roll up their sleeves for others. Screams would have come from a few of their mouths. He could hear the screams. Stop. Stop. Marina, first of all would have used hot, unforgiving words. Murderer, she would have shouted. Daddy you are a murderer, without noticing how she had scalded him with her burning accusations. It would have been a struggle to keep her from leaping from the speeding car, if he had not stopped. Susan and his mother would have been quiet. They might have suspected his carelessness, but they would have accepted it, as long as he went through the motions of helping, of dealing with what had happened by turning back.

Luigi regretted the sympathy all of them could feel for an animal. He was grateful none had been on the seat next to him. Marina's seeing a dog's head torn off might have turned into weeks of that moody mock anorexia. And Maria Grazia, even before she was pregnant, loved mothering. Even when she was following minnows, she followed egg periods and when batches of eggs died she thought she saw grief in the mothers shown by their lack of eating. She wanted to write a paper and even recorded grief moments in minnows. Her cats. Oh God, Luigi thought. I hate hysteria and do-gooders and whom did I surround myself with?

Luigi parked the car. Just for a quick drink. It felt good to put his feet on the ground, one after the other. The palms, so ingeniously telescopic, were sending out the first date pods. The mad stream rushing through him was dying down. Sadness washed in. Shame bubbled and gushed over the killing. It was a strange feeling, knowing something had happened that no one except he, himself, knew. Luigi felt numbness in his fingers from the tension, the white-knuckled holding on. Suddenly he swooped down to check the front plastic bumper by running his fingers along it. Relief. No cracks or imperfections.

Leaning closer to where the animal probably was struck he saw no smears of blood on the unmarked barriers. He leaned over again and felt ashamed to be checking for tell-tale signs. Forensic experts could sniff out blood even in a speck of dandruff, but the naked eye, at least, would be appeased.

You looking for something?

That was the old caretaker approaching Luigi and taking off his cap.

Nothing at all, he said, covering his eyes with his hands and straightening up.

I saw you bend over.

Luigi felt an instant alert and changed the subject. Are you at the museum?

The old man nodded.

Must be a wonderful place to work, he said.

The guard looked at him wondering what he was trying to hide. He had seen plenty of men that age coming up to Fiesole. A certain sheepishness meant they were waiting for a date they shouldn't be having. Another look was more nervous and that meant drugs. Even men that looked like doctors. Professors.

They certainly could build, Luigi said, opening his arms in the direction of the amphitheatre. I mean the Etruscans. You are probably just the man to tell me, why it is that the Etruscans came to Fiesole and went no further? Just a few kilometers down the hill and they could have founded Florence. Do you have any notion? Why is it that a culture goes so far and no further?

The guard studied him. He was like a man out of a movie. People below were standing on the un-mortared Etruscan walls. He waved his arms and gestured for them to descend. His eyes stayed on them and when they failed to move, he took out his whistle. The white-haired man's attention had turned. Signore, there are books you can read, he said, as he tipped his hat.

Signor Caffo was walking back along the shaded road with the waterfall when he saw the whole scene. He shook his fist at the Lancia and tried to get its number but it blurred by, and his head was full of pounding shock. Maybe he saw an Fl but the blue car was gone, evaporated in the blinding sun. He shook his fist and by then had reached the white dog whose neck seemed to have been broken. Fresh blood was clotting on its fur. The dog was still warm from its life and warm from the sun that had been beating down on its hot sunny nap. You were old, old lady, he said, never surprised any more by the cruelty of people who seemed like ordinary people. You were old, he said, watching blood drain from her mouth and pool beneath her grayish muzzle. Instinctively he held up his hand to wave down the four-wheel drive Land Rover coming towards him. A youth in baggy shorts stepped out. I need help, said Caffo. We should drag this poor beast to the side of the road. And he motioned to the tall brownish green grasses, bowing and bobbing with seed. Then, and his eyes wandered, I don't want to just put her in a bin, he said, shrugging off the reality of the dumpster. Seeing the deep tear along the setter's neck and remembering the sound and speed without any braking at all that had left the dog on the road, the old man's head seemed to shake. His body memorized the violence, as without purpose, and it offended him. He could let the news out at the bar. Someone would know whose beheaded torso that was. The young man, tall and self possessed, seeing the dog's head nearly severed from its body turned toward his trunk. I can get a blanket from the back of the car. Let me do that. We can at least wrap her up, he said, eyeing the tits splayed flat like stems.

No disguise crossed Milli's face as she looked around the room. She'd seen this moment in her mind. Not just once. But fleeting like an evil spirit that had entered someone's body and had now taken over the emptiness that was mocking her. She knew Farina was gone. She knew then that not only was her protection gone, it was wrong. It had let evil in. Let in that side that she had been baptized out of.

She thought she would faint. Would cry out. Would scratch at Igor who was looking at her with some sort of question. But she felt and remembered that she had to transfer an animal into herself. That was what the Ogoni did when they didn't want to become slaves. They invited animals into their souls. Invited in ferocity. Cunning.

Where were you?

Do you expect me to answer without, and she could hardly find the words, telling me where Farina is?

She felt good hearing her voice. Less so, when he grabbed her arm.

Did she go out? Milli felt the pressure on her arm as he twisted it. No one was there, but they would be. The room was never empty for long. Maybe she could distract him.

I said, where were you? We don't need the police in this moment. We don't ever need their attention but now it is something we really don't want.

She had never seen Igor up so close. Never seen the pores of his skin. The teeth that were so white in spite of his breath of tobacco. Who was he to himself, this man who was pulling her arm.

Milli wondered what beast she had invited inside her. It wasn't a mouse. It wasn't a lion, either, she thought as she felt tremors in her legs.

Where is Farina? she asked trying to look him in the eyes. Trying not to look pleading, lost, trying to look like her mother, Bene, calm, not willing to back down. Her mother, who had asked her not to quit school. That head of such purpose, with the eyes of no half-measures.

He threw her arm down. She's not my responsibility, he said. You don't appreciate me, he said, much to Milli's surprise.

You think many people would take a Nigerian and a child? Without asking anything in return? They wouldn't. All of you, but you above all, don't recognize what a choice I had to turn you out.

The words burned Milli but she didn't answer them. She wanted to be clever about the enormous risk and uncertainty that was all around. What false steps to be made that could cost her time. The telephone on his desk beckoned to her like a jewel without price. But it was off limits. Off all signs she could emanate that she wanted to use its power. Milli couldn't believe the telephone. How much power, like the Ogoni said, how much power lay in these tools. The telephone was her way to find Irene. To find out what the story was. The cell phone the police had kept, she had never seen it as more powerful in defining her life than a condom. But that was its power. It had power beyond anything that could be seen in its small shape. It was a god, connecting her to a life she couldn't reach or find, any other way. And it was so easy now, easier than a prayer, if she could just get out the door and into a phone booth. The numbers would find Irene. The numbers would go across the city and end the nightmare.

That's when he said it. She's been sold.

It was difficult to know what he expected by saying that. He was a careful observer of energy, when it was off and when it was on. He was not free with his words so he knew an explosion would occur. Probably he thought it was a way of repaying her for not calling last night. Difficult to know if he thought the words traveling up her spine would be enough to send her packing, to make her pick up her things and take the little one along, out of his charity and patience. Out of his sight and his long tolerance, letting her exceptional state in, when she was all belly. Not one crazy man in a million would have done that. Are you serious? What kind of work can a pregnant woman do and what has she done since?

Milli looked at him, then felt hate come up in her. There was that moment, then, when it felt like Wole holding her arm, when they were on the ship, when from his metal cup he was giving her water and some of his bread. When she had heard they were not going to be washing hair. The way the waves below the ship called to her and he held her arm, dug his nails in. The memory of Wole telling her she should live, shouldn't be ashamed.

I can't tell you where she is, Igor said.

Milli drew her head back. She still had the chance offered by the phone. She threw her eyes towards the ceiling and would have prayed to it, to the heaven above the room.

Igor was impressed by her silence. It was nearly as spooky as the child's. He had expected her to start yelling. Throw herself around like Linda after a party that had gone wrong. He thought her eyes, too, were scary, nearly like a starry sky under an eclipse. She was different than he thought. She was making it difficult for him to accept his own little joke.

Why don't you go and look for her, he said.

He wasn't sneering and saying Florence, why don't you climb the tower next to the cathedral and look for her there. Why not? Why wasn't he sarcastic? Milli knew they could not talk about it. Could not repair the danger. Farina was not in the room and it was not worth losing a second to scratch out his eyes.

There were many things to consider, professor Milandri thought as he held a slide of Santa Croce up to the light in the Chapel of the Cross. And popped it in the machine. Its travertine green and white marble never disappointed. How many did he need to show to make clear that the great cathedrals had the same east west orientation? Santa Maria del Fiore. Santo Spirito. They faced outward toward the city itself as a social pact but they all lined up on an axis that was sun determined. From that point he could move on to the bifurcation that occurred between astrology and astronomy in the world of Copernicus and then Galileo. A few steps forward before turning back to Toscanelli. Once Galileo came up, it would be a pity to not make a slight detour and bring in the charming story of Sister Maria Celeste, Galileo's second daughter, who was buried with him, but this morning there was no time for it. He looked at the plump nun's keenly intelligent uncomplaining face. He, too, would sacrifice her. He put the slide down. Her sweet letters to her father and that one where she tries to send him two pears, so close, and yet her own talents were sacrificed to a convent because Galileo was too poor to support her and her sister.

He was tempted. As he was tempted by the passage from the libretto from Peter Grimes.

> *Now the great Bear and Pleiades where earth moves*
> *Are drawing up the clouds of human grief,*
> *Breathing solemnity in the deep night,*
> *Who can decipher*
> *In storm or starlight*
> *The written character of a friendly fate—*
> *As the sky turns, the world for us to change?*

He could use that piece to lead into the sixteenth and seventeenth and eighteenth centuries when the Church lent itself to measuring the sun as it slowly acknowledged its mistake.

> *But if the horoscope's bewildering*
> *Like a flashing turmoil of a shoal of herring,*
> *Who can turn the skies back and begin again.*

Professor Leonardo Milandri loved the question: Who can turn the skies back and begin again? It could lead right on into physics but he needed it to stand for astrology and the bifurcation with science. But maybe the flashing turmoil and the shoal of herring were too baroque. And the question had a moral direction and so that was confusing, too.

Better to stick to the basics, he thought, flipping the projector and putting up Galileo himself. Galileo said: 'The heavens declare the glory of God and the firmament sheweth His handiwork'. The fact is, Milandri thought, that even today with all our precise instruments we cannot approach perfect measurements. Although the number of atomic oscillations of cesium bring the year's length pretty close.

Sir, would you mind if I asked you a question?

Milandri turned in the dusky light and nodded to a fairly square American face, rather distinguished and clearly not a scientist. Something in his voice sounded as if he wanted to say we are alike. We both have degrees. It was easy to observe his unskeptical wish to be included.

Was that a picture of Maria Celeste, Galileo's second daughter?

He knew however he answered, the man wanted to open up a conversation. Show what he knew. All right, be included.

Are you visiting Florence? Milandri asked, moving back towards sorting his slides.

Have you ever seen her letters?

Milandri smiled at him without mouthing the obvious. My work actually involves infrared waves. Using computers and telescopes in unpolluted sites in the southern hemisphere. Nothing, I'm afraid, as human as those letters. Although my father, who was the head of the observatory here, used to take me into Galileo's house and let me touch his telescope. It was a beautiful way to begin a passion. Looking out at Jupiter's moons, thinking of his lens, where he put his eyes.

I can imagine, Thomas Simpson said, sincerely. I feel that, too, when I touch the parchment of a law defining how those dying from the plague shall be buried.

Historian? Milandri asked and tried to look even busier. I hope you won't be too hard on me this morning when I try to do my thing. You'll probably think I'm skipping pretty fast. There is so much, he said, lifting his arms in mock frustration. So much and while usually a talk can spill over, I have to do my best. Toscanelli was precise. And the least I can do is to be coordinated so that when the ray comes in, and he gestured to the wave of dark netting covering the windows, I'll be on time. See that bronze shape? It's nearly three hundred feet above us. Sunlight will pass through it and finally cross this disk on the floor, calculated to measure the sun's angle.

SIX

I T WAS INEVITABLE that Susan jumped when the door opened. She was washing her hands, putting her face under. The kitchen window was closed. She hadn't had time to open it.

Where did you come from? she said, relieved, glad, all rippling into place as she saw the face with its turned up nose and what might well be a sharp tongue. I thought we'd agree you'd call if you stayed over. The feeling of freedom she had felt in the garden, the explosion of her decision, pitched her forward.

Marina's ash green eyes darkened and then she laughed, puckering her lips in exasperation. Will it make you any happier if I say that I won't be home tonight or tomorrow?

Sparring. Her daughter's poking motions stirred Susan up. One minute peace and then this new young woman was pointing so that the choice was a smile or letting her go with a shrug. Marina butted her mother playfully, pushing her with her hip as she reached for a glass.

You're not the only one who's hot. Florence is crammed. Everyone's guzzling from plastic bottles. With the tourists dragging their bags like little wagons, I thought of baby bottles. She puffed out her cheeks with satisfaction. It's like everyone has turned into a bunch of children. Down went her short curls under the faucet as water trickled through them. Oh. Great.

Susan opened the window to let a breeze edge in. Marina's head was all wet now and she was shaking it like a puppy. The drops striking Susan felt good. Marina entered a room and expected even the music to change. Here she was, exuberant like a child but not to be treated like one.

I was in Florence this morning.

And you didn't hand out any more of the fliers?

No, I was translating for a prostitute.

No kidding. Good for you. I bet you really gave her a hand.

A swallow of surprise hearing the tone. Its enthusiasm something of an insider's, as if they had both been on the side of social problems, were both veterans of groups and protests.

What was she like?

Susan looked at her daughter's Puck-like hairdo and saw a range of expressions that had never happened before. The half-adult who spoke was speaking with a voice of a new person coming alive.

There is a choice, Susan thought, before she prepared herself to interject. They could exchange, while Marina slipped in and out of the house, taking her things with her, some pieces of why the interrogation collapsed. But that would mean telling Marina how she had lost her temper. Or she could lead her out to the garden and try to explain the hole. Or tempting fate, she could ask about Carlo. Judging the determination in her daughter's stance, Susan adjusted her own. There was no point in imagining that Marina had time to see beyond where her own mind was going.

It was a mess this morning. You know how much I care about abused people and yet I didn't help at all. The woman was from Nigeria. And I wasn't satisfied with the judge's interrogation. It was utterly ineffective.

Marina suddenly gave her a hug. I'm sure you helped her,

122

she said. Who's the rose for? she asked, reaching out for the long stem rising from the fluted vase.

Guess. It's a day old.

Marina rattled the cellophane still puffed around the bud like a glass cage and reached for the card. Extracting it, she studied the words. The curve in Carlo's C was small and she didn't like it too much. It seemed timid. She wished vaguely (and then it scared her like the pimple on his cheek) that he could have been more inventive—even making his signature with a soupy heart. Love, that's all he said. Just like he did this morning.

The way Marina crumpled up the envelope caught Susan by surprise. Marina looked so determined in her shorts and yet nothing of the little girl. As Marina turned, the raw excitement in her daughter's straight wide shoulders was palpable. How was a mother to judge the crumpled paper? Maybe crushing it was an expression of something that was fundamental. Purposeful, seductive and alive, Marina rushed past.

In her room, the angular young woman decided to change her shoes. The white leather sandals her father had paid for had tassels that he liked and she wasn't convinced about. Looking around her room, the flock of silver frames on the desk, herself on a horse with her American cousins, herself alone with Luigi in Athens, her mother handing her a cob of corn from the garden, she felt the divisions in her life. But the rest of the room made Marina feel at home and slightly nervous about leaving it behind. She didn't want to go back into the kitchen. Her mother might want to pry. Without even trying, sitting back as if she had nothing in mind, she could extract so much personal stuff. It probably wasn't deliberate but her training in listening to patients still resulted in delicate soliciting. By the time the small gold buckles were fastened, Marina felt torn. The rhythm and confidence she possessed coming in had been absorbed by the worry of trying to please. A few minutes facing her mother and she felt cramped, restless, and in her attentive presence, a wish to get away. The way her mother smiled there was not enough difference between them. Marina wanted to make it clear she would never be as spontaneous and shapeless as her mother had been. She would try her best not to make her mistakes. She would avoid if she could with Carlo the complications of her parents' traps. She would never be a hippie like her mother with bare feet and hopes no more solid than a sandtray speaking like a ouiji board.

Mom, I'll see you later, Marina said, smiling. She reached out to kiss her mother on the cheek. She wondered, seeing her inquisitive eyes, what her mother really thought. Marina didn't want to ask. Certainly not now. But her mother, poor thing, hadn't been much of a teacher. Her determination was useful but as a qualification for dealing with men it didn't work. Love you, Marina said, as she pulled her face back from the surprisingly hot cheek. The hurried words were often said from Susan to Marina and now they snapped open mirrored and reassuring in their familiarity. When they would see each other next, Marina couldn't be treated in the same way.

And call, for God's sake, Susan said. At least once every twenty-four hours.

Susan found herself with her head in her hands. The soft sobs came out like marmots she'd seen in the Alps peering out of holes. Looking around. It was useless to link the reaction to Marina's exit. The empty house if it were just a matter of Marina would feel lifted, aerated by the cloud of perfume and her swinging beaded bag. Something in the day was pressing on her. Catching her breath. Susan went to the sink again and splashed water on her face. I better not stop, not even a minute. Outside of the kitchen window the cicadas struck up their notes. A horny scratch with dense pauses, the comforting and tedious sound of nature and its mating nets captured her ears.

The answering machine blinked its red sign. Stop. Stop. Susan's hand was leading in the direction of the study. Put the tape from her mother away. The handwriting was so correct. Why not listen to what she had to say? Susan spun the squat package around. Imagine here was a voice, her own mother, and she simply parked it on a shelf. A familiar voice and she only wanted to turn it down. Instead Susan suddenly wished that the short elegant woman had come and was just standing normally, drying a dish. And then she formed a more distanced thought. What if Charlotte's tapes were buried and dug up centuries from now? What would they say about life? Not just about her but the world she came from? Who could understand? What could they hear in her stories of when she waded in the Mississippi? When she drove her father's car at age 12. And what would it matter? They couldn't ever hear Charlotte from the inside, hear the howl of death and how it shut her down, sealing her fate as a shallow low flame. How would they ever know that her independence stopped once her husband's death hit her like a Tsunami. Hearing the tapes would they picture Americans as happy people with stone houses who talked proudly about their Presidents? What was a Republican? Who could put all the pieces of her upbeat stories together? Where was the rhythm of work in the old voice? Work that had been Susan's support and tool for touching the world. And the rivalry? Would they hear that? Unanswerable, Susan sighed, relieved to squeeze the tape in after the others on the shelf.

On the way out of the house, already dressed in shorts, carrying a stack of Xeroxes on prehistoric women's roles, some exciting images on Roman tombs where women are depicted as holding styluses as well as mirrors, she stopped in front of the blue Chinese lamp and decided to listen to the messages blinking underneath it. Last week three patients cancelled. Most shocking was Eraldo, a veterinarian, who called it quits.

Said he'd rather spend his time day-trading. At home, in his parents' living room, in front of a computer. Day-trading, Susan thought, sadly. His solution. Trading time. Maybe it's a definition of life. Susan could close her eyes and still see the blockage, the unrelenting tumor that he traced like a headless snake twisting through the sand.

The illuminated numeral waivered. First call. Luigi. His mother's anniversary. More likely he was just nervously dialling because Maria Grazia had shut off. He could wait to hear that their daughter had come home.

Susan pushed the button again. The voice was hesitant and then in its weariness it began as if he were standing, slightly stooped, in front of her. Vaclav. Susan wanted to stop it there, thousands of miles away, but, of course, it continued. A little slurred with a trace of complicity, certain of the forbidden brightness that would follow. It's probably just as well you're not in. I hope you and Marina are fine. It annoyed her that he assumed no one else would hear the message. Imagine if Marina were still in the house. It would have rocked what was just barely stable. The voice assumed, as he always had, that his presence posed no threats, only delight. That she was without responsibilities as far as he was concerned, since he had no intention of breaking up her life. But that was years ago. Instead the weary voice now was alarming.

Let me say it Susan, you know as well as I do, we were made for each other. Probably that still haunts you as it haunts me. Susan tried to interrupt the tape, punching the button to move to three but the voice continued. Forgive this being a message. But I accept that. I want to speak to you because I don't know about tomorrow. Maybe you are in the next room with a patient. Maybe in someone else's arms. I dreamed about you. Dreamed I sent you a rose. *Paradiso* came to my mind, when Bernard finally asks Mary to intercede for Dante. Where light becomes love. Tomorrow I am going into hospital to be operated on. Nothing fills me with more sorrow than knowing that I can't touch you one last time.

His voice sounded stressed, weak, under siege. The ponderous side that some called supercilious was there. Odds are I will not come out of the anesthesia. I don't say this with pity or regret. That isn't true. I am scared, angry, but (I hear you laughing already) I am sure of what I am doing. I cannot live. Unless I pass the test, unless it is meant to be. My life cannot fork out into another wilful branch. I'm not a transplant human being. It is not a sense of social justice that made me refuse the chance that my privilege obviously offers. No quite the opposite. If I thought I knew how to live, believe me I would have said yes. I would have taken the first plane out and put myself under the talented hands of a London specialist.

Susan almost covered her ears.

If I cannot be saved on the operating table in Prague because my heart can't take the shock of being back in my own society that is a sort of truth for me. My heart is worn out. My faith thin. If anyone might understand that as sincere and unself-pitying it is you. If not you, the marvellous woman with the painstaking eyes, you as the penetrating therapist should. In Prague my life is a business of politics. In my own family I am seen as an egotist and a burden. I cannot help you. "Marie and the Clouds" reveals I am unaccountable to reality or fantasy. I am a parody of authenticity that once seemed an aspiration of mine. Loyalty is a complex master.

You were always stubborn, so certain about what had to be the way. Stubborn. Proud. Blinded by ethics too narrow to consider asking for a divorce. Susan found herself talking to him as he spoke. Resisting the news and the invasion his voice provoked. She had her defences, but this plunge was difficult to censor.

All around I have reached limits that I cannot supersede. Primo Levi argued that he was not a suicide and then he jumped from the stairs. I can understand that. Understand how he fell completely against his will. The doctors tell me I am being a fool by staying here. What do they know about the man who is tired of being dissatisfied with himself. Even the great Havel came by two days ago to try to convince me to place myself under care, and then a foreign doctor. As if I deserved special First World treatment. You know Susan how our story fits. I have never been so completed as I was with you. But there too I reached a limit. Not love's limit but life's. We touched the God in ourselves and it is that very God who asks us to be true to the earthly life we have been given.

Susan's stomach unexpectedly lurched and closed.

Look Susan. I am doing the very thing you so rightly accuse me of. Monologuing. But you are not in and I am alone, a rare lapse on Elsa's part, so I think this is the time and the form given to us. I don't know if you want to say good-by. You and I are so close and yet never closer than when there is touch.

Susan tried to breathe and found her stomach resisting.

His voice broke. It was a voice she had no remembrance of. Calm and choked.

If you do, Jean Paul has already asked to escort you in those days or hours in Prague. The funeral will be enormous. You'll have to forgive me if the operation succeeds. Then this dramatic talk will be a joking prelude to the life I will have to take up. But assuming otherwise, the funeral won't be Victor Hugo size, but big. In these years every symbol is being used. In spite of my exile, I am a political figure of projected hope. Elsa is hysterical. So is Elisa. She didn't want me to make this film. She wanted me at home.

Susan felt his concerns start to suffocate her, his explanations even in this intimate moment turned to himself. Now he was swinging back to his wife. To the woman who used his credit cards and wanted a bigger house. His words in a rich accented English were still faltering ahead. Susan thought she had to run down the hall. She tried to calm herself, to look out, out of the sweep of windows before her and the terraces and the valley. The sky was an engaging Della Robbia blue. Improbable. She grasped at its quietness, like Marie in "Marie and the Clouds"—that dreamy, contented painter, that balanced muse, he presented as her. Susan's feelings lurched again. She felt dumb and stalked. If she didn't move her feet she would soon be vomiting on the floor.

Luigi felt steadiness enter his fingers and slow his pulse as the car climbed. The country roads were stunning composites, mosaics of dry walls and contrast of bare soil with the vines above, with green leaf and articulated shadows on nearly white soil under the sun. He'd always loved the steps, the bite the terraces made into the land. Terraces. Not exactly a startup business. Backbreaking labor. Lifting and building the platforms for the grapes. How long could the peasants keep this life up? Luigi snapped the radio on. *Today more accusations of genocide in Rwanda.* What about canicide? he thought, unexpectedly gripped. And infanticide? he thought, feeling nearly afraid. My own flesh and blood. Me. An unsuspected killer. Yes. Me. On the road.

Luigi moved the radio onto music, even though most disk-jockies and their habit of English bothered him. *Hel-lo Florence. It's going to be a hot one today. A scorcheroo-oo.* So back it was. But the definition they were giving of genocide was annoying. The way speech was used, the ignorance, made the radio, too, an offence. Genocide was not new. Everyone, instead, should remember that the term came about in the First World War. Then the Second World War took it beyond human imagination. But anyone who wanted to open his mouth up on the subject of extermination should look much, much earlier. Africa. Where humanity was born. Genocide meant group identities. Trying to eliminate a people. A different goal entirely from trying to win a battle. Luigi nodded at the irony. Making those distinctions was how he had been trained. For what it was worth. *Niente.* Once it mattered if you read Croce or Gramsci. But not now. Distinctions had become perversely light. Distracting marketing tricks. Decisions as brand names. His mother's father's company. Five hundred thousand lire for the chance to hold less than a meter of parachuting nylon over your head. Or a purse with the leaping hare branded in the leather. Historic craftsmanship. For two million lire a bag, the back alleys in Buenos Aires provided the tradition once alive in San Casciano. The Lepre brand. What did his darling daughter Marina call them? *Heaven.* She called the purses heaven.

Luigi took the curve, let his foot off the gas and his mind relaxed in the same way, until he accelerated again. Such breathtaking vistas and yet what was the valley really? The base of Florence, *per forza,* gushed with blood. Weren't they, modern day Florentines, considered the people of the valley? And weren't the people who were there first really Etruscans? Who wiped out their stories if not the Romans? Who cancelled their language? The people who painted themselves burnt red must have left their amphitheatre in Fiesole and wandered down the hills. And been exterminated. Or stripped of their beliefs. They disappeared. Except for the unstoppable drive of genes. And the persistence of their enigmatic statues with mysterious smiles. Luigi punched the dial. *Hel-lo Florence. Hang on. The news is coming up on the longest day of the year...* He'd hit another gap around songs. Hey fella, Luigi said over the upbeat voice, I've got news for you. Even on the longest day of the year, we're all beasts. That's *belve* in Italian. Animals in English. Throat slitters. Dog killers. Abortionists. We don't want anybody else's history. We're sons of the sons of Roman—he took his voice low—murderers.

Passing by a long line of slow cars descending in the other direction, Luigi looked for the glass and gold of a hearse. A small Romanesque church of white chiselled sandstone rose up. Place did touch him—silence, incense, the transformation of the host—but he couldn't sit passively in a pew hoping to be part of the Catholic Church's higher meanings. Why pretend to ask for forgiveness? Giada's family had strong relations with the Church. Tina had annulled her marriage. Quite a piece of work once one had produced three rather odd children who now control the board. But not quite so difficult if your father has helped an Argentinian Bishop. Umberto, his grandfather, was always ready with cash. It was Cesare, his father, the son-in-law who minded. His family had not come from the land or the Church. Luigi's favorite was a great-grandfather who carried print in a carved wood box strapped to his back. The gazetter walked between Arezzo and Florence, making broadsides for people who wanted texts printed. Set up lines of gold letters backwards to spell out laws, marriage decrees, written power on demand. In his imagination the man seemed like Father Christmas appearing on the crest of a hill. A dust covered, snow covered man—was he wearing a cloak and brimmed hat?— disseminating order and the minimal records for Unification by using his own hands and feet. Susan had always liked his story of printing an announcement for an assembly in Arezzo with Mazzini.

And could it ever be much more? Could there ever be more than stories of the valley? It all flowed backwards and dropped off. Was there ever such a thing as the beginning? The furnace sun shortening the deep shadows into black blades said, if so, it was way before Unification. Before the Renaissance. The Romans. The Etruscans. Way before Yaweh. Way before there were marine pines waiting to be plowed under in frozen glaciers. That the distant light went back so far, Luigi thought, was justification for why no one need account precisely for the blind, laboring flame even he—just a hair short of an atheist— called a soul.

Luigi grappled for his phone on the seat beside him. He wished the plastic toy would ring. Call him and squill in vibration with the elusive thought of his soul. Its pleasing mysterious joys and wretched sobs. Ring so he could utter the word, soul, yes, soul to Maria Grazia, so she could remember that once she had not found him a heartless monster. On the meandering road to the cemetery Cesare, his father, faithfully traveled with Giada several times a week back and forth to the grave. They'd stop for a glass of wine. Stop for two. The truth escaped when he told Luigi one day, I do it to keep your mother company. I don't believe in life after death. But you know, neither does she. She hopes.

How was it that his mother, Giada, had such a hold over calling him to the tomb? So that for these long weeks death and honoring hers had been an obsession? Did she want a Mass? How was it that no real commands from his father remained? Only his brief observations, like white drifting broadsides, practical comments and technical ideas turning and twirling uncollected in Luigi's mind. On the long winding road where one could look south down on the city and catch the fantasy of the dome, where was Cesare, his father, who had tried so unsuccessfully to outvote or direct Giada and her sister as the umbrella factory grew? Where was his voice if not buried by the leather purses and high profile stores in Florence and Rome and Buenos Aires, by the cash that sprouted and grew so profusely from key chains and brief cases until they could have considered themselves rich enough to have bought more villas and more shops with Tina's kids.

Luigi thought hard about the language of his father's secular line as he drove through another piece of narrow road and high hand-worked stone walls. His father contrasted so radically to Giada's father, Umberto, who never let go of the reins. The black gates with shining bronze orbs along the top were ahead. Lines of cypress behind, uniform in height at about six meters, added rows of somber notes. They had been planted, as far as Luigi's eye could judge, right after the war. Could he remember them as striplings set in the bare and war shattered landscape of those years? No, he could not. Although he could date the time to riding in Umberto's black Alicia Lancia. The slight bend in the crest of the cypress now, their broken shaggy tips, was sad. Hel-lo Florence, Luigi thought, slapping the wheel. Has anyone in the city government read my report on cypress canker? The answer was the passive refrain he knew from his job. It would take an epidemic and some ugly photos of bare hills before any deal would be struck. And then it would be an exaggerated contract for replanting the whole of Tuscany with trees from the nursery of someone's relative who possibly kept double books. No guard was in the tin-roofed hut. The parking lot, empty. Luigi felt suspicious even though the shady place seemed peaceful. Prudence urged lock the car. Buttons were so easy to push.

Deep within his ears Luigi heard the trees sounding around him, light drum roll movements stirring the silence. Hearing that slight movement of trees wind-milling was a familiar part of his life. Often he picked it up in forests or even in a garden at a party. That energy, that kinetic power, was as convincing and pleasant as anything he had ever experienced. Luigi's eyes were still filled with flaming patches of magenta, the bucolic vision of a white cow tethered to a tree. Relief trickled through his stiff body as he shook his legs and stretched. The inner gates were wide enough for hearses and were open, without a single guard. Eyeing the glistening white gravel, he connected to it. Luigi imagined he could find the tomb by going straight ahead, then, by skimming the semi-classical tombs, the section that had retained the Fascist Roman altars, passing the glutted block of aspirations to social class, the heroic renditions of Honor and Wisdom as if their swords and kneeling postures reflected a commitment to real justice, and reach his mother's grave.

Silence, not unpleasant, moved like spirits around him as Luigi walked briskly. The short broom snatched from the trunk pointed forward like a flashlight, possibly unnecessary. Surely someone had been sweeping the tomb for the last few years. The vision of a white edifice caked in soil and screaming of neglect panicked Luigi. But Dinizia wouldn't allow that. And it didn't matter if his hands clutched no flowers. Luigi chuckled at his cultivated inadequacy. How many times, regretfully, had he seen Maria Grazia's face betray disappointment when he had not brought flowers? So what? No one is perfect.

The marble was even more pretentious than he had remembered. The tomb, which had two curved colonnades like Bernini's entrance to Saint Peter's, held the names and caskets inside. While Luigi lifted his eyes to find his mother's name carved in marble he could not overlook the stiff vases filled with flowers, red roses, fresh as new blood, on either side. Someone had come and gone. The empty vase next to their intense color caught his eye. The hard metal vessel, mute and solitary. Facing him was the drawn suffering vision of the small man who died so quietly in his sleep. Cesare Augusto Dell' Istante 15 Marzo 1921–29 Giugno 1974. A clamminess came over him. My father. Why was he not buried with his people? The quiet efficient administrator seemed forlornly silenced in his marble box. Lost in the umbrella spokes and the deals his mother's family made with the growing side of business. Swamped by the blaring roses.

Luigi felt the obvious. The duration between the beginning and end points. He put his finger to the dry marble as if to tap its truth. The company, its powerful expansion as unregulated as tanning hides, was a sincere part of Cesare's life and it killed him. And he, Luigi and his mother, Giada, rarely talked about how it happened. Or even him. Cesare had been knowingly or unknowingly covered up. Like the chemicals and enzymes the company had poured into the Arno for decades, the brutal urine and lime concoctions that ate into the stiff salted hides and broke the molecules down into skin finally smooth and desirable after turning them black and slimy, hides decomposing in the gripping stench of corroding softeners assaulting the coverings that had covered the tough and starving animals that had come from Yugoslavia, come in illegally to join the mess of making brand name purses and belts. The lethal wash was dumped weekly by the workers in the wee hours of the morning—*stai zitto*, be quiet, stay down—into the Arno, up above San Casciano. The toxic dumping that asphyxiated the schools of perch and left them bloated and belly up, floating islands of death, and eels and finches and wrecked the food chain for carp, the river victims when the lids to the vats were unscrewed and the operation, among others, made bribes a part of the business. That was only one of Umberto's impositions.

But his father had already signed his son's part away by the end of that struggle. Withdrawn. Signed Luigi up for income and tax benefits but out of any awkward decisionary power. He'd signed Luigi off to protect him but also because Luigi seemed indifferent to practical realities. Cesare's death blinked on like another silent part of Luigi's soul. His father had been unable to stop what he considered wrong attacks on society itself. Unable to curb his wife. He had been choked like the fish and Luigi had pursued his research and his mother had gone on as if the family belonged to Umberto and Tina and the Lepre, the leaping Rabbit, brand. Luigi rubbed his fingers across the dates and felt pain like an electric shock. They hadn't missed Cesare's silences. They hadn't missed the way cognac bottles stopped piling up. Just a few minutes ago the visit to the tomb seemed as if all would go smoothly. Now Luigi felt as bad as when the white dog arched its back trying to get to its feet.

The tombs around theirs were massive. The wings of angels darkened by shadows from large oaks. There were tombs backed on tombs until there was a look of a city of ashes, with a Colosseum curve behind and the cypress again. Blue green. Maybe I could say a round from the *Rosario*, Luigi thought, awkwardly. For both of them. For the wordless mystery contained in the endings of the flat boxes with their names and dates. His anger died down, and the thought of prayer brought a vague picture of his parents closer, almost peacefully into his breast.

The gravel behind him squished. The squish, squish of feet pushing on it and pushing it aside got nearer. Oh, you already took my place, Gian Franco said, waving a sheath of yellow roses and patting Luigi on the back.

Without thinking about the mood he was breaking into, he stuffed the stems into the empty container to the left of Cesare's tomb. Why not? I remember your father, too, Gian Franco said. He used to think he could talk us out of our plans for changing human nature.

The plastic surgeon looked short of breath, emotional. He plucked a red rose from one of Giada's vases and put it to his face. He closed his eyes as if taken by the scent. But Cesare was not notable like your mother. She was unforgettable. He paused, almost overwhelmed. The plastic surgeon's fringe of hair looked mussed and foolish.

Luigi felt thrown off. He wondered if Gian Franco was taking something. He was sweaty. What was he leading up to?

You didn't know it, and Giada didn't, but her way of caring for me made me compare her to my own mother. Your mother was elegant and she knew. She knew how to be a lady. She had knowledge. She didn't complain.

Gian Franco paused again. He hesitated as if he was looking for the right phrase. As if he had rushed to a place that now he could not retreat from. He touched Luigi with the rose. You were so lucky Luigi. Gian Franco's lips quivered. More than for your money, you were lucky for the mother you had. Mine was deformed by her early life. The rats that used to crawl under the door when she was a child. Her unending sense of not having enough. Want twisted her up. Her anxiety was like shame that she wrapped us in. That's the unwritten story of Italy. The trauma of poverty. Its grip. Its denial.

The words struck Luigi as if Gian Franco had broken a window with a stone. He felt invaded as much as hurt. He didn't know why because his own thoughts were certainly not that reverential. But he resented the innocence snatched by the man standing beside him. He was mixing the past and present like a dog digging. And Gian Franco's confession about his own mother was like offering a stained house-key to his life.

What is that sound? Gian Franco asked, turning around.

Silence. A thread of wind in the leaves. Then a hollow pock, pock, pock.

A woodpecker, Luigi said. There are some pileated ones left. Maybe because most of the cypresses are dead. There's plenty to eat in rotting trees.

So it's not all doom as the Greens would have it. Good to know that the planet isn't as ideological as the Left. Luigi, as I drove up I couldn't remember ever having had such strong feelings.

Luigi almost wanted to shout. He could see the feelings in the crazy way Gian Franco was acting. Maybe he was going to jump off into what was bothering him. Square up for a change.

In my work, saving women from the ravages of old age is not exactly a pleasure. I'll tell you handling adipose tissue until petri dishes overflow is not inspiring. I see a lot of faces. They have become slightly scary to me. Maybe it's like Polanski's Repulsion. Remember that eye? Terrifying the cut. You see lines of worry. Of excess. Gian Franco stopped as if amazed. It's true. I see a certain vulgarity growing among women in Florence. I never see a face like your mother's any more. Can you understand what I mean? Noble. Just think about her cheeks. And her breasts, he said, with a slight wildness. I just

137

see dried out old tan sacks. Or overripe tan tits. No upper class woman in Florence has white breasts anymore.

The president of the country club had just strayed onto forbidden ground. If Giada knew her cheekbones were being examined at her grave she would have had a good laugh. She would see the irony that Gian Franco didn't give a wit for all her hours of civic lessons. But her breasts. Gian Franco was lost.

Be careful, Luigi stammered. You're talking about the dead. Shut up for a while. Take a break. Luigi couldn't think of anything else to say to get his attention. Life was so strange. Like Gian Franco and himself. Like the colors of the flowers. Clashing, not what Giada would have picked. He couldn't touch the subject of his mother. Gian Franco had sucked up all the air. But Diniza wouldn't have bought red roses. She would have picked daisies or iris from fields along the way.

After what seemed like an interminable time without speaking, Gian Franco asked, Shall we go? He asked lightly, using the tone he did when calling for a vote that was already won. Having been stopped short by Luigi, he felt saved, as if the imposed silence had mercifully washed his hands and feet. He let Giada go. Let the wild gaffe go. As far as I know, the trees aren't wired. If there are judges, they have paid their dues and are two meters down. What about a walk?

Luigi glanced at Gian Franco's retreating face. A rivalry that had never been expressed had been spilt. Giada from her tomb high in the wall beckoned to Gian Franco. She beckoned to Luigi, his deep need to answer her call. Did she like fomenting the jealousy? And where was Cesare? Luigi felt eyes resting on his shoulders. Eyes that noted broken promises. Luigi didn't believe the eyes were there.

My father might have liked what the judges are doing, Luigi said. He must have had many days when he thought that bribes were no way to behave. Or to build a young democracy.

There was no point in kicking the back of the glass booth. The phone didn't take coins. Milli yanked the snaky silver cord and wanted to scream. She skipped all the writing on the walls, the black scribbles and heavy words. There was a hammer and sickle, that word *boia*, executioner, which sent chills up her spine. Writing on the phone booth walls. Only reaching Irene's cell phone would put the day back into its place. She needed to buy a phone card. Or perhaps just go to the river. That was undoubtedly where Irene had gone. The question *why* plagued Milli some. Why had Irene gone out, she thought, as the people on the street swirled past, and a young man tapped on the window, asking if she was finished.

His dull eyes looked like a carp's. Milli hated his push on the door. He had money and was of this place. He was one foot away from her and had no idea who she was. The air was growing hot. If she was to get out, he and his blue baseball hat had to step back. She pushed the flimsy door open rapidly, without looking up. A small rush of satisfaction swept through her. It was slim, the sigh of satisfaction, but real that pushing him back. His pasty face in haste stepping back for her.

Now all she had to do was enter a tobacco store and buy a phone card. It was simple but it seemed a ball of tangled knots. Nearly impossible. Milli calmed down by remembering what she and Irene had said would happen if something happened. Nothing would happen. That's what they had decided. Nothing brutal would happen. Farina always obeyed, even when she was tired, and whined a little, churning on her mother's lap, she would behave. Irene made all those connections, surely, when it turned past nine o'clock.

Farina, Farina, Farina. You are my little piccina. Birbina. All bella bambina. You have magic in your knees. No, she would laugh. Your toes. No. Your nose. And they would touch, the game being never enough. You have magic in your occhi, occhi, eyes.

If Farina was not sitting in her wooden chair, it was because

Irene had grown tired of waiting and they were at the river. The trickle of the river over stones, even though there had been some ugly threats, some knives, the spot under the bridge consoled her now. Irene and Farina were waiting there. So it was a matter of buying a phone card and telling them, when they found each other, laughing by now about the long boring night, the man with the rough cloak, the irate American lady with the red hair, the theatre of the police station where they just wanted to be told lies, it was a matter of buying a phone card. Or just walking to the river on foot. Maybe there was no point in going back to a tobacco store to buy a card. Maybe it was better just to go on. To find them there. To join the two of them on the river bank. To rest then, under the bridge, out in the air, out, though, of the heat making her sweat. Milli pushed the sweat back into her hair with light brushing movements. The slipperiness reminded her suddenly of when she was much younger, when her sweat was not a secret or a surprise, when it was a part of her on a tropical day, like a forthright gift. She was smooth and Meniki might kiss the drops around her neck. Or lick her belly with his playful cat-like tongue. And rain was nearly steam. It was too complicated to buy a phone card. To waste time standing in line with people buying cigarettes. It was quicker and less making-her-heart-beat just to take the bus and then to walk there. That decision to move forward, to hold Farina in her arms, to forget Igor and the law trying to catch her in its claws put Milli in a good mood. Instead, her fine featured face, directed by worry, gave no sign that she was looking ahead.

Professor Melandri could not say it more clearly than by forcing his eyes onto his watch. Couldn't the American see that he couldn't lend him more time? The American's face was not unsympathetic. But different. Unmasked and unbefitting a man of his age. It was untempered. Perhaps it was only a matter of seconds before he would ask with his white teeth if he could extract an email address, a point of future meeting. It would be a small price, if it would make him withdraw from his hovering over the slides. Professor Melandri had learned from his contacts with American academics that when they seemed unsophisticated they were usually focused as experts. Single-minded. And tireless learners. Childlike, but absolutely not to be dismissed as the ex-Communists would like it. No this firm determined jaw—if anyone wearing such a loud striped shirt could be on the Left—might have some insights. Or he might reflect those stripes and just be a Puritan square. The American's face brought back the earlier problem. Melandri couldn't pull out his handkerchief, but it sat, a shock, wet and crumpled in his pocket. It wasn't clearly an attack. But a close call. And he found himself diminished, less of a humanitarian than he would have wished, after the prostitute had passed him and spit. She was like an ostrich hurling a ball of phlegm. And the fury that arose in his breast was frightening. Far from the indignation of being hit by a pigeon and writing a letter to the *commune* about its policy of protection. No, it was a horrible revulsion for one's fellow human beings. The amazing experience of such violent anger nearly ruined what he had been anticipating for months.

I can't say I know a lot about it, but it's always struck me that the Catholic Church encouraged science but covered their bets. Wouldn't you say Toscanelli is a prime example? Or am I wrong? Essentially he's a Thomist: *with this science we can know our bad inclinations and keep ourselves from many sins and errors.* But he was also an astrologer.

Melandri didn't know whether to respond. Seeing the glint in the American's eye, he wondered, how would he have absorbed the unexpectedly unpleasant glob. His naïve face suggested that he might well have been shocked by the Nigerian, especially after she turned to spit again. Poor fellow, Melandri thought. You probably would have feared catching AIDS. Feared being touched. The public was funny when it got close.

Close enough to puncture one's balloon. As the barrier rose between the American and himself, Melandri cooled his arrogance back down. Wasn't the public the reason he was in the cathedral fussing with a carousel? Wasn't the story important? Melandri personally liked the experiment's elegance. But theatre, the ray's arrival, made the lecture intriguing. Pure, endless, shining, flashing, dancing, guiding, streaming, showering, suffusing, peerless. Light as an actress. But light as truth, concrete reality. Since ancient Greece, theatre often showed people reality, taking something complicated out of the dark. And dramatizing it, not as legend but accurate report.

The American historian was still stiffly waiting for a response. In my lecture, I hope you'll see how versatile Toscanelli was. He aided Christopher Columbus with maps. He helped Brunelleschi with his calculations for this very dome. But the thrust of his work was in service of the reform of the Julian calendar. That's the power of a reasoning mind. Astrology was a big part of that interest. But now, he said, intently staring at his pile, I'm late. The face of Giordano Bruno was in the next slide. Melandri didn't want to lift it up, in case it stimulated another attempt at a professional relationship.

Thomas Simpson knew he should clear the space, but hope made it difficult for him to retreat from the clatter. This easy touching of a learned man, like wandering in the Uffizi past the Botticellis, offered the greatness of Florence. A greatness that came from belonging to a friendship with a Florentine. These months in the new archives there had been no special lunches. Just depressing conversations with archive clerks. Who challenged him with every fact in the American cover-up of the Iran Contra affair. Although it was foolish, even an offensive way to proceed, the sensation that the astronomy professor was his last chance made Thomas Simpson ignore his feelings of begging. He had always wanted to see the observatory in Arcetri. In fact he had looked out over the valley from the observing station, spotting Galileo's red house. That anyone could enter. But the feelings of the secret passageways, the family letters still in drawers—the backstage, that's where life-changing energies lurked. In Des Moines, he had linked the moon's glow in his backyard more than once to Galileo. Galileo was surely the Italian version of Hamlet. And the Gregorian calendar was a topic that he never could get straight enough. In the Julian calendar the moon's cycle was thought to be separate from the celestial where all was forever and forever. The Julian calendar used the sun. The American professor's heart lifted as he let his eyes swirl in Vasari's dark cycle of bodies in the dome. They had real weight even so far away. The distance to the frescoed ceiling was ambition writ large. The black cloth covering the window where the ray would pass did its job well. The light was choked off for now. He felt foolish wanting to believe that the astrological aspects of Toscanelli's ray might be of use to him. Yet, he needed good news.

Virgil stopped, although he couldn't stop, stuffed as he was. The shadow covered his brain. His talons stopped pushing. He couldn't see what was above and he couldn't move, or hop over a few rough clods for a deeper covering of his dappled brownness with the soil under the tomato plants. He was tired, caught and suspended, gripped by poison sacks that were swelling, engorging and might explode. Virgil stopped and waited in the semi-dark. His heart pounded, speeding along. The shadow pressed on him, pulsed down and rose. Death was blocking the sun. Death was freezing the light.

Round, round. In hypnotic rhythm. Round and round in a raw way. Close and lift. Now. Hawk wings. Hawk shadow. Heart pounding. Heart beating. Less shadow. Now. Less air moving. Now. Less. Now. More. More light now on his head. Clear unfiltered sun. Hawk wings gone.

Virgil was tired and only half-way, wearing two skins. He

was out of the high moving death shadows, the circling, searching, dark wing beats and back into the garden of clods. Sunlight was falling on him light now day now space sun sky clouds enormous heartbeat and task light flooding him and turning him golden. Warm.

High. Strong. Nearly straight light. Tired, his talons fingered and felt, touched and tugged, moving skin again.

Signora Caffo called the retriever back, but scent was a joy stronger than her mistress's words. Marta's brown wet nose nudged the walk-in-gate open. She pushed further and was into Susan Notingham's yard and wagging past the pots of white impatience before any more futile commands were released. The garden stunned the bow-legged woman. At first she was worried that Marta's tail would swing and snap off the daffodils or crush the anemones with her thoughtless paws, but it was only a matter of seconds before she realized she herself was inside, her skirt rubbing against the spice of the basil as she proceeded along the path. Not catching the dog but taking in the way the sweet peas were tied, the way the auburn cherries got enough sun. Signor Luzi, the gardener, had never said much beyond a grunt. He had never told her about the beds of lavender, the dense swoon of perfumes. Never offered her a cutting from what were hundreds of begonias. He gardened for Signora Notingham and chatted about worms in her fruit trees but had never let on how grand an operation it had become.

The dog was wagging on ahead. It was not Agnese Caffo's custom to find herself in other people's yards, trespassing or spying on their goods, but the thought of Arvon made Agnese Caffo feel a strange entitlement. Arvon drew her in like a magnet once the gate moved. It was a discomfort she didn't like to face, gazing on other's luck, measuring the fortune of this garden with the iris and zucchinis in hers, the fortune of people who have the comfort of swings and grandchildren with normal minds. It was the twisted story of Arvon that had led her into the yard. The sin was envy. That horrible corrupting feeling that she didn't want to feel. Agnese Caffo made certain no envy lurked in her heart. They had a respectable green Fiat. They had good beef on Sunday. They had snap dragons, too, with double blossoms. She and Signor Caffo were as well provided for as Signora Nottingham. It was Arvon who had felt envy. He was out of place. The Persian prince was the one not happy with his lot, that of a working farm. He had kept trying to join this place. Arvon was the one who was punished by wanting to be a chicken.

The resolve to bring her peacock back overtook Agnese Caffo then. Her conviction grew sturdier with each step. It had not been her intention when the door was pushed open, but now it was destiny. Around her neck like someone chopping it with an ax, she felt the humiliation of allowing her bird to stray from home and knew it must stop. Signor Caffo, her husband, wouldn't make an issue. He refused to come to the Signora's yard and insist that she lead the bird back home. But it was wrong to let Arvon stay so foolishly with the hens. Signora Caffo glanced over the yard that she hadn't seen often since the old Signora Dell'Istante had lived in the villa at least part of the year. With the old Signora she had furnished eggs and caned baskets. They often met down below in the church for morning Mass. With the new Signora, right from the beginning, such a young girl with the Signora's young son, the conversations stopped at the gate. She had her own pressed oil. Her own tomatoes. Even in the last year with Arvon's blue and green tailed flights over the fence, his red eyed fights and squealing, she had never been invited in. The old Signora had offered bread. But not just bread. Not that she had accepted, that she expected or needed it, but the table in the kitchen had been offered. And presents of clothing. Those were different times. Hunger was met with common courtesy, like saying *Buon giorno*. A tip of the hat. A common touch. The priest then, too, asked and knew how to make hearts burn with guilt until they reached down into their pockets. Now the pews were empty.

Agnese Caffo's heart pounded. She tugged at the gold cross around her neck and stretched looking for her prodigal bird. Her worried eyes searching for him widened at the opulence. They were stopped by the thick trunks of trees with glass tables underneath, and a bronze fountain that trickled water. Nowhere was there need in the garden. Not in the dry stone walls covered in violets. Not in the large oven for bread. Or the hammock with its large wooden stand. There was no need in the garden. No need. It almost made her laugh. Agnese stood still, trembling now, nervous for how far into the garden she was. Where was the dog? If she stood still maybe she could scan the hedges and pathways for Arvon.

And what did Marta have in her mouth? What was making her tail wag and what was she shaking and dropping. Covered in skin. A toad. Trying to jump spread eagle and rolling away. It was better than when they are mating and stuck to each other. But strange that transparent webby ball. Toads can burn the lining of your mouth. Marta, she cried, trying not to stir up the straits that were deepening. The dog disappeared beyond a pile of soil. Ran straight up it like a tractor with treads. When Signora Caffo reached her, Marta started to bark.

Quiet. Quiet, she said, raising her hand as the dog, now wet and a bit muddy, whirled around. A steep edge and then a dry deep orderly hole. Oh, Agnese Caffo said. Oh, and it felt deep like a moan. The large deep hole surprised her. Its neat walls. It was nearly like finding a body. Oh, she should have been minding her own business and here was digging. She knew by the gaping hole something terrible was going on. She put her foot on the edge and felt crumbling underneath her shoe. A deliberate hole. It was hard to believe the Signora was after illegal treasure. Suddenly she felt she could twirl herself, lose her footing and tumble in, right to the bottom of the crime.

Agnese Caffo's mind stalled. She had no intention of spying or any idea of such cheating going on behind the iron gates. But here it was. An excavated hole. A lapse. One more unbearable stroke against the Signora who had never gone to church. Agnese Caffo glanced towards the towering villa and wondered how long it would be before someone came out and faced her. Facing the hole was nearly as shocking as the long ago fresh soil of two Fascists buried in the woods. The soil nearly shrieked on its own and set the heart pounding during those years. The horrible lapse of finding civilian bodies pushed into shallow graves, still nearly panting, and knowing, that was the thing. Knowing more or less who in the village might have been among the killers. The dry deep hole was substantial enough for Roman glass and amphorae, deep enough for a tomb. Gold beads and bronze statues. Money. Agnese Caffo hadn't seen holes so deep outside of the cemetery. Water bubbled at the bottom. It must be holding large treasures. There were kings, they had always said that, unfound Etruscan kings with golden hens, and golden eggs, buried throughout Tuscany.

Wits. Signora Caffo whispered to the dog, gesturing in a deliberate way that she hoped might convince Marta to follow. But she didn't want to leave Arvon. That was the reason she had allowed herself to trespass.

If only she could see the bird. If she could get somewhere else in the yard in case the Signora came out. It was standing over the illicit hole that made her entry a problem. A compromising discovery for the Signora. Awful what people did. Agnese Caffo's knee ached. More than ever, she had to get her bird out of this yard, where beauty seemed to be important, but really hypocrisy was lurking in every shadow.

Agnese Caffo scanned the trees as she turned her back on the scandalous hole. What did she expect? Oh, she knew she still expected to see Arvon, his tail a magical harp of iridescent colors, a life that stunned with its magnificence, blues and greens swooping from a tree, his head cocked when she said his name. She scanned the trees and in a far pine, with laddered branches, she noticed the ruined bird, torn-up, his tail plumed shreds. Her heart sank. He was cowering, in her opinion. Not asleep. Not ruling the roost. He was hiding, without the strength to protect himself. At first Agnese Caffo felt bereft. Then she felt shame. Anger at his withdrawal. Her bird and his foolishness. Arvon needed to come home. To stop going away.

Signora Caffo felt dizzy turns in her head. Her mouth went dry. She was not young. The pine tree was tall. It was only a matter of minutes and Marta would bark without mercy to get the bird riled. There was only one choice, she thought, looking at the pathetic fowl that was hers. Judging the way the prickly branches had been chopped, testing her feet, her bowed legs with knees that caused her such pain, they still might just get her up there. A few branches off the ground. Then it would be up to him. How her arms could embrace such a big, but thin and mangy bird, would be a question only God could answer.

Agnese Caffo looked up into the tree and eyed Arvon. Are you going to come down? she asked, or will I have to come up and get you?

In his eyes, a blank frozen stare. In hers, cold condemnation.

The peacock shook the bony joints that were bird shoulders and gave out a harsh, lonely cry. Flapping his wings, which were licey and full of broken quills, he stiffened, lengthened, poked his head out in a scolding position. He blinked and ruffled up. Then he plunged and landed on the branch below. He waited, turned, and then fluttered to the rung below that. Another and another. Hopping skilfully.

Arvon touched the ground. Agnese Caffo's strong hands reached out in joy. As she stroked the odd greasy feathers, her arms trembled. The sense of possession was like no experience she had ever had. A glow transfused her or him. Arvon rested in front of her with his small, unyielding eyes. She felt unworthy of such a reward. Unworthy but also vindicated. She didn't dare to think, though, that she could say 'follow' and that Arvon would. Marta was already sniffing and troubling him.

Agnese Caffo opened her short strong arms. Here was her angel to struggle with. To wrestle with, to overwhelm and capture, bend, if need be, backwards and forwards, not letting go. She would carry him, wings and legs as she carried so many other loads, from rough, twisted logs to her grandson, Luca, when he fell unconscious and was blue. Arvon stiffened but didn't try to scratch with his haggard claws, push with those strong blackish legs. He nearly walked straight forward into her outstretched arms and went limp.

Agnese Caffo felt awe. Her heart beat like a soft drum under her ribs, as she raised the long scrawny bird. She had to rejoice, grasping the prodigal, whose head, with its cocky ringed eyes, was nearly blocking her sight. On bent legs, which now were shaking, she had re-captured what was hers: Arvon's not resisting body dragging his green and black peacock plumes. God certainly would help her now to balance and to carry her precious load as far as the gate and, with a push, to click the metal door shut with her muddied shoe. Then the hole could rise up like a huge black sack and still not trap her inside. Its nefarious secrets, which she didn't want to know, would follow her, though, and she would pour them out, all the shock and implications of what she had witnessed, once she got home.

SEVEN

T HE RINGING SOUND gave Irene hope. The nightmare was over.

Igor's voice took charge of reversing that. You were fifty short last night.

The astonishment of him reaching her on the grass while she was wavering, still hesitant to decide, was awful. His voice, so much to be avoided, having tracked her to the riverbank sounded bad.

Of course, he couldn't see Farina sitting there. He couldn't hear the water or imagine the spot he didn't know about.

But he was imposing himself like the slave driver that he was.

Where are you?

Irene shook her head.

A client asked for the one with fingers that solve anything. He's having a smoke and I told him you'd be ready in half an hour. Igor didn't want to know why Irene hadn't appeared at the door, her nerves excited. Half an hour, Irene. If I hear you're doing tricks, I'll take your neck in my own hands, find the veins pulsing. Cuckoo. Cuckoo. You won't make cheap decisions after that.

Irene wondered who she was arguing with. As she said yes,

she knew. She had been arguing with herself but that was over. Igor had tracked her right into her brain and threatened her on the grass. Igor had found the way if not the words to make her realize that it was inevitable. His cruel insistence pushed her. She was glad he couldn't see the clouds moving, see Farina, sitting as quietly as a preacher.

She would think of a speech as she lived with the dead feeling passing down her arm into Farina's small hand. But by the time she neared the Piazza della Annunciata, she had thought of nothing to tell the child. Pigeons jaywalking crazily didn't part for them as they climbed up the steps. Irene thought nervously that she should arrange her hair. Perhaps she should brush Farina's as well, before knocking at the convent. Of course her little cotton dress with flowers, that drooped, too, never having seen an iron.

Come on, Irene said, pulling the tired child up. Feeling her warm presence as a sensation of uncomplicated smells of bitter grass and day old clothes, Irene almost forgave herself. It would be good. The sisters would feed Farina. Keep her clean. But what if the first face she saw had a tight chin and hair coming out of it? No there would be someone kind, some old nun with a jolly face. As the sun beat on them near the top of the steps, sitting students shooed the headstrong pigeons away. Farina roused herself for the flutter. Irene felt alone. Looking at the cans that had been dropped, she felt the sensation of being cast away. What if the nuns started to ask questions? How did she come to have the child? Where were her papers? Those non-papers that changed Farina's life in every routine in the city. Paper was stronger than a rearing horse.

Farina, what if I buy you a toy?

Why, Farina thought, as the pigeons wheeled again with their blustering fuss. After such a long walk and so much worry in Irene's face that looked elsewhere and almost wildly, why?

Toys were not even chatter. They weren't forbidden. They

simply were not part of Farina's existence. She hardly knew what they might be. She certainly never longed for any stuffed toys with button eyes. She had her bear that was never far from her in the room. He was not as careful as she was. Farina found going down the steps difficult. Without a hand to steady her, her body teetered on her short leg. She was tired. Her shoe hurt. Where was Milli and why were they turning around?

Would you like a toy?

The resolute child shook her head negatively while also searching for an answer. She was disappointed that her head shook no. But she really didn't want a toy. She frowned. Farina thought it was time to talk. Her thoughts ran forward about her mother and her worry and her wish to get out of the sun and back into the dark familiarity of the room with the clothes lines and her bed. She sensed Irene's distraction. Farina didn't know what to say except, where is momma?

Don't worry, Irene said. Let's look for a toy.

By then, with the Duomo rising up at the end of the street, blocking it like a giant orange air balloon, Farina felt pee-pee trickle down her leg. Surprising, terrible, a stream she could not stop, so she let it drip down and tried with her hands to wipe it off her legs. While people passed around her, Farina felt tears start from her eyes. She could hardly bear to move another step in the light.

Irene caught in one glance what had happened. She didn't know how to use the experience as a brake on her deed of giving Farina over to the nuns. She saw it, instead, as a sign that the three and one half year old more than ever needed a roof over her head. But how could she give over a child with wet pants, unbrushed hair, and a face streaked by weeping?

The two figures were passed by shoppers, mostly tourists with bare legs, while Irene held Farina's forlorn little rump over the curb. Irene looked like a prostitute, in the tight slick curve of her clothes, a pulsing aura of lack of shame. Her dyed black hair sprung out boldly, her sling backed shoes were sharp. She knew she cut a dramatic figure leaning over a small child who was lame.

I want to go home, Farina said, suddenly putting her arms around Irene's neck. She felt the acceptance in Irene's emotions, her anger in retreat.

Irene, too, felt back in touch. Holding the child with the grasping arms she felt melted and different than before. She almost knew a part of herself, a furnace of energy that could not give in. She felt stokings of reprieve, of rescue, but knew that they would not last.

I'm going to get you a toy, she said, pulling up Farina's wet pants and deciding to carry her the rest of the way.

Inside the store there were more cold eyes than in Craiova when the Roms came in on horses and their dusty wagons, tired, thirsty, holding back their plans. A clerk with thin penciled blue eyebrows indicated with a fast look that she was their shadow.

Do you like this doll? Irene asked, picking up a Barbie that she rather liked.

If you just tell me, the clerk said.

Farina shook her head. The doll was too hard and pink. She looked like Matrushka, the funny woman who sometimes gave Farina a pat on the head as if she were a ball.

The clerk leaned over the long counter covered by the puff and gauze of dolls, their nylon hair, their elegant gowns. She hovered and spread her arms, acting as if they were a collection of real women who needed protection.

Irene seldom brushed against the public in stores. She shopped in large open markets where you could plunge your hands into the piles and pull tight red elastic bunches out or black shiny crushes and press them against your body and imagine. She and Milli bargained from stall to stall where weather was all around and not stifled with perfumed air. Sometimes she lifted a plastic jewel, if the crowd was busy enough. Irene despised the clerk's masked face.

Farina's eyes darted like a pair of hummingbirds from fuzzy cats to long red cars to airplanes hanging from the ceiling among the lights. There were tables of books. Farina felt amazed. She studied the pink fur of a chicken wearing a hat with a bow. The plaid ribbon was fascinating. But she saw pots and thought they might be paints. And boxes that she thought might hold pencils.

If she had known she was about to leave Irene, she might have chosen the chicken with the big hat. In spite of its broad back and funny tail it could have been hugged at night and, in the morning, its bright orange beak tweaked for a smile and its hat set right. But she didn't know anything except that Irene wanted her to have a toy. She was naturally attracted to objects that linked pages to magic. Words leaping in her book—Red Riding Hood and *Cenerentola*. She wanted a set of colored pens. Farina pointed to a colored plastic envelope of markers. Her face broke into a smile.

Anything, Irene said, knowing, now, that the time for separation would soon come.

The pens are waterproof, the clerk said.

Irene held up a tawny doe that she herself would have loved. It had a pert set of eyes.

I said do not touch. *Per favore.*

Do you want this? Irene said, handing Farina the doe.

Pens, Farina said again, knowing that lines would follow from their tips. Colors would come out like kite tails. More than once she had picked up a pen that Igor had let fall and for the time she had it, before he stood over her, nodding and holding his hand out, she could make it spin across a page. She could spell her name. She could spell Milli. And apple. Wolf. Red.

Irene was both disappointed and proud. She thought of

getting both, something soft and the pens, but that might break up the charm. Pens were a sign that her decision was right. Farina did not need solutions that had her growing up under a bridge, with Florentines staring. She needed to fit in, even to the stupid world that the toy shop clerk inhabited. She needed books. The nuns always honored books. And Milli would appear and the two of them would get the papers they needed. It would be a question of hours, no more. Milli would come and there would be no problems with the law because the nuns would help the little child.

Will that be all? the clerk asked with a trill of relief.

Irene raised her palm in a gesture that was in part pacifying, in part itching to accuse.

Wrap it as a gift, she said to the clerk. Then she turned and came closer with her hand raised toward the clerk. This child, she said, this child, and the words that came next rushed out so forcefully that Irene believed them. This child you will not forget. Someday she will be famous. Irene wished she knew the name of a TV program where there were judges and leaders talking. That's what she would have told her suited Farina.

The sister who opened the door had a young face, optimistic, still fresh with a language of helping. She was just going back to her room, having called Susan Notingham, a woman therapist she knew, about the Mother Superior's state of ill health. Not finding her in, she left a message on the answering machine. Sister Morena held out her hand to pat Farina's head. Her pat was neither personal nor harsh. It was educative, perhaps a bit hungry for touch.

Irene liked the brown eastern face. She wished she could roll her responsibility up like a handkerchief and stuff it in the nun's sleeves. It was too large what she was about to do. She was aware now that the carved door opened further and further that she would have to run. How could she pull the little girl out of her arms and where could she place her on the brightly washed marble floor? How to thrust her at the sister. To unpry the hands so tightly pinching her neck.

Come in. I'm Sister Morena, the woman said, as Farina pulled her head back and tucked her chin in like a turtle. Beyond the door there was a desk, stained glass windows casting green and red light on the floor. The stout nun stood slightly perplexed, flexing her toes in wide sandals. She'd taken in many children in the shelter in New Delhi. She'd taught breast feeding and although it wasn't allowed, she'd spoken of AIDS. Are you coming in, she said with a gesture as crisp as her cap. What's your name, she asked as Farina closed her eyes, snapped them actually, and held them closed.

As Irene stepped into the cool entrance soaked in muted colored shadows, five stories burned on her tongue. They sizzled and went out. The cool patience of the brown eyes might not let her go.

Do you have a toilet? Irene asked.

The nun pointed down a hall. The white hall vibrated with regular interruptions of children in native costumes. They were official photos and the children were red cheeked or wearing cornrow braids. No face said unhappy or lost or without purpose. Irene hoped with all her heart there would be a window. They were on the ground floor. The stained glass ones facing them in the entrance with a white clothed Jesus and blue, red and yellow robed disciples were large enough for a covered wagon to pass through.

Irene didn't expect the lightning jolt of sadness and panic to strike her so brutally as she put Farina on the floor. It electrified her. Without an explanation, without a kiss, with only the hurricane of regret and hope and confusion churning and roaring through her body, she put Farina down, pushing her some to make her let go. She pushed as she wanted to hold her tight. She faked coolness as she felt flame. She said to her, I'll be back with a mouth so dry it was like the pillows stuffed with wheat stalks that she used to bury her face in as a child.

Farina looked up startled but Irene was already clicking down the hall. Inside, there was no time. Irene locked the door, turned on the water in the sink, turned it on full force and didn't dwell on the dark circles in the mirror where she witnessed the extraordinary sadness shooting from her eyes. The window was possible. It was surprising that the nuns hadn't barred it, or even made the curtain opaque. Like the best signs of fortune it was large, not a peep hole saying maybe. The window was so low Irene didn't have to stand on anything. It was a trusting window, chaste like the whole whiteness of the room. White tile, scrubbed and white curtains. Yanking up her skirt in the light of day, the bruises on her legs sickened her. Her life and who was responsible for all these bruises? Up on the sill, it was a short jump to the sidewalk. No one was coming in that minute. The frame in the window made Irene duck her head and a rush of stealth, of giddiness she had seen in her people, after they had left a house and were sorting through what was worth keeping, gave strength to her arms' push. She scraped her spine as she slipped down the wall. If she crossed the street, in thirty seconds she could be gone. There were doctors of law, of music, Irene effused, landing well. Why not a doctor of windows where centuries of Roms' fingers and feet hold a way of life that can't keep them out of windows?

Done. She rubbed her scraped back. What did she expect? Irene turned the corner and realized nothing was done. It was as if bats had sprung out of a box and were screeching like those at the Ponte Vecchio that twitch close at evening. The sky then is sunset and beautiful pinks and oranges but the bats change all that with their screeching diving moves that cut the sky into upper and lower. She was below the lower sky. Caught with the lowest haunting twitches seeming to pull her hair and then flipping away. Farina had been consigned.

Irene didn't know where to go next. The sensation was as strong as the current she had swum against. Worse. Higher. At least the waves she could smash with her arms and the cold battering current was something to resist. The window was one way. It was deep and flapping shut. She had closed herself on the outside of the little girl's sober smile. Irene didn't know if heading towards the center, getting into the rush of Florentines and tourists with their clicking suitcases, if she could reach any place of safety. One simple knock and now Farina's life was in someone else's hands. And her friendship with Milli was brought towards a battle. The police might come in. This might mean she was a traitor. A traitor who betrays the secrets of a group.

Irene reminded herself that there were many good reasons. Igor was one. His hate was pressured enough, hiding and festering, so that the pus could burst forth and to wipe it off he would sell a child. But he would not choke her. Irene knew he would be glad when she came back without Farina. But that was no reason to forgive him. Or the world that let him order the eight of them into following his cruel warnings—Milli, Kristal, Linda, Matrushka, Stella, if she thought of any of the women, they were all orphans, having parents who gave their seed but all of them burdened and harassed by neglect. Her own father was darkly silent and thought that she belonged to him and his rough life assumed her submission. And that was not even the whole of the world that forced her into putting Farina in a white place of tiles and stained glass windows where officially they promised to look after children. For the first time what Irene was living seemed as threatening and shadow-filled as the fear she felt as a child in the creaking wind-filled forests. When oaks seemed bodies with suffocating ancestors gathered like mocking spirits in the leaves that then rattled off and drifted.

How could she climb the stairs again, put her feet on the

worn out crookedness of the marble steps leading back to their shuttered room and know that Farina was alright?

Irene tried the phone. Milli's was still off. Farina must be worried by now. Irene didn't want to picture her gentle profile. The nuns figuring it out. Irene realized, then, that she had exploded her own world. It was in jagged pieces floating in her mind. She had shaken her own routines of accepting the days in the dark room and the nights in cars and as they brushed her now, she recoiled. Exposed, nothing was the same and nothing could be discussed. If she went back and took up Igor's client as if nothing had happened, what if the unknown was slipping away in those moments? What if those were the minutes someone was killing Milli? Irene knew of two prostitutes who had been dumped outside the city, and the police never found more than the signs of hate—shallow, persistent wounds with a knife. And there was a monster loose in Florence, a man who hated couples and probably seeing prostitutes he lost his mind in guilt. He strangled women.

Then Irene could almost feel Farina's panic. The child's wide eyes weighing up the emptiness left by Irene's silent disappearance. She could see her quietly chewing her lip, waiting as she so often did. Irene could feel her own panic tingling on her neck and racing up and down her arms. Cutting so deeply into someone's life to change it left her with a sense of fear greater than a sense of danger. It was like the strange yellow sky of a few weeks ago. Clouds clogged with sand blown all the way from the Sahara and holding the sand so the sun made the sky a horrible yellow. Like the whole world was ending. This was the unknown. What was next was not like riding bareback. It was like holding the reins of galloping steeds running in different directions. Galloping and having no power whatsoever to turn them in a single direction. What if Milli was in danger? Irene wondered if she should go back to the nuns and ask for their help. Explain that Milli, too, was in danger. And that she was. She was herself in danger.

Danger was like a leaping fire. To imagine that much danger burning when all she had done was to remove Farina from danger. How could that be? Irene steadied herself in front of a window displaying some purses. They were yellow and had rabbits stamped into the leather. Stiff creatures with stick legs. Small and useless. She had skinned hares, uncovered the braided muscles in their hind legs. Her eyes couldn't believe that the purses cost as much as five or six men must pay. Irene didn't feel hate for those who bought the boxes with little yellow strings on them. It was about the same feeling she felt for the men. The world had strange conditions. The ugly little bags, the way a man's penis could be made to rise with just a few strokes. She didn't know what the link was, except money—money that held neither much comfort nor happiness for her.

Farina watched Irene go down the hall and wanted to run after her. She didn't dare to look up at the woman who was talking to her.

What's your name? Maria?

Farina heard the words and decided not to shake her head.

Anna? Why don't you tell me?

Farina.

Sister Morena clapped her hands. Farina. That's flour. God's gift. But that's not your name.

Mine is Sister Morena. Can you say it? Your momma will be back soon.

Farina didn't like to hear her say something that wasn't true. Irene wasn't her mother. She didn't like the cool woman without a smell.

Shall we have a look for her?

Farina nodded, even though she knew the lady with a blue scarf was confused. Irene wasn't her mother but Farina couldn't think of a word that identified her. Irene was perfume, green eyes, red finger nails, Irene was someone else. Not a friend. Irene was like a bird.

In front of the door, the problem grew. Could you call your mother? Ask her if she needs help.

Irene, Farina said.

Signora, the nun called as she lightly tapped on the door. She could hear the water running. Its waste struck her immediately.

Sister Morena knew the child should not witness whatever came next. She had seen slashed wrists in New Delhi. She had found people hung. She knew what doors could hide when people left children like bundles for others to unwrap for the prizes they could no longer enjoy.

Anna, I am going to take you to a room where there will be a nice bed. You can rest and Sister Gertrude will come. Then your mother will be back.

Farina fingered her dress. Irene, she called lifting her voice.

You mustn't shout. Here is Sister Gertrude.

Irene, Farina shouted as if she was going to be dragged away.

She will come. You go, Sister Morena nodded. And Sister Gertrude, please ask Sister Catherine to come with a screwdriver.

Dear Lord I commend myself unto your hands, Sister Morena found herself saying once, twice, again as she wiped sweat from her forehead. Then she lent her mind to the child, to her solitude, and then moved forward as her heart flushed with consequences in all directions. Sister Catherine was lifting the door off its hinges using her considerable strength. She was worried and dumbfounded that Sister Morena should have been so naïve.

There was water running. A small crystal stream of water pouring like a throat of song. There was the woman across from the convent watering her geraniums on her terrace and peering to see in. There was sun illuminating the walls and the room's emptiness. Sister Morena caught her breath. Even if God had willed this, the emptiness of the bathroom, the water rushing, the escape shocked her. As she turned the faucet to stop the flow, the open drain caught her eye. Who could throw away a child? She calmed her mind instantly.

We cannot judge. Moses was found floating in the reeds. Some lives are cut dramatically from the very beginning, at the beginning, out of love. She felt pity for the child with her thoughtful eyes. Sister Morena could feel problems on all sides, starting from Sister Catherine. Sister Morena's chest, which had hosted TB, ached as it often did when she felt pressure. Their mother superior would be furious. What a pity, she thought, although she knew that she should have felt hope. But Mother Superior was ill. Her sciatica worsened with stress.

In New Delhi the lucky ones, the ones with enough sense to hope that a convent could feed their child, the ones afraid to ask, they did what the mother did this morning. They dropped the child and ran. In New Delhi it was more difficult to draw the lines since so many children lived on the streets. It also was easy, by talking to those living on the streets, to get children and mothers or families back together. It happened often.

Her husband was beating her, but she's better now. She's sleeping at an aunt's but she'll take the child once her broken arm mends. Down two dark alleys, past the parrot cages, the narrow stairs, she's there.

Instead, the child in Florence would fall under the laws. In Rome, where Sister Morena had spent six months, two children had been brought in. And the sisters with the Mother Superior had decided together to keep them for a while, keep them and not call the police, hoping for a miracle. They called their mission the Catacombs. But now, Sister Morena sighed, ashamed at the sigh, she was in a different time and place.

Courage, said the voice softly. Farina studied the old wrinkled face. It had chins and two teeth missing in her smile, back in her mouth two holes. Her nerve was failing. She tried to not create trouble, to follow and wait, not to despair but this was all new and frightening.

Don't be frightened, the white head said. Just collect yourself. God likes us not to hurry. Take your time. Nothing will happen to you that's bad. My name is Sister Gertrude. I know something about being lost.

The word lost made Farina pull back. She couldn't say where she was with these bright colored windows and Irene missing but a voice told her she was not lost. Her mother would come. She was not small and worthless and she was not lost.

Sister Gertrude nodded at the straight back, the pride, the strong dignity emanating from such a small child. Sympathy, like a piece of bread slathered in honey, welled up in her. She touched the child's head and Farina felt a sureness that was like branches of leaves brushing her. Farina wanted to struggle but as she was led down the hall she also wanted someone to trust. She didn't like the young woman who was looking for Irene. She would not smile until she saw her mother again, but the woman leading her through the kitchen with the smell of soup was new and the only one she could find.

Farina's mind scoured the room that loomed hundreds of times larger than she was. She had never seen so many flames and big pots both dull and shiny. The flames came up like dancing blue hands under their giant bottoms. The pots are half her size. There is sound chanting somewhere and she has never heard it before. Never heard a Mass. Sister Gertrude offers her an apple from the counter. As she hands it down, a fly touches it. The apple cut open moves into her memory like a boat finding an anchor. It moves into her memory and forevermore will prick her nostrils, when she smells that smell which no one around her even imagines as a smell. The crack of the skin being cut, that sound, she will never forget that snap and without knowing, hearing it, will feel her body stiffen for attack.

What's your name?

Farina, she says softly, like laying her bear to sleep.

I can't hear what you said.

Farina.

Farina studies the old gray head looking down at her with curiosity, her glasses covered in steam and her eyes hidden behind. She has told the old woman her secret, why can't she hear? She has said her name and it left her, with its beaks and claws, its bear, its narrow bed and new colored pens. Her name is out and flying. Why can't the old woman hear it?

That can't be your name. Farina means flour. Are you telling me you want bread? Sister Gertrude's large shoulders hunch as she rises to stir the beans. You're probably hungry. What if I give you a piece and you tell me your name?

Farina.

Sister Gertrude doesn't want to smile at the determination in the little face, although it pleases her. Farina frowns. Why can't the woman hear? Farina's name sits in her head. She hears her own voice saying it in the secret world where she lives, like a bird under the eaves. She hears Milli's voice calling her and Irene's lively and excited one. For that second when both images are close beside her she feels the brown color of their room, the sound of the brown river under the bridge, the flesh of the brown faces she knows.

What if I call you *Bella Bimba*?

The water rises and wind wildly sweeps the sky, clouds swimming in speeding clusters, while the moon bounces and then drops into the flooding water. It tumbles, the whole moon, and goes under the water, as the waves rise. Then absolute calm.

The brakes snap and are gone, and Charlotte holds the

wheel that stays on. She can steer but the street full of people jump out of her way like exploding bombs.

Now on a boat, there is calm, and the water shimmers. An owl hoots in a tree. It makes an inquisitive sound. Charlotte dips her paddle and now a chief wearing a silver headdress of feathers stands in front of her. He beckons, with his hand, to follow him. She resists his large flowing robe, his hundred feathers moving like pages in a book. Leonard, she calls, Leonard, she calls to the wind. It's cold and empty. And she is Scarlet O'Hara.

Charlotte opened her eyes and intense moonlight, bright, almost lemony, was polishing her sheet. She tried sitting up and her head started to swim. Not just spin but roaring twirls like an engine that was stuck. She considered calling the desk. A few more minutes of this and she would consider this as an attack—heart or stroke or she wasn't sure what—and then she saw the owl again. Heard its feathers. She couldn't stand up and she knew there was no chimney in her apartment. The owl if it got in came in through a window. Or, she thought, her head spinning until she put her face down and hoped the unpleasant dizziness did not take her away, unless this was a dream.

Her head twirled a few more times. It tossed off a certain pleasure like the distant dim memory of when she fell down thrown by spinning all kids did. Over and over magically lifted from their eyes and feet as the sky twirled like goblin clouds. Then it stopped. Charlotte's eyes seemed to be looking straight. One foot on the floor and she felt steady. The dream was not one she had had before. It was new. What had not changed from so many dreams was Leonard. Leonard was certainly missing.

Saying his name, Charlotte felt a painful rush that filled in for her husband. It wasn't there right after he died, but it was a mood that came to be his place in her thoughts. It was like an abandoned track she ran around. She never stopped running and the beginning and the end were quite the same. The starting line and the finish line left no satisfaction.

His incomprehension was more of him than anything else he had left. Charlotte knew how little Leonard had ever known of her and how that possibility was nil now that she lived her life alone. How little he ever knew still shocked her. The government and U.S. Bonds paid her what he had provided, but he certainly had not prepared for death, prepared her for his sudden departure, leaving her with bills to pay, and children who didn't need her. Charlotte felt the cage drop and there she was reviewing forty years of her life that compressed like one hundred pounds of plums boiled into two jars of jam. The trouble with Leonard was he had never seen her as a body. He had his own version, and even her body was nothing he knew very well. Every day she said the same things to herself. Everyday, as the country marched on and new buildings got built and the people all around her got richer and the Native Americans started running Bingo parlors, she said the same things to herself, while she talked mainly to women, and now Don. Don had experience even with unemployment and men who beat up independent truckers. Don had never seen her even in her robe.

The owl still seemed to be in the room. Charlotte walked forward and there it was—in the corner, near a wastebasket, a small white owl, with round yellow eyes, staring at her.

In her dream the owl was haunting, annunciatory. But hidden. It called like something from the Romantic poets. Darkling. Dark and hidden in the leaves, calling. Charlotte was terrified seeing its crest fluff and turn there. She wanted to laugh. She wanted to tell her friends—oh just the cutest little owl. But he did not meet her standards for experience. It was nearly four o'clock in the morning. He was real and demanding a solution that she couldn't imagine. She wanted to phone downstairs and tell them to take it away.

But he hopped onto the chair in front of her TV.

Don't you soil it, she said.

167

He lifted his wings, small as two pieces of melba toast. Then terrifyingly ashy and wide.

She could see his claws.

She said she wasn't afraid. Just as she told herself she wasn't afraid to drive through the inner city at night once she had rolled up her car windows. She thought she was absolutely unafraid, but the owl abolished all that. He was unnerving.

The owl undid her, somehow made her feel her life was predictable and empty. That grimness she didn't like as an accounting. It wasn't pleasant. Instead his presence was really a sign of forgetfulness, leaving the window open, the tree trimmers overlooking a branch that scratched against the glass. That is what she preferred to think the owl was about, having to cope on your own as a senior citizen. Having these surprises like owls flying in and no one around to help. Charlotte was even willing to reach for her children and even blame them, although blame was wrong, blame Susan and her brother Bill for so respectfully keeping their distance. The owl moved slowly across the floor. He walked like a spirit or a gnome, walked on feet. He was shorter than a Pekinese, and moved like a chimp.

Charlotte felt a scream rising in her body. She wondered why the owl had come in from some real tree outside. If she shooed him into the hall, he might start to fly, to bang into a picture, knock down a lamp.

She saw his face as rather strong. The white ruff was like pine cones and a dress worn by Queen Elizabeth I. Nearly like the Indian chief. She wanted to call the desk now. The intensity was fading. Yet she knew the owl was important. It was amazing how sad she felt seeing him and knowing that she would tell the story tomorrow. Even put it on tape. She would say, imagine, Susan, your own mother just whisked the owl right back where he came from. She would tell the girls who fixed her hair. She would call him cute. She would call herself brave. She would invent a scene.

Oh little owl, she said, it is pointless that you expect any-thing of me. Charles at the desk will put you outside. Why did you come? Why did you pick my window? The questions pricked her a little, like all questions where she felt resentful of ever having been picked. I haven't done a thing. Leave me alone, she said, hearing her own ridiculous distain. Yet it was in that space of moonlight and dream, a slant that was like a slot suddenly acting as a warning or a luminous suggestion, she felt she was destroying something by lifting the phone. She was robbing herself, and she felt that. That sensation was difficult to remove, although she knew once Charles came up, the pleas-ant familiar feeling of her living room, even in its unpicked-up state, would return. And she could let this complicated reason-ing go, although the moonlight falling on him was very beauti-ful. The cloak of light on glistening feathers was so beautiful it struck her that it was as unusual as a cactus that blooms a white milky flower only once and on one night.

The rain was blowing, instead of its usual straight drop down, like buckets thrown from on high, thrown one after another, straight down on the dust and then in an hour gone and rising in humid undulations, the rain was flying. Aki wouldn't have minded getting wet, having the rain even soak him, with the bad news on the radio about the strike and the arrests that kept rising. He didn't like the way the radio warned people to stay in. Yet what else could they think, and it was in this very moment that Ramada had decided to go off looking for solutions on his own, in villages where blood was being spilled.

He almost did walk down the unpaved road, to feel the wet slashing against his chest and legs, flattening his clothes against him, but what was the point. Just to get off the cinder block porch. Even if he walked all the way to the river. Stood on the pier and listened as long as the soldiers hadn't cordoned it off. What would he hope to hear even about the strike? That the government had been victorious. That the trouble with the young men in Saro-Wiwa's group was many were thugs? *E-sho-be*—blood must be spilt. It was flowing, in many directions, and the villages were full of terror. Ogonis were killed every day and women raped.

Where was Ramada's mother? Why was this on his shoulders? Why was she having it easy, her life in Italy? He had no letters from Turin.

Down at the river, Aki knew there would be mostly obedience, fast walking, no loitering, and the police boats going in and out from shore. The river would be only that boated, oiled, turmoiled and patrolled water he could see from far away. That stupid way one could not even stroll freely down at the comforting strong flow. There would be anxiety at the river, that feeling of being herded away, of not being able to gather. Often he did go to listen to the poisonous tales of beating, of blood. Often he stood and collected the horror and let it fill him up with resentment and anger. Sometimes, he liked standing there; it was more than being helpless. It was like hearing rain on the roof or standing in it. Either way it wasn't doing much. But with Ramada gone, he didn't want to stand and listen to rumors, especially about the boys in NYCOP. If Ramada had been beaten like so many of the boys who were herded up at roadblocks, and accused of being the ones to run kangaroo courts, word might or might not travel to the door. If someone knew, it would not be because they had seen him run. More likely it would be they had found his body. And even then it would be at night, in the dark, an appalled, winded man whispering and leaving quickly. But no one had come.

Aki turned to go inside. Fucking government. Fucking prejudice. The government, the oil companies were trying to eliminate the Ogoni. Inside the air would be close. Two women would be chatting, if not arguing, and where would he go? The boy was beyond his hands. The boy might even be safe, but if he had reached Bori, he might have reached an ambush. Okuntimo's security force was run by Okuntimo, who had boasted on television that he personally knew two hundred and four ways to kill a man.

Aki stood at the door. He kept his fountain pen in a small mother of pearl case in the back of a set of drawers in the bedroom. The crusty bottle of ink was there, too, under some papers, the deeds, the baptizing certificates. With the rain falling, the little suction tube pulling ink up was one thin line against the universe. Yet he was going to write a letter to the nuns. He was going to write for news and give news to his daughter, hoping that she would listen for a change. That she would come home and fill the wound she had left in him and in her son. If she didn't understand, it would be pain that he didn't need. If she had disappeared, unbearable. Aki wondered how she ever managed to leave the bickering house where he still slept and Ramada still kept his shoes and pants. It was hard for her once Meniki drowned. And easy to believe that Italy was better than this honeyed, oh but brutal place. Aki didn't care about her excuses. He wanted her home, in her country, with her son as he tried to make something of the oil and the land for the Ogoni. Although there was no peace, at least she would help complete what had been driven apart and separated under his roof. Aki didn't want Sabula's razor tongue to criticize his efforts to contact Widu. He didn't even have an address. Yet. But just as there had been years that had passed, time changed and ended. He had always expected closeness from Widu. The rain poured and steamed, and the wind puffed in the bedroom window twisting the curtains.

Close them, close them, Sabula cried, waving a spoon. She rushed to the light frames, pushing them, catching the cloth that was wet.

Are you looking for money? She asked, seeing the open drawer.

What do you think? he asked.

We've paid the rent. We've paid the water. The electricity. There's no money in that drawer. Aki scowled, knowing he could not confess he planned to write to Widu. The impotence of not dominating even the weaker of his wives stuck in his throat.

Have you heard any more about the government's suppressing the free thinkers? he asked sarcastically, knowing that would send her into shrieks. The familiar, ineffective sounds would help him tame his pretending.

Piero decided to leave his paper on Maria Grazia Bobanelli's desk. She would read it and perhaps if Professor Dell'Istante didn't have time, he could start from her support and position. Piero felt strange leaving it without her being there. But it was a common thing. On her clean desk, she couldn't miss it. He wondered if he needed to clip on a note. 'Please read,' he wrote.

Piero had heard that she was having an affair with Professor Dell'Istante. He didn't want to imagine it. But he could in some way see the interest that moved underneath the surface when they walked down the corridor. Not that he would have seen it, but being told by some girls who also kept track of the class attendance, it was possible to decode what was an unusual formality and read it as a cover-up. It was difficult to imagine that someone at least his father's age could be touching an assistant like Professoressa Bobanelli. She was kind and knew molecular biology as well as he did. Piero didn't want to think of her pulling her lab coat off. But once he did, he could see she had nice breasts and envisioning her unbuttoning her blouse, he could comprehend her attractiveness, unsettling, and her skin glowing with warmth.   .

Piero knew he would miss his bus, if he didn't put the paper down. He was surprised to find that imagining his two teachers in bed was almost intriguing. His parents were so stressed out and lived side by side as if any change were a psychological earthquake. Sex, if it went on, must be rather perfunctory. Like their toothbrushes lined up in a snapped case and the toothpaste rolled perfectly from the bottom. That's why he so upset them. Any time he said what he thought, he slapped their past and threw it in their faces. At least according to them.

The neighborhood was the latest tragedy. Piero curved through the northern section of Florence every day on the bus; the people selling on the street and the Chinese kids playing soccer were new elements. There was renewal in the neighborhood as far as he was concerned. Not the fast food. Nor the Italian pizza made by an Egyptian family. No, renewal was the spices coming into the stores in yellow envelopes and red ones. And the head scarves. And the roller blades. And the black saxophonist who had moved into their building. He brought Arab melodies, and some confused bits of American blues. Piero had to admit sometimes the shrieking in the halls sounded crazy. But solos about loneliness, the saxophonist was especially good at those riffs. Piero wished the long hoarse blasts and the soft mewings could emanate from himself. His own mouth making sad wails and then wild honks. It was true the fellow seldom finished pieces. But he was worth putting up with. When he was high or whatever got him into a good mood, his sounds, were all mixed up and that was so new. The mix was exciting coming out of windows. On a street built up by workers after the war, with one beige dull building after another with their green metal railings and internal plumbing added in the fifties and sixties, they were sounds people didn't know or want to know. People on his street didn't know what kids felt all the time.

His parents didn't realize that Florence wasn't cloth makers any more and the war was not the Second one but the war on ethnic cleansing and the ozone layer. The bus doors snapped like mantis wings. There were plenty of empty gray bucket seats. What really scared his parents was to say that the Moroccan saxophonist was original. That made them lose control. Piero had said it innocently. Saying the saxophonist was original, while his parents were faithfully buying the Saturday newspapers holding cheap CD's with lessons on Beethoven and Bach, he drove them into despair. The world moved.

Traffic was clogged by belching trucks trying to cross the city. The bus rocked and surged and stopped. Piero didn't feel like concentrating on two formulas of organic enzymes. His problem was his parents' tolerance in general. His own inclinations, which were far more traditional, climbing up the trunks of trees until the sap made him feel suctioned to the cones and the needles, checking for pollution, trying to argue about the dangers of magnetic fields, his respectable studies hardly made them any happier. His father threatened to strangle him, when he pushed his plate back and said, No meat. No son of mine is a sissy. His father's anger was serious enough to have disturbed the atmosphere until Piero stood up and left. His mother often blotted tears from her blue eyes, not happy at all that her son was non-violent. Not interested in hearing that she was not neglecting him by not feeding him animal flesh. Sitting at the table with his parents making loud noises with their knives scraping the plates as they cut their meat, sullen and disappointed, and trying to pretend his position was a discovery, every day, when his mother put out the chicken, steaming and brown, or the Florentine steaks. You always like them. *Liked*, Piero reminded her. The tension of sitting at the table was so great Piero considered asking if he could eat in his room. They faced him, glum and nervous, looking desperate. Yet Piero could see fright, because they both knew, although he had no wish to exclude them, they didn't understand what was going on in his head.

Buddha stood before the ficus religiosa: in his heart he recognized that he had reached the spot where his journey would finally fulfill itself. When he saw the kinky branches and glowing gloved leaves, a breeze overcame him: the tree bowed and moved in such a way that the day hushed into a centrifuge around the great life rising toward the sky from the earth. To pay homage to the tree that would shelter him and host his search Sidhartha walked around it seven times. Each footstep was carefully placed over the ripples of the roots as he looked at the gray bark; through the puzzle pieces of the heavy cover, he looked up at sky. The silence was not silence but insect snappings and the call of the monkey and sturdy loon. A bare-backed reaper, noticing how even the wind had stopped as the prince walked around and around the tree, offered him in silence and honor, eight bales of hay. Sidhartha bowed at the gift and spread the soft, fresh prickly hay out as bedding under the baobab tree. Then, turning to the east, he lowered his body to the ground, assumed the lotus position and said to the spirit confined in his heart: "Even if my skin dries, my hands cripple and my bones melt, I will not stir from this place until I have found true wisdom."

How can we in our western civilization understand a passage like this? Trees are one of the earliest symbols for life and in their longevity they represent a different dimension in historicity. Trees themselves in the way they metabolize are an example of meditation in nature. Many in Italy are patrimonies that could be used to suggest ways of uniting human beings. With life spans that exceed ours, they are, unlike monuments or ancient human remains, or unlike stone and mountains, which have only echoes of tectonic convulsion and hurling fire, trees speak of the mysterious greatness of life that is not human. With roots that flow and fasten themselves to the earth, with branches that reach towards the sky, these living plinths show an attention and attentiveness that could help us scale our presences on earth.

Maria Grazia felt the first smile of her entire morning. The paper Piero had left on her desk was a breath of fresh air. He was a young man in a cloud in most ways, but you couldn't say that he didn't care. Why the words that were not really acceptable in a science paper should please her so much at first made her think it was subtle revenge. She could already see herself bringing it to Luigi and when he said the boy's got a problem, she could imagine herself taking up his defense.

Her eyes skimmed down his text. They stopped here and there arrested by the tone.

St. Francis sat under an olive tree on the hills of Assisi. Christ passed his darkest evening in the olive groves with his disciples. Pliny tells of how elephants in India pluck the boughs of spring trees and wave them in their trunks at the time of the equinox in order to communicate with the new moon. To put one's body into the hands of a tree like that in S. Nicolas di Luras, where it has stood for nearly three thousand years, there must surely be something to be culled from its having witnessed the elements for three thousand years. She liked his quest. Young people were after something quite different from her generation, which had been concrete, social in their explanations.

If like Buddha we could hold this question until we understood its 3000 year old answer, besides the way we used nature for remarkable cures—like cyclosporin and penicillin—perhaps we could accept trees' way of circular growing. In Italy few of these Methuselahs remain. They are living for some special reasons. If we could focus on that question of extraordinary age, could it answer any hypothesis for us? And this is only one question. These trees offer vertical stratigraphies whose economical systems live in vibration with the air and its quality, the earth and its mineral elements.

Maria Grazia wondered where the graphs and tables were. Around page 16 there was a plan for sampling. An outline included types of wood in the dome, and Brunelleschi's use of chestnut chains. What was intriguing was how forthright he was in presenting his case. Luigi had not succeeded in showing Piero or any of his students how a paper should be written. On the other hand, Luigi probably was disinterested in considering such a loose and holistic point of view.

The creature in her womb was nudging her very slightly. Down inside her, he or she was making some movements like puffs. Puff, puff propelling. The phrase 'circular growing'. She didn't know what Piero meant by that. But she could easily ask him. It was a phrase that struck her as valid beyond his obvious moral wish. Piero was well mannered, always ready to go out into the field. Maybe she should ask to take him under her wing. His work might prove to be if not alike, akin, to hers.

The baby inside her was giving her heartburn. Maria Grazia shifted her hips trying to accommodate the ever-present sprig navigating. Mistake? Trap? She liked Piero's sentence for the trees that had lived so long they had seen literally hundreds of thousands of sunrises and sunsets. His conclusion: they must be living for a reason. There were problems to solve, but this child would survive. He or she would stay with her, not feeling that he or she came only because the door was left open. The strong rainbow coming from the prism, how interesting that it was falling across Piero's paper.

THE METAL BOX on legs containing sand she could move, press, gouge, pile into heaps, let lightly pour through her fingers, the sandbox was the only place in the empty house Susan could turn to. There the day was clean and had not yet scattered. Touch existed in the thousands of grains in the sandbox and was as close as she could get to the physical sensations Vaclav's message had released. The sand, receptive and giving back images, might yield help. To strap herself in a seat to fly to Prague, to appear open faced to meet Elisa and Elsa at his funeral, to touch his soft mouth one last time while he was still alive, only the last was an issue.

The day was strange, not Alice in Wonderland strange, but almost. Starting from that ungodly squill at six. From there events twisted and it was as if tapes were moving events and spinning them off their spools. The useless tape of evidence that broke up the questioning in the judge's office to the tape from her mother that she had been strongly tempted to put on. As if the relationship had changed. To the latest one, unbelievable, except if you knew Vaclav, and then it seemed natural—the tape pre-announcing his death. These were messages that provoked, that dug under the skin. It was so strange, really, these disembodied voices that were not flesh. The answering machine was daily and tapes, in general, nothing out of the ordinary. Like photographs. They captured people and time but were not flesh. Susan shook her head. Even this kind of pseudo-philosophic thought belonged to an earlier period of her life. She could have been twenty years younger and sitting in a Buddha posture while Gian Franco and Luigi argued about the power of images and Marxist uses of them. But it didn't matter. This morning tapes, magnetic ribbons, bothered her because they were not flesh. Not the people themselves but weirdly affecting. Because events bombarding her in all directions arose from voices, like flies in amber, caught on tape.

The room couldn't have been more still, her own shoes left in front of the television last night and still there. But her life was disturbed by words said from flesh to flesh but not flesh. This morning most of her life had centrifuged to other places, far from the plans she had. The way Teresa reappeared from her long winter and spring of sleep and would be settled. The way Vaclav's voice reached right into her guts and made her retch. The library with its stillness was laden with feelings and events touching her but she couldn't touch them. Certainly the heaviness of hearing Vaclav's weak voice was not about what, if anything, remained of her adulterous young and stunning affair. The chains around her were grief. The grief of flesh and mourning. The illusion she had of knowing his most intimate life.

Outside a dog barked. Its yelp playful, close, but now the frantic yip stopped. It was as if a wagging dog had gotten in the yard and was nosing through the dried up tulip and iris beds. No dog could get into the yard. Yet oddly, it seemed one was nearly under her window.

Susan took the term centering into her mind and closed her eyes. The sour taste from her stomach's reversal was witness to how deep the news had driven. It had been years, even more, since she had stood in front of the sandbox considering herself as a patient. Entering concentration until an image, anything from a volcano to a leaf, turned into a direction.

As Susan looked down at the sand, the emptiness around her, especially in the red chair where she usually sat, drew closer. No one with benevolent eyes was keeping her company as she kept her patients company. No one was listening, attentive, studying the silences, the facial movements, the crouching shoulders, the jerking legs, participating in the patient's investigation changed by the interaction, as she so often was changed, as the one who kept watch. With the leaded windows closed the library was rather cool.

Her work. From the day she had told Luigi she was going to add the sandbox to her studies, he had stepped back, as if he knew her outside world, which was already filling with differences, would separate them. Yet it made good sense to her. He didn't like her traveling to Rome for the training, but more pertinent he found the sandbox itself a joke. He didn't like psychotherapy. It was an indulgence, a hobby for the upper classes. He found her discussions irrelevant, didn't like the crowds of women talking about spiritual possibilities and where was her political fire? Where was the rigor and scientific accountability? The sand, instead, was the marvelous dimension she had been looking for. Patients talking about problems was not enough. In drawing, in sand, the hands expressed images before the mind could slow them down. In poems, in dreams, images were ancient portals. The sand was a sea where images made in freedom, in darkness, floated to the surface. They expressed contact with the body's perceptions of memory and thus, some of the most unuttered pictures of the self.

The metal shelves bulged like Noah's ark. Putting back a plastic Mickey Mouse or a rubber worm, sometimes their odd insignificance made Susan marvel at how they could carry projected energies from ancient stories or archetypal symbols. Almost all of the seemingly random arrangements had delivered insights at one time or another. The green dragons, the crystal drops, the pieces of broken mirror, the cows with up turned tails, the beds with little flannel sheets, knives, swords, spoons, the blue eggs, the rubber babies, the giants with black belts, the ladies with scales for weighing, red devils with pitch-forks, golden cats, bells from temples, butterflies, ants' nests, plastic whales, drums and silver horns—nothing bigger than a finger. Grass huts, chariots, lanterns, tigers, ladders, airplanes, sail boats, *madonnas*, elephants, wings. Any story formed from them would be the right one, the one that needed telling.

Dry or wet was often the first bifurcation. Did the patient want to add water to the sand and work more directly with shaping it, wetting her hands, and touching the body of sand as it compacted and acquired thickness and shape? Or did she wish to work with figures in dry space? The sand wet was often an earlier connection, shaping out events lodged in the body without words. Choosing to add figures, the work became more relational, more narrative, more headlights shining on the everyday roads.

Susan picked up the crystal pitcher and went to fill it in the room off the study. Luigi had left tools there for fixing minor problems in the house, screwdrivers, drills, a solderer. There had never been much rancor. And now it hosted an ex-ercise machine. An ironing board. Tied bundles of "National Geographic." Lavender was drying. *Origono*. Shelves of *pomorolo* and apricot jam. The water rushed up over the top of the lip. Vaclav had not used water in the few months he had come as her patient. He had ended the sessions for good when he followed her into the small room, coming at her, cupping her breasts from behind, as she filled the pitcher. She resisted, told him to cool off, but it was nearly the last time she gave him an order as her patient. They had made love right there on the floor. It was probably close to the last time she saw him as his therapist. At least that unacceptable lapse quickly closed.

After that her explanations were as a companion, and sometimes her enthusiastic discoveries turned her into an unwilling muse. He often took her knowledge, like he tamped his pipe, not noticing he had just packed her perceptions into his own artistic pouch. But she held her own. Water. For as long as they knew each other, they both understood water as a symbol for love. A basic element his characters often discovered. But so did her patients. As the spirit. As flow after dryness. As turbulence. As flood.

The water in the pitcher was appealing. Even in the dark room it glistened like a gem. But Susan didn't know if she wanted to use it to wet the sand. To proceed mute. She had not been looking for an erotic relationship, and Vaclav too, with his tenderness, his outlaw side, his artistic work, his childish pride, perhaps didn't expect such sexual feasts. Yes, he had shown Susan her body, down to the roots of her hair, the insides of her fingertips, the thirst in every corner of her dry chasteness. But then asking deepened and expanded, and he, too, grew surer in the way they understood happiness for a long period as infinite passages, more ample and more intimate explorations of one another. They became calm. Accepting of when there was hardly any fire. Vaclav had shown her, the Minnesota girl, without any intention of showing her—because they existed outside of their marriages—herself far beyond the prudent and needy wife. Vaclav had healed her temporarily of her childhood, her father's death. But then she no longer needed a teacher. And she had become his. Interchangeably. And when he left, as they both knew he would, not having the courage to leave Elsa, Susan felt violated, electrified. But she could stand. Outside of the bruises and loss. Even driving in traffic, thinking about patients, she had somewhere to go. Not Vaclav telling her, but her recognizing a shore, a battered place, where she would come back.

Luigi had been no match for her, deeply raw from the break.

With his cypresses and his young reading of life as a mild rebellion with the certainty of science and his family's money, it was as if he were on another planet. She tried to understand and go slow, taking her sense of guilt as the rudder helping her to accept the days she was living. Their physical relationship was young, inexpert, something that could not be started over. And that was one gap in the end: her knowledge of her face open to Vaclav's and then open to her own uncovered self matched to the scaled-down, blank routines of wife and mother, while Luigi would be pounding the table and Marina, with her helpful little hands nervously tried to put down the spoons and forks in the American way. But it was only one.

In spite of the pain, for a long time, Susan saw stones and kicked them. Kicked them, hoping Luigi would bend down and notice either that the path was destroyed or that her feet were in a mood to kick. But since he hadn't noticed in the years she and Vaclav met at least twice a week, and talked daily, almost always gratified by the charged attention, it was improbable that in her moodiness, imbedded in impatient intolerance, he would have stirred and understood. Her ardor, when she expressed it, made him draw back. Susan always hoped that they might have added another child, slowly joined not just through Marina's progress in school but from a common flow of the past, a day by day routine with Luigi's money making life easy, except that she did not want to live a model of adjustments, or as an ironic character like one of Vaclav's half-baked political dissidents who accepted an enormous sense of inner failure but convinced herself she was living a higher morality. It was too late for that.

Susan, in the first year of Vaclav's going back to London for good, didn't feel misunderstood by either man. It was up to her to make herself known. Vaclav wanted more possibilities than she could offer. He wanted the torment that came with having two lives. And Luigi was too young to be let into her world. He was caught up in the words about changing human nature, but as an armchair anarchist, rich in theory, and poor in actions. She, like the sandbox right beside him, brewed individual changes that held no interest at all for him. Luigi liked certainties and the only change he would allow had to be out in the world where he talked about political changes, talked, back then when Piazza Fontana set off ten or fifteen years of political and cultural radicalism as if he could be a Feltrinelli, perhaps carrying bombs with his conflicted body. But, of course, and thank god, he never got that far.

Water. She would use water. Susan poured it into the center of the sandbox and let it puddle. Then putting dry sand over it, she made it cohere and glove her palms. She closed her eyes and felt Vaclav's body, her memory of it, in the box. She didn't open her eyes, didn't put words to the feeling of rubbing up and down, patting the sand into solid rising shapes. She smoothed it over and could feel his legs, white and hairy, rough, and now rubbing still against hers. Digging into the sand, she could feel the hollow down at the base of his spine. It was strange feeling so helpless and hearing his voice laughing above all, smiling, and then fading, wanting a notebook. Susan rubbed the sand and shifted it, knowing Vaclav was dying and she was helpless. Her heart was helpless. With both palms down she let her hands rest. Still and unmoving on the sand. Vaclav was dying in another city, and with all the windows shut, she could still feel burning indignation that he was in a distant room. Probably with open windows. She could imagine his eyes, demanding from her that she hide her grief. She would cherish standing near him. How right it would be to look out together over the beloved valley, taking in the silver olive rows parched by summer light that nearly erases them into whiteness and shrouds the peaks of Florence. How much he, too, would revel in revisiting their chaste room in his old apartment with its stale ashes, TV, screens and scripts, mussed up leather chairs. The apartment Elsa threw scenes about once he started flying back for years after the film "The Fountain" had been finished, until they decided, she, Susan decided, to have him turn in the key.

The sand under her hands was firm and packed. It was moist, almost cold under her palms. He was dying. Taking some sand between her fingers, rubbing it like loose salt, is as close as Susan can get to him. She lets it fall away. Eyes closed, tears coming like talk, she takes handfuls of sand and knows they are not heavy enough. They are not heavy, like his big boned body, cradling hers. Like his legs wrapping hers. It would take six men. Susan's hands touch the sand, lightly finding a pulse. Women didn't carry caskets. They washed the corpse. Wept. She does not know if, even in six, she would be able to hold up her part of the bier and his weight. She would like to. She would like to carry Vaclav. Like to walk openly across the Charles Bridge with people applauding a bold life that gave colors and symbolic meaning to silence. Who explored, so-matter-of-factly, lives that had chances to discover or lose their souls. Susan waits until another impulse comes from the rhythm she is tapping on the sand. If only she could hold her lover, her friend, of so long ago, from underneath, scooping and digging in the sand. Like loose salt he still stings her heart. His words, once large like colorful pheasants, strutting, ebullient, surprised in the bush, now are faint and small as they were on the tape. Small and sick like crushed birds. Susan's hands stop moving again. Something else had settled now, feeling so near to him.

The light pouring in the four windows was a lease from the day. The room, its windows closed, still was bright. What had taken place in the sand could mean something only to her. The sand was churned very deeply and mounded up. She would not go to Prague. Would not call and leave a disembodied message: words that were not flesh. Her clarity spread.

Undoubtedly Vaclav would search for her call, her message. And he would notice the silence. Surrounded by friends in Prague, people desperate, admiring and circling around him in his chosen life, he might lift his ear as they kept talking and wonder as people kept entering the house, where her voice was. Most likely he would not think of her as afraid to take the risk, or as without anything to say, but in noticing that she hadn't called, she hoped he, with his perfect pitch, because he did have it and probably in his decision was truly giving it space, might understand. The sorrow and joy. He might remember how often they walked in silence, near the house on the winding road below the church. Awakened. Emerged. Inseparable. Reborn. That touching of infinite reality was the gift, the energy lifting a curtain for both of them. No use stressing that in the day-to-day world, their story was of an infant with a deadly cord around its neck.

Susan could well imagine what a terrible patient he was, resisting Elsa's attempts to make him stop lighting his pipe, or to lie on his pillows and to put the telephone down. He would be making appointments, calling people as if there were scenes to conceive, sending friends and admirers out and in, with scripts, props, petitions. She would have gone to Mostecka' street, if she could have been alone with him and claimed him, claimed their ecstasy. If she could have been alone with him and shared his moments of panic, his impatience with others, his night-watch for the dead he expected to see gathering, she would have gone now, and stayed close, sitting through a heavy night, not leaving him, remembering. Remembering rivers swaying with light, roses batting against each other with scents. She would have gathered what vivid knowledge they had shared and, as the sun rose, would have tasted with him the bitter power of their kisses. And would have kissed him again. And met his haunting eyes that would still be capable of wonder. And when he said enough, she would not have believed him.

Not one drop left. Ramada held his glass bottle to his lips and found it empty.

Not only was his water bottle empty. His pockets were too. It was killing that feeling to say no until someone grabbed your shoulder and a rifle jabbed your ribs. The *naire* had gone, twenty at a time. The sun was high. It was late. Yesterday was gone. And today, that same uncertainty, but with empty pockets. What Saro-WiWa had said was true and would be true. It would never be over until there was power.

You must pay to use the road. You must pay to farm. To get to the market. You must pay bribes to those who should protect you, but are driven to drive you to extinction. You must pay to have no roofs on your schools, no medicines in your hospitals, no petrol in your gas stations, because the oil that is yours is not yours. It belongs to the agents of death, and you have no rights to self-determination. And when they feel like exploding and putting you under arrest, they will.

A woman with hair tied in a ragged scarf studied Ramada suspiciously. They'd walked around him curled asleep in a bush. A pup. He was too young but you never knew exactly. She had assumed they were more ferocious, loose, more nervous the NYCOP youths who had beaten Kobani, Badey, and the Orage brothers to death. For the last weeks, all there was in the villages where there was talk of standing up to the government and getting the oil out of the water, and the flames out of the air, of giving the Ogoni their pride, all there was were terrifying stories passed on by villagers on all sides, of soldiers beating the elderly, beating the children, forcing themselves on women and raping them, entering houses, everywhere leaving sounds of death, of being frozen by the sound of automatic rifles fired in the air and then, with raucous laughter, firing at people shrieking. That witch hunt without any end in sight was thanks to the NYCOP youths.

The short woman, with her blouse knotted above her waist,

pounded her orange wedge of wet cloth, slapping it against a rock. Why weren't those black swirls music? Once creek ripples were nice fish and crab music. The boy washing his feet wasn't old enough to even have a blade of whiskers. She turned her back, bent down into the water, hoping she was right, but not wanting to sing out to him, your name. What are you doing out on a day when the police are striking people on the head in Harcourt? But it bothered her deeply seeing her face in the water so troubled, so split into circles rippling off. It bothered her that she wouldn't even offer a word to a boy, who like them, probably hardly made a living.

Ramada sensed how uncertain the land was. Down near the creek, with its dusty greenish empty flat space behind, the water didn't feel more peaceful than the unhealthy pollution around Port Harcourt. The water stank. The black oil had seeped between his toes. He wasn't sure even if the woman, who turned her back, would run him out of town. Were those barefoot men he saw at a distance elders? Should he hide or could they tell him if Bori was safe? Where might he relieve himself? The garage where he worked seemed modern, alive, even more brotherly compared with the extreme timidity of how people walked.

Ramada had been beyond Elme before, but so much had changed in the last six weeks since President Abacha arrested Saro-Wiwa. He had. Maybe these villagers had. Saro-Wiwa, who had heard the Voice of the Spirit of the Ogoni, was locked up. The god Wiaor five years before had called to Saro-Wiwa and told him to put himself at the service of the dispossessed, dispirited, and disappearing. That a man on TV could be called by a god was an idea Ramada had heard fiercely debated. Aki and his old friends disagreed, agreed, over just who Saro-WiWa was. Five years of Ogoni struggle and killings, years when he was such a small boy he couldn't understand at first why Aki cared that the man had been pulled off of his television show, or why his writing had been shut down, but now he felt there were things he could see with his own eyes that he could not hear on his grandfather's porch. People were lost and frightened. They were as poor as thorn bushes. Suspicious of their neighbors. There were hundreds of dead in the last years and, as Saro-Wiwa said, the Ogoni were so deep down in the well, they could only be heard by shouting.

Why is your face so long?
Why is yours so satisfied?
I saw an old dog hit, run over by a blue Lancia. Her neck crushed. The driver sped on like a hoodlum. Signor Caffo closed his eyes and the lines around his eyes and mouth met through a connecting channel of lines. He beckoned for a glass of water. The climb up the hill had been hot. The spectacle of the lack of respect or concern for what might have been an accident had not lessened. It was a climate in Florence. Useless to put words to it, calling it young people or indifference. But he wanted to explain it to himself. He could see that his wife was really not listening.

He put his rough hand out towards hers. Hold it, he said. I feel that bad.

Agnese Caffo was surprised to have the hand in hers, squeezing it hard. She put her other hand on top of his and rubbed it.

Did the dog have a tag? she asked, thinking of Marta's.

No, he said. Probably we'll just see a photo, tied to a tree. I stopped at the bar and the men could only remember how many accidents had taken place on that road. A lot of them had been drinking the first glasses of the day and they didn't seem to think it was important. What they said was beside the point.

Agnese Caffo sat quietly. It was difficult because she was exploding with news. Yet it was so rare that Signor Caffo asked for some affection that she thought, even with pots on the stove, she should sit.

She did and there was a lovely moment in the room. There were no flies and the oil on the tomatoes was pungent. Added to her feeling that Arvon had returned, even with her husband's tragic story, and the shock of the hole, the balance was good and must be how cats feel when they purr. They are happy in that moment to be creatures. Not that it could last. The chard had to be stirred or it would burn. Arvon would have to be chained or he would probably fly right back. Yet she didn't want to chain him. She didn't like that path.

Agnese Caffo had to decide how to tell the man holding her hand about their neighbor's excavation. He would be shocked as she was. He would ask: how deep, how long. The pressure would rise as he drilled her: Are you sure? Did you see any Roman lamps? Couldn't they be putting in pipes?

The irritating period of questioning could be as steady as how he chopped wood. Once she told him, he would know immediately what to do. And she hoped she would agree. Sometimes she backed down because he refused to change his mind. The room then could fill with sullen upset that made the room grow quiet and cold.

It pleased her, although she was feeling restless, that his hand was still in hers. In the morning. In June. Just simple and on the table. Probably he would be insistent about calling the police or the superintendent. He tended to believe that following the law was right, even when he didn't like the government.

The hole was such a disappointing and cynical surprise. The American who jogged up and down the hill, who waved from time to time, had never seemed as if she was hiding things, promoting sales of stolen goods. She often, in fact, seemed the opposite. Promoting peace, with petitions and who knows what.

But to turn a neighbor in was serious, worse than unpleasant.

It brought back the war. Both Signor Caffo and she had faced those awful decisions. That moment when something was understood about a villager who seemed to be with the partisans, and then it was understood he was not. Unbearable moments when betrayal engenders betrayal. Signor Nando's being shot had changed both of them. Something they never mentioned but never wanted to face again. And didn't want to open up to discover if it had been their observations of when he came and when he left the stable that led to the order. Or if, it had been someone else's spying out in the woods. At the time, the Fascists managed to bring about reprisals, so in the end Mario Ghetti's son had been driven from his bed and sent to Germany. What good had the war done anyone?

Agnese Caffo looked at Signor Caffo's face, shaded under his hat, and wondered what he would say. He would doubt her. But if she described the four earth walls, he would listen.

She herself thought it would be better to telephone Signora Notingham, rather than the police. Better to give her a chance to explain.

But her husband, tired of rotten people, he might just insist that the police and the courts would be the place. The dog's death had come at a bad time. Certainly if he caught the killer driver, he would turn him in. It was difficult facing someone and making an accusation while his eyes shifted. Priests always take refuge behind curtains and screens. That's how they speak so directly to the one not telling the truth.

You haven't told me, Signor Caffo said, shyly, why you were smiling. He tipped his soft hat.

The older man brought her back to the joy she had planned to spring on him. Arvon came home, Agnese Caffo said. He answered my call, she said, without adding another touch, although she could envision his descent, branch to branch to branch, as if Arvon's obedience was from a film. He recognized me. Walked into my arms.

Irene's phone was ringing. Milli, once she reached the Mugnone and found it bare, white clouds, stones and rivulets, no child and Irene sitting there, she picked up her mind, quickly, traced her steps to a tobacco shop, bought a phone card.

Where are you?

On the bus.

Get off. Let me talk to Farina.

Irene wanted to remind Milli that she was six hours late in dialing and to scold that Igor was furious and expecting her to meet an appointment in a few minutes. In fact, she, Irene, was already missing the appointment because of the amazing tempest of the morning, caused by *her*, Milli. To accept the excruciating business of explaining what had happened in those hours seemed unfair. Why, besides taking the responsibility for the little girl who was under the danger of being sold, why now was she going to face a scene that would be worse than when the Roms prepared for a funeral?

Get off the bus, Milli commanded from a telephone booth near San Marco.

Who do you think you are getting us into trouble? This isn't a joy ride. I work. I'm late. You're in trouble too. Irene knew she could turn the phone off. Just snap its lid. Like blowing out a match. Even if Milli rang again she could have turned it off. But now she knew Milli was alive. A missing cadaver had got up on its feet and started dancing without even knowing to feel relief. Without knowing the disaster and alarm she set off. The crazy lady didn't apologize or even seem perturbed. Just impatiently ordered her to step off the bus. But. The crazy lady was alive. Alive.

Irene wanted to be left alone. Not just for a few minutes but for a few days. Left alone away from everyone. Put her head down on her arm and go to sleep on the bus. Block out the reasons to rejoice and those for weeping. But her life was all marked, by thistles that hook on with vicious seeds. She was marked. Anyone looking at her could see she had been through the brambles and they had stuck to her. And they had to be picked off. Milli's voice was commanding, blind to how her ship had gone out to sea. Her voice revealed her worst mistake. Thinking she was the captain.

The plane trees along the boulevards were still. But really they were steaming hot jets. They were blowing fires like volcanoes. The thorns stuck to her, making her bleed, were in large part due to Milli. Irene decided then that she would get off the bus. Like someone entering a battle, she would face her opponent. The Roms called each other enemies when they decided to settle points of honor. She would meet Milli and end the mystery that the Nigerian mother still didn't know. Enemy or not, the woman was blind, still waiting for Irene's reply.

Where are you?

Near San Marco.

I'll meet you in the bar directly across from it.

Let me talk to Farina.

Irene snapped the phone shut, like a glove thrown into the ring. Like a glove thrown with her thin patience.

The woman coming toward her was one. One head. Two legs. There was no child in her arms. No one behind. One skirt. One black head of hair. No little pair of shoes. No small hands.

Dirt was the word Milli felt first. Irene was dirt. There was no time for fine points. Where was her child with this piece of dirt?

The Ogoni animal she had been praying to—its energy settled once she heard Irene's voice—awoke and tore through her. It was biting again. Biting her eyelids as they blinked.

Irene, her friend, was not carrying Farina. She was coming toward her and looked sober, not hurrying but waiting for the light to turn green.

Irene spoke first. She struck, before the startled face could attack. I thought you had forgotten me. You might have called, she said, coolly.

Milli's animal growled and stormed and pushed her forward.

Where is Farina?

Safe, Irene said. She's safe.

Where is Farina, Milli whined, half crying. Then she screamed Farina's name as if a sun had exploded inside her. The sidewalk in front of the bar was crowded and people were pushing to go in. The machine making ice mountains was popular for drinks. Milli couldn't ignore the sibylline comments. Pretend she could slink along in anonymity. She saw the poisonous spider web. A dreadful plot had taken place. Irene had ordered it. The strong face she had counted on had done more than disappoint her. She had sneaked into her life and cynically, ruthlessly changed it. She had taken all her hallucinations and done something with Farina. She had brought ruin on Milli. The exploding sun voice burst.

Milli swung her fist and Irene saw it coming.

Irene snatched Milli's wrist and twisted it. She's fine, Irene said, trying to recuperate some order where they were standing. Under gathering public observation. Milli didn't retreat. The feeling of being robbed took her over, and like anyone stunned by that rough yank, she screamed after the thief. She wanted a crowd. She swung again taking aim at Irene's chin, and this time a young man tried to intervene, grabbing her arm. Milli tried to kick Irene, and Irene stepped out of the way. A few merchants as well as the man from the bar came out. Tourists, the younger ones, stopped.

Irene decided to creep step by step backwards towards the stoplight. But it was as if they were on stage. People were around them. Hands were trying to catch her hands. Milli was screaming, *Puttana*, prostitute, you prostitute, as a policeman started walking towards them.

Irene knew she would run. Flap her arms the way Roms did, flap them until the people around were slapped, confused, were hypnotized, and thus stepped back. She raised her arms and Milli, aware or unaware, pursued her. The people standing around parted a space and watched them run. The small gathering settled down, as the policeman shook his head, watching the two women sprint on high heels, like riled storks, shrieking and scratching. The bar man observed what he could understand about the fight. One had stolen the other's flour. The energy of two women going at each other was admired, abhorred and then the incident disappeared as they did. Way off past the Accademia they could still be seen waving and lurching. The sidewalk calmed down. *Gelati* overtook people's thoughts about the open disturbing skirmish. No one imagined that one of the women was so desperate she might take her own life.

Gian Franco and Luigi were rounding a bend, where a tomb recorded the plight of a couple who had died in a shipwreck, *O Mare Crudele/* return to peaceful waves, when Luigi saw a rather distinct figure with a headscarf. Diniza. She had a walk that had never been graceful. Her feet paddled just a bit, yet recognizing it as her walk, Luigi's heart felt glad, even attracted by it. She was bending over, picking some of the *margherite*.

Gian Franco had just mentioned the word, more than the word, the mechanism of little kickbacks that he had set up several years back, with salesmen, medical suppliers, but then with the national health service, too.

That's where the problem lies now, he had said, obviously untouched or unwilling, at least, to show guilt. The commission. You must see it in the university. That little tip added on, every time there is a sale. And of course, they have grown pretty large. Especially for the ones at the top. The judges have pulled up a carpet. Mind you there are more.

But now he was being solicitously quiet, waiting to be introduced.

You remember Diniza, don't you, Gian Franco? That's the order Gian Franco expected for the introduction, but Luigi reached out towards the woman who had lived among them for so long, and said, Diniza, how sweet of you to remember my mother. And surely, although he has grown older, you still remember my friend, Gian Franco.

Standing in front of her, Luigi wondered what it was that made Diniza so important to him. Her hands were still red and chapped from working too hard using buckets with cleaning chemicals. She often appeared in his dreams. Sometimes she seemed to walk in the halls of their house. It was her solidity. In his mind, she seemed to not to reflect their problems but to maintain her own life while somehow radiating care.

Looking at her smart eyes, her expectant quiet, the thought struck him that perhaps she really did mind their faults. She had been absolutely determined to leave once Giada was dead. Maybe she had had enough.

It's good to see you, Signor Luigi, she said, her small mouth curling sweetly. She squinted from the bright sunlight.

I thought you might have already come, Luigi said. There were some roses.

Your mother had lots of friends, she said. I'd be surprised if by evening there aren't more. Of course, she said, people are growing older.

How is Signorina Marina? she asked, after a pause, which like most of her pauses, seemed to be full of thoughts.

She's fine. Growing fast. Even fast enough to have a boyfriend, as far as I know and her mother tells me.

Diniza smiled radiantly. Don't worry, she said. I remember your mother and how she worried about you.

Did she? Luigi—reminded by how much Diniza probably

knew and could tell him about his parents, things he had no idea about—wanted to know more.

And you, Signor Gian Franco? How is your family?

Perfect, he said, smoothly.

Luigi didn't want to go on in front of his old school friend. He imagined that in Diniza's eyes they both probably looked respectable. So why did he endow her with the capacity to perceive that they had just been discussing bribes?

A sheltering instinct burst from Luigi. He realized that he mustn't force anything. But maybe he could take her home and close the door on Gian Franco's conversation and open up another.

Will you need a ride?

No, she said, the bus takes me back. I come often, she added, with a spurt of gladness in her voice.

Then she said, Your parents were so good to me.

Do you need anything? Luigi asked.

No, she said, surprised and embarrassed that he thought her compliment was a request. She loved you so much, Diniza said, as an answer. She was proud of you. She didn't want you to live alone.

It was hard for Luigi to understand what he felt hearing that last sentence. What did she mean by alone? He knew Diniza had been given money by his mother. He had handed her the check at the settlement of the will. He was sorry he had ventured into the area where so many types of insults and misinterpretations could arise. Luigi doubted if he could even invite Diniza to visit the apartment. He doubted if she would come in or would sit again in the kitchen and talk. Or, if she knew anything about his father's real state of mind, if she would say what she knew.

Awkwardly, he kissed her on both cheeks. She smiled, warmly, and turned in the direction of Giada's grave. After she had shaken Gian Franco's hand. She walked away from

Luigi as if she was disappearing forever among the trees. She was walking towards his mother. Probably both women had shared each other's secrets. As he watched that sturdy walk, a woman comfortable with flowers, folk medicine and basting meat, a woman who could have been a doctor if the war hadn't driven her from Sarajevo, each plodding step made him wonder if they might have once changed his life. But it was she who had pushed him toward Susan.

NINE

O N THE WHITE WALL there was a man on the cross. He was stuck and probably hurt. Farina didn't understand what she was to do in the white room, with a white bed, with the door closed. She didn't like the room. It was the opposite of her room, with its dark blanket, and its busy clotheslines. With all the women coming and going. The fat sister had said she would be back. Farina didn't know what to do. She had never felt such hollow fright and defeat hooting in her life. She had never been alone. She had never stood in a room, without other faces she knew scurrying to dress, or chewing on a chicken leg, or chatting on the phone. She'd never been alone without cigarette smoke, and shadows in stripes coming through the shades. Or been without her bear, her chair, her pot near her in the room.

She looked up at the wooden statue. The face had a crown of flowers and the man had blood dripping down his face. Farina knew the man must be hurt. She minded him. He had an awful face. She would like to climb up on the bed and take him down. But she knows her shoes are dirty. She knows she probably could not lift him from the wall.

These thoughts are new to Farina. Climbing on a bed. Walking around the room, touching the walls. All the way around the room. She feels curiosity tweak her. Then her overwhelming wish for her mother. For Milli to come. She feels like throwing herself on the floor and hitting her head.

The fat lady had told her to be quiet. Farina knew well those words. She wondered if this was a hospital. She had heard Irene and Milli talk about hospitals where sick people go. Farina felt so alone she decided to open her pens. Irene had wanted her to have them. She knew how to make the world go away. The screams. The hurry. She didn't think but knew the pens would make the room grow smaller.

Farina drew out the red pen and with both hands popped off its top. She wanted to see it work. She knew, because inside her she heard 'no' over and over again, that the white walls were not for pens. But she felt she wanted the color to come out. Maybe it would call someone. The M was easy. Farina felt how fine the letter was going up the wall. Milli. It stood brightly on the wall and gave her some sense of comfort. All the long letters were straight as a house. Maybe the fat sister would realize then that her mother had a name. The word on the wall shone and was appealing. It made Farina forget her worry about the writing. She felt proud as she took the blue pen out. Her name was next. The a was too little. Then Wolf. *Lupo*. And with a black pen, she felt a surge in the line and she drew a large set of teeth. With a yellow marker, she drew eyes that were fierce and large. She drew a long tail with a loop and decided to fill the whole body in, black circles swirling up and down, even outside the lines. Then a scarf to turn her into a grandmother, before Sister Gertrude opened the door.

Under her arm, Sister Gertrude held a clean set of clothes for the child, and a nice rough towel to give her a scrub before lunch. The shock was great, added to the commotion that was taking place among the nuns.

The wall, which was so perfectly white before, made her gasp. The silence that had been broken had never been so clear as when she saw how a child had put graffiti on a space that really was not so much about peace as about order and rules. The long red letters were like dripping candles. The little girl could already write. Her name was Milli. An ugly name for a child with such determination. Unless Farina was her name. Farina was a more uneven labor of blue, yellow and purple letters that rode uphill and then back down. Why couldn't it be her name, since she said it was.

The world inside children never ceased to amaze Sister Gertrude. A wolf was in there, a wild fellow at that. His scrambled yellow eyes popped like cartoons on TV. But the surprise was the unfolding revelation. Imagine that secret of writing, real writing, across the walls. It was like discovering a prehistoric tomb. The sisters weighing up the future of the little girl—police or no police—to baptize or not as if the plague would snatch her before the afternoon—they were overlooking the child herself. Whether or not she needed a Christian name. How dare they worry about such things when the young concentrated face already possessed hands that knew how to write. Even to express her dark fears through a wolf. In the hysterical meeting that was going on, the sisters had no idea of who this child was. And what her resources were. They had overlooked her. As they had overlooked Providence.

Farina put the pen behind her back and kept her eyes on the floor. Rickety anticipation made her keep them down. She knew the large woman might erupt into a scold. She glanced up and caught a round face that looked like a moon friend.

Sister Gertrude laughed, in spite of problems that were multiplying like eggs being laid. She caught the eyes studying her. The wall could be repainted. Instead, the whole group should be called in to witness the little radiating mural. Witness the energy and endless goodness of God. His creatures large and small. There was nothing wrong with the little girl except her poverty. That's the truth. She could, given time, explain her own life.

Sister Gertrude thought to say, we don't like children to draw on walls. To begin Bella Bimba's education. But she had left the child alone. The girl hadn't cried. She had, instead, set about her own work. Like Jesus in the temple.

Bella, she said, putting her hand under the child's chin and pulling it upwards. *Bella,* she said, although she shouldn't, pointing to the wall. *Bellissima.*

Farina hoped that meant that she could see Milli. She hoped that the large woman would take her now to her mother. Farina felt space in her body, kindness that might lead her. But instead the moon head said, we are going to take a bath.

In a few minutes, as the hot water poured out, gushed and splashed, Farina clung to her clothes. She didn't want the dress pulled over her head. She had never seen steam. She wasn't going to get into the water. She took the sister's sleeve and tugged it. She shook her head and held tight to her ruffled dress.

We have to wash, the nun said. We will eat soon, and you want to be clean, don't you?

Farina shook her head. No, she said, firmly. Clearly. I want my mamma.

Get into the bath, the nun said, pulling the dress up, not hard, but until Farina's eyes were covered and she was half way out and half way in.

Sister Gertrude felt pity for her. Children had no power. They had so little say. She didn't have anything to comfort the child with. Who knew if they could find her mother? Who knew how long Mother Superior would put up with the chaos? There was no choice but to force the little girl into the water. Force her kicking and letting the water splash on her towel and even on the walls. An angry child had the force of a mule.

But Farina didn't kick. She drew her eyes inside and stepped in, helped by the nun. The water was hot and frightened her.

She didn't look up when the woman scrubbed her back. She sat in the tub, straight and rigid. When the woman told her she would lift her out, she went stiff and left the water like a papoose.

Farina didn't know why her mother had left her. Why wasn't she here to see her dressed in this new pink dress? Why wasn't she brushing her hair instead of the lady whose hand kept pulling her hair? Farina didn't know who to obey. She didn't feel bad being clean. But she was exhausted and wanted to close her eyes. She took her shoes and buckled them alone. She worried for her mother. Her mother with her soft bones. Her mother who let her ride on a horse on the merry-go-round. And was there to lift her off the horse. Where had she gone? And Irene. Why had she left her in this place she had never been? Farina folded up her towel and wished she could hang it on the line. She knew she could not formulate the things moving around inside her. She didn't know what death was, but some feeling of darkness and abandonment came over her. She knew how to get herself out of bed. She knew how to use her pot. She knew how to observe when a person was like the grandmother who was a wolf. The river this morning had been nice. She wanted to go back there. The river, she said. My ball.

The slide of Giordano Bruno was a winner. The statue of the monk, cowled, but not blindfolded as he must have been when he was burned as a heretic in Rome in 1600 stayed in the pile. The cowl was of his order and yet its ghostly covering over the centuries looked like the image of repression, hooding so much of human history's attempts at truth telling.

Melandri had seen the statue innumerable times walking though Campo de' Fiori in Rome. Its absolute darkness always affected him. Far more than the brass circle in Piazza Signoria, for example, in Florence, which marked the bonfire, the annihilating ire blazing from corrupt interest groups who ordered the heaps of logs, where poor reforming Savonarola went up in smoke, the cowl spoke as only images can. Of course, the shoulders helped. Not defiance, but not resignation either. The burden of a single man operating in good faith. His crime. Positing that the origins of creation were so vast they were unknowable except as relative to our time and position in space. There were no limits to the process of knowledge. The brooding statue looking down on fruit stands and flower stands over the centuries passing in the square had not even shaken the monads and pantheism from his thought. His view of the universe was now cosmic theory. He was a man who had perceived a kind of perfect freedom.

Who would he be, now? A Nobel Prize winner. Maybe. Melandri knew that the thought of Giordano Bruno driving a Land Rover towards the Altiplano in Chile and climbing to six thousand meters where the oxygen barely kept them awake was amusing but not the way it was. No one today worked alone, much less with only a writing tool, a few key ancient texts, the help of Kepler and Copernicus and his brain. Certain pieces of theory, now, are like stars themselves, bursting with energy, modeled millions of times. And the skies he studied then were clear as glass.

Twice last summer, Melandri had seen skies over Florence clean enough to actually have merited the risk of taking Galileo's telescope from its resting place in Florence and fiddling with the focus. Twice only had it been worth it even to imagine asking for the unique and historical privilege of using it, seeing through a peep hole luminous sky opened so much further once that genius had grasped the idea of a lens. Twice only had there been atmospheric conditions unpolluted enough to hold up any hand-held telescope and to feel the small and vast power issuing from a narrow wax paper chute, standing where Galileo stood in his house in Arcetri. Melandri used a brass instrument his father had given him. A magic tool that held in its slightly battered barrel a closeness that when he brought the sky down brought his childhood with it. Wandering down the road in front of Galileo's house, with the moon illuminating it brightly, Melandri sampled and touched the sky all the way down to the church where Galileo's two daughters had struggled to survive. Melandri felt choked with emotions standing there, with Brunelleschi's prophetic dome below. His father had stood beside him there, always citing the citadel of philosophers starting from Ptolomy. Melandri, when he found the one clear summer night to revisit the sky in the old way, invariably felt love for his astronomer's life shaped by former lives. A specific sense of Galileo and his father intertwined and lightly weighed on his shoulders as he stood in their place in the courtyard.

In a ritual he couldn't explain, Melandri always plucked a pear leaf from a thin, struggling tree outside the convent. In the starry darkness he took away with him its resistance, the tug of the green leaf until it could be pulled off only by pulling nearly the whole tree in his direction. Alive, not letting go, it made him feel love for his father's curiosity, and for Galileo's genius, for Florence's native, acerbic pioneers. Sometimes, one circulated in his cardigan pocket all summer long until it crumbled into brown, prickly dust.

Only twice last year did the city scud and atmospheric pollution clear and lift enough to permit him to look at Betelgeuse and feel the night as a fabric of named fires so mighty that man could imprison man for speaking about its ultimate meaning. He had looked at the moon and enjoyed adjusting the eyepiece like those before him looking at the moon's dry Maria. Sea of Tranquility. Lake of Dreams. Sea of Nectar. Not the terrifying marvel of the universe that armies of astrophysicists gridded out in isolated observatories, retrieving computer data, running numbers and numbers to have access to events occurring after its origin. Galileo, who saw the same moon through an eyepiece, was right not to waiver in his faith. Not to disclaim it. But last year the scrawny pear tree was dead. From frost. Pollution. Parish oversight. The funny ritual, dead.

Melandri, in a semi-shade still cloaking the chapel, was brought back to people milling, a few settling in chairs. The monk was nearly beside the point. Once a slide locked into its slot in the machine, it was as good as five minutes of information and spin-offs. Reveries. Great heights.

What it would take to burn another astronomer like Bruno? Water on Mars. It wouldn't be a Pope's order but a government's. Defense. Property. Aliens. It was perhaps even easier now than then to fan the flames of cosmic insecurity. To focus terror as an outside evil. Melandri put the Bruno slide down for the second time. With reluctance, he passed it to the rejected pile. The Sea of Discipline.

Keeping time was something he had learned from American colleagues at conferences. That rough way they had of ringing bells to interrupt as if there were a fire. Or actually cutting off the sound of the mike. Twenty minutes, they said. Twenty minutes they meant. *Esagerato*. Fanatic. Rude. It seemed like that, the first few times. But now Melandri found that idea was part of him. What are you trying to say? That was the deep issue.

Time and light. The appointment in the cathedral was a way of focusing the sensation of awe that came from touching one ray of cosmological order. Not the dust and fire explosions that astrophysicists saw in reassembled infrared images and numbers from the sky vigils kept by robots. Not the tremendum, the orders of magnitude that were beyond apocalyptic language. No, he wanted the heart-breaking dimension of light falling on the earth. The sensation of mystery transmitted through a hand-held telescope. The eons of searching for a calendar in the specific rhythms of celestial bodies. The Sea of Crises. Of Fertility. The Marshes. Marsh of Sleep. Marsh of Decay. Lake of Death. Sea of Gold. Of course, he couldn't get off on the moon.

Melandri picked up a slide with a ray of sunlight falling like Cupid's arrow rushing to the floor of Santa Maria del Fiore. He had other slides of rays. One from St. Petronio in Bologna. He might project five or six of those in rapid succession, like fire-crackers exploding just before the ray in the church reached the wall. Once the dancing fire got down to the level of people's eyes, he would have to turn the machine off and get people focused on the motion and speed with which the earth was spinning and, thus, how the light traveling on its curved path was moving, moving like a live shimmering presence, a liquid hand. And they would all be witnesses, like Toscanelli, of light and its long, fruitful marriage with science, registering its presence with their own eyes.

When neither woman could run much further, Irene stopped first. Not that far from the convent, she put her head back against a beige sandstone wall and panted. Her black dress, slicked with sweat, heaved up and down with her heavy breathing. The sun burned and she turned her face. As she looked away from Milli, a tragic song of painful moments in her life encircled her head. The excruciating notes tugged at her heart and sense of failure. Yet pride pounded inside her breast, toughness and daring edged out into her legs and feet. She was not one to be subjugated, even though every night she put herself in others' hands. It was destiny that she learned to escape rather than to conquer. She could take any loss, and turn it around, remember later, how sad it was.

Milli panted too. Taller by a full hand, running had emptied her of the ferocious animal she needed. Facing her friend, she could hardly stand on her legs, much less tear her apart. Running, the anger had run like a gazelle in a hunt, chased, outpaced, and deserted, leaving her with mouse-like feelings or a small dog's quarrelsome yip. And no breath. Gasping, in and out slowly, Milli looked at Irene's familiar sharp-featured face and around at the stucco buildings in full daylight. She absorbed the alien place as if it were a harsh desert, where for the first time, Farina was not to be found. The walls and sidewalks and the church bell that was clanging back and forth were a new world unknown to her. She had been robbed and deceived until nothing was left. Farina was not in the room with Igor and she was not in Irene's arms.

Milli blinked her eyes and felt empty of her child, terrorized by an amputating machete having split off any minute of connection. The worlds she had wandered through. Cut off. On the other side. The warm dusty soil and jumping fish. The water where suddenly Meniki was taken down by cruel powers. The damp, dark living room where her mother was washed for burial. All that Harcourt held had been spread over by Florence and the job she did. By Irene, her dark and lively energy, her flashy skirts. Her life had started over with the passing of time and the gentle stories offered by Farina. Now it vanished in mocking grief. In Irene's empty-handed presence that life vanished. Farina, Farina. *Bella bambina.* You have magic in your *occhi, occhi,* eyes.

Milli had never imagined a moment without Farina, not one minute where within her radius of thought, touch, smell, the girl was not the accompaniment to her plans. Never on a lovely shop-filled street in Florence or under the sweaty body of a man in its deserted junk yards had she felt she wanted to fit the city's world. But the world was there like the moon, like the Mugnone trickling. The world was still there in Florence. And it was influenced, lifted and warmed, cut into invigorating little pieces of joy and glitter, by Farina.

Never before had Milli felt the world to be without Farina. Her brown eyes, her way of licking her lips, her furtive smile when Milli appeared at her bed, her finding words and thinking that Milli would want to learn the words for the green trees, the shoe made of glass. Would want to know what the word was.

Scarpetta di vetro. Glass slipper, she said, always getting caught on the s. The way Farina's mouth slipped when she said the word like a whistle now assumed a magnitude like a star.

Not that Milli remembered Farina in her every moment. Not that she didn't leave her to Irene. No, Farina was in that same line as having ribs or toes, or hair, even hair. You don't think of it, but you feel it's there. You know it's on your head. It's a deep feeling, deeper than hair or fingernails. Deeper than anything that can vanish. It's not a spirit. Not a ghost. Not tricky, coming and going, like voodoo. Milli could say Farina and from anywhere, know what it meant.

Irene had changed that.

Where were you all those hours?

Irene, without thinking, had refined the refrain, refined her haughty way of slipping off and facing Milli squarely. Where were you all those hours?

What are you saying? Do you want to be paid? What do I owe you for my child?

What child, Irene intoned, coldly pulling herself up straight, and mouthing it with harsh disapproval. What child? What child would have you for a mother? A mother who doesn't call or check in.

Irene was surprised to be saying what she was saying but she felt power surging inside as if she were dancing in small steps around Milli, closing up the circle. Small flashy steps that were cruel and meant to impress, to cast a spell, so that she could lead her confused friend into the trap, into the portal she needed to pass.

What child? she asked again.

Now the face in front of her had changed. Now Milli felt as if her anger had changed again to something where she had to run away herself, to get away from the cruel madame in front of her, the cold eyes of a woman like the turbaned woman in Turin who had first taken her money and made her sign away her life for a contract of slavery. Irene, on this street in Florence, crowded with passersby, had emptied her world. Her daughter was on the other side of a wall that Irene knew and was taunting her with.

Farina, Milli said softly. And she wept.

She couldn't say anything. But it was as if, in a way that didn't fit into words, the skeleton in the yard was being explained. Sometimes, with patients, it took years for them to accept a truth that their hands told over and over in the sand. The violation and buried nature of her relationship to Vaclav. It was like staring at a ghost, not being able to admit that unknowing could extend so far. It was like staring at a ghost and not wanting it to recede. In some odd pairing Teresa and Vaclav had come together. A deep buried part of her life was now apparent to her as love—vanished and yet hauntingly real.

Susan looked over at a picture of Marina gazing up at Luigi and herself. You know nothing of how far away I was from you both in that photo.

TEN

LUIGI WAS SORRY that Diniza had left. Her rounded back looked like a safe that would not be easy to crack for its secrets. Watching her disappear through a wide opening in the trees he felt her independence. She lived in rooms he had only seen twice and both times he had met a strong, solid man with broad shoulders called Jacobo, who stood up and shook his hand. He said he repaired shoes. The way Diniza's eyes sweetly filled with tears when she left made Luigi wish they could serve as a mirror to show him himself. It was a weak thought, and one he would not have formed as a young man. He wished immediately, head down, that he had thought something stronger.

You see, Gian Franco said, Diniza holds your mother up as a goddess. A signora above all the rest. Now you can't find servants like her, can't find loyal people willing to become part of the family. We have one from Moldavia, and she is out every night. And she wants more money. And in the end, she's so homesick that she can't even clean. She watches TV and says she is learning the language.

Luigi couldn't resist. Do you feel proud standing in front of an honest hard-working woman like Diniza? I must say I wondered if she suspected the gist of our earlier conversation.

213

What an odd idea. Gian Franco cocked his head, amused that his friend was so predictably gloomy, incapable of measuring what really was going on.

She saw you as your mother's pride and joy. She saw me as someone who became a doctor. Do you really think that sturdy woman had any order of second thoughts? People like her never realize anything except that powerful people are usually bad. But she saw you and me, by extension, as part of an ideal life she led with the good people of Florence. The Dinizas live their days within the small circle of their own good faith. People like her are content to live satisfied by the idea that they are honest.

Luigi didn't consider that worth responding to. That arrogant analysis chilled him. On the other hand, probably not only Diniza, but he himself, had not a very clear picture of how bad things were becoming. He didn't exactly want to know. He certainly didn't want to mix up his stories with Gian Franco's stories. Yet here they were, walking on the gravel paths, with the cemetery as a sober background. Such an awkward situation and yet Luigi couldn't exactly take the high road. He couldn't just look down on his old friend's lapses and condemn him as an exemplar of the new atmosphere. Somehow, what was happening in Florence was not as simple as corruption. It was not as simple as saying a human stain, either. Never to be escaped. Luigi felt some dread but he couldn't resist continuing the conversation. It seemed as if he would never get out of the trap of the odd day if he didn't puncture or penetrate the differences between the two of them. Did he have any right to think that he was better than Gian Franco? It was odd, but he wanted to think that. Wanted, and the word made him smile, wanted to prove, as if he could do that with logic, that he was better. Luigi felt how his mother's approval was driving this last thought. The rivalry that had leapt out from Gian Franco's declaration of love for her was a troubling and very young feeling. Luigi picked up his pace.

His phone twittered, poked in with its sound.

The company he had been seeking for interminable hours was in his hands.

How are you? Luigi said, so unexpectedly glad to hear Maria Grazia's voice.

Luigi thought of taking a few steps back. But the low walk was empty except for the two of them. Going in any direction, Gian Franco would hear. The eagerness, the shy wish to hear about her day. Yet standing in front of him, feigning a routine response, he had probably already picked up a tone.

Luigi couldn't say, I am busy. He didn't want to say where he was. He didn't want to interrupt Maria Grazia's initiative to reach him. It was a pleasure, a joy.

When are you coming back into the office? she asked.

His watch said near noon. An hour. Luigi thought he was safe then. He could close the conversation and yet leave it open. The trees were glistening in light. The intense heat of summer, of being outside, was liberating.

Instead, she turned the phrase. I thought you had forgotten me.

Luigi heard the voice of the expectant mother, the voice of the fertility god mooing and insisting on space. He couldn't head into that space with Gian Franco standing so near to his side.

I'm in the cemetery, he said, fearing that she would question that. She knew for weeks that he had said he wouldn't go. She had listened to his lecture on the hypocritical cult of visiting graves.

I'm surprised, she said, as if she thought he was alone and could develop that thought.

I'll be back in an hour, Luigi said, again, hoping he would not have to answer her abruptly.

Is someone with you?

Luigi immediately registered that Maria Grazia would imagine him with another woman. Phones were terrorism. They chewed up context and privacy and for every bit of control that they offered, they extorted something. The sky was so beautifully blue.

He would just have to end the conversation. He would have to hope that she would understand and not be too harsh. That she would extend to him again the opening that she was offering now.

I have to go, he said. I'll see you soon. Luigi felt he had to gasp for air. He was cutting off what he had dreamed of for more than a week. Her initiating a call to him. Her reaching out, searching for contact. It couldn't be as disastrous as he thought.

Gian Franco smiled knowingly, sniffing the conflict and moving into it with the assumed right of an old friend.

Any problem?

No, Luigi said, walking faster, as he put his phone back in his shirt pocket.

The university, once in a while, actually needs me, he said with a smile. We sign papers for everything. Sign and sign, hoping that what we are signing is true. I for one never read the fine print.

Gian Franco took the lead, as he put his hands behind his back. He was willing to gently move back into the ugly territory that was giving him trouble.

Did your father ever tell you how the system worked then?

It's funny that you ask. I had such an unusual experience this morning. Almost a vision of his innocence and determination.

What do you mean?

Luigi stopped walking and turned. The woodpecker started up again.

Have you ever thought what his head must feel like, Luigi

asked. They drill and pound with their beak, if you think about it. The beak takes the impact and so does the entire head and the vertebrae. It's hammer and nail in one. Just to live.

No, I hadn't ever thought of it.

Think of it, Luigi said.

Okay, done. Gian Franco said. Now what did your father have to say about business then? Did he have any friends? Or was he full of enemies, like most people who try to change the system are?

Charlotte opened her eyes again. She heard a rustling in the room. Now she hadn't dreamed about the owl. She was dreaming about Susan. Their last meeting in Minneapolis. Distant and unpleasant. And then her daughter had smiled with life in her eyes.

Charlotte could hear the sound. It couldn't be the owl. Charles from downstairs had come in. He had carried a large straw basket. He was business-like. To the point. He kept his eyes down because she was in her nightgown. He had thrown the basket over the little owl. It had flapped its wings under the reeds. It had made a low sound almost like a growl. That had not been a dream. Her watching him slip a large plastic sheet under the basket. The owl had shuffled some. And Charles had turned the basket right side up and carried it out.

Tomorrow, ma'm I'll release him in the arboretum.

Yet the sound was back, rippling and folding. Charlotte reached over to the light stand. I guess it isn't quite sunrise. I could pad out to the kitchen and make a cup of coffee. Wake up from this dark. Imagine seeing Susan. She could feel her daughter's eyes so alive and then almost filled with pity blessing her. The rustling seemed very close. Down under the bedspread flounce.

Charlotte reached the earpiece of her glasses. They were heavy on her nose, heavier it seemed to her each day she grew

217

older. She hated the weight leaving red marks on her skin. Everything broke or bruised or burst. You had to wear scarves to cover the waddles of the neck. Awful, just like her mother's terrible waddles. And when one put on a bathing suit, the little burst veins were enough to make one feel like a road map.

There. They were on.

Charlotte's heart nearly stopped.

Facing her on the floor was the small white owl.

It was very close to the bed. She feared it might fly, trilling its wings, onto the bed and then what?

Charlotte didn't want to move. But she gripped the sheet with her fingers. That way she could pull it up over her head, if the owl tried to land on her.

The white ruffed face turned slightly to the right and then to the left but didn't seem to want to fly.

Charlotte closed her eyes and wished the bird away. Willed it out of the room. She was used to willing things out. It was a shame and sometimes her indulgence embarrassed her. But if she didn't feel like getting up, she didn't. If she didn't feel like vacuuming, she didn't. The world didn't care about her dust. About the only thing she really didn't do just as she pleased was eating. She had to eat. But otherwise, if she felt cramped or limited—forget it. It was a mantra that she rather liked and since she lived in these retirement flats, it was useful. So many old people complained and felt duty bound. Worried, even about other places. What was the use of that? The children were grown and had their own lives. Her philosophy, if you could call it that, was live and let live. Miss Pekard in the fourth grade had said that the Stoics thought something like that. Or maybe the Stoics thought you had to be brave.

Now she heard Susan's voice. I wouldn't have left you if you would have been willing to be a mother.

Charlotte opened her eyes.

The owl was there. It now looked very real to her. It was solid, sober, and seemed to be growing bigger in the room. In some way, although it hadn't lifted its wings, it seemed to be an owl that could fly, quite far.

Charlotte wanted to order it to leave. She realized that was funny. She could open her window and try to shoo it out. But the owl seemed to convey that he had come back. That he was not about to leave.

Charlotte considered turning off the light, rolling over, and hoping when she reopened her eyes that the owl would have disappeared. Gone away the way he had come in. But she understood that was not the message coming through his fierce yellow eyes. He could fly very far. He could move and fling himself into the sky and then dive down with night eyes to carry off a mouse.

The sensation reached her that the feathered creature was waiting for her. It was as if he had come out of the sky, stopped like Santa Claus over her rooftop and come in, for her.

Charlotte froze with this vision.

The owl. She wanted to say the Owl and the Pussycat. The Owl and the Pussycat went out to sea. But the impish, quite imposing face staring at her was not that owl. She felt a choking sensation in her throat. She felt depressed and pulled her night-gown closer. There was nothing sadder than an owl's song, that night song she had not thought about for years.

Can you speak, she asked suddenly feeling brave.

The owl didn't move.

Charlotte thought then she could throw a pillow at it. It couldn't talk. It was just something like having a little too much to drink. It happened rarely. But when it did things could seem, well, out of whack.

She narrowed her eyes in a threatening way. Get out of here. You've ruined a good night's sleep and I've had enough of you. I have my own problems and my own plans for today. How am I ever going to drive or even imagine driving that truck for a few miles, if I am all tired out.

The owl didn't move.

Oh owl. If I think you are real, what am I to think? If I think you are a shadow of my mind, it's really no better.

Charlotte felt her temper rising. She thought somehow Susan in the dream and her way of insisting on life beyond ordinary life had brought this troubling scene on. She felt angry at her daughter, so angry she was nearly boiling with anger. Then Charlotte thought she didn't know what she was thinking. Whom could she trust?

What does it mean bringing an owl to Minneapolis into my bedroom? I don't know who said that. Some Greek said that. Owls to Athens? What did that mean? I used to know who said that.

The owl hunched its shoulders, fluffed up its wings. It lifted a claw and shook it out.

Charlotte was afraid to get to her feet. She was afraid if she stood the owl would disturb her even more. That she would discover that he had some dire plan, like those Indian myths where the owl sings the penetrating song of death.

That was the thought she hadn't wanted to think. That the owl was here to tell her that she had no more time on the earth. That the room with its alarm clock, and her dressing table with her parent's pictures, and the old Maine farmstead, and Bill and Susan, her two children, and Leonard, so young he looked like a movie star she was incapable of resisting, that it was a fling that had all taken place and now it was coming to an end, without her having any say.

Charlotte was afraid to close her eyes. She saw Don on the road and he would be waiting for her. Don was such an odd piece of her life, a part that had appeared like those pregnancies that happen when one is close to fifty. One needs at that point no children. It hardly is physiological, and yet the body and, sometimes, even the heart, are willing to give it all one more try. Even if he was fifteen years younger than she.

But it was ironic, Charlotte suddenly thought, panicking, if the room's four walls with a stack of last month's newspapers piled up were the end. Nothing had been accomplished. Nothing had been finished. The whole way she had indulged herself, she had not scraped even the surface. She'd never seen the pyramids. Not even read the whole Bible. She had not left a mark, even on Charles downstairs. Oh, he thought, like they all did downstairs at the desk, that she was peppy, pretty sharp for her age. That was the thing about women from her era. They counted for nothing. The words sent stinging tears into Charlotte'e eyes. If he came up and found her dead in her bed, he probably wouldn't blink an eye. What did he know about her.

Charlotte couldn't say I am ready. That was something at least she had planned. When she was really old and the children were gathered around her bed, when they were whispering how they had loved her, had remembered when she had gathered them in her arms and–What? Tied their shoes? Brushed their hair? Ironed their clothes? When she had told them how to live their lives? The word 'live' sounded like the most haunting melody. It was beyond description that feeling of living as the most precious unending thing, gifts and secrets hidden everywhere, under the table, on paths beside the Mississippi River, in prom dresses made so long ago of rayon, walks with Tulip, her childhood dog, the leather smell of the back seat of the car with her boyfriend, Rodney. Charlotte could see cherry blossoms, and waves then, waves that grew higher and higher, tormenting waves, frightening, and no one was around her. She couldn't see Leonard, or Susan, or Bill. She saw boxes and boxes and boxes of stuff, of letters, of bills, of junk mail and campaign literature, and it was all closed and mixed up. She couldn't imagine why she hadn't thrown out boxes or opened them. They made her feel like they were empty nests and she wanted to hang a sign on all of them. To be burned. And that will be very sad. Charlotte struggled with that feeling. She didn't want to feel it deepening. The sadness, too, was like a wave washing over her. Taking her further out to sea. And why had Susan ever moved to Italy? And why had Bill married that public accountant?

I loved you, Leonard, she said crying out in the room.

By then she felt the owl lifting her, determined to carry her over the trees, the baseball field, lifting her over the apple orchards, the beautiful path where she could see her mother still wearing a magenta dress with shoulder pads. And her bearded father leading the family into a park where there was a circle of picnic tables made of wood. Is this it, she thought, is this all there is? Where are the mosquitoes, the lemonade, the bringing together of all of us, bare footed and excited, lifting our skirts and placing our feet on slippery rocks before stepping into the energy of the great Mississippi moving at a splashing, glittering speed?

Having heard Maria Grazia's voice and having shut it off, the jolt of how he was living his relationship with her seemed stupidly obvious. It was so arrogant of him to want his way. Yet he was helpless, really, to change things. But Luigi did want her to call him. He did want to see her at night, and more than see her, to make love to her and taste her black coffee in the morning before they went to work in separate cars. Or she on her bike.

Walking around in the cemetery was a rather foolish thing. It was certainly not his habit to discuss problems as if no one could hear. He had been with Gian Franco for nearly an hour and that sticky way his friend had of making him feel guilty, as if they were Siamese twins now annoyed him so much he didn't see how he could continue exploring the subject. What did Gian Franco know about his father? And how could they possibly agree on the issues of corruption.

Gian Franco looked over at him. He was glad to have such a fuzzy headed friend, still loyally linked to pasts that were gone. He wondered if Luigi still had his father's connections with the banks. The banks were fairly secretive about who was handling the papers and how they had to be destroyed. But he knew some of the names. The vice president at the country club's brother-in-law was a banker who had connections to the right people in the foreign ministry in Rome. And if Luigi knew the same names, just a word, just the right word could help. Or if not help, at least get him in. The paper shredder he had used was surely one tenth the size of those being used in the banks. The times had suddenly exploded in unexpected ways.

Have you ever heard of Dr. Venegri?

In what context? Luigi asked, turning to avoid a chalky Roman temple with a faux column fallen like the beginning of the Apocalypse.

Banks, I believe.

Luigi had heard of him. A fox with a medium bad reputation and a weakness for villas. But the idea of admitting it, of opening up a door in a fraternity that in some ways was like the cemetery itself, was not for him this morning. There were systems of alliances and movements built from free masons, sometimes. Sometimes, networks through political parties. But they allowed for an endless amount of space for adjustments that could turn to scandal, and then blackmail, here, and blackmail, there. No one who stopped in his office in the university ever really imagined how much that so-called business world he had turned down sickened him. Luigi reached up and snapped off a cypress cone. Its small intricate compartments were still full of last year's seeds. He put it in his pocket without illustrating its capacities to scatter up to one hundred versions of itself. He put his hand around it and felt a distant sympathy for his father. His father's antipathy to the steps his business life required.

The light blinded, when it found an opening in the trees.

Luigi had never really asked his father enough to know him very well. To know how much it cost him not only to leave the business, but to find himself emarginated. To go into a retirement of white tennis shorts and too many drinks. Of years of traveling back and forth to the cemetery and doing his wife's beck and call. Because it was not suitable to stand up to one's father-in-law. It was not possible to resist the pressures that forced one to play the game or otherwise to be considered a troublemaker, disruptive. To ask for transparency was to disrupt. Not just to be disliked, but to be seen as repugnant, abhorrent, a threat, who, at the same time, was dangerous. Irresponsible. Anti-social. The problem was the very Italian idea that one who wanted reform was irresponsible because he was jeopardizing so many—was threatening to ruin so many others—who never considered what they were doing was actually wrong. The conformists were only responding to the way things were done.

Luigi turned to Gian Franco. I don't know Dr. Venegri. Personally or otherwise. And unfortunately, my parents are no longer here to tell us, if they knew him, or more probably if they knew his father or mother, what passwords he responds to.

I'm sorry Gian Franco if you are in difficulty. But you should have known better. Taking little cuts is no way to behave, he said, feeling the arrogance in his words. Feeling a distain that was hollow and spilled back onto himself.

I'm surprised, Gian Franco said, genuinely hurt. You have your villas, and you begrudge someone else the same chance? Do you really believe these judges going after us are impartial? That they aren't driven by political motives and answering to whom they wish to keep in power? Do you think if they force our new prime minister out of office things will be any better or different in ten years time?

Luigi didn't want to answer. As much repugnance as he felt for Gian Franco's words, he also felt the long and disappearing set of days that they had shared. He didn't wish Gian Franco ill. He didn't wish him a judge's summons, nor did he want to know how far in Gian Franco was. The country club was full of people who were part of the world in Florence that was under pressure. He wished that Gian Franco was strong, and that what they had once professed, the heartspoken compassion for social progress, he wished it were true. But he couldn't say that either.

I can't help you much, Luigi said, succinctly. It's too bad we can't sit down under a tree and share a bottle of wine. Life goes up and down. I hope you will get out of whatever is on your back. Good lawyers matter for these things. You know that, I'm sure. You need a lawyer on good terms with the judge. It's a question of money. And if you know the right bankers, it's the same as knowing a cabinet secretary.

Luigi was sorry he said that too. To admit so frankly and without indignation under a blue sky that everyone, including himself, knew how things worked. He motioned to Gian Franco to go ahead. I think I'll stop again at my parents' tomb. Saying that Luigi felt relief.

Gian Franco looked at him seriously. You've always been weak, he said, as his eyes lit up a bit. Too weak to decide for yourself. I am as sorry for you as I am for myself, he said, laughing. Really, we never wanted to think it, but we are just like everyone else.

The phone. Susan decided not to run for it. The words could wait like a train in a tunnel. Then she would hear them, judge if she was up to facing the person on the other end. Now it was ringing again. She ran.

Sister Morena, of course I remember you. You crossed my mind this morning strangely enough. How are you?

Sister Morena spoke softly. There were ears everywhere and she could hear the excited voices humming like bees, many of whom would sting.

Forget the other message, she said covering her mouth. The one I left on your answering machine. No, not forget, she giggled, but she couldn't imagine how to explain. I was wondering, she said, feeling how she was breaking the rules, the tight order that reigned in the convent about keeping conflict inside the walls, if you could come over here. We have a problem with a child and I hope you might give us an opinion.

What kind of problem?

A child has been left with us, and many here think we should turn her over to the police. As soon as she eats.

Of course, I'll come, Susan said. But I have patients this afternoon. Probably I can't get there until close to supper. Will that be in time?

I hope so, Sister Morena said, wondering why in the world there should be any question of time with the fate of a girl in the balance. Maybe nothing could save her, but the idea of turning her over to social workers, putting her into the reed basket where she would be found by foster parents, it was too soon, for that. She could hear Sister Gertrude's voice rising. I hope she gives them the fiery speech about responsibility, she thought. She had seen her silence all the petty complaints when some of the sisters murmured about wanting better soap, better fruit last week. She reminded them that economizing was a privilege, a joy embedded in simplicity. Not given to everyone, she had said, but given to us, that chance to live so simply that we can taste things, touch things for what they are. We are the real mystics. The sighs that flowed around the room were as loud as if women were lifting heavy baskets to their heads.

Susan looked at her watch. Nearly noon. She wondered if she really could do anything for the child this afternoon. If the Sisters had the mother with them, there would be lots of things to do should the mother consent to be helped. But each case was different and whatever had made a mother give up the child in the first place was unlikely to be resolved by diplomacy.

226

That tool didn't work among strangers in less than an hour. Evaluation and then a plan were the way to proceed.

As she hung up, she knew that her head was in too many places. Even though her patient notebooks had not been opened, the feeling of the sandwork was calling her back for another round. She wanted more visions into the fierce feelings that were coming out of her. The rake made fast work of the mounds she had shaped. The tool of making worlds visible was a powerful one. The wall of figures was so like the way she wished to see the world. Multiple truths leading to a core. Its bulges and potential were nearly the antidote to the way she once had always been told to hold her tongue. One follows rules. Fine but stifling. The dwarfs made her smile. The pipe-stem cleaner trees. The images of plastic, paper, metal were so extraordinarily kitchy together. They were like a thousand carnivals of bad taste. But one or two plucked out and they became endowed with energies that are in needs, loss, conflicts but remain hidden until one pays attention and tells that story to oneself.

Susan wanted to push on. Mentally she touched lots of the figures, and then closed her eyes to see if any came to her with her eyes closed.

Often her patients stood dumbly at this point. Trying to pinch their eyes shut as if they were children told not to peek. Standing there, often with shoulders slumped, they looked strangely disappointed when nothing came. As if they were in a test. As if someone from the outside was going to approve or disapprove. Tell them the answer. Alone with themselves with their eyes shut, they expected magic. They hoped for shooting stars or words uttered from a god.

Susan turned her mind back to her own heart. She was in the dark with no other sensations. She opened her eyes and reached for a small porcelain owl, leaning on a pink umbrella. It was a salt shaker. Her great aunt Mary had given it to her as a child, when she admired it on her kitchen table. And her mother Charlotte had chastised her for hinting that she wanted it. Susan was surprised to be holding the old owl with gold rimmed eyes who, when she became a therapist, had joined the sandtherapy symbols. Minerva. The owl who was also Athena. Minerva, who warned poor Demeter that her daughter Persephone had been abducted.

Susan was taken by the sudden set of links. From the tiny cheap treasure of an owl she had been plunged into the story of one of the oldest mother/daughter myths. She didn't have any explanations for that. She didn't know what the compensations would be. But she had reached for that figure and that was where the story in the sand would begin.

The ceramic owl sat near the center of the sandbox. It looked as if it were on a desert. Susan chose some pine trees. Five, six, she put a little forest around the bird's left side. Then she reached for an apple. The dimension was that of a gum ball. There was a word she hadn't thought of in fifty years. Gum balls of all colors in those round machines that for a penny divulged two balls down the chute. An apple. And then she picked a fire made of plastic, with curling painted flames.

Susan began to work with the scene, pulling the symbols into relationships with one another. The cicadas droned outside. Her analyst's mind worked like a capable student's. It wouldn't stop. So easy to fire off associations and learning. Susan didn't know if she could enter the necessary state of abandon in the time she had. But if she demanded more than ceremony from her patients, she must now demand it from herself.

Mother and daughter. Daughter and Mother. Charlotte. Marina. Susan was pleased that after using water to work with her feelings for Vaclav, she had been returned to her own image. The story she had picked, with the extreme distance in the sand between the apple and the fire, was almost a photograph of what her mother had wished for her. Charlotte insisted for

Susan on a blind repetition of her own pattern. She wanted a helplessness that consigned her to a flat, traditional life. Without the powerful spirituality of a Teresa with her driving mules. Or the lapses of experience. Or the fires of sex. Poor mother.

Susan felt energized by the dynamic. It was as if a part of her inheritance was showing up before her eyes. After nearly thirty years abroad, the skeleton of her American life was being uncovered. The word 'skeleton' gave Susan goose bumps. Teresa. The experience as it started to grow seemed distinctly part of her earlier meditation. Teresa, to Susan, was many things. This kind of perception was what Vaclav called the Divine connection. Susan didn't know, but she assumed it was what St. Teresa called her visitations. Jung said synchronicity. It was a lift into a level of opening attention that languishes day to day. Its clarity, no matter how shocking, was solid and the experience of attention, beauty itself. Truth was a million things that then simplify with attention into a living story.

Susan used her eyes to play with the owl, the dark forest, the apple, and the fire. She put her fingers to her lips. Who was there to let her feel that she was being watched, guided? No one. Yet, she thought, the work has gone on forever, way beyond this room. Or my patients. Sand itself has been made into images by priests for millennia who, arranging a single mandala for a year, watch it, then, blow away.

ELEVEN

I T'S NOT A compost pit. No white maggots, she said. If you understood, you'd get right off your chair. The hole in the earth is cut perfectly straight.

Amadeo Caffo waited.

How long has *la Signora* lived here?

Dai, Agnese Caffo said, wrinkling her face at him. You're forgetting when they got married in folk clothes. Ever since.

Signor Caffo didn't know what to think. Signora Notingham, if he pictured how slight she was, how energetic, nervous like a hummingbird, burning energy, the way she never really stopped on the road, staying in motion, shaking her red hair, bending over to touch her toes, lifting her knees as if she were a majorette—she seemed, *ecco,* American. Younger. From a film. Did he imagine she would sell prehistoric treasure to criminals you read about in newspapers, who cover their heads with black jackets once the police sequester the marble satyrs in their trunk? He couldn't really see her doing that, with her pretty daughter often at her side; couldn't guess why she would be drawn into something illegal like that. On the other hand, she wasn't helpful about returning Arvon. Did she fear snooping? And it was true, whatever her work was, people parked on the hill, coming and going all day long. Still, her mother-in-law,

Signora Dell'Istante never found it necessary to gossip about her even after her son took two moving vans of furniture and left the villa for good. And he had noted that the *professore* still parked his blue Lancia inside her gate, which, in its way, was a strong comment.

For a minute, the images of delicate crowns of gold wired with gold laurel leaves and the lustrous bronze statues of animals that were neither bird nor beast stopped Amadeo Caffo. They had an authoritative book on Etruscans and the finds spread from page to page were enough to give you shivers. The famous bronze chimera that was lion-headed with the feet of birds. His back bent like a striking snake's. The statue cast a spell. Amadeo Caffo knew he would love to be the one with the luck and force to uncover an ancient king. Under his shovel in the vineyard he had found a large uncracked terracotta jar, but from the eighteen-hundreds. Healthy and round it squatted next to the hearth. And a couple of coins, corroded and rubbed until they couldn't be given time nor kingdom, had turned up when the earth spit them out in a drought. Rusty horseshoes. Oil cans in profusion. Broken plates. The whispers of plastic for the last ten years. What hadn't been dropped and forgotten in the earth? But the shock of reaching into the ground and opening up a frank and sacred world that now could not be imagined gave him chills. As did the idea that a frescoed tomb could be smuggled off. That plaster and paint carrying Italy's real life history could be moved into the hands of strangers while dollar prices grew as the treasure migrated north on the *autostrada* made his blood boil.

A hole as deep as a mine. Amedeo Caffo could feel his hand shaking should he ever be the one to lean over and see the dusted glow of gold rubbing through the soil. Or the edge of an urn bearing a terracotta couple. Or pulling, undestroyed, the life-sized extraordinary upturned pointed crescent eyes and smiles energizing a clay man and a clay woman with pointed upturned crescent slippers. It would give one a place of honor in Florence. Yet it would be a serious temptation to want more than honor.

Signor Caffo glanced at his wife. Her lips were firm. He looked again at her face, for the vanished rosy flush, the bright embers she was holding when he came home. She had pulled her fingers from his and the room appeared more like the rough stone walls.

The determination lining her face made him unexpectedly sad.

He didn't know what to say. Signor Caffo stood up and automatically shifted his belt. He had always heard tales that Etruscans left complete tunnelled settlements on other hills beyond Fiesole. Came back for a last round once they were being defeated near Rome. The question was the soil covered so much. It was unlikely that Signora Notingham had found the king. Even more unlikely that it was the golden hoard. Luzi the gardener would have aired the tale of digging long ago, if there had been so much as a pin out of place. He often made *la Americana* into a conversation at the *bocci* court. Mopping his brow between sets, he exposed the lack of oil in her car engine; how she dried her sheets in a machine instead of hanging them in the air. Her odd ways provided a little humor when his scores were low.

She has created an infection among us. Our village is being ruined, Agnese Caffo said, waving her arm like a sword. She prints fliers—no more war, no more bombs—and look at the peace she lives. She wanted to add, she's not a Catholic. She does not go to Mass, but she knew her husband had never been sympathetic to that. And neither, really, was she. But it was an explosion—that someone different was actually different in her intentions. In her easy smile, how could one read treachery? It wounded. Created doubt.

Agnese, that woman has already caused you lots of unhappiness. But Arvon's home now. At least that.

He took his wife by the shoulder. Why don't we go out to the shed?

I'll tell her that I entered her yard, Agnese Caffo said, needing to break free. When I see her jogging on the road.

His wife knew as well as he did it was dangerous disturbing day-to-day events. That's why there were police. If we confront her, it's best you don't go alone. In his pocket his hand clung to a key. If there was any gold—a necklace, a cross-hatched thimble, or more unlikely a single golden egg, the money would be extraordinary. Not like the three-thousand lire a case he got for grapes. His six months work until harvest, the bad weather and hail, locusts, the neighborly tension of price-setting in the co-op, not to mention backaches that ruined a night's sleep, burning blisters bursting in his wet boots, cramps in swollen fingers that curled like the woodiest tendrils in the vines. Humanly, it was to be expected, to compare lots, but when the mind caught fire by comparing—the money from grapes with the lustre of an ancient jewel—the contrast left a hammering feeling of discontent. And a feeling of shame afterwards.

Would you talk to Padre Livio about it?

Let's think, Signor Caffo said.

The sun in June cast light for fourteen or fifteen hours until the vineyards were like one-hundred shows dressed and undressed by shadows. Each change unveiled remarkable sturdy colors that never grew too bright. With all of Florence, the proud orange dome and the straight white facades off in the mists, it was his favorite time. Still not too hot or burnt by winds, the world around them, especially in the early morning, felt benign. The yard, too, lifted from its more tedious and petty ways. Why couldn't the hole be something good for the village instead of another lapse?

Agnese Caffo reached in front of him for a slice of bread. She spread it with a thin mantle of dark plum jam. Before he could ask for one, she left the room.

Signora Notingham is foreign, he thought as his wife walked through the door into the courtyard, bright with light. The sensation struck him like a spade in the head. An error, where the abrupt blow hurts and one still feels slightly stupid. The *Americana* was not like them after having opened and shut her gates on the same hill for twenty years. One deep intrusion behind the wall and she turned into a *straniera*, a foreigner. Agnese's one journey around her yard uncovered the generally polite woman and turned her into someone like a splinter infecting the body. Because she was not Italian, she didn't care if she sold its treasures. The suspicion pouring in his mind was unfamiliar. Amadeo Caffo was amazed. Different from Agnese's thought, but *la Signora* was a fast spreading infection, if suspicion was. Two hundred meters from their own stone borders, he had never felt betrayal surrounding them. Never worried about what was happening behind the walls. At least never before except when the *Tedeschi* were in the woods. The distrust seemed a dangerous nuisance that could only grow worse. The runnels that split open the dog's body had shaken his hope. They, though, were left by someone else. This killing fever welled in him. Now he was in the courtyard, walking fast to catch up to his wife with her slight limp. Some uncomfortable sensation made it seem like a rope was tying his leg. All of a sudden, he imagined, for a moment, that Signora Notingham's ex-husband drove a blue Lancia that was darkly familiar and fishy.

Agnese, we have no choice. We must cross the road and ring her bell.

The Mother Superior had dialed the number herself. Giudice Pingello's cell phone number was in her black book. He was *disponibile,* the husband of her second-cousin, willing to help the convent in matters that now came up all too often. Exiting the room, she could hear the voices around the table still rising. The pain she carried stabbed her in the neck, down her spine, the long and unending trials of the body made the ordinary events nearly vanish from her head. Her body, should anyone see it, was a robe of dry reddened sores.

She would quell the movement that was forming. For reasons of common sense. For political reasons that Sister Gertrude and Sister Morena could not understand. The child needed to be handled by the law. It was too great a responsibility to let her stay like a kitten or a puppy that everyone adored. And then what? Just when she would be settled in, if she would, she would be isolated in the convent, and probably given over anyway. The Bishop had urged a more formal participation with the civic structures. Their function was education.

Guidice Pingello, I'll be brief. We are looking for a social worker. We have an abandoned child with us. We'll baptize her. She seems in good health. But you can give her better tests and get her into a family, even by tonight.

Why not keep her for a few days, Pingello said, turning his back to Benedetta Livi. Why rush? he asked, offering the Mother Superior the space and approval he assumed she needed.

Can't you pick her up?

Her request made him curious. Listen, he said. I'm just about to start another interrogation. The plump, short prostitute looked destroyed. Ripped skirt, torn grass-stained blouse. But not holding her head in her hands or staring at her rounded lizard shoes. She seemed aware of her disheveled state. Aware to the point of having normal eyes that met his. Pingello hoped it was true. Later this afternoon, Madre, I could see what might be done.

He had that complication in himself. At home, he left the table without picking up the dishes. Walked out of a room while his son was striking too timidly the notes of his recital piece. His wife said it was only at home that he said no, holding himself in reserve like a silver tray to be used for higher things. What was the difference? she asked. Why is the chaos of Florence preferable to us and our mild requests? It wasn't rhetoric he could answer but there was a difference between the quality of disappointment he felt at home and that which he felt in his mission in the Questura. In the dusty room there was always the chance he could turn the tide. Even the law. He could bend it slightly if it seemed helpful. This afternoon, Madre, he said, why don't I stop in? It's too difficult to make arrangements over the phone.

He was on his back, inside the skin. As he struggled to right himself the sense of where he was, vaguely joined earth, insects, a worm moving. Where he was was nowhere. Or it was the dirt where he lay on his back. Virgil's heart pounded so hard he could not proceed with his task. Down somewhere, there was his skin, in his mouth, and in his throat, and over his eyes, his own skin, slow as mud to remove, to digest and chew, to chop up and get down into the stomach. Virgil was hostage. He'd flown and been licked, nearly chewed, covered in slobber and dropped to roll in his own poison. Bounced and tumbled. And landed. The shadows were some he did not know.

His talons fingered the skin, fingered it as far as he could on his back. No knowing whatsoever where he was since he had been spit out and dropped. To turn over had still not happened. It was the first thing. To nudge his back legs and not hop but push and roll. To acrobatically, inside the prison web of his own skin, roll over and not stop.

He tried blindly through the veil of inhibiting wraps. It was dark where he was, cold. The sun was somewhere but not where he was. He was underground. The leaves rustled some-where. Birdsong. He was buried and gagged by his cloak, his year of life. And danger echoed through him. As long as he was in between. Or worse, upside down. How tiring it was. To try. Again. To try.

The creature inside her moved. Maria Grazia could not justify why she thought Luigi would turn around. For how many weeks now had he been unable even to make love. He had lain near her, last weekend, with the moon keeping her awake and then said, You know, with Susan, I didn't mind the awkwardness. I was surprised to find I liked making love to an ever changing woman. As she grew rounder, I learned to put my arms around her in different ways. Hurt, she had been hurt, and instead of saying so, she had sat up in bed. But Luigi, my body is still smooth and taut. How can that be the problem? I can't explain, he shrugged. He acted as if she were mountainous. Then he turned his unshaved, warm bulk onto hers, but she turned away. She turned. Then he turned away. Silence. It was terrible linking Luigi and their love to cold emptiness that left no hope. Then she had got to her feet, wanting to be busy to calm the sensation of having seen the end. Should I make some camomile tea?

Maria Grazia looked at her watch. The absurd vision of the tall man nervously trying to find the right pose, bowing his head, dusting the marble carvings, before a tomb he had called for several months a colossus, hypocritical, pompous, made her grateful that her parents had their parents in simple boxes in the *Commune's* cemetery. They never believed in stage acts. Or even ritual. But if Luigi went this morning, why hadn't he taken her along? Why was this intelligent man so impulsive? Who was with him? That same thoughtless quality promised she could be almost certain in the end he would change his mind about the baby. But the way he said, I don't know. I don't know really if I can, made the eventual reversal not much of a victory.

Maria Grazia turned on her computer and the colored cube spun. The colors were a brief cartoon. She could invite him, say Luigi, come here. She could roll on top of him. She could smile and wait, coax and forgive, but she didn't want to. Other friends of hers, they gave advice as if women still had no choice, no dignity. Just bend and he will bend. And once he sees the baby, he'll change. It was ancient myth that way women had of waiting and twisting men around their fingers. It was folk-lore as far as she was concerned. Once he saw the raw little wet skull, if he couldn't respond, why pretend? She entered the password without thinking. She could see what messages came in. Vaclav Slovecki's films with commentaries would be the university series in July. A faculty meeting for new chairs. And an e-mail from Piero Lunardi.

Maria Grazia knew the biology of the fellow she was carrying. That was her rosary. Maybe Luigi couldn't be curious beyond a certain point. Maybe small children bored him. Her uncle Silvo wouldn't even touch Titania and Camilla until they were walking and talking. He disappeared while his girls were wailing and tempestuous. But when they could follow orders he taught them things. Took them out to see his bee hives and finally to collect the honey. Told them stories about Hannibal's crossing the Alps and had them walk a piece of the San Bernard pass in snow. There were men like that. But Maria Grazia couldn't say that was true in Luigi's case—if Luigi had been a particularly good father to Marina once she could talk or he could reason with her.

The film series was free. Her mother liked Slovecki. The Czech's last film about the woman painter had beautiful scenes. Emotional and without the shadows of secret police. But something had been lost from the remote and stoic endurance of his early films. And it was more than a switch from black and white. The world he described had collapsed. As had the dignity of his characters to endure. At least she thought so. Maria Grazia clicked on two more messages. And Piero Lunardi, what did he have to say?

In a way Luigi was coherent about his feelings. She couldn't imagine him, like her own father, sleeping on the floor, lying next to her, when her boyfriend in liceo, Matteo, had been killed by a car. Her father curled up, stayed close, helpless, without explanations. His warm hand every so often patted her back and then the loud sound of him blowing his nose. And that spoon her mother tried to feed her with, all week, the *minestrone* whose comfort she refused. Luigi's parents seemed egotists incapable of any simple feelings. The way he described his father and his mother and her sister—how they dressed—they sounded like dolls and soldiers. And his grandfather, a general. Maria Grazia didn't like the vision but she imagined Luigi's parents with their bulging brief cases full of family business, having one thin elegant Lepre case for family, with files carrying labels like 'Human Affairs'. And his mother, from a photo Luigi kept near his bed—of her laughing, but correctly, her lips holding back her teeth—she could only imagine his mother as making Luigi feel weaker than he was.

Luigi had stabilized in a life that didn't include a wide space for family. However true it was that he wanted her, a younger woman, but perhaps, like so many men his age, only in a handsome sport car with two seats only. It might be that his strongest drive was to move forward where he did not have to face any of the old things, which made him feel a failure, like his independent daughter and ex-wife. Death was to be escaped not by procreation of another generation but by growing more carefree himself.

The mailbox had four more messages. Even with the echograms, the probe passing through skin and walls, Maria Grazia did not want to know the baby's sex, although it was clear in the cloud created by sound imaging. One message was from the gynecologist who was a little too pushy. Maria Grazia was primed for following her baby's progress and yet for its sex, she chose slowness—the dark unknowing—she felt this as more natural and hers. It was like the ancient women's tales she resisted when they labeled women seducers and yet, in this case, it was part of her. She wanted the long unknowing.

Until the child was born, nothing could be matched to her father's nose or Luigi's long thin feet. No idea whose skin color the flesh would carry. No idea if the little being would have her uneven temper. No thought of saying oh that flash of silliness was like Zia Mina's smile or surprise seeing that Zio Silvo always held his head cocked like that. Until the child was born only health was followed by new probes and tests. This baby's health was abundant, its health tracked everywhere in the growing multiplication with tempests of splitting and explosions more and more specific to his or her reality. He or she growing always further out of non-existence. Assuming enough form and sufficiency to be born. How curious she was to know if, from the tiny motions she felt, its first howl would be a lusty one.

Maria Grazia returned to Piero Lunardi's email. There was no reason to wait for Luigi to tell her, as if she couldn't see the assumptions herself, what was wrong with the lad's paper. She would give Piero an appointment. Give the eager boy time to discuss what he had written.

It was the next thought that surprised her. All wrong and yet it made her smile again. Piero's propensity, if it was a serious intention to learn, made her think of showing him the perplexing numbers around her female minnows. Why was there a principal component that suggested, well, she called it mourning. You didn't have to be Luigi to make a face at the word. Yet that didn't necessarily mean you couldn't design an experiment to explore it.

Almost as clearly as their first kiss, Maria Grazia felt Luigi teaching her, as a student, the power of method. Maria Grazia wondered why she was entertaining the idea of showing Piero those egg numbers. Piero had a complexion that easily turned red. Not a slow blushing, but fast and bright. An obvious innocence that she was playing into. But he had a mind that explored areas like the new physics that Luigi considered subconsciously religious. She liked imagining Piero's earnest thinking and then disliked the voice she heard in herself, mocking or doubting Luigi, because she knew Luigi fought, harder than anyone she had ever known in the university, to operate seriously on the students by teaching science and thus to lift the country, Italy and Italians—he did believe that—a notch or two in the global world.

Are you ready to listen? Irene asked, her eyes widening, as she stepped back giving Milli some room against the wall.

The harsh sunlight burned Milli's eyes. Someone way back in Harcourt, in the beauty shop where she once worked, that shop with the little tin sink and the rubber hose for water came up. Ullele. She hadn't thought of her and yet oh there she was—flashing eyes, wide hips—clear as ever. She used to pull hair, and laugh as the customers cried out. She did it so often it was difficult to believe anyone would return to her, but they did. Ouch. You pulling my head off. And she never said anything. She just pulled and rolled things up too tight. Just as if it had to be done to make the hair straighten out. Irene was like that, but worse.

The sun was high in the sky. It was nearly noon and the tar, when Milli looked at it, seemed to wave. It rose like the air was beating and folding, rising. Off the blacktop street the heat was rising like waves dancing before her eyes.

Milli shook her head. If certain words came back to her ears she would fall dead there on the sidewalk. Or murder Irene. Standing in the sun made her sick. It was time to find some shade.

Why don't we sit down, Irene said, almost like a person Milli once knew, but narrowing her eyes.

Why are you making your eyes like slits?

Irene stretched her arms out to their full length and then brought them back and cracked her knuckles.

Milli could feel the animal coming back in her. It felt good. You look so mean, she said.

They moved, walked down two tarred streets shaded by shop awnings, without saying. At the first bar, Milli and Irene each pulled out a white metal chair that scraped as if the sidewalk would come up. Under an umbrella, the extra shade dropped like a cool net, expanded and settled like a forest's shade, like a mangrove's circle. Drew them inside of it. Under the umbrella, eye make-up smeared and worn off, skin dry and tired, they eased their bodies down.

Pathetic, Irene said, pointing at the wilted rose in the vase. Its coral head drooped like it had a broken neck. They sat across from one another, in silence, while in between on the table were the dead hours that had flayed and exhausted them completely.

Milli rested her eyes on Irene's eyes, which were not unknown. The light nut-color with a radius of darker brown. Milli didn't know she wanted to feel comfortable, because she was still exploding with anger, but seeing the familiar eyes, eyelashes stiff as sticks, eyes not clouded with disaster, she checked herself to steady her shoulder that, perhaps, was shaking. She was ready.

She asked softly, almost as if she didn't care. As if she felt too sorry for herself to care. As if someone else was asking. The words, wrapped in the ache of holding Farina, her lovely head against her breastbone, hard and real, as she leaned against the cement pile under the bridge, came out.

Farina. Where is she?

Irene wanted a flashing answer. She wanted Igor's deed clear. Not dangling like so many thoughts that never got finished. She would force his intention to make it the twisted-lost-night that it could have been. She wanted Milli to know the whole earth had been torched.

Igor tried to sell her.

Stark in the shade with the little breeze and motorbikes,

low conversation around them, the words still hit Irene like the power in the can of mace she carried in her purse. On a street with people going home for lunch, the words, if sprayed, could blind people who didn't know they were blind. Farina the innocent. She had saved her. Irene knew and not just believed that the deed had taken place. She knew that she ripped the child and saved her life from an end that was far more violent and against all laws, more gouging, more maggoty, than all the scandals she could think of. Stinking breath. All the fetishes and human weakness. Begging to be jerked off. Biting into someone's back and spitting out the skin. Stealing. Stealing looked like skipping rope. Nothing. Nothing bad. The veins in Irene's neck stood out as she squared her jaw. Her thoughts smothered her. Nothing like a child, a smooth body with a trusting head, falling into the hands of a seller. Farina. And then more terrible hands tying her or forcing their huge dirty member into her helpless innocence. Igor tried to sell her. Milli, you stupid bitch. He had a man there ready to pay. I saved her.

You're lying, Milli said, scared by Irene's angry face.

Igor's as hard as Florence is. He was already counting the money. Everyone knows it's true.

Irene wasn't going to list what everyone knew. Wouldn't waste her breath on a world that was lower and more degraded than the one they found themselves in. Wouldn't add more chaos to the steel truth she had laid down. The bottom of her feet burned, scorched by the sidewalk, where she had kicked off her shoes. It was like touching coals, taking an oath.

Milli couldn't find the socket for the plug. She could see Farina in a box or a cage. The box was closed. Suddenly she could smell the piss and bodies of them when they were kept below deck after they left Lagos. A young woman had died then. She hadn't known her, but the feeling of when the word passed around was throat-closing. They had thrown the body off the ship. Milli didn't know what she could have done to

244

have made it any different. Any easier. The curled up woman had been stabbed. The freighter with its Nigerian flags flipping like ribbons had pulled away and there was no Aki holding Ramada's hand. They have Jesus in Italy. Hadn't she said that? The phrase made her wrinkle up her lips as she looked at the round white table they were sitting at. When they stayed below for eight days, unsure of what would happen next, with the friend of the girl who died moaning like her mind broke down, Milli didn't know if she should pray to Jesus or if she had to pray to the gods of her land who she had offended. The dead woman had disappeared and no one knew her once she fell into the waves and their own lives were crammed into that small space below deck. It was Wole's kindness, his experience at staying calm through trouble, that got her to think about her own troubles. And the ocean they could see through the port hole day after day, it often covered the window with water so that they saw the dreaded thickness of water and being under the ocean all around.

Irene appreciated the fear rising in Milli's face. She liked seeing it grow, finally, *Dio Mio*, waking her up and pulling Milli to a place where the woman could actually understand the logic in what took place.

She's safe, Irene said, as a truck roared by.

Ready with your order, *signorine*? a young man asked. Irene looked at Milli and Milli shrugged.

Two beers, Irene said.

Italian beer? She nodded.

You can get her back, Irene said, not stopping to sweeten her voice. Fear was singing at the table. The woman still hadn't asked her what happened, with her thin slumped shoulders. Fear was singing like a frantic violin. It was not that Milli was weak. But it reminded her of other times with Milli. Vague and dreamy. Not pouncing on the fact. In some ways, Milli would never be able to be independent. Like now. She was like a stone that had been rubbed too smooth, too thin. And was like glass tossed into the air. Skip, skip, skip was the way a stone hopped on water. Not touching. Skimming and floating. Like Milli.

Milli, wake up, Irene said, impatient now. She was late and could just about imagine Igor's wrath.

Irene didn't want to be hit or humiliated. Didn't want to justify herself to that pimp. He was short two girls. He would be intractable. His eyes, bloodshot with fury.

Irene regretted that she was thinking through the mind of a man who could hardly present himself as representing anyone. Igor who was impossible to know or understand. But Milli wasn't anyone you could lean on. Milli, who had made Irene feel ripped out like an oak pulled up, torn from the ground as she left Farina, while the child's eyes burned on her back. Just thinking about Farina made Irene endure a pain that was as close as she had ever been to jealous rage.

Milli, you must go and get her from the nuns.

I knew it, Milli said, waving her hands like they would fly. I knew it. You always wanted to do that. To take her from me. Even when she was born.

Irene grabbed one of those flapping hands. You don't have time to accuse me. This is Farina's life.

You're hurting me.

You're hurting yourself, Irene said standing up. Then she sat down, turning like a slow graceful screw.

Are you going to get her?

I don't know.

Milli, it's not the time to stop, to lie down in the grass, to give up. To slow down. To sit with your legs crossed. Not now Milli, but I can't help you. You must do it yourself.

TWELVE

C OME OVER HERE, she said to Ramada, seeing
him still standing near the road. She didn't like him
still standing there, but didn't like how Adele and
Mubiki walked right past with their baskets on
their heads, snooty and not answering. That's why she'd followed him. That is what had been destroyed along with the
torched villages. Believing even in a boy's reasoning had been
changed. A vulture sat in the banyan nearby. She knew the bird
was waiting, and who knows why because vultures were not shy
or polite, for the fish putrifying in the green and oozy shallows.

What do you have in mind? she called out to the young human figure. There were mats of mosquitoes around him. Boy,
we don't want trouble here and if you are smart you'll go home
and get there before dark. She knew if she said much more,
people would come out and scold her. They were like the dust.
All around and nothing. They were determined not to make
concessions for all their suffering. They didn't want trouble,
even that which came from helping someone from the same
tribe cross their lands. The priest no longer came every week.
The compass for the order of things was broken. The military
had broken them into powder. People were like dust. Worn out.

Ramada didn't want to ask the woman with the orange

t-shirt anything except was he right to think Bori was just a few hours ahead. He was hungry. He was damp everywhere in his socks and pants, his shirt. But he would only take food if it was offered. Her eyes didn't look like that. At the meeting, there would not be much more than broken chairs but certainly they would share the little they had.

She had thought about him. Watched him get up. Leave. He was the same boy going through her mind. He looked like a lost cause. Or she thought, maybe I am.

What are you doing here? She asked, again.

I'm going to a meeting in Bori.

Oh, she said, rolling her eyes to the grey sky above and waving her hands.

Oh. Boy, go home. Don't you know that they only want to kill boys like you? Then they come here and take our chickens. And smash our houses. You should be in school. Our school is shut. That is where the crime has gone deepest. They are taking you boys and letting you turn your heads into ideas that will get you killed. I went to school and they taught us what was our neighbor's was not ours. And they taught us Muslim law was not our law. But they have it in the north. In our land. They taught us British law was just and look, she said pointing to the horizon and red scorching flame. So I say it's the Ten Commandments. Do you know those? Thou shalt not kill. And look, she said, pointing to the red flame on the horizon to the west again. This is our wealth. This river full of the black curse. I'm pretty near crazy, she said, laughing loudly and slapping her knee. I don't think I make the sun come up. I don't. But someone does and school is school. There is where you should be.

Ramada looked at his shoes that were no longer white. They were big and on the long walk had rubbed until he had blisters underneath and on his heels. He didn't want to ask her for water. Her hands looked dried and old. She was not like Sabula who polished her nails and put oil on her hands. He thought for a moment to tell her, what he told his friend, Tiku, that the Ogoni had to go back to their old ways. He wanted to tell her about Ken Saro-Wiwa, but her scowl stopped him. The flame and who owned it was what he was going to hear about in Bori. A helicopter's drone made him look up.

Where's your mother and father that you are out here?

Ramada found it funny hearing that sentence said so indignantly, like he had parents who told him what to do. He stood up as straight as he could. And lied right over the unexpected hole she had poked into. They want me to go. They think it's a good cause. And no one heard him, not even he himself, thinking mother, thinking father, where might Widu be, since she never wrote. And his father was a little grinning head, holding some utake, standing with his uncles in a photo Sabula tossed out. They do, he said, telling her to mind her own business. My parents want me to go.

The thin woman threw her hands in the air and laughed. Oh that's good. A good cause. Boy, I heard on the radio this morning they are arresting anyone that they think is a resister.

Who do your parents think you are? Samson? Who would let a boy like you, without even whiskers on his chest, let him walk to a meeting where there is only going to be trouble?

Ramada didn't like hearing the words. Didn't like being mocked. A rust colored mutt, hearing her raised voice, came towards Ramada, baring his small yellowed teeth. Ramada jumped.

The woman bent over in laughter and slapped her knees. How are you going to fight if a dog scares you? The vulture rustled on the low branch and shuddered its wings.

He's hungry too, she said. That bird would eat the dog if he could. It's growing dark here. It's strange. Don't listen to your parents if they told you to go and fight. Go home, she said. Look at this place. It's dry. It's dead. Without another word, she turned and said almost shouting, It is a mighty bad world when the elders and one's parents aren't just either. Go to school, she said, but not where they teach you lies. This black oil has done us no good. Her heart felt unable to say what could help a boy who thought he could be a soldier. The helicopter now was stirring the trees. She wanted to pick up her feet and get out of the unpleasant way that the blades churned the air. Away from the eyes studying them like the vulture. But she would stand, making certain the soldiers didn't come down low to make the boy run like a joke in their game.

The black curtain shirred by two ropes, one on each side, dropped and it was time to give the sign to lift it off the hole so that the sun could begin pouring in the window and pass through the bronze ellipse fastened underneath the window. Nothing was precisely the same. Fixed first by Toscanelli, the measurements had been redone and the marble and brass relaid on the floor in Ximenes's time. Although the gnomon screw marks were there, there too, calculations put it slightly to the left of the original holes. And European Summer Time added another shift.

Melandri signaled to a technician on the walkway nearest to the latern to lift the curtain. He looked at his watch. The crowd was there. Florentines for the major part. Ester Bobanelli looked fresh, waving from a middle row. People were even standing against the walls. The slides were in the carousel like racing cars.

Not many knew to look but he did as the curtain rose and the light popped through, high, still far from hitting the marble floor and its meridian, but soon to travel toward the north chapel of the cathedral. It was light darting like a pointer, a wild pointer on the wall. But no one knew to look for it yet. They waited for explanations, orders.

How full the dome was. Vasari's universal judgment, the

neat rush of divisions, angels and the figures from the apocalypse, hell and the universal moment of measuring. An astonishing cast of characters. One phrase only, in the fresco. *Ecco, here is humanity.* The ray would be all they could work on in the hour. The frescoes would be something not even to mention. They were amazing and took, if one thought about it, so much math to meet the curves and to smooth out the saved and condemned bodies across the concave surfaces. The dome itself contained calculations that still were not understood. Technical mysteries of how they bridged the *vastissimo* space. But the solstice was today's chapter. Melandri settled on the American's face. He was holding a pencil, like a good schoolboy ready to take notes. Melandri could foresee the eager face crowding him and fingering books on his office shelves. If he asked an intelligent question—after all, that was the pleasure of ideas—his request would be easier to fulfill.

Farina was barely visible in her chair. She was not eating.

Sister Gertrude was clicking a glass.

Not now, the Mother Superior indicated over the hum. No more speeches now.

Sister Gertrude leaned over and, instead of tapping Farina on the head, she brought her fingers together, pinching them and separating them, opening and lightly soaring as if they were a butterfly. She made an arc over the child's head, hoping that she would smile.

Some of you know her name is Farina.

Her eyes squinting through glasses searched the child's alert face for a smile but there was none. Solemn. Listening. Then looking down and sighing at the beans.

Mother Superior Benedetta shook her head more clearly. Why couldn't the meal hurry along and be over? Sister Gertrude had never distinguished herself as a rebel. But that seemed to be where she was going, as the trolley stopped to stall the clatter of the dishes. She was heading, without any sense, into undoing the neat guidelines that existed for this kind of case. The ice cream in cups was being brought in.

There are so many sides to our mission, Sister Gertrude said. But the deepest gifts are those that make us open, like children.

Although as novitiates we interpret our lives as before and after marrying Christ, this morning in the face and the talents of this child, we are at a point where there will be a before and after. We need time to understand the child we have been sent. For her. It is not up to our will to decide. She may not be inevitably a citizen of Florence. Or even of our Lord if we insist that our Lord can be called only by one name. If the bright faced nun had been drinking Chianti she could not have been racing and trampling over more treacherous borders that had signs saying stop.

I myself—and she felt a blush passing through her body, while the clatter of the business of clearing plates—Sister Monica, scraping loudly and making the dirty forks and spoons crash into the box to hold them—resistance, looking down, some even standing up to leave, while she decided to go on—I don't have any answers. Yet this child has come and spoken to me, starting from her name.

How did it come to be Farina?

Farina suddenly looked up. She put down the spoon large enough to lift a *rosetta* roll she hadn't eaten.

Her eyes brightened, hearing her name. An answer came shooting out, her tongue happy and sure, without being able to stop it.

My mamma, she said, her strong voice surprising the nuns who were still sitting.

Farina knew the story. Knew part of the story. The part Milli told her—often when she was sitting on her little chair. You have a good name. And it comes from the earth and from the sky.

How many times Milli had told her the story of her name. In different ways, sometimes leaning on the bed. In my land manioc comes up from the ground. With a hoe. And it is crushed. Pounded. But *farina* grows in the air. It bends and waves. And its wheat seeds are gold, and tiny, and what's left is blown away by the wind.

Farina is an important name, Milli said, sometimes serious, sometimes smiling. It brings luck. It's like plenty. Like wealth. Milli'd rub her fingers as if money was in them. Farina knew that. Knew what wealth was too. It was Milli's big black purse. It was like the castle in her book. Like the girl who had mean sisters.

Farina knew her name was important as bread and she felt proud. Her name was cakes with balls of sugar in shops. She felt like a queen when her mother told her Farina was a name from Italy, from the place she was born in. Its suggestion came from the river as the sun came up on the day she was born. Farina had no idea that people thought her name was odd, that it made them shake their heads once they heard it. She didn't know that Farina, as the name for flour, made her absolutely outside of the Florentine path and creed.

Farina had seen snow once in Florence. That was the best time she had ever had with her name. Milli had said, that's your name, that's flour when it gets cold. Your name is a heaven name. A whirling name that no one can stop.

Farina felt the drops of flour pricking her face and melting. Sharp little pieces, icy and then water. From the sky and from the earth, that's your name. Farina lifted her face upwards, put her tongue out, and the flour fell, white and flurrying, making her shut her eyes and close her mouth as the pricks of ice kept falling. In my land, flour doesn't come from snow, half the year, like it does in Italy, Milli said. Manioc comes from dirt. All the year. From hard, hard work. My mamma, Farina, she hoed. She pounded.

We all have experienced empty times in prayer, Sister Gertrude said, haunted for a minute. I am not the only one who feels dry periods so long that even a black insistent fly is welcome as a sign of life.

Mother Superior was standing up. Even if there was foment, she thought, it was useless because at a certain hour Guidice Pingello would come and the law would take over.

I wish you all would leave the table. Otherwise there is little reason for this early lunch. You have tasks, the floor must be swept and washed, and don't forget the judge will join us at four. As you know, I need to rest. So I shall go, she said, looking astonished as she eyed napkins still not rolled into their metal rings and sisters who didn't seem about to be pushed from the room. Sister Gertrude, she said, adding nothing more but hoping to freeze her in her mistake.

Milli, Irene said, I'll take you as far as the door.

Wait, Milli said, sure for the first time that Irene might really do that. Walk her to the door with the nuns who had her child.

What am I supposed to do?

Are you asking me? I made this path for you, Irene said, suddenly recognizing it. This is like I built you a bridge. A life. Igor is no place for you.

What am I supposed to do with the nuns?

I don't know but they will find you papers. They will make you promise to believe in God. Your mother already did that.

Who has Farina? What did she say when you left her?

She said to bring you as soon as I could.

Do they expect me to raise her? Am I supposed to get on a boat and go home?

You're free, Irene said amazed that Milli could really leave the dark compound.

And if I left her there?

Irene finished her beer, lifting the glass, tilting her head and letting it all flow down in a rush.

Was she supposed to sit courteously while the crazy lady mouthed her craziness?

What if I leave her? Give her to them. What if I gave her over to them and they found her a place, like you thought, a place with books, with manners? Then Milli could barely breathe.

Irene looked at her watch. I'll take you there.

No, Milli said. Even her name. I wanted something good for her. Different from me.

Irene wanted to talk about Harcourt. You can take her back to your father. To your son. You can get out of here and find a way again.

I can't, Milli said. I have gone too far, now. You gave her away. I don't see how I could get her back.

Milli, Irene said, forget your scars. You can't leave her there.

I always wanted something good for her. You can't imagine, Irene, the house my father lives in. You can't imagine how I could feel going back there with who I am. Who am I? she said as tears filled her eyes. Maybe I must give the child a chance.

Milli, Irene said, you are out of your mind.

I have a son who I dream of. I want to see Ramada.

Milli, she can go to school. She can know her brother.

Milli shook her head. You did it. You took her there. For her own good.

Sister Gertrude stopped. Nodding her head, she wished the Mother Superior a deep rest, and then watched her slowly take her painful walk past the long table. Inside herself she felt no confusion.

Farina's writing on the wall burned with divine energy like the burning bush. A clear command. A gentle reminder of faith as waiting.

In this very convent centuries ago, children were put in a wooden box and a wheel was turned. The child passed from the outside, the blue sky, maybe the plague, maybe bruises and blows, but in one turn of the wheel the child entered another world.

I don't have any answers, she said. I cannot say many things because our guest has eyes and ears as sharp as radar beams.

Sister Gertrude looked down on Farina who had let her ice cream melt into a chocolate pond. She was listening to the heavy nun and watching all the faces around her. The lady who had let Irene go was listening. Farina was moving back and forth three sizes of spoons. She had never seen so many spoons and glasses. And white bowls and big plates.

We all know about drying dishes, pantry cleaning. For the last months I have done all the paper work for what our meals cost, what our soap costs. We've all been pitching in hoping to lighten the load of illness in this moment. I have done what I could of my share, but nothing whispered or prodded me with an inner meaning. Until I saw the writing on the wall that this little child did.

Sister Gertrude lowered her voice.

I don't have any answers. But we don't need to provide the answers, she said folding her hands across her breast. Imagine this as a crossroads, our little stopping off place, here in a city. Our work is education. It is frightening, absolutely terrifying, what can be the results of the before and after of this child. Imagine the parable of the talents. What is inside a child? What could we possibly do if we decide to change her life? If she finds a new home. She was left with us. Her mother left her. But she may be back. And if her way of life isn't easy or the best, what should we do but hold out our support. This child already is someone. Someone in the clearest sense of our Lord's plan. And any break will sow chaos, not that she can't overcome it. How can we help her?

She looked out at the nuns whom she would have expected to approve. Sister Mary Catherine was yawning like a cat. Sister

Morena wanted to say something. She seemed to agree.

Imagine this crossroad, Sister Gertrude said, as the trolley pushed by. She put her index finger down for Farina's hand. She hoped she would grasp it. I know there is illness and shortness of temper, fear, even in our small community, of admitting that we are afraid to say she can stay with us. Afraid to say that she doesn't even need to be baptized. How can we if she has a faith already?

Yet, murmured Sister Catherine, shaking her head in disapproval. Not today, but surely tomorrow, she does need baptism. You aren't offering her anything unless you offer her the cleansing of her original sin.

Farina didn't like the tension and worry gathering as the women shook their heads. The tablecloth was so long and white. There were still many faces wearing glasses at the table. She slid from her chair. She looked up at Sister Gertrude. The tablecloth followed her slide. It tugged some and the steel cup with her ice cream toppled.

It didn't break, Farina said, quickly, in a high voice, putting her hands behind her back and wincing before Sister Gertrude could do anything to stop the chocolate pool darkening the cloth.

Sister Gertrude picked her up, heaving her into her arms. She speaks, she thought, feeling moved by the thin ribs she had already felt lifting her in the bath. She knows more than we do. What if one of our sins is that we believe we have the right culture. Our words and prayers must serve an essence deeper than that. What brought her to the door is just poverty. The poverty that's always been. The poverty that held my parents with fifteen children to having us all shift rocks hoping to find soil. The child is tied to people who have carried her in a good way.

He hit the key before he could stop. The email flew off in the direction of *Professoressa* Bobanelli. She had already answered. Given him an appointment. What he needed to say to her was: Thank you and I'll come at nine. That's all. The assorted notes that had just flown off were not for her eyes. Yet something had made them escape from his fingers.

He had a file for 'tree bark.' Had a file for Ötzi, the Stone Age traveler who had surfaced from a glacier melting along the modern states of Italy and Austria. Ötzi wore a cloak of bark. He had seventeen kinds of wood in his arrow sling. And there it was again, another voyager last night, wearing nearly the same bark cloak five-thousand years later. A beggar asleep on the far wall of the Duomo. Who knows what the *Professoressa* would make of the file for 'Feet.' Roots and feet. Feet rooting like great trees. Celts. Hindus. Cosmic root/energy systems. He himself didn't know where the links worked.

Piero had been standing at the cathedral to revisit the Madonna of the almond shell. The beggar had been lying against the wall, underneath the marble sculpture of Mary ascending. He thought, until he noticed the beggar, that he needed to check the shell to see if it displayed the naturalistic markings of an almond. Just like confirming that the buckles holding the chestnut beams in the nine circles of Brunelleschi's dome were made of oak. The dome was lined with forests. But the wood was buried. Hidden inside, ring within ring, it bound the whole structure.

Yet it was the beggar who struck him. Those crusted cracked feet were not an illusion. He found it difficult to use the word destiny. The feet held a life of experience. And where in the constellation was birth?

Piero could feel his mother standing behind him. He felt her shadow fall across his heart. Your father wants you to sit at the table. You must try not to upset him so.

Pushing back his sleeve, he saw that his watch said five-twenty.

Charlotte was more than twenty minutes late. Don Gorovitch had wondered before what had ever made such a handsome lady look at the likes of him. Women like Charlotte were late. They had noses that needed powder and who knows what else took up their time. He had never imagined someone like Charlotte would look at him. Yet from the beginning, he had wondered if she was serious, or if it was just curiosity or boredom. She had one small side of her hitching up her skirt asking to be lifted into the high cab that seemed capable of enjoying herself right to her core, but it was a very small part of her. She wouldn't ever be vulgar.

Meeting her in the mornings, out on the highway, was the most unlikely scene. And largely it was innocent. Having a woman who went to ladies clubs and concerts sit there beside him, trying to settle her hips into the seat. Trying to find a comfortable place to hold her breasts high. He had imagined that sooner or later, her friendly interest, her questions about life on the road, might dry up. He had imagined that on a beautiful peaceful morning like this one, with the sun almost up and floating near the grass, the trucks heading out to Iowa, and the early cars heading back into Minneapolis and St. Paul, this reckoning might come. A day when she simply would not show up. And leave him with his stiff shoulder and his bad leg.

It was a strange thing, how it had started with her coming out of church with him sitting on the curb because his truck broke down, almost from TV, her purse dropping and him with dirty hands picking up keys and lipstick, papers and a brush, hairpins and how from a minute when their eyes met that she too seemed to enjoy, from then on, at least sometimes, his company. As odd as it was, there were smiles on her face and he couldn't say that she minded being with him, though the word lover had not surfaced. But he was bold enough to think it was there, in her mind. The way she would kiss and squeeze back. It was like TV all the time he had to try to figure out what was next, or in his case, how not to offend. With her talking just when he thought she might let go. It was a challenge except when he felt she was putting him on.

They did converse. They talked and their conversations opened up worlds as different as day and night. She was the kind of lady he had imagined was a lady. Different from a school teacher. Less strict. More of an actress. She'd said it more than once, nodding her head at him. Just think that we live on different sides of the city, and spent nearly our whole lives not knowing each other. Not just each other, but I was taught to think that labor unions were dangerous and that workers on the whole had no discipline. And that Catholics drank too much. It makes me blush, she said. Such hard work you do. All grocery shelves are stocked because of your work.

Maybe he loved her voice, even more than her eyes. Her perky discovering voice, insinuating that he had talent. The way she listened when he told her how drugs for many drivers were part of the job. How he decided not to carry a gun, although he had been beaten up on the Pennsylvania pike. His other women had their own terrible hard luck and didn't find his road life much to admire. They knew about scars, the law. She was an unbelievable woman to happen, like he was some big deal. She made him feel like a sheriff when he wasn't too embarrassed to admit it. Her own husband, she told him, had lacked physical courage. That was believable, although he didn't like hearing it. He didn't like thinking that Charlotte had not been tended to and fussed over by a man with balls.

The steady stream of trucks and cars was building up, moving towards rush hour. He couldn't say he was surprised. She didn't owe him anything, but it had been the most unlikely occasion. Having a woman on the other seat, who was pretty damn good. She let him guide her through the gears. But then, those diamond rings flashing, she pressed down hard. She liked it and she could shift pretty smoothly. Better than he would have expected.

Better not think too much, Don said to himself. He was disappointed that she hadn't told him. Disappointed that she hadn't had the courage to say it was over. Unlikely. That the trip they were planning, maybe this summer, with her doing some of the driving out to the coast through Mount Rushmore, through Death Valley. It was just a dream.

I guess you weren't as courageous as I thought, he said looking at his watch again. He was loaded with forty tons of spring water destined for Iowa. He didn't like carrying water. Transporting water was not unstable but it felt that way. It was like transporting her, he thought. She was only going to drive for a few miles and then they would have had bacon crisp and scrambled eggs somewhere. Coffee and rolls. And then she would have called a taxi for the ride back to her car. He had the ten dollar bill to press into her hand all ready in his shirt pocket. Folded in four. That should include a tip, he always flourished as he tucked her in.

You don't owe me anything, he said to himself, opening the door to his high cab. He shifted hands to accommodate his plastic bag with a new cassette. Pavarotti someone had told him was very good. An especially warm Italian tenor and Italy was where her daughter lived. He'd planned it as a surprise. Even for himself. He'd kind of always wanted to see Florence. And maybe he'd imagined someday they might have even gone that far.

The long lines of cars were thickening and covering the lanes in all directions.

It was hard to take. He turned on the engine, pumping the accelerator until the exhaust could have gotten him a fine. His fancy socks were too thin for his shoes. Time to put on Johnny Cash. To let in his music and the broken-heartedness that was part of life on the road. To stereophonically wrap himself up in the tried and true words of his people. The American class who felt things and carried the country on their broken backs and got beaten up. And somehow endowed the rich as being good. Maybe Charlotte would call. Or maybe she found him foolish and found herself foolish. And, he thought dryly, putting in the tape, waiting for the inevitable words to envelop him, he could always call her. Try to fill in that silence and recapture the sincerity he had told himself was a mutual attraction. And no, it wasn't false. It couldn't be. Charlotte was not a lady who was just curious. She was not a pigeon feeder. Or a stray-dog collector who had tired of tossing scraps to a flea-bitten one she'd discovered in front of the church.

His brain urged him on and his body responded. The danger was extreme until he was right side up. Inch and fall back, brace and squeeze on soil where pebbles knocked his spine. Thump and hurl. Hurl and not rest. Virgil rolled once again and found his face smashed down. With his front legs pushing, his back legs and his belly touched the hard earth. He was back on all fours. Back. The world below and the light above. His head up, with dirt scratching his eyes.

The prong of his front talon climbed into the fold of skin. He gripped it and stroked, pushed, nudging and coaxing the old covering from its attached place until it was loose and free to be eaten. Urgent, clearing space over his nostrils, skin was tumbling, tangling. Coming off. In light. His brain hived light tapping him somewhere. The one time day was lengthening. Virgil knew what he could know. His entry out of his skin was over his eyes still. He could die of thirst. Sunlight was abundant, signaling, falling somewhere over the hole. Virgil labored and twisted. Tugged.

Underneath him was a rough piece of metal. Poking up, its jagged edge pierced. Virgil dragged himself beyond the sensation of sharpness. Away from the blunt broken cutting tip of wheel-spoke that reached through a surface after centuries of not rolling and bumping along, pulled by a Mongolian horse.

THIRTEEN

I'LL TAKE YOU to the front door, but then I'll go, Irene said. Once you know where Farina is, you can sing your own siren song of tears. The idea of turning on her phone again and hearing Igor scream at her was repulsive. Yet she was ready to go back. To leave the stage to Milli. The tension of the morning was so bad she almost looked forward to a client. To drifting off, to climbing onto a shelf in herself and looking at the poor man pulling up his pants and taking the money, and washing herself off, without any thought that it mattered. That it was anything more than a lapse that barely distressed her in comparison with this.

This drama caused by a friend was a trial different from her work. It roused her feelings. And if it went well, it would take her friend away. Hastily remove Milli, not just from sharing their cheese and onions and loaves of bread, take her off not just from the rare afternoons in the market, lifting a necklace, or the river times where a cigarette and its smoke rose and twirled into a certain kind of chatter that was only with her. She and Milli knew stories about their beginning lives. The Niger River and the forests near Bucharest. They knew flashes that, maybe, were better forgotten but if they were forgotten, Irene's parents and Milli's son would fall into a bottomless pit where no one had a memory. No horses. No drowning. She and Milli knew what it was like to have rain coming down their backs soaking their clothes with a man on top and other times so easy that the man might even carry a clean white handkerchief. Irene shut her emotional thinking down. She could imagine Igor's face, his foxy teeth, and probably he would force her to pay Milli's debt. Hold her responsible or try to make her think she was.

You're a monster friend, Milli. Letting me pay. Pay for the beers. Letting me take the weight of Farina. And Igor. What shall I do about Igor? Have you thought about that? Irene waited for Milli to protest, to fill in the silence, but she feared from the blank look on her face, her eyes fixed, that the woman was hardly capable of getting to her feet and walking to the nuns.

Milli said, take me there. Irene, take me. Then I'll think hard and try to clear my head. This is so big. You just take me.

Luigi made it obvious to Gian Franco that he had nothing to add. That it bothered him to talk about crime and certain judges and certain bankers. By turning his head, walking fast and three steps in front of him, Luigi signaled without saying anything or being offensive. But he wanted to turn on his phone. To call Maria Grazia back. To exchange a few intimacies, under the blue sky and with her sitting captive at her desk. He couldn't wait to turn the phone on and say things he hadn't said in more than a month, let them flow into her ears only, and if someone was sitting in front of her, too bad. She could blush and he hoped she would be pleased hearing affectionate words meant for her only. Preparatory words, courting words, cooing irrational dirty words that he hoped might let her allow him back into her bed.

Luigi, how long are you going stand there? What else is there to do? Maybe we could have a few beers in town.

Gian Franco was crowding him. Now fussing with the flowers that had been added to by Diniza. The irises, nearly wilting, were lovely tissues of purple and white. A gift from a natural heart. Gian Franco was oppressive. He had no idea what he wanted, really. He was hoping to put their destinies together and to convince himself he would not be punished. Probably he would not. The judges in Florence certainly were divided among those who wanted this cleaning up and those who didn't.

A car with a loudspeaker on top, playing a record, pumped its message into their surroundings. Sometimes they were political messages, sometimes announcements of party *festas*. The recording that was scratchy and blaring held the economy of scale from his childhood. *Attenzione.* We are in the neighborhood and can sharpen any kind of knife, those for meat, those for cheese, scissors. We fix gas leaks on the spot and repair umbrellas. *Attenzione.* We are in the neighborhood and can sharpen

Gian Franco smiled suspiciously. Who do you think are their customers?

It struck Luigi that he was hearing the fading sound of tradition. Imagine repairing an umbrella. The offer rang like a chime as he heard the words for the third time. The fifty lire blade that held the umbrella spokes up. The twenty lire spring that sometimes wore out. Umbrella shaft repair. The same countryside that once poured milk into buckets and took it home to boil. An active sense of scale and measure. Real respect for cost. The politics, too, that had people roasting pigs and sides of beef on spits and pouring wine while someone played the accordian, local politics all used to be like that. Someone played a record and someone knew he had to respond. Either it was the enemy camp or it was one's own. But the system was known. People held to group roots. There was a chasm, real and deep, between the Right and the Left. Workers went to the workers' festival and drank the wine of a future society where everyone had a chance to hold one's head up. To proclaim the essential role hands and backs and hard work played. His father had objected. Being careful not to bring up all that the funny nostalgic touch of the record suggested to him, Luigi decided it was time to push Gian Franco out.

I need to pray, he said, already imagining the stupor.

Come on, Luigi. You?

I do, he said, putting his head down and not being sure of much except that Gian Franco had to leave and that this gesture would irritate, no, insult him deeply.

Farina was walking on her own feet down the white hall. Silently moving her hands and her mouth as if she were talking to herself, suddenly the little girl started to cry. She didn't like the rush of feeling making her sad and lost. But she felt frightened by the long time she had been in the white walls and at long tables without anyone she knew. The children in the mountain and jungle pictures on the walls were far away, even above her head. And the strange faces, too glad, too close.

Farina had never cried in her life until her chest went up and down, until her legs shook. Never choked on her tears until there was no more air. Never felt uncertain that she could release whatever was inside because she didn't know where she was or what was expected. She moved blindly into a slippery state that was not freedom or helplessness, but a protest against the unbearable change that the new women all around her didn't understand.

Farina opened her mouth and when Sister Gertrude bent down, first for the child, but secondly to contain the piercing sound that was traveling in the halls, waking up the Mother Superior, jangling her nerves, the old face with the big nose and teeth clicking close to Farina's face made her howl, unable to bring the other world back.

Farina. Don't.

Sister Gertrude thought of picking the child up, but her insistent touch infuriated the thin little girl. Her rage exploded and she screamed in a series of sharp staccato cries. When Sister Gertrude tried to get her up, reach under her arms, Farina kicked and moaned, threw herself on the ground and thrashed. Her back went rubbery and heavy, squirmy and limbs kicking.

Several faces frowned down above her and they looked not like Milli, not like Irene. They didn't frighten her, but they were like big dogs standing on top of her. They had glasses and when Sister Gertrude bent again, Farina tried to pull the frames off her face and throw them on the floor.

You're having a tantrum, Sister Gertrude said, growing more insistent as Sister Maya came running down the hall.

Sister Morena leaned over into the huddle. Watching the kicking, pounding imp full of energy, she offered to help get her up off the floor.

Hold her legs and I'll take her arms.

Farina couldn't stop crying. She would have bitten anything she could sink her teeth into just to hold on. She raised her voice.

Ma. Ma. And she sobbed.

You're hysterical, Sister Gertrude said, shaking the kicking whirlwind.

Stop or I'll slap you.

The hand passed strongly across Farina's cheeks. It left red marks on a flushed wet miserable face.

Farina raised her voice to a higher scream.

Take her outside, Sister Maya commanded in alarm. Mother Benedetta is trying to sleep. Not one of the nuns could laugh, although the child was so small that her explosion was easy to forgive. Or it would have been if any of them felt less frozen, fearful of accusations of selfishness.

I won't ask, Sister Gertrude said, not surprised by the raw

force in the wriggling body. Farina, I remember. I do, she said putting Farina's legs out in back and holding her tightly under her arm, like a bed roll that was moving and resisting.

Farina, I remember feeling as worried as you do. Heaven will help us if I can't. But you are like a pig, a squealing pig, she said tightening her grip and putting more weight on her hip.

Going towards the door, suspended under Sister Gertrude's arm, Farina screamed until every room in the convent heard the sound—a voice beseeching, tired and tried but not giving up. Protesting, violating every room, it entangled the nuns.

Awful to be awakened.

Awful to hear fright so unlike prayer.

Awful to imagine the engine of untamed energies, the will needing to be tamed.

The truth. This is the truth, Sister Gertrude thought, her arm raw from the child's vehemence. Imagine the pain of unanswered truth moving through these protected halls. Abandonment. That is the truth of this terrible sound.

Farina couldn't cry much more without choking or throwing up her lunch. She stopped crying before Sister Gertrude reached the door because she was afraid and confused. She stopped making her body rigid, and sobbed as the sobbing became rhythmic. Her kicking the air was half-hearted.

Finalmente, Sister Gertrude said, lifting the child as the weight became all gravity and limp. The air outside would be good. Turning the body until her head and wet face rested on her shoulder. Just putting the child down outside and letting her recognize her surroundings might help. Do you want to go out? she asked, her hand firm on the knob. There will be sunshine and children. Eh, Farina?

Farina rubbed her eyes. She didn't want anything. She rubbed her eyes with her fists, gouging them in. She could hear her own sobs, feel them striking her and passing, striking her chest and passing. And that upset her into weeping again.

I'm sorry, Sister Gertrude said, smoothing her hair, patting the head on her shoulder. It's bright outside. The sun is as bright as fire. Maybe it's too bright for such swollen eyes. Too hot for such an upset little face. Let's put some cool water on you. You've been strong and now you let all that business out. It's not so pleasant, hearing the truth, she said, nodding nervously. We don't hear it often enough, do we, Sister Morena? Truth catching us with its upsetting force.

Never had Farina cried so hard, sensing an end. An end to her mother. An end to the familiar grass she had known and the river. To the room and her bed. To the song she was often sung. It was past or lost. It couldn't be seen in the white halls. In the arms of the sister who had slapped her and was carrying her. Her mamma was not there to take her in her arms. To smooth her head. To cut an apple. Just these new heavy arms. Farina shut her eyes, not knowing what to do. The crying had left her. A cool empty feeling with no wishes but to sink made the room in front of her walls she couldn't resist. She wanted to go, softer and softer, away to sleep.

Bed, she said, to Sister Gertrude, who was talking to another nun. They were whispering in a little crowd. Some looked angry. Some ready to fight. They were different in their dresses, all the same blue color, from the dresses, black and spidery, her mother and Irene wore. In the sea of faces, there was worry. Sister Gertrude's face was kind.

Milli sat down on the steps not far from the convent, once Irene left her. Two hundred feet away was the door. The carved wooden door to the convent. Two hundred feet. She wondered if she could crawl on her hands and knees, slithering her stomach on the ground to reach it. Like a pilgrim, she had seen them, like abased humans, crawling up steps towards a church.

Let me in, she thought she heard. Let me lie in the shallow cool waters.

Milli looked over at the tall, shut wooden door. Now why did Irene have to go and do that? Put Farina inside. The door was more than she could do. Why had Irene asked her for more than she could do?

Milli stood up, shooed off the pigeons that were circling round her, and pulled back into shade where students were smoking and laughing, loudly, making nasty comments, she hoped not about her.

She could see the way they looked at her they were making fun.

All right, she said, spitting. I'm just as good as any of you.

Eyes, she saw wide eyes mocking.

I can read, she said. I've got an upper primary certificate from school.

More eyes. More ogling.

Why are you staring at me?

We're not, said one of the boys, feeling bold.

We're just seeing if we have enough money.

Milli stared hard at the face with a strong nose. Those awkward boys that were certainly not the worst. Most really wanted to know how it was done. And that was better in her opinion, healthy, almost like home, that they wanted to know their body inside a woman's. But here in the foolish excited pack of young people, it was out of turn. It was trashing her to everyone's delight.

Milli shrugged as if she hadn't heard. They were stupid and young. Not innocent but raw and conforming. Rich kids who had no idea that life on the earth was hard and humiliating.

She needed to think. She turned hoping to find shade. As she turned she heard someone say *puttàna*. Prostitute. And laugh as he kicked a can so that it bounced down the steps.

She nodded without plunging in. She would walk away smoothly, head up. What was another minute of acting in this cold city where she acted always on her high heels.

Where could she go? She didn't need to keep the wooden convent door in her sights. She could get back. The answer that she heard was the river. Sit in your space by the Mugnone. Sit and rest. In the dark shadows cast by the Duomo's vast white and orange eye seemingly closing off the street, Milli had the sensation, in a rush hurling towards her, that Farina was crying. Milli tilted her head and could hear it—angry and rabid, lonely, frightened. The sound whirled and tossed her into a panic. A long cry that was unending. A cry that said life on the earth was hard. It couldn't be Farina. Farina didn't sound like an angry witch. But the eerie sensation entered her skin.

Milli looked around in the crowd for a face that would match her child's. The cry was flowing and rising. It made her speechless. Made her forget those stupid students twirling her around.

The child was in her mind crying and screaming. She had held two children almost alone. And all their cries were in her head, alone. Only she could hear them, and her mother's voice, and Meniki's and she held nothing at all except bitterness. The cries of pain and desperation, and now this child screaming like she wanted to spit life out. It was a voice like a cave witch who was cursing those who had come upon her. Driving out those who had disturbed her plans.

I have to decide, Milli said, pushing herself to go faster.

When she pulled the damp plaid blanket out, put the newspapers down, the sun had warmed the grass and she wanted the heat to enter her body. Lying down, looking up at the sky, Milli felt unexpectedly calm watching the clouds move, at great speed. Vast white clouds that she never saw in Harcourt. White ships that made her know she was not of this place. The sky had its beauty here. She had even thought that, puffing on a cigarette, the morning Farina was born as the sun rose like a pink shell cracking open.

Useless to think. But she'd thought then, holding the tightly wrapped child, how'd she return to her father's house and all the same how she'd stay in Igor's. And the scale stayed even.

Luigi was alone at last. Gian Franco had stood for a certain unmeasured time and then he left in silence. Was he offended? Who knows if the ridiculous fellow was offended by the feigned show of reverence.

He was gone. And it had been a deliberate gesture on Luigi's part. Perhaps Gian Franco's too.

Allora, Luigi said, taking the phone out of his pocket. Nothing. Maria Grazia's was off again. Would the stupid game of cell phones ever end?

Attenzione. We are in the neighborhood and can sharpen any kind of knife, those for meat, those for cheese, scissors. The fellow must have made a loop around the area and was on his way back. Still making his pitch to the dead. Next I'll hear the woodpecker, Luigi thought. Then it will be time for my parents to speak.

Exhaustion, like the shade over the tomb, seeped in and quieted him. He didn't feel like joking any more. Didn't feel like supporting the tension of making any concessions. His head and what had taken over needed to be cleared out. He was not going to rush down even for Maria Grazia, another appointment or to fight with her. He needed time to get some perspective and to deal with the visions that had swirled into his consciousness since this morning.

The graceless marble tomb. It didn't even feel oppressive at the moment. The flowers hadn't altered it. It was the way the family was assembled like a neat set of books. Each a volume and each now relatively quiet, settling into an order that was about microorganisms as much as anything. It was about decomposition, if you will, going back into nature. At least, if you were not orthodox. It was about re-cycling. Except that the tombs were for appearances. For saying that one occupied some space in society and maybe in people's hearts. Graves claimed space for memory. And the bodies never reached the soil.

His grandfather Umberto had insisted on appending an idealized photograph. He had a straight posture that you could see even without including his stout chest. It was posed when he was in his thirties although he died close to eighty. The immunity to time suited him. There was nothing but purpose, determination, obsession showing in the slightly ridiculous fellow. No doubt showing, nothing but the hard chinned drive that propelled the only child of stockyard parents until he was the proud owner of factories.

Cesare died twelve years before the older man had unpredictably had Mazzini's "thought and action" carved into the marble. The workman finished chiseling the revisionist message after Umberto was buried and the high Mass with priests with a contingent from Argentina was behind them. And then came his mother's insistence on having the last word, some comment, to establish their place among the more pious Florentines. "Lo I am with you always, even until the end of the earth." Could she have possibly chosen that line without noticing how it fit her sense of herself? Even before the casket had been slid in, some people had raised this link, sympathetically, of course.

Luigi found much that was fascinating in focusing on his mother's ambiguous eyes gazing upwards in her photo to *nonno* Umberto's unjowled confidence. Cesare's blank frame must have been an adherence to a wish, but it was striking seeing two black and white portraits whose bone structures resembled each other and nothing, no image, on his father's compartment.

The lacuna was a message in its way. Even twenty years past the fact, the silence and solution of his father's withdrawal still showed between his mother's hatted pose and her father's face, younger by half than hers. By the gestures they both made to

273

convention and to the relatively powerful associations her family had within the Church and beyond it. Their similar physiognomies probably meant they could read each other's minds.

Luigi liked Cesare's lapidary stone without a photographic image. Liked the name and dates, factual, and no longer hanging on. His choice would be the same. No interpretation. No professorial pose. Yet the legacy he had been left by his father was rough. He had hooded his face. He was unknown as if some terror held him hostage. His portrait was like the brittle Carrara marble backing the empty frame. He wore the same tailored Cisternino suits chosen by most upper class Florentines but he was different from most men of his era and class.

No one thought would sum him up. But Luigi did remember, beyond the glass doors, how adamant he had been about staying away from the party members Umberto patronized. How he favored keeping the Christian Democrats with shadowy links to the last regime out of their permits and permissions. And how he lost over and over. The old links with the Fascists were as deep and effective as cypress roots and Umberto was not afraid of them even in Communist Florence. Cesare used to lament how he could guide neither Umberto nor his own son. How he hated, almost as much as Umberto's moves, every step Luigi took towards the Left. Now that was haunting. How Cesare opposed the Left hunched near the Communists. If he could see Florence today he might think he had more justification than ever to have worried. To have doubted and withdrawn. The Left, once the Berlin wall fell, looked as perplexed and unprepared as anyone. Their language became all at once like Latin. Used all across Europe but not current. And prone to the deals, the cronyism Cesare dreaded.

Cesare—the day version—acted like a soldier, a man who insisted on rules. Judging the fine-featured man by his rigidity—someone from the outside, like Gian Franco, but like he did, as well—his father seemed like a Fascist but he was not.

Not even as a joke would Cesare have shouted as Umberto often did—Underneath everyone still wipes his hands on a Black Shirt. No if anything, he was a liberal in favor of a secular state, like Mazzini.

That was stunning, really, now, when truths seemed to be so hard to pin down. Rules seemed so far from truth. Rules seemed far from anything. But there had always been different kinds of truth, Truth today. Truth yesterday. Yet—independent of that flux—there was such a thing as truth. Political or otherwise. How to establish it rationally was the way Luigi fixed his sights. Cesare, in his silence, probably saw things in that light all his life.

Luigi didn't waffle about truth when sampling a patch of cypress. Always, in the same way, it was the key. The whole question was how to establish parameters. If you picked up a thousand cypress cones, so what? That was the point. What were you seeing? A phenomenon of shedding shock? Or something natural? A thousand cypress cones could mean ten trees or twenty trees or fifty trees had dropped some cones. Or all of their cones. What told you if the area you were measuring had meaning, or if the wind was a factor, or if what you were collecting was the contents of a village dump where farmers left all the cones choking their courtyards now that prosperity meant they were not needed for fuel? There was truth in that patch of sampled forest, but what was it? How could you figure that out? And was it necessary, for science, what you thought of as a brilliant discovery? What he loved was finding order and linking it beyond one's own puny head by adding it to the community. Not cheap truth. Not proving a point, but something that uncovered what was there.

Luigi liked the slight echo with his father's unbending side. Cesare had strict ideas about what a purse business should be. Grade four leather. That's grade two. He had clear ideas about what an umbrella should cost, that's tin, not steel, and who should make it. He didn't want unending growth. And he thought business had truths that could not be measured only by incredible balance sheets of profits.

Someday soon, Tina, his mother's sister would die. Tina would not be buried in the box saved for her in Florence. An era would end. And the Lepre brand would leap into her children's hands. The life twist his father's life had taken would almost be over. He had put Luigi on a side road, taken him out of the running, like he himself. There were no phenomena to measure in his decisions. Cesare had quit. Even if you were trying to measure reform, Cesare had never succeeded.

Luigi had to admit his grandfather Umberto's omnipotent mustached face was still a kind of truth. An unashamed look that didn't hide his origins. You could see beyond the style of the photograph itself, a Fascistic side. He had served and succeeded, used every means possible extracted from the loose and desperate links he had to those who were rebuilding in those years. He used party hacks, Bishops, priests, used bribes, ingenuity, new language, old Fascists. He used it all mixed together as the whole world around Florence slowly pulled back from the brink of desperation, starving, dictatorship. He was tireless. Never accepting no. He was more than willing to put on a new set of heads, like the Romans did to their emperors' marble bodies, new looks to old concepts after having voted out Italy's king and the Communists. Just by a hair.

Giada's face was strong featured and not so much of that early era. The way her eyes lifted warily under her brimmed hat there was more evasion than pride. A masked fear. Poor thing. In a certain way, Luigi thought, not feeling proud, he and his mother were each other's slaves. They both served each other in response to Giada calling Cesare a cold man. Served each other because Cesare refused to put his face in focus beyond the shadows of a mask.

That was the thing. Not just about science or what was true

in Florence for politics and economics. Life and what people felt held different truths. Not what they believed like an ideology but what they felt. It was relativity but without the rigor of testing. Everyone could tell a truth in theory. Even if it was just a miserable market trick. Or an attitude broadcast to others in the family that sent them in the wrong direction. Cesare was considered, without taking any steps back, as a cold man. But it wasn't true.

The Florence flood of 1966. That was just that kind of revealing moment. A point in Florence that could not be erased and went as high in people's memories as the eight-meter mark in Santa Croce. It was a coming of age seeing those brown angry waters sweeping through the streets. It was a collective trauma, rushing to destroy everything precious in the city, and for those awful, swollen, pounding days everyone was pulled out of their personas and pushed into the muck of joining ranks.

Cesare emerged in those days in a different light. He, like the ripped up buildings and pouring currents, the sloshing madness in the streets, the rows of sunken cars, seemed a man whom no one in the house knew. Susan had been with Luigi as they went that first morning to present themselves as volunteers. Against all the rules in Florence, they were living together. Coming down the hill past Fiesole, on his scooter in the blinding rain, they didn't know if they could even reach the center. Umberto, on the first day the waters exploded over the bridges and terrorized the city streets, forced his workers to report for work. To sit at their muddy benches and thread their machines. His shacks were caked in mud and horridly damp from the rain, but back from the river in San Casciano. After those terrible days, his shop became a synonym for mud and profit. For forcing people to concentrate on piecework while the city cried out. Even in last night's dream, San Casciano was thick with mud. The dried goo and mold held on and returned every so often like a morbid revelation. Giada had backed her father, Umberto, while Cesare had insisted that workers should be free to help in the city or to stay home comforting their families.

Cesare lost. Luigi and Susan came across him in the Duomo piazza. Wet, exhausted beyond that crazed look he had when he drank. Another person, as well, from the man in tennis shorts, the immaculate one.

They had stood in a small circle, hunched under the pounding storm while deep water sloshed over their high rubber boots. Rats swimming. Broken tree branches. A bike zooming on its side past 'Or San Michele. And a pervading smell of heating kerosene, which created a sensation that one lit match held over the livid waters and the city would be set on fire.

Get out of this dangerous place. Go home. That was Cesare looking like the figure in Lear's storm.

We're okay. Luigi was raising his voice to get over the thrust of water rushing. Susan and I are at the Archives. You wouldn't want to see the manuscripts. It will take one-hunded years to get them back. The shelves are underwater and the *pergamene* swollen like sheeps' bellies.

How many are you?

Three hundred, at least. And you, *Babbo*? What are you doing here?

Look, he said, as the rain poured on his lifted face. The officials knew last night. They knew when the dam in Pontesieve was clogged. We were warned to protect our things. But the telephone lines were down. We knew you were on ground up there too high to be flooded.

You were at your mother's breast when the Germans bombed the bridges. You can't remember what the city felt like that morning. The planes came in thick swarms, breaking up the city by lighting and crashing the bridges, letting them fall into the Arno and the whole sky was black with planes and red with flames. It's like that now, his arm sweeping through the rain pouring down, this rendering, and his voice broke.

Susan had tried putting an umbrella over his head slick with water. He pushed her arm away. I don't need one of those. I don't need it, he said as a dog nearly as wet as he was swam past. He laughed. Shrugged. An umbrella. A Lepre umbrella.

You're soaked.

I don't need babying, he had said, pushing her away. Susan used to repeat that, how adamant he was, how crazed and resistant to the idea that he should need help.

There was such violence in nature that day, nature's unstoppable violence, and his father responded to it in a way Luigi never saw afterwards again. Umberto had stayed at his factory and Giada with Diniza had moved things from the basement to the apartment and its covered terraces. Susan and he remained there for a week. Later Giada would join with more than the myths, but it was all blurred that first day in the rains, when she stayed in the house and looked down on the desperation and Cesare, worked for more than thirty hours, running shifts of teams with shovels and pails and wheelbarrows, fighting back the scandal, the desperation, proud history and beauty challenged by the angry and vicious waters bashing Santa Croce.

Unshackled. Responding to some just purpose. The scent of his father not whiskey but sweaty, human, timelessly courageous. It mixed with the soft scent of iris, floating from Diniza's flowers. Clean-hearted Cesare was someone he missed.

Milli turned Farina around and around in her mind. Turned the small legs learning to walk from the Mugnone around to the Bonny River in Harcourt. Milli had never opened up the thought, seen it flat out, walking back into Aki's living room, with Farina, and Sabula raising her hands, had never felt being back again in that cement room.

Widu. That is what they would say. And would they turn off the radio and put down their spoons?

Widu.

Milli staring ahead at the stone wall covered in sunlight, the swift flow of water over the stones, could feel it wasn't that hard, the room with the electric wire running along near the ceiling. It was easy in its way, like tying a piece of blue ikat around her and making the knot at the breast. It was not that hard. Being back.

And Farina would get behind her at first, hold her head in her skirt, and then the brothers and sisters of her father's third wife would come forward. Bandela would be tall enough to teach her and maybe would take Farina into her own arms, like she must have Cochi and Kerila. She must have been asked so many times to wash their faces, add their numbers up.

She surprised the whole room and no eyes snapped at her. No eyes knowing much about Widu except where she had been. She'd pay the taxi and the neighbors hearing the word would rush over. She could stand in the cool damp living room and they would wait with shiny eyes for her stories. Italy's full of golden streets. Their churches are as tall as mountains but they have the cross like we have here.

Saying that the room would divide. Milli knew Sabula would click her tongue, and Aki would send her to the kitchen until he could tell his daughter that he allowed the goddesses in the living room. He allowed her shrines although he had once promised his first wife that the gray swept living room was for Christian gods.

Milli turned Farina around in her mind. Turned her words around and the color of flour and the newspapers she read. Farina did read newspapers. Not really. Milli couldn't say that to anyone. It wasn't quite that much grandness, but she did. And she could read—recognize 'police' and 'boats' and 'Italy' and 'elephants'—and like the ants that scurried over the newspapers Milli sat on, she could pick up other words that caught her eye on the pages. 'Car.' 'Soccer.'

Governo. Government. She had asked Milli that. The rulers. Farina didn't know what a ruler was. The leaders. Milli had explained. There was no place on earth where people got what they hoped for. From leaders. Her parents had learned from the war in Biafra. Learned.

Ramada. Where would her son be with his broad shoulders? He'd be at school when she came up the path. But the taxi she paid would be seen coming down the unpaved roads and messages there traveled by words. Or maybe by cell phones now. He would hear because someone would run to tell him. Or ring him. Your mother is back. And she's bringing you a camera and the big floppy shoes all the boys in Florence wear. She's come and she's broke and she's got you a sister.

Milli wondered what was coming into her mind. The flood burst. It wasn't sweet like she was remembering. There was no room in the house for her. Not even a box under the bed, once Sabula stalked the rooms.

Widu. The name made her question if it was her name. It was as far away as guitars to dance to and yet easy, too, just walking back into it. Like the woman thrown overboard, swallowed in waves, lost in the ocean, maybe Milli could just drop off and Widu could come back, and what would it be washing heads again and finding a shack, because it would be that, for Farina and Ramada. A shack where nothing worked.

Florence had more things than she had expected. Not that Milli had money for them, but Florence did. The markets were different, with gold apricots and watermelons, and black olives and green olives, and whole half cows without flies on them, and fish on ice, and even the little dresses she put on Farina, they were different. There were mountains of much and more. Oh, if they went back, if Farina went, not back, but to Nigeria, not home, but to another place, where they would not make her change her name, she could be Farina, anyway. She could go to the missionary schools, with the new laws, that made the country prevail. The nuns could no longer just teach religion.

Her mother, Bene, a Christian, strict enough, still liked the local ideas of religion. She'd say, with a voice sweetened by wisdom, nothing is religion purely. The whites gave us Jesus but Jesus is in the earth. If I take this wood and build it not into an idol but a god representing the earth and trees and wood, if I let it return to the earth, let it break down instead of worshipping it, that is us, Ogoni. If I create a god and am grateful to the earth for its wood and I let it go back to the earth, that is us and it adds to Jesus. That takes us and our ways to leave them at the foot of Jesus. We take our secrets and feeling for nature and leave them quietly in the church.

One season her mother took up the charge of an homage in the village to Allah. Because Jesus wishes us to be friends. She left Aki for four months and lived inside the walls with four women who were Muslims. How many mysterious weeks passed as the ten women lived inside the walls molding aspects of life, creating statues from nature. Widu had fed her mother through a hole. And other women had. Gifts of food brought in everyday and given to the women who lived like priestesses. And in the end, the walls came down and the beautiful trunk-like statues were unveiled to live until the termites and damp took them back to the earth as slivers. The never-ending-always and mightiness of God.

Milli could see her mother's face. Not dead yet, but alive, wonderful high bridged nose and eyes that could pick up a trick passing between the ears, passing as a thought. She could read it like it was a big egret opening its wings right on your face. Now Bene's body lay on a table in the living room and Aki had not had the strength to have a simple burial that was Christian.

The prayers Sabula said were blasphemous. She couldn't see the difference between the work her mother did just once to Allah and the voodoo she was proposing. One was dark magic. The other a hymn.

If Farina stayed, now, the soap-smelling nuns would put the cross around her neck and Milli would have to bow and nod. If she went back, where would she go for Farina's schooling, except to the nuns. Everyone in Africa tried to take up the role of interpreter. And Farina would need the nuns so that what she knew, her special life, would remain.

Widu. Milli laughed saying it. Her name was a desert on the other side of something. Not like the wall in front of her, but as vast and changed. Not like Farina in the convent. But the same because she could not be reached. Widu would stand in the living room, with the flies buzzing, and everyone would have a hand out, waiting for the riches to be dropped in. Waiting for the ceremonious payoff of the return.

Silk? And they would look for a scarf. Shoes? Gold rings?

Sabula would be making her circles and raising her hands, already saying, We don't have room. Where are we going to put a child and Widu?

Milli turned Farina around. Tried to imagine her in one of those white rooms in the convent where she was at this very moment. She could see the quiet face of her daughter. How she looked at things. Where would Farina be if those white dressed sisters looked after her and gave her a book. It was different the book they would give her in Florence, it would not be dirty and torn, not one for a hundred sets of hungry hands. It was different reading the history and being there. Different than the history she read, that was over the ocean, and the history of her land. It was young and full of caste systems and untouchables, full of tribes and fighting. Full of colonials. Not like Florence, although she knew from the statues Florence wasn't like painted flowers and gardens and golden crosses. It wasn't. There was no art in Florence like her mother's art. That nature art, that ritual that dissolved, like the pulpy seeds into the swampy mat where they fell and waited and rose again as trees.

In Florence reading a book of history, Farina would be told it was her history.

Taking her back, what would her history be?

Milli looked at her lined palms. The thoughts she had were taking her in circles. If Farina had to go to Harcourt as she had gone to Harcourt, like Aki, her father, because there was too much poverty and trouble in Ogoni land, what was she going back to for Farina.

If she turned Farina around, the way her mother Bene had turned her around, her mother, so tired from the difficult life they had in Harcourt, would she have said Farina was like Widu. Those bright eyes so curious to read, had Bene seen them too?

Her mother was calling her. Widu had never felt a day more difficult except for Meniki's death. The world of the dead beyond the world they were in, was calling her. Bene had never been able to help once she was dead, and the Christians did not believe in ghosts, but Milli could feel her close by, giving her strength. Standing near the wall by the river, as if she was making a statue, as if she had been behind the wall of the Mugnone for months, taking gifts from the community, but working in silence, working on a piece of art.

Her mother had just stepped out of the ceremony after months. The walls were coming down. What was the strong woman wrapped in blue and red ikat saying? What was she holding in her blistered hands. She had said to Widu when she stepped out the first time, when Aki was upset, when the children were frantic, Bene had said, look at the statue, it alters you and it alters the place it remains. Everything is altered by everything else. And the gospel alters us more, wants us to love. But love doesn't kill what alters in other ways.

There were fruit trees in Harcourt. Peacocks and gardens, emerald green, and British and American and Yoruba people laughing in those large colonial houses. The oil people and the government people. Igbos. Dutch. And where could Farina fit?

Maybe in the servant quarters. Maybe she, Widu, could bend her proud head a little and work in that compounded place in Harcourt. For the people who had a lot. She could live there with Farina and Ramada, and work quietly, bending and serving tea, for one of the women in one of those houses.

If she turned Farina around the face she saw was Widu's face. Widu listening to the shouts rising over her head as she sat on the cart and her parents moved into the slum in Harcourt. She could turn Farina around and where was she turning her from really? The room with the slats. The cruel eyes of Igor. This very grass with the broken bottles and pieces of plastic. If she turned Farina around and put her on a dusty street in Harcourt at least there was the sun and the smells that Widu had known. There was a library. There was the university her mother had wanted for her. If she turned Farina around she could feel Widu's eyes reading those books about the wars of independence. She could see her eyes following the rivers, the great rivers of Africa, and when the camels came and the Muslims came to the north and when the Portuguese came, and when the Catholics came, and she could see the walls of how her mother wanted an orderly, kind house that was Christian. She could see the goats, their babies frisky and romping, and the pigs and hear the sound of small boats lapping in water. She could see, with Widu's eyes, the way she was going to go on to school. And see Widu saying goodby to the river life, to the rafts, to the circles of women, to the night life that snapped on in Harcourt, to the moon that came up and changed the smell of sweat from doing work to dancing and going out. She could see Widu saying goodby. Goodby. She had heard it in the bars, heard it in groups of soldiers, the way to keep power is to keep people down. Goodby, people, goodby. Goodby my dear Menike. My dear.

Milli stood up and walked down to the stream. A frog with eyes like egg silt was sitting on a rock. The green of bright jade leaves, it was still and the sun was warming it. There was a story about frogs somewhere in her days in the streets that she hadn't walked in for so long. Stories were so good for telling you how you could go wrong or right. The frog had too much pride and he pretended he was not a frog at all, and he courted the ladies, sang songs with his warbly throat. He wanted their gold, and when they asked if he was a frog, he said no. No, I am not. He thought that was showing his abilities, that shrug and strut, confusing the ladies. And in the end, they ate him up, and he left a bad taste in their intestines. And that's that. A sharp story with equal parts. Like being stung by mosquitoes—one gets a red swollen bite and the other dies from the swat.

Mill couldn't see her face in the water because there was mud, long grasses, rocks and altogether the water was cloudy, except when it was cleared by so many rocks there were little rapids.

Mother, she said, what statue do you have to show me? What is there behind the wall? If I turn Farina around is she me? Will she wander down the streets in Harcourt like me, and will I be reviled and snickered at? Will I be able to be any better than what I am and will Sabula treat her like she treated me?

Like a slave in my father's house.

Milli sat down and wondered if it was possible to get into the water and lie down. Face down. Or on her back and lie as still as a corpse. Or as a raft that had sunk. To put herself in the muddy water and let it fill up her lungs. She didn't know if she felt that bad or if Farina would then go to a good home, like those colonial houses, that had lawns and books, and could take care of her until she was a lawyer. If Farina could enter a house with a piano in it, and tea served in glasses with ice. If they would buy her books and take her on travels, not in the bottom of the airless ship, but on planes with seats that rolled back like carpets. If Milli could just enter the water and let it enter her, crush that spirit that was pushing up and down, slower and slower, let it enter her ears and go up her nostrils, then it would be finally like soil that would enter and cover her. The rocks would pierce her back and slowly the water would press and enter, and she would choke and grow heavy with the sun burning out her eyes. And be like Meniki. Bloated and cold. Snatched under and taken away. And then the dust and the maggots would chew and cover and she would sink back into the earth.

The frog croaked and jumped. Feet splayed, it splashed and swam fast with pumping legs.

Startled, Milli fell back off of her heels, where she was crouching. Her butt hit the soil. The frog had entered her intestine and disgusted her. The green frog wasn't an elephant. Not a lion. A frog plopped and it scared her. Got inside. She took it like a rampage, a stampede. Fell over from the amazing surprise. Her elbow scraped, her hip hit the ground. Lightly knocked from the sleepy and dark kingdom of dying by a frog's splash and plop.

Her head snapped. Her worry drained like waste sucked down as she lay in the dust. Giving in then, and putting her head back and wondering if ants were crawling in her hair. She laughed with her mouth wide open, her voice hooting and the tears trickling from her eyes and falling back into her hair. She laughed and rolled over on her side, and pulled her legs up near her chest. All the questions going in rings and then going the other way stopped. Still. The stone wall in front of her, the one rising to the street and the bridge, seemed to hold her up. It seemed to say she could climb right up its brown protrusions. What was she doing lying on the ground with ants tickling her skull? She would go back to Harcourt. She saw her father Aki, sitting on the porch rocking. How that idea got in her head so strong, like a shoe that fit, she didn't know. But she was quite sure it was present and speaking. There was Sabula talking behind her back. Milli's hands pressed on small pebbles and dust. The dust. Its dryness suited her. It matched her palms. Its soft scratch said home. Dust that took anything back. The smell of the earth, grass, and a whiff of sweat, the dust close to her skin was hers.

The nuns would have to help and help her take Farina back. There was a ritual in Harcourt for the return. All of Harcourt in a shiny sleek way knew there was going out of the port and coming back, just like the lap, lap, lap of the water itself, filled with junk and gleaming light. The nuns would have to give her money and silk scarves, tickets at least second class, and they would go, wearing their crosses and believing in them for the fact of the tickets themselves. They would believe in the universe and the light of stars.

The porcelain owl was compelling. Like a herald, like the all knowing observer, prodding poor Demeter, Susan understood that the white china shape with the yellow eyes and pink parasol was a figure who announced. A childhood toy, a memory, who in the stories, besides announcing death, explained how the daughter and mother would live separate from one another six months of the year. The myth of Demeter and Persephone held an endless irreducible set of truths told over centuries— told until the contradictions were the truths. How Zeus was the father of Persephone, and gave her to his brother, Vulcan, but how he was also the husband and brother of Persephone's mother, so that who was betrayed, above all, was Demeter, the mother, the wife, the sister. Yet who brought sterility to the earth itself, who took all crops, and stilled all growth, until the deed and secret was revealed was Demeter, the mother, the wife, the woman grieving about the inevitability of power, of relationships, grieving and, at the same time, imposing her own protest over her daughter's descent. Winter, that season of regrouping, of absorbing death and loss, to prepare, then, for the return to life, to playing the game of life and love; it was Demeter who imposed winter on the earth.

The owl's eyes were rigid and fixed. Observer. Seer. Susan held the owl in her palm until its smooth coolness was warm. Midwestern salt shaker from the past.

A strange feeling made her fist seem leaden. At first it was obvious to associate it with Vaclav and the vertiginous closeness she had experienced by working in the sand. Susan felt a strong wave from his life washing over her. There was no term like love for what he had left. Winter and death. And spring. Never before and probably never again in the city where she now lived would she ever feel the intensity of where love had taken them. These pulsations now would die down again. Some people who perceive their lives must follow a strand that is there from the beginning. Hers had been one where it was necessary to break up the life many times just to favor that one strand. Break through the frailty just to let the essence of her life flow out. Susan found more tears, no longer honoring the banks holding them back. Her impulse was to stop there. To not go any further in the unassisted free association she had led herself into. It was a dark feeling. Then she sensed it had nothing to do with Vaclav.

It was her mother. Charlotte. She was hearing her voice. Charlotte who had never been a Demeter, who had never looked for Susan anywhere. Who had nearly no interest in a daughter who grew beyond the confines of her own horizons. Who didn't want Susan to have dreams. Charlotte, who existed outside of myths or tradition, who stopped tying the knots in rolled up beef, and gave up the piano because she didn't want to practice chords until they stood up, cleanly. Who didn't ever hear music but pushed her stumbling peppy fingers forward hoping for familial applause. Charlotte who lived without questions, except the startling one, if you believed her—Maybe, someday, will I know who I am? Charlotte had entered Susan's mind. Driver. Buyer of frozen sandwiches and prebeaten eggs. Nonhair-dyeing auburn bleeding into gray, not dyeing it like

Susan did as a flag of life and contradiction, hat-wearing lady, who couldn't garden, who once Leonard was gone, eviscerated him, shredded his memory until he was to blame for the shape of her life past and present. Storyteller. That was what was hard about the tapes. How Charlotte could take a memory and invent it. Re-invent it. Endings put on that pleased or sounded better. Like Susan's birthmark on her arm. How Charlotte fussed and tried to cover it up all of her childhood with make-up, with long sleeves, with sighs and frowns, how she looked at it and conveyed that its imperfection was not from her, not of her. Susan would go to school and wipe the make-up off.

Charlotte's relationship with her daughter fit exactly with that continuous hounding when Susan came home, her arm exposed. The purplish sign was not pretty but its existence on Susan's left arm was a life-giving lake in the end. She met her mother's frustration and fear of her own life there in the dark blood vessels that spread between her wrist and half way to her elbow. The purple birthmark, which Charlotte would have hoped to erase, which could have given Susan any number of complexes, only strengthened her will. The birthmark was not a source of shame for her, but a sign of another world. Her mother wanted to cover it up. Susan wanted to let it be what it was. No big deal. And that really was Demeter. That announcement of imperfection, that decrying of cover-up.

That was where Teresa came in. Susan knew now that returning to the excavation this morning was touching what lay beyond patients and professionality. It cut close to finding Virgil in the garden shedding his skin. Eating it. Swallowing his last year. That coincidence was amazing. The unfinished work had come to a certain point, the unfinished work of leaving the skeleton in the soil, of fantasizing about her, and now she had separated completely from what Teresa was really: not her task. Not her life. And no one had made her do it but herself.

The reasons were endless once she began. The layers in

Teresa. The way Teresa was buried, and had lain for so long. The whole story of digging her up was not a story of exposing the figure. The woman with a chariot, was and was not, a need to reach back to the land, to the earth, for an image to hold, to rescue. The excavation was fascinating and like so many fascinating things was a false turn to evade the hard truth of simply living her own cumbersome, lonely, amusing and elusive life. The skeleton was not her past. It was her imagination's need. And now its many possible connotations were shattering like mercury when touched.

Susan checked her watch. The flowers on her desk needed to be rearranged before the patients came.

Suddenly that ridiculous claim of Charlotte's, that throwaway line she would haul out even at the grocery store and laugh about with check-out clerks, turned poignant. An ironic judgment on herself as well. Maybe someday I, too, will know who I am.

All the identity buried in Charlotte and passed on to Susan and now probably stewing and brewing up in Marina were dependencies and reluctancies and matters unknown and always possibilities for breaking silence and determining to speak. Charlotte, her mother, was someone who saw herself like a face on a passport. She was that name and photo. She belonged to that country and place of birth. And Susan really didn't quite belong anywhere. And Marina had all the chances in the world to reveal herself to herself. As she did. As Charlotte did. And the story of Persephone and Demeter was strongest in the part where Demeter knows she must freeze the earth in order to get the attention of the god, her husband and brother, and to tell her story.

Susan loved Demeter, loved the way she could suffer and make seen what had been violated in nature. That force in Demeter—the way Greek myths showed the self as multiple parts that you might never fully separate—was pretty much the way Susan saw not just her patients, or her daughter, or her lover, but an unending thirst she had. Susan had crossed paths with a prostitute, all nervous and probably in danger. And she had been unable to do much except upset the institutional attempts to get to the bottom of things. The judge's room had been filled with real procedures and she had grown impatient with them. And she had not offered, not even believed, in that setting that help, other than her own view, was possible. The sandbox space she offered others she had forgotten was not her own power.

When Maria, in "Maria and the Clouds" chooses not to go down into a courtyard and help a crying child who has been bitten by a dog, Vaclav had her return to her painting. Maria continues deepening the greens in her painting, glorifying a tree lavish with plums. It was a literal moment that seemed a secret message from Vaclav to her. And at the time, seeing the film, besides all the disturbing personal references to the life they had shared, Susan had thought he was really talking about himself. Depicting the contradiction of the artist and his helpless favoring of art over life. She had not really seen until now that he might have been signaling that she, too, had Maria's weakness: a self-absorbed lack of doubt. And that she was as shaky as the next person, when it came down to the difficulty of knowing how to live. Professional and observer were words that required constant humility and cleaning.

The owl was really her aunt Mary's salt shaker. And yet it was now Minerva, the witness who had been transformed and transmitted in stories for more than two thousand years. The sandtherapist herself.

The sandbox was like the winter when Demeter froze the land. It required going underground. So was the hole in the backyard. It was the hole where primal life whispered secrets that would never be fully known. Demeter froze the land, as a permanent feature of life, to notify the gods, and to make certain that the daughter knew there were seasons, times for life and times for death, times for reflection and times for action. Times for mistakes and times for forgiveness. There was no elsewhere. That's the doorbell ringing, Susan thought. But it was too early to be Emmanuel, sad eyed child, whose mother believed he lacked an image and was ridiculed at school. But it was, without a doubt, the bell. Maybe another rose for Marina. Once that kind of long ring might have been a telegram. Telegrams brought by men on little scooters who used to be the exotic penetration of everyday life. Susan could remember telegrams and their faded yellow importance. The words counted out, hurriedly cut, pasted in and special. How long had it been since words as money had that parsimony? And that monumental sense of announcement, important news?

There was surprise on both sides of the gate. The black and white dog had already crossed the road and Agnese Caffo had to reach over and grab her by the collar so that she wouldn't jump.

Buon giorno, Susan said. Silence. Are you looking for your peacock?

Amadeo Caffo patted the setter's head, wondering just how to phrase it. He and Agnese hadn't really discussed it since they had been seized by the impulse. They had rushed to turn off the chard but not explored how embarrassed they would feel. Signora Notingham was almost pretty seen up close. No wrinkles and her eyes certainly didn't look that hard. He felt obliged to say something.

Would you mind if we stepped into your garden? he asked.

Susan felt the awkwardness of their standing in the road, the dog nuzzling her legs. But was there a reason they should come in?

Certainly, she said. She hoped that their innate sense of place and her sense of timing could keep them very close to the gate, although there were no chairs there. It was not an occasion to offer them a chance to sit down. Not because they were not welcome, but her young patient and his mother would be at the doorstep soon. That's what she thought, although she knew the uncovered hole, if they saw it, would be difficult to explain.

FOURTEEN

T HERE WAS SOUND in the chapel, human voices, settling, with the chairs scraping. His assistant, Gioanna Regete, was giving him the signal. Melandri thought it was up to him to nod his head and not the other way around. The microphone wheeze and as he tapped it, that amplified thud pounded through the random noise. The ceremony would begin.

Melandri looked at his watch and his concentration gathered into him. By physically shutting out the faces and entering into himself, an excitement and anticipation collected, nerves and ideas ready to branch out. First slide. The dark shafted by the appearance of an image and there it was, the bronze loop, the gnomon, positioned like a burnt frying pan on the screen. The instrument that had been used by Toscanelli and was attached ninety-eight meters up behind the backs of the people in the north chapel opened the story.

In 1475, Melandri said, the world and, for world I mean Europe, looking primarily at itself, was on the verge of many discoveries. Of course, it depends on your point of view. If you want to see discovery as physical explorations, we are on route to discovering the Americas and Africa, or if you wish to see the steady cracking open of a re-emerging scientific attitude, we are more than sixty years from Copernicus's sure and radical theory to adjust the earth's position, putting it as the third, rather than as the central sphere. In many different ways, from different angles, the configuration that the earth was round and at the same time not the center of the universe—two ideas that are not only new but unsettling—are on the fire, alerting and de-stabilizing existence. But at the moment this gnomon is being bolted in place in this very church, neither idea has been proved or, at least, made an inroad into the city of Florence, or any other European city, for that matter. There are intimations of this world, and the intimations are vibrating, because when ideas are discovered or re-proposed, usually they are alive in other parts of the collective world. The common ground is math, in this case, and fighting dogma, and finding new markets, as well as trying on theories that were intrinsically threatening because human beings are conservatively insecure about changing ideas about the cosmos, as well as being energetically curious and greedy about commerce.

What you see in the slide and, if you turn your head will find in the southern window of the lantern, is an instrument that weighs approximately two kilos and has been forged from bronze. The place Toscanelli affixed it was reconstructed from scrupulous research by Jesuit priest, Leonardo Ximenes, in the eighteenth century, when he used it again to establish a fact about the earth's slight movements within its axis by measuring the alteration from year to year of a ray hitting the brass and marble disc you will all see this morning on this very floor. The gnomon was a simple tool used in many churches in Italy and one in France, in the span of three centuries, to compress data by making experiments about the earth's motion with regard to the calendar year. The aim was to focus light so that it fell on a meridian that had been established by some criteria on the church floor. Next slide. Here is the meridian in Santa Maria del Fiore. Next. Here is another type of gnomon. Two were erected in Florence, and one in Bologna and one in Rome by an ambitious and gifted Domenican, Danti, who eventually knocks a hole in Santa Maria Novella in Florence, a south facing church, so that he can measure the arrival of all four seasons marked by the sun's position. You see, in this slide, the instrument appended to the upper left corner of the façade today.

The touching fact, at least to me, is that all of this science was bubbling up in Florence because the principles of ancient learning were being revived. And this branch of measurement was an outgrowth of the Catholic church's administrative interests fitting well with scientific exploration. They wanted to know, since the Julian calendar established by Julius Ceasar had been becoming ruinously longer for more than two centuries, when precisely Easter could be celebrated all across the world. That issue, different from Christmas, which had been declared a fixed date, was a real mess that was caused by many things, primarily lack of knowledge about the order of our solar system, but also because of the original competing cultural ideas about how to measure time. The Jews used a calendar that was calculated by using full moons. The Roman-turned-Christian world used the sun with some moon measurements. Easter had no fixed date. The Christians tried to follow more closely the Jewish idea of Paschal, a feast determined by the appearance of a full moon after the spring equinox. In theory, in a tribe, in a village, one has only to observe the full moon and declare the following Sunday Easter. The authority, and its concomitant power, however, derived from a local sighting. Instead, the Church needed to announce the moon's appearance years ahead in order to prepare Bishoprics across the world.

Melandri wished the gnomon in front of Santa Maria Novella was still not on the screen. He should have thought of a slide like the moon. Moonlight shining so that they could imagine the idea of local time. Nevermind. But, *i signori e le signore*, this local system was of little consolation to an institution that aspired to world unity. The Catholic church wanted to know ahead of time, even years ahead, when the spring equinox took place, so that in Christendom, and I mean, in a global kingdom that was not even fully mapped, but was being conquered, the Church wanted to have Easter, and the story of its God, be celebrated at the exact same time, or at least a time it declared, all across the earth. Which, as I said, and you are free to laugh, was really a huge problem, that if we were searching for an equivalent is no longer how you tell time but perhaps the power of a unifying language—which like English today keeps trying to assert its hegemony over the whole world. The Catholic church was willing to invest in a research line using instruments like the gnomon to measure the discrepancy between the sun's cycle and the Julian calendar. Next. Here we see this very chapel being leveled and adjusted, with water run over the floor in order to meet the conditions necessary to insure Ximenes' experiment in the 18th century. The line on the floor was measured against a level in a basin of water. This chapel for those months functioned as a physics laboratory researching a different problem.

Next slide. Enter Toscanelli. Here we have dropped back three centuries from the physics lab. Toscanelli was a man for all seasons. And as the astrologer for the Florentine Signoria, his ability to predict the stars' movements and the earth's positions had a value in planning initiatives, in thinking about military attacks. The wish that humanity nurtures for making cosmic life certain has not abated all that much. Even an American president like Ronald Reagan consulted astrologers. Nothing to be proud of if you are running a complex modern state. Melandri could feel the urge to add a few more digs, and wanted to slip in a few facts about star wars and the costs in Toscanelli's time. He hoped he could stop his tongue from pushing on by changing the slide.

His eyes peered out into the dark and back over his shoulder.

Instead of a drawing of Ptolomy's design of the universe, the pearl of the earth floating in the center, a slightly jowely face that loomed across the screen could only be, with those intelligent eyes, and fat homely cheeks, Galileo's daughter. Melandri hesitated. Here we have a concept that caused more conflict than can be imagined, and, although Ptolomy's thought had come down into Latin through Arabic translations of the Greek, this interesting idea has been ground to a halt by the large inquisitive pair of eyes you see before you. Ladies and gentlemen, I am afraid to say that a piece of modern scholarship is facing you. Well, we can stop here for one moment, since she has insisted on being recognized. Whom you are seeing is Galileo's daughter, Maria Celeste, who is really known now because of feminist scholarship that is unearthing so many stories that were not told when it was considered appropriate for fathers to place their daughters in convents.

Melandri snapped his fingers at his assistant.

Next. The machine made a sound, lurched forward, the slide or presumed slide of Ptolomy's world whizzed past and then Maria Celeste's stolid face appeared again, like a mischievous saint holding out for a hearing.

Who can blame her for wanting her revenge? Next. We must go on. After all, we have the earth that will not stop for us and our human errors. The sun's path has been calculated and the ray is on its way. But if you will just turn your heads and look against the north wall perhaps you can see the first signs of the sun's appearance, while my technician pulls out Maria Celeste's portrait—with all due reverence to her story—and lets us proceed.

Melandri was growing hot and irritated. It was time for a cooling drink. The noise of the crowd was considerable and two or three people had gotten up to walk with children on their shoulders. A particularly blonde little boy pointed to the light once his grandfather showed him what to look for.

Look, he shouted, loud enough to make heads turn. *La luce.* Nice, thought Thomas Simpson. Nice. I wish Melissa could see this. His own daughter was too old, too much into TV and her peers to be convinced to even sit through a ceremony like this. History for her was Whitney Houston's last disc. Oh, that will pass, Thomas Simpson thought, almost feeling lonely and strangely ready to go back home. He loved Melissa's chubby insouciance that distance had made charmingly sweet. He wished she had a name like Livia or Giulia, and that she could appreciate Artemisia Gentileschi's paintings but she didn't, freckle faced and marvelously disinterested as she was in anyone outside of her group of horseback-riding friends. The astronomer was not a particularly good speaker. He strayed and strained. What was he trying to say? The way time was fought over, how it became political, so that England ran three hundred and seventy-five days behind the Catholic Gregorian calendar at the height of the struggle over how to measure time, just because Protestants did not want to appear as if they would give in to a Pope. Wasn't he trying to talk about meridians?

Thomas Simpson didn't balk at that thought of absolute stubbornness. For some reason it gave him a sense of relief, an unexpected poignant signal that he was actually missing home. The weight of human nature was flatter, more rationalized, in America, and, that was not a virtue, but it made it easier to decipher sets of emotions. For the first time in these exquisite and frustrating weeks, he wished to be in his own back yard looking at the moon from the standpoint of a simple wooden deck, with the garbage cans in the alley, and the crickets. His own place. The idea of time as local was something he knew deep in his bones, and often felt like a dull confine. For months on end he lived in his head, counting the days until he could get away from the narrowness and the blind spots in the measuring faces of colleagues frustrated because they were obliged to keep politically correct smiles on their lips. How he loved every brick in the long memory of Florence and the sense that he belonged to something larger than the self-censored faculty meetings where no one mentioned the secret deals with Saudis or the revival of Savings and Loan scandal tainting the ex-President's son for fear of losing points. For politeness. For consensus. For officially accepting that every one had a right to his point of view, however tedious or delusional it was. Yet living in someone else's country boiled down to nothing more than charm, escapism, pain for being a stranger in a land that was not one's own. Time was local in the end. Systems were reckoned, for better or worse, by the place one lived. Sorted and ranked by basic symbols called roots. It was odd, really, that he had invested so much in hoping to be joined to Florence this morning via this disorganized man who might be a splendid astronomer but was short as a lecturer. The professor had bitten off too much. That was the way European history went. Interconnections made nearly any story a raging river. And it didn't help that Italians were not taught how to teach.

Melandri's watch said that eighteen minutes had run away under the circling whisker of the second hand. And where was he in compressing the story into a few brief minutes? The face of Maria Celeste had made him lose his place. The context of meridians, both as science, as data collection, as a way of continuing to measure astrological truths while the Church officially declared Galileo's calculations heresy, the agreed upon fiction that Copernicus' theory was a convenient fiction—he must follow a line as straight as the meridian sunk in the chapel floor.

Next. It was the black and white engraving of the German nut tree. This, too, was in the wrong place. He'd forgotten to write down what kind of tree it was. The gnarled branches were a nightmare. Pope Gregory XIII who had called for the calendar's reform cited this tree's blooming on the same day in the old Julian calendar and his new Gregorian one as a sign of the rightness of his changes. Melandri would have to swerve to fit it in and who knew what slide might come up next.

Melandri had nearly no uncertainty now when he traveled to observatories. In La Palma or Maui the observations were hardly human in a hands-on-sense. One stepped into a world completely controlled and monitored by the computer infrastructures and machines opening a precision world of lenses and screens, beams and wavelengths brought to the hushed focus of a shrine. Each gold-plated costly second was mapped and recorded, by computers and monitors organizing infrared images day and night to make maps of what was there when someone was not looking. The continuous probes of primordial rings of dust and gases farther and farther out towards the questions of origin itself were planned years ahead. Not parity, but a minor parallel mirror lay in the light years it took for the light of galaxies to arrive and the way modern scientific probes were twenty, thirty years in the making. And here in the chapel a well paid technician had managed to confuse his simple and earthbound slides in the ten minutes he had consigned them to her lovely, pale white hands. They carried the curse of human error.

Here we see, and he paused with a searching sigh, a tree adopted by Pope Gregory X111, when he was lobbying for acceptance of his calendar. He sent pieces of its branches to various protestant German princes, and argued that the tree's blossoming proved the universal rightness in the nature of things—given that its flowering was on the same day in both the Julian and the Gregorian way of measuring. Couldn't Easter promise to reintroduce the same natural rightness even if they switched to a new system?

Dear Widu,
Putting the salutation on a small piece of paper felt like writing in blood. Aki looked at her name and it burned inside

him. He wondered what remained of his brown-eyed daughter. The disruption that led him to put her name down was so great that if he didn't lift the pen up, it would make a black blot over the top of the page. And what would that mean? What would it look like to her, except that his hands trembled and that he was no longer even able to push a pen with some clarity across a page.

Once he saw her name, enclosed in his rounded strokes, he saw lots of things, mostly her mother, Bene. One side of him wanted to write about just showing their abilities, as if they were doing well in Harcourt, in spite of what she might have read. Widu did read, often under the window, when Ramada should have been followed, or the kitchen out back needed washing up. In spite of marrying, Widu was not without books. Nothing much in the house now of books, but as a young girl she used to go to the priest and she stayed reading there for hours. Aki was sorry. He didn't think he could stand hearing the word scratching in his ears.

If he stood up some evening and tried to list how he had no money for her books, no strength for her mother's wishes, how his moves had only kept them like skinny cows yoked to a stick pulling someone else's cart, it would only make things worse. Sorry was a reaped crop and worthless, bending him in a way he didn't like. It was better to sit rocking in the chair, Sabula's voice firing over his head, and somehow let the feeling like tears come in, as he pushed the rocker back and forth, like breathing. Letting himself remember, although he hadn't maybe even known at the time, how much he loved Bene, and Widu, and the others too. How he was clumsy and couldn't express how he loved them all in spite of the dark and tough daily grind where all you could wonder is, where are we going.

The return. It was deep in Harcourt. The Ogoni themselves a tribe that was looked down on. Particularly by haughty Igbos. Not only did they kill them outright, but all over Nigeria Ogoni was a name that was not exactly like calling people Judas, but it was that heavy. Ogoni were scapegoats and considered nothing by a lot of people. Considered arguers and loudmouths. False people. And even once he had converted to Christianity, respectability did not just fall to him. Public opinion ran high against the Ogoni. Unjustifiably. And that is perhaps why Saro-WiWa was such an incandescent figure, so troubling and so mesmorizing. Because he told his people to defend themselves.

Aki looked at the brief sheet of paper. How could he sum up the defeat of even one day or the danger now to Widu's son, or the degradation of his people, or the water's smelly loss of life? How could he possibly put into words the bursting he felt inside?

Return was always a celebration in Harcourt. The sacrifices repeated that which had been done in the beginning, although Sabula with all her witchcraft still wouldn't kill one chicken for Widu's departure. He wouldn't mention her, but he would say they were waiting to celebrate Widu's return.

Celebrate. With bright dresses and the local string music you could get so that they could dance in the back yard. Celebrate, away from the soldiers, down by the river. Celebrate. An exile, that is what Aki thought flooding his mind. They could drink themselves sick with palm wine, the palm wine, and wake up the next morning ready to start over in their corner of Harcourt that wasn't a city. It was a compound that every day had to be swept up, and ordered just so that they held their place in as dignified and honest a way as possible.

Aki looked up and the storm cleared sky seemed calm enough. Bright. Not a sky that particularly looked down on a looming battle.

How could he ask her to come home? He could, because he had honestly invested his energy in trying to make something better. He had kept Ramada and it was not all shame that the boy hoped to change things and make a new life. Aki didn't want him at risk. He didn't want to put the boy on the line without his being on the line. Without his mother being home to counsel him, although he was so tall and independent, his hands having earned money for more than two years, he was to be proud of. Aki did know that Ramada had learned from him not to be part of any corruption. Sabula didn't particularly think Aki was right for that. No gold medals from her. She felt she lacked because of his stubbornness not to truck even with the local dockhands. But she couldn't seduce him or trick him into thinking that he should enter into some of the little networks at the pier.

I'm not that buffoon and stereotype you wish me to be, he had told her more than once. I am a real Ogoni. That was one foolish sentence he could say and feel he was laying it gently, like a ritual cloth, at the feet of his dead wife.

He couldn't write Widu's name again. Couldn't tell her about the military repression of this government. Or about the abominable politics she had missed. The stories of international shame, those stories that spread across the world, like the oil blackening the water. Seeping in its sticky suffocating way into the water and like fire in the sky when even airpilots from all over took a detour to look down on the port in Lagos to see the ships full of cement going out for miles. She'd heard him complaining about that. Widu was still around. How the world laughed as the port filled with boats that were there just to feed on the government's false promises and made them the laughing stock of the world. Aki knew other parts of the world had their corruption. But they didn't tell it. No cancelled elections. No dishonest votes. They liked to laugh at Nigerians, at the Ogoni, they liked to pretend that they had no problems. Americans had problems. Italians did too. They just liked to say others were worse. So much needed to be destroyed everywhere but not the family. And the politics now were much worse.

Aki could hear parrots razzing one another in the next yard. He couldn't imagine why he was thinking about troubling his daughter. But Widu was a lot like Bene. She was smart, good, until grief turned her thoughts into running away. He was angry with himself for the sack of sorrows he allowed himself to carry. But he could feel anger, too, that wanted to set things right. He had converted to Christianity and had a set of rules to follow. And if not in this world, the next would set things right, again.

The dogs down the road were yipping. What if he wrote Ramada needs you and by the time Widu answered, Ramada was dead, turned up, different than Meniki, but dead? What if he was calling her back only to stir up her pain? Widu's spirit in leaving was something way in the back of his mind he admired. She could not be crushed. Ramada was her son. Didn't that mean he was safe?

Pulling the wooden door open, Sister Morena didn't know what to expect. The bell had sounded as loud and long as a fire alarm. It surely would arouse Mother Superior Benedetta and, perhaps, in spite of her infirmities, bring her frayed patience to an end. Mother Superior seldom lost control of her own temper, but she also seldom lost control of the convent itself. She knew how to hiss down little frissons of excitement, knew how to forget kind acts and to stress lapses so that the sisters tended not to gather, tended to focus and hurry along. She made her moves without hesitation.

Milli studied the capped face in front of her.

Yes?

Milli's heart pounded and she wondered if the world could possibly turn in a good way at last. The cool dark air was pouring out from behind the nun as if from a cave. Milli wanted sharp words to come out. She wanted to slap the nun and say whatever she felt like. How dare the olive shaped face under the clean blue cloth stood between her and Farina.

Yes? Sister Morena asked with more authority. It was almost certain that the tall doe-eyed woman—who could not possibly imagine the whirlwind and chaos that had sprung from the child and seized the convent in these hours—was looking for her daughter.

Sister Morena felt joy radiating from the story of the prodigal son. The woman's face was alight with alarm. Return. This was one of the moments that connected her all the way back to Delhi. The opening that suddenly flickered in the heat with hope cutting through the dust and dryness. Her mind since she had been outwitted this morning focused completely on the woman before her. How in a few seconds could she impose a direction? There would be a crowd of faces in minutes and the noise would surely bring the Mother Superior this time to leave her bed and castigate them all. Hesitant to leave the tall, taut woman standing, since she might run, like a camel fearing a kick, the physical question of where to place the woman, inside the door, or in the hall, while she convocated Sister Gertrude. And perhaps Susan Notingham should be called. No chair was nearby. No time opened like a sweet fruit. Like a pomegranate with seeds.

Space was generated by these few thoughts and Milli reacted to the complication and the nets in the silence, feeling her feet swaying under the impact of feet trudging up a gangplank walking toward the ship. The electric yawning space in front of the door grew too long and trapping.

You have my child, she said, her voice rising, snapping and on fire like an uninsulated wire about to short. I believe you have my child.

Come in, Sister Morena said. I am afraid you will have to stay here, she said, leaning over and closing the door. The sisters are resting at this moment, she said, whispering in a voice that grew so soft Milli began to feel suspicious. There was no chair in the lobby. The green palm bursts in the stained glass were lit as was the blue of Jesus' robe.

Where is she? Milli asked stepping forward and raising an arm that Sister Morena caught and gently put back.

Sister Morena didn't want to make another mistake like the one she had introduced this morning. She didn't say the child was sleeping, although she wanted to say that. Wait one minute, she said, hoping the woman would not bolt after her.

Sister Gertrude had been lying on her back, on the bed next to Farina's. The body of the sleeping child was small on the white sheet. It reminded her why people felt so willing to sacrifice for children. They were so small, so easily hurt, and yet the intensity of being new to life meant their energy, which was surely a divine source, often vibrated like the green of branches. A little tough but hard to snap or break. It was amazing to see that vulnerable young life as a remarkable one, a child who could see into the intrigues of life, but one who was not going to give up easily. The way she had held her own without collapse until her energy had run out would help her in the years ahead. *Give her the fruit of her hands, let her own works praise her at the gate.*

Sister Gertrude wanted to close her eyes and meditate. She needed to believe that Farina would not be abandoned. The child's dark circles so unexpectedly put in proximity to the convent's resources, surely there would be a way to give support to her growth. But now she wanted to approach the deeper and nearly knowable sense of divine. *All the rivers run into the sea; yet the sea is not full.* She wanted to rest in the deep silence of prayer for as long as she could.

Her finger was at her lips. She made a soft calling sound. Standing in the doorway, Sister Gertrude could read from Sister Morena's expression that the reason for her appearance was a significant one.

Perhaps the Mother Superior was about to come down hard.

But Sister Gertrude could read faces from her years of silent assessments and as she processed the look of concern, she knew it expressed altruism inside the almost panicky sense of urgency. It must concern the child.

Farina was asleep on her side. She had never sucked her thumb and her hand was touching her face. Her body was half curled and one arm flung wide and holding her packet of pens. There was no center or circumference to how she occupied the bed. She had nothing of Leonardo's famous drawing of the Vetruvian man, with his two sets of legs and arms generated from a central point in the solar plexus. Farina, her small frame and small bones, has no papers as she lies there. She will not turn around, over and over, like the baby in Maria Grazia's womb, still floating serenely outside of life. Farina is asleep with a wonderful mind and strong spirit. The little girl is loved by Milli, and loved, now, by Sister Gertrude, and by Irene, who is with a man, an old client who has paid her many times to make love to him and his wife. Irene at this moment when she is caught and pushing and stroking inside the tangled pawing arms of the two of them, in their house, in their bed, Farina glows and flashes in her mind. Irene can see Farina this morning in bright light when she ran for the ball. And trace the thud of landing once she jumped from the window, leaving Farina, because she admitted and addressed the fear that entered her gut-understanding of Igor's restless glare. Open-eyed to the sad filthy truth, only she, and not Milli, had snatched the dagger threatening to tear open the child's precarious existence. Irene, now finishing off the woman and listening to her grateful sobs, can only think of how disgusting—no pathetic—the two of them are, pitiful and weak, fatter than the month before, and so grateful, so willing to pay. The man was trying to bite her ear. *Basta*, Irene said. It was over and she had done her part. And they could lie there while she collected herself and removed her limbs and face from them. Straightening her blouse, quickly darting a glance at herself in the mirror, and not minding that they seemed nearly drunk with their kisses, she calmed her mind, lifted her presence from the closed shutters and wrinkled sheets where the two of them moaned, by picturing Farina and how she was in a clean straight place where her delicate face and innocence could find expression. The lovely child smiled back. Irene reached for the bureau. In the brutal wave of clear vision, as clear as her leap into the Danube that cut her off from her tribe, she leaned hard on its square ledge; it seemed that her hand's instinct to steady her body was all she had to hold herself up.

But in the morning seeping towards first light, starting with the swifts gathering insects and screaming out over the sky, swooping down over the Arno and then treading currents and livening up the sky before the central hot core of the morning arrived to this now, perhaps Farina is the most mysterious and perplexing. Innocence. Her unrecorded birth and existence is the nearly forgotten measure of what human life in a city, in a country, should concern itself with. Asleep she is cocooned only for minutes. She could be tossed anywhere and not find her way. That small body is indeed the most central and forgotten question in Florence. Who is she? Where is she going? Does she need an identity card?

Every church has an image of a child, a Christ, sitting on its mother's lap. Every church in Florence has a mother, and some have as many as ten madonnas posed in a thousand versions of sweetness or alarm or teasing insouciance, hung as art, as stations for prayer, paintings famous or local. The Baby of the Birds. The Baby of Sorrows and Dreams. The Baby of the Golden Pear. The Baby of the Black Orb. Which one is Milli and which Farina? Can she still be sold and abused by a craven mind? She can speak and even see, but that baby on a mother's lap, what would any exceptional child of three and one half years say she knew? She would still be blind to her own life. She would want to help her mother. Farina would say she wanted to help Milli. She would want to wipe worry from her face. She would wish her calm. She would not want to think that the sorrow on her face was caused by her vision of the future.

Sister Gertrude stepped out into the hall and thought she heard a click coming from further down the hall. Perhaps Mother Superior was getting up.

Sister Morena put a hand on Sister Gertrude's shoulder. She faced her squarely while her tongue went dry. That made whispering difficult. Tensions were collecting like clauses that would have to be addressed. Time was hope and the sense of time reduced to an impoverished handful of minutes.

In a few minutes the mother waiting at the door would undoubtedly make a move. She would raise her voice or disappear back into the city or perhaps appear in the halls, inspecting for herself the metal bed where her child lay. The thought of another scream shooting down the halls temporarily stopped Sister Morena.

Sister Morena nervously scratched her head. Farina's mother could not be left alone for much longer.

You go, Sister Gertrude said. Stand with her, talk to her and see if you can understand her interests.

I'll wake Farina and come. *In much wisdom is much grief.*

Marta pushed in again. Agnese Caffo thought, without plotting it, that if the dog escaped they could easily near the hole. It would be a natural way to get so close to the pit that bringing its existence up would not be awkward. Or not more awkward than necessary.

Could you hold your dog? Susan asked, suddenly seeing the entire garden from the inquisitive eyes of her neighbors. The little fountain whose sound she so appreciated was bubbling and it reminded her of the beauty she had forced from the dark cypress-covered places. The garden had been her task, one of so many that she had elaborated until anyone would hold her breath at the planned beauty.

How can I help you? Susan asked smiling, thinking how, once again, the day was unlike those before. What was the old couple doing after nearly twenty years of silence? She had attempted in the early years to make contact but they were stand-offish. So they had never trusted her petitions. When the mental hospital closed, those cramped gulag rooms with five-thousand patients often straight-jacketed in San Salvi, she had tried to interest them. But she couldn't make them listen to why it was too drastic to close the hospital all at once. They mistrusted her. They were offended. They took it personally. Then the divorce. Patterns got set in the village.

In. They were in. Amedeo Caffo looked over the yard and was stunned by its grand walkways and banks of flowers. It was a rich and complicated garden. No wonder she was not one to go to church. Father Livio would ask her to give.

Agnese Caffo released her fingers from Marta's collar. Come here, Agnese Caffo called authoritatively, but the dog had taken off behind a hedge.

I'm sorry, Signora, the woman said stepping out onto the graveled path.

She'll be alright. Now, are you here for the peacock? Do you know that he might even kill one of my hens?

No. He wouldn't kill. And he's in our yard now.

Well, I heard him fighting in mine this morning, Susan said. Even now there was resistance in the couple and some great emotion underneath.

Amedeo Caffo couldn't get over how the yard had changed since he was last in it. Maybe even twenty years ago. No wonder she might be considering selling stolen goods. The yard could have belonged to an Arab sheik.

I am afraid I have a client in a few minutes, so I can't offer you seats in the garden. Tell me, what brings you here.

The old man's eyes looked on the ground. It was frightening to accuse. Inside the yard in front of a young face that didn't look crafty but out of place, he felt how they had carried their own kitchen, their own twenty years, across the street, where this other life had been going on. It was so strange that Arvon, like a magnet, had been drawn to her style. That the peacock had not stayed with them, not helped his mistress who valued him so highly. This yard was an aberration, indeed a lavish den.

Signor Caffo motioned to Agnese to go faster, to absent herself from the discussion, and to get the dog. My wife entered your garden this morning to bring the dog back.

I thought I heard barking, Susan said; I did.

The gate was open. My wife wasn't trying to enter, only to catch Marta, our dog.

There was a problem my wife came across.

Amedeo Caffo wanted to pin the crime on her in that moment. He wanted to take his weariness about the crooked way no one cared about the poor or dead dogs or what used to be a clear sense of limits, of what was yours and what was mine. Overcoming his sense of shame, of being displaced, he wanted to have the nerve to accuse a woman in such an excessive garden of breaking faith with society. Signor Caffo said, hurriedly, Signora Notingham, my wife saw that you were excavating. She saw a deep hole.

The words out of his mouth were not carefree, like Marta, who was leading his wife for a chase. Marta had decided to go her own way and, nose down, was following a scent.

The words he had just said to an American surprised Signor Caffo. He felt they immediately elevated him, because he had certain ideas about American bravery from films. And certain ideas from their Presidents. And in all cases, just as she ran up and down the hill and carried petitions, he had not really thought about her much, but now a lot of reshaping was taking place by accusing her and waiting to hear her answer. The excavation was worse than a landslide. It was loss of civic sense. Pollution of the spirit. In Florence everyone knew it was political parties, and rarely individuals, who decided what could stay or what counted. He realized she might well be protected. Even by officials in the department of antiquities itself. That was the worst of the doubts flooding him as he faced her. The trembling anger that made him doubt he had a right to accuse her of anything. It wasn't an accusation, he told himself. It was a question.

Please catch the dog, Susan shouted. She shrugged. It was useless to deny that her neighbors had caught up with her invisible fantasy. The feeling that she couldn't explain herself to them was a horrible one. She wished she could. Wished she could straighten it out by saying, probably it is difficult for you to understand, but I wanted nothing from this excavation. I wanted no brooches. I was not looking for gold. I was following a vision of an unburied, unresolved image inside myself. I was touching a woman whom I wanted to give birth to me. But that was barely plausible even to a therapist and not something that would explain anything to the distrusting couple. Identity? Looking for clues in a prehistoric woman? We dig up soil, Signora, around our potatoes and zucchini. We work hard and would never steal.

Class judgments rested on his tight lips. Pride that carried pain. He was not looking to be bribed like so many people who felt they had nothing. No, Susan thought, he was sincere.

Put it down, Agnese Caffo shouted. Put it down.

All morning Virgil had been struggling and once again he was mortally trapped inside the soft dewlaps and drool of a dog's mouth. Agnese slapped Marta's muzzle hard.

Down, down, put it down. The dog whined from the burn of poison stinging the red lining under her tongue. Virgil dropped, and the old lady gave the collar a yank. It wasn't her wish to save the toad. It was an instinct. A fear, too, that Marta might ingest poison.

In a minute Susan Notingham was at her side.

Against her will, the commotion and scene had brought her running into a clear propinquity to the hole. On the gravel, the small stone-brown creature dragging bits of translucent skin was moving. Without thinking, Susan took the old woman's arm. The impeded hop most probably belonged to Virgil.

Thank you so much, she said, relieved that the nosey dog had obeyed. That the peasant had chastised her own dog. That Virgil had survived.

Agnese Caffo nodded.

She lifted her eyes and gestured towards the planks nearby. She thought her husband had probably explained how she had entered. I saw this, she said, sad to view the neat soil corridors. She looked down and the tomb-like walls made her shudder.

Susan felt she must wake up now. The dark cypress shadows cut the deep hole in half. All the morning was shutting down and she knew that she must stand near the hole and be brave. The light was blinding and the shadows deep. This underground adventure was wide open. And it was alright, she told herself. No way to keep them at a distance.

No old days or new days. No saying that they had no right to snoop in her yard. No, the hole was an open door that she had prolonged and they were all standing beside it. Susan wished it felt more like a beginning. More like a festivity. That the solemn faces were guests. That they could speculate about chariot burials and how the gods were vivid then. But they weren't toying amateurs. They were waiting for why she had broken the law.

She really didn't mind that they were standing there so expectantly. The hole looked as neat as her kitchen, the cupboards with their ball jars, and yet it was hardly domestic. It was as if a meteor had crashed into the ground. There was no knowing really what was underneath until some expert came with trowels and picks. And her suspension of her digging wasn't a blunder. It was as deliberate as Demeter's freezing the earth. But she couldn't say that. She suddenly felt stabbing grief for Teresa. The bones, the chariot rider, who had seen the sun. She felt her nobility and her majestic death.

What could she say? It was not a hole about which she could make conversation. Anymore than she could explain how lifting Teresa out of the ground would perhaps be more pain than she could bear. Would she be able to say goodby to the soil-rivered body that held a real world, alive with myth. Could she let go of the woman who had ridden over these very hills, heard nightingales, kissed someone in a world animated by a world beyond death?

Agnese Caffo studied the open-faced woman. She looked ruined. Signora Notingham was absolutely ruined, caught like a thief knocking a hole in a wall.

Without explanation, Susan asked, What would you do?

That voice, so light and unashamed, querying him, made Signor Caffo look down again. Her silver voice was as foolish as her petitions.

Silence overtook them all, awkward gloom except for the business of the dog who had jumped down into the hole and was moving her paws, eager to dig, tail sweeping.

What if the dog did? What if Teresa's bones started to scatter? Please, Susan said, call the dog up. And the dog leapt up, following a plank.

Would you like me to alert the authorities? she asked, again, not certain who to call or what the effect might be.

Signor Caffo had seen the police take people by the arm and lead them away. That wasn't what I intended, he said.

Susan Notingham laughed. Everything was circling, but she wasn't afraid like he was.

She felt open to the next step, to baring the hole and the woman so long ago riding on the earth. What could she say? No one would know what she felt, how torn and relieved, how ravaged and prayerful she would feel as she watched whomever it would be touching and chipping and carrying away the Etruscan.

She had to be brave in front of her neighbors, who would not believe her. She had to stand, brave in shorts and shirt. I don't mind, she said, only partially bluffing. Let me call the authorities. You are welcome to come in while I search for the number. That way you will believe me.

The words filled both Amadeo Caffo and Agnese Caffo with discomfort. She was already turning toward the house, with that brisk walk.

We don't need to go with you, the old man said. Quite certain she would call. He looked at Agnese his wife. The hole was the intolerable difficulty of all that was outside of their realm. The Florence of privilege.

But Amadeo Caffo did want to know that *la Signora* would call. So that he impressed on her that he was not afraid of her or her wealth. Burning with embarrassment, dreading each step, he agreed to go in, swallowing embarrassment like pools of water and air, but he would cross her doorstep, wiping his feet on the mat, and nodding his head to show he had respect, as he entered the cool halls so beautifully lined with paintings. He would enter on his own two feet and listen while she called. But first he would wipe his dusty feet again on the mat.

When Farina opened her eyes, lifting them as another hand reached out to touch her damp head, the world in front of her was familiar and hers and her arms, skinny and eager, reached from their resigned position around Sister Gertrude's neck and hooked themselves, pulling her body, which Sister Gertrude firmly supported, as she handed her over to the open arms. Arms, arms, arms. Without a word, Farina hugged her mother as the order in her life fell back into what she knew. The sheets and long tables and the sisters fussing were over and the old head was over. Farina felt her mother's skin and hair and clung and stayed still in the humane, delicious closeness and didn't want to accept that her mother was going to put her down. Down on the floor. After the whole world had been made still. But she felt Milli sliding her down her hip.

Put those legs out, Milli said. We have to go. Farina, where are your shoes?

Sister Morena and Sister Gertude exchanged glances. The child rolled out of her sleep and as they all stumbled to find a way not to force the situation, the two nuns both knew who the steps belonged to in that drumming they heard at the far end of the hall. The trouble was how to interpret the signs in Farina's mother and the shuffling friction in the steps coming closer. Both nuns wished, standing side by side, that they had a revelation other than what they knew about the convent in this moment. Its own turmoil and pessimistic vision. Its wish to simplify and follow the rules. And that the woman in front of them looked more amenable to suggestions. That her stance wasn't so shaky. That her determination didn't seem directed by fright. Sister Morena had seen a few such vexed women insist on crashing into a wall.

The solution, the song, the prayer was the child. Farina. The light that needed to be extended. Both women knew it was not enough to accept her joy at seeing her mother as the only outcome. But it was the outcome standing there in front of the door. The reunion was real and not sentimental, at all, the way that Farina's mother had the girl standing on her own bare feet. It was the only possible element to be deduced from the morning, should the child fall under the Mother Superior's reforms. The reunion as solution was too smooth and simple-minded to say it would turn out for the best. No one knew. But the spirit in the corridor, in the prayers, was that Farina was in God's hands. Waiting even a few more minutes, the child could easily be taken away in the arbitrary reasoning about her interests and be put under the law. That was the risk of letting the pair stay until the footsteps reached them at the door. The law, which was conceived to be above the weaknesses of human beings, fit a plan that might well remove the child and place her in another Florentine home for her own good.

Ugly and difficult the story. Modern as the new world.

Sister Morena looked at Sister Gertrude. The two sets of eyes met firmly in the concordance of their impressions. The hope was slim, nearly an illusion.

But we should ask.

Who?

Sister Morena nodded her head at Milli.

Milli didn't know what they wanted her to explain. The small hand in her hand, and the body leaning against her legs was restless. She sensed danger in their faces and squinty eyes. Would they give her tickets? Would they give her money to get home? It was awkward to ask the heavy lady with glasses. Where were Farina's shoes?

Sister Gertrude nodded firmly at the tall, dark mother. They must leave. Leave before the nets dropped that would surely entangle them and most likely tear them apart. She wished she had some holy word, some token or blessing to leave with the mother, some trace or sign of what she felt in the half day she had spent with her child. The little mural Farina had written and drawn on the wall. She would keep the wolf with the yellow eyes alive. Keep Farina's and Milli's long colorful names alive. Maybe they could find their way back. But the mother might have taken her own action by then.

Sister Gertrude wanted to lean down. She felt the inner bow so strongly it was like falling to her swollen, painful knees. There was no use (since she was pushing them out), to tell Farina how she would remain in her heart, like a special altar, and how her prayers, morning and evening would follow her wherever she went. God, if Farina would look for God, she would find God, because she was so intelligent and alert, but

God had already found her and spoken through Farina's gift to read and write. Why was life this split between the cool air inside and the hot air outside, the city of unceasing traffic, the young people swarming on the steps? Why the sordid rooms where the bodies of these women were paid for? Why was the Mother Superior sick and bent on having her own way just now? Why was she, Sister Gertrude, pushing them out? Why the fierce feeling of love, like a clap of sublime thunder that was forcing her to feel as if she knew. Why was the thrust clear that they had a path?

You must go quickly, Sister Gertrude said, not wanting to elevate her deed. Not wanting even a moment of parallel authority as when Christ's parents were sent into Egypt. Go quickly. God will help you.

Farina looked up and liked the words. The old woman's face was almost crying, but soft. Soft and constant as the music she had heard in the white halls.

Sister Gertrude swept the child back into Milli's arms, as she postponed answering the voice of the Mother Superior calling her name.

You can call. But now, go, and get far from here, Sister Gertrude said, pushing them out and closing the door. Call? Where was she now? In pain, leaning against the wooden door. Her troubled feet on the cool floor with the colored light from the stained glass falling on her face. Standing in the true desert again, since she had no idea if she and Sister Morena had done the right thing. The hard sacrifice of pushing Farina and her mother out remained in her arms. She could feel the strained push. She would have to answer, when the answer was hardly obvious, since Farina's mother had come to the door and had been waiting for guidance inside the convent. Instead she had pushed her back into Florence, into the night world and world of the poor. Pushed her blindly into difficulties, without knowing. The leap, which she had to call faith, was now darkness again, a cliff, a falling off. Hope. Hope that the mother and Farina would have a place to go where what had happened to-day would shelter or shine one ray on a different path.

Sister Gertrude did understand Mother Superior, who, having reached them, looked as if someone had snatched her purse and left her muddled and still confused. She was in her sleeping gown. Her drawstring dangled and she looked sorry, almost as if she would like to enter the chapel to pray.

Life was not just sacrifice and knowing, Sister Gertrude thought, preparing her defense. Life was not. And although she couldn't say that, the mother's face, and Farina's absolutely pure happiness seeing her again, were signs that insisted on a concomitant amount of trust. Whoever they were, Farina and her mother had come this far. And they were re-united, like her own feelings of faith after such deadness. Florence was a dan-gerous place. And Sister Gertrude knew she was pretending if she thought otherwise. But wherever Farina's mother and she were, her presentation of herself at the door showed that they should remain together. Sister Gertrude wished the rest of the conclusion was certain. Instead there were only invisible trails.

Sister Morena was speaking. The mother was young but it was clear who she was; she came for her child. The young nun had no trouble stating the event as she did. They escaped. They ran away. We didn't want to cause another scene. There were only two of us, and she was strong. But she might come back and we could always help her.

Mother Superior Benedetta, standing with her inflamed chest exposed, her hair uncovered, almost despised them both. She had to think before she could say how she might bring the matter to a close. I know you tried, she said. Sometimes those prostitutes, am I right, was she a prostitute, they are so deter-mined, there is no way to stop them. You did well not to force them, she said and turned to walk back to her room, along a corridor that was silent and cool. They can bite and scratch.

AIDS. She wrung her hands at the perilous *percorso* of living a modern life. We will include the child and her mother in our evening Mass.

That which is done shall be done. There is no new thing under the sun.

FIFTEEN

I T HAD BEEN Susan's kind of day, the familial memories jarring, like refuse on the river, bobbing up, as Luigi stood rather empty-handed in front of the grave. Now a Vespa puttered by, making its way illegally inside the gates. Luigi could feel Susan's un-ironic face looking at him, hands on her hips, remonstrating. She had always said awful things like—Dante turned right upside down before he could leave hell. It upset him that she still appeared like Beatrice in moments of real confusion. That was her priestess voice. Tell me. He'd had young, lean years of that. She'd preach, coax and promise hope. Luigi, she'd say, if Dante found illumination in his life by imposing the discipline of exploring his torments and his inner direction, why not you? That was only the lead in, once she found the psychoanalytic channel. She would drag out her books and follow him as he tried to settle down in the next room. She would find a way then to herd him around the sandtrap. How she could rely on symbols when there were facts?

Women. Still, Luigi had to nod approval at Susan even now. She was a thoughtful mother and he and she got along better than most people with their own families. Women were not Florence's sickness. It was the men who were wrong. The turgid compromisers, the split sly minds that gave in too fast and let themselves forget about real hard truth. The bankers. The politicians. Luigi wiped the sweat from both sides of his nose. His mother would have been already saying that she was worried. Get out of the sun. You'll burn. But she would have meant she didn't like him swiping his face with his sleeve.

I'm going to change all the towels in the house, Luigi said out loud. Every single white towel is going to go. No more showers where the slightest grime of mine is left to show on the white fluffy pile. No more handprints left and then the linen discarded.

No more of those white things hanging in the bath after I come home today and take off my things as I enter the house, dropping my shoes, and loosening my belt, and dropping my pants, and wiping off my sweat. I will walk naked down the hall, and my penis will lie heavy between my legs, and after soiling them with my errors, I'll stuff the towels in a bag. After today, no more traces of me left on impeccable towels, with quiet but unending dread that I have just sullied the way the house is to be. Leaving marring imperfection. Those white spy surfaces sopping up all signs of life demand that when I wash I am to wash all lapses off and emerge, immaculate and perfumed like a good pink man. *Per carita*, no telltale sign left of the dog's blood, or my jealousy for Gian Franco, or my weakness in the face of Maria Grazia. No more. The white towels will vanish. No chance remaining after today for you, mother, to sample me and my moves as I wash, drown myself, at least once, with the showerhead turned to hard, the wasted water pounding my chest and my butt and my thinning hair, the water marking me. Stepping out, dripping like a hairy male should, I will wipe whatever dead skin comes off, the scabs and scum, the patches of sweat and semen and leave it on the towels for you as evidence of this morning's flagellation. Then out they go.

Having orated that, Luigi wished that he felt less foolish, less regret. Less wimpy. Could Darwin have reached the decision to throw out his mother's linens as the culmination of years of tormenting scientific doubts? Could St. Augustine for that matter? Or Gramsci from prison?

Seduced. Softened and domesticated. Sold out for the long deadly call of stability by allowing oneself to be seduced. That is the story of this very moment, Luigi thought, sadly. Men are missing. Clones are in and wired to be seduced. Seduced by the slight of hand that makes the illegal legal and the word 'culture' a kind of science that belongs to the black box in the living room where marketers have shoved in an incessant stream of adverts and American pop songs. A slight of hand and hypnosis and although the judges are asking for clean hands, for hands to stop taking their suitcases full of lire and the cuts that now have Gian Franco in difficulty, there is a feeling that money is almost irrelevant. Money's okay and a part of life and there should be plenty for all, just like in America, in Dallas. Spoil sports those judges, if by catching the politicians, they stop the money from flowing freely everywhere in the city, flowing without being restrained by legal measures and taxes and rules.

Fraud. Deception. Hot accusations. Yet everybody knew and knows. And while now, they have suddenly become the focus of the judges looking at the banks and the politicians, already the people in togas are being driven back into their dens. Already, the arid singsong of TV and buying—culture as nothing—is taking over houses and leveling any capacity to measure the truth. My father, Luigi thought. He always objected to celebrity and money brandished. To bribes and the mix with politics that Umberto with shrewd and, not completely cynical, faith pursued. Cesare objected to falling, although he fell, he objected to falling down to the level of a money-worshipping beast.

Luigi touched his father's name again in the dry marble. He

rubbed his fingers along each crisp letter. Cesare had a shy integrity. Not like the grit and self imposed steel of the judges in this moment. Not like me, Luigi thought, as he saw himself favorably in the miniscule minority at the university. Not like the luminous thread of science that could be picked up, regardless of how pitifully it was handled by people who had entered the university by bribe and by agreement.

Cesare might well have enjoyed this moment of glory for the judges. And in the twenty years since his death, what would have changed for his father? He would not have been among the accusers. He would have been satisfied by the turn of events. But not convinced, just as he had been skeptical then. Every minute is a possibility for losing ground. And he would have sadly pointed to the new elections and the new wave of banality, as the obscuring of truth.

Maria Grazia's phone was off. The metallic voice, which was made of silicon, insulted him every time. It was emotionally depressing to hear it and to think Maria Grazia could switch on or off. As well as he could. Switch off or on.

Maria Grazia was nearly everything and not just because of the work she did for him. But she was brilliant. She could easily, if she would ever leave Florence and leave the borders of Italy itself, she could easily do solid work that would soar in the annals of tree genetics.

She had said to him, just once in recent weeks, it cuts both ways.

How irritated he had felt. It was a declaration of some independence that made him feel uncomfortable, even unloved.

Why it had remained festering in his mind he didn't know. She had said, love cuts both ways.

Cuts. That was what slowed him down. That harsh, slightly under her breath, threat. But now in the light falling into the green algae clamped to a few of the letters cut from the marble to form his father's name, he saw cutting was what released the name. The strength of the hand tapping the chisel fascinated him. The C with its ancient curve. The E going back to Greek.

She would not change her mind. To the extent that she loved him she was not one for tolerance. Tolerance was for a dying man. Tolerance was the way unchecked stability could produce languid robots or stupid slaves.

Luigi wished he had something to tell Maria Grazia. Something that would make her bend. He didn't want the child. And they couldn't go on repeating that conversation.

But it was already on its way into the world. She would run it, and he would make adjustments, if he had to prove a point. Luigi wrestled one red rose from Giada's vase. Another.

Luigi knew he was going to live with the strain. The intricate strain of love. It had its compensations. But they were difficult to hold onto as long as both of them could turn the switches off and on.

The cypress that Piero was finally thinking about. The brooding trees standing like dying Etruscan warriors all around the cemetery. What his student was looking at were precisely the switches that not only gave but took. He was looking at an exchange, not like the politicians, who took, or the doctors or the shopkeepers who made their calculations and took cuts on an exaggerated basis, nor was he was looking, in a simple minded way, at the exchange that you must give to get. No, Piero was finally clicking on an idea that had been waiting millennia to be tested. Trees had found enough mild aggression to live. He was onto a tree language that had to do with giving off to the atmosphere the most necessary element for the lives of others, a generous beneficence for the health and peace of all life, while subtly taking in, not only because it was unused, but because it was a way of supplementing the long journey of nutrients coming up from the roots, a cocktail that it needed from the air. How long that subtle grasping set of gulps had taken to develop.

Piero had some promise. It was comforting to think of him rising like a star, of taking the boy in hand, who, perhaps, was focusing for the first time and pointing his inclinations in the direction of real science where patterns lifted up above human ideas like injustice. There was seclusion and solace in discovering a specific response to stimuli that had not been explicated before. Luigi flinched, startled by the thorn pricking his finger, as he tugged another rose from the vase. Maria Grazia might like directing part of the work. She could plan the analysis of the volume of plant intake from the needles. Not exactly a proposal with a diamond ring. Not precisely a cradle. Luigi nearly regretted that he got such joy and could become another person when, the minute before, he had been devastated with sadness and guilt. Science made it easy in some ways. No wonder Maria Grazia would flash him those intolerant stares when he smiled thinking that logic would justify and enrich his offer to her.

The red light was blinking when she stepped in, followed by her neighbors, who made the dog sit. Realizing the muddy animal should never have entered with her long swinging tail, Signora Caffo ordered Marta out. Out, to sit in the garden.

It was a message again. She'd missed the moment, by being in the yard. There it was, another message in a day of struggling with messages, flesh that was not flesh. A blinking red light. If it was Vaclav's voice, if he had called again, the decision had been made in the sand itself. The sand had stirred her memories up and now, two hours after she had thought the opposite, she would call him back. Susan felt the uncontrolled flood rise. She would speak to him. She would tell him how she could not reach their life, any more than he could, and yet how it lived in her blood, in her cells. If the voice behind the red light told her, sorrowfully, that Vaclav was dead, if it delivered that cruel blow, she would return the call, asking to be met. Saying somehow that she would find a flight to Prague. Teresa's imminent exhumation was giving her something. Susan was touching deep sources in her own buried life. Touching them and not pushing them back down. Even if the voice was just Luigi's, or Marina's, before calling the *Belle Arte*, she would ring them back. They were dear to her, dear. She turned to Signor Caffo. Do you mind?

Why she had not expected it was normal. As normal and not magic as why she had begun to look at the story of Demeter and Persephone. Why the sadness of the day had gone on and on with an intimation of unheralded change once Teresa was acknowledged. The day, in some mysterious way, was carrying, in that revisited grave, the gleanings of her life. The voice, not one she knew, was telling her, kindly, awkwardly, that she would never be whole.

Dave Sanecki calling, from Silver Leaf, your mother's retirement home. I'm afraid, Ms. Notingham, that I have some real sad news.

Melandri asked his technician to turn the slide machine off. In the six or seven minutes left he wanted the screen retracted and the whole chapel given over to the light. The light was moving down the west wall. It was shaking and jumping since the currents near the lantern window that was letting it in were moving.

If you will all turn your heads, but please remain in your seats or otherwise people will be blocked from getting a view, what you see brightly concentrated on the wall is light from the sun, brought into a shape given by the gnomon. It is not a ray. Light travels in waves at the speed of 299,792.8 kilometers per second, but we are not seeing a wavelength or a ray. A ray, *un raggio*, is a word with a Latin root, radius referring to the spoke of a wheel. A ray is in the eyes of the beholder. Radiating and radiant, we bring about a ray and the way we conceive of it as an arrow. There is no such thing except that we see the white light we have funneled through a slot. Really this intense swab of light on the wall, which is seen as a column in space, is dancing particles if anything. The ray, if anything, is a sign that is man-made. And while the light from the sun has been traveling towards us, the fact is that the earth is spinning on its own axis and also moving in an orbit around the sun. The blotted brilliant sunlight moving on the wall moves because we are moving. The earth is moving and we have nearly no sense of it. But as the story I told you today said, measuring deviations in the position of the earth's movement on its own axis was Ximenes' experiment. And the earlier readings taken of the meridian were to declare the summer solstice when the light actually struck the line as opposed to the predicted calendar time. And you will all see this now if you arrange yourselves around the meridian.

It will come very fast, this traveler, expected and predicted to hit the line for more than five-hundred years. It will come down today, too, and sweep across the floor, hovering and it is easy to see why light held and holds such power. How human beings ponder over its appearance and disappearance. And how we gladly accept its mantle. Melandri stopped speaking and watched the faces of the group around him. The barriers to the meridian were being strained. People were pushing, and the usual inequality appeared obvious between the first comers and the late comers, the short versus the tall, and there was the American standing nearly a head above the people around him. And Ester Bobanelli, he couldn't even see her.

Please sit down those of you in the front rows. Otherwise no one will see. The fact is that Toscanelli more than five-hundred years later has made nearly perfect calculations although now they are really of no use, which is not to say that their truth is of no use, nor their inspiration. The dome still stands because Brunelleschi made the right, absolutely unimagined, conclusions. Toscanelli, too, was accurate and reached as far as he could go. His predictions are very close to what modern math foresees. Nevertheless, because of complexities in counting time, and the slight alteration of the ecliptic, the axis the earth spins on, this ray is now arriving at approximately one sixteen, modern Italian summer time. The true solstice took place at eight o'clock this morning. And the light is a spectacle, a part in a ceremony, that we human beings can only witness, and even today, never wholly penetrate.

The sunlight danced like a dervish, a goddess that didn't want to stop. The revolving color at once the yellow of flowers, of daffodils and sunflowers, and golden silk, a nimbus snatched from Giotto, a set of glowing fires seen in a goblet of white wine, a color that was not common to Florence, light being not the subject of the way people were seen, the yellow golden presence was awesome, intimate, intimidating as it teased and rubbed, vibrated, took up all the attention that its wordless dancing attracted and it danced on, nearly touching the floor, but still staggering and lingering on the wall.

The light poured through the gnomon anchored at the window from a mass of light pouring from the fire of the sun. The sun outside Brunelleschi's dome shown on the orange tiles, beat down on them. It had long slipped into the room where Michelangelo's river god was stretched and floated light on the long lap of the god spilling. It pounded goldenly on the mold that he had made from mud and sticks and bronze. It shown on the Niger, catching in the long wavy puddles of slick oil, going out in iridescent flares. Not yet up for many hours to warm the city, it meandered and collected in the white soap-suds eddies of the Mississippi near Charlotte's retirement home. It struck the backs of ducks in the water and the truck cabs of drivers like Don Gourevitch driving west on the freeway.

The sun was hot in Florence and hot in Susan Notingham's garden, where the Caffo's dog sat, hot in the convent, hot in

Igor's explosively closed room. It stifling presence added to the airless feeling in Piero's house when he stood up from the table and his father slapped him. It laid itself inside every ripple on the Arno as boaters pushed past and swirled it around like painters mixing hues. Down it filtered through the sick cypresses in the cemetery.

The sun was shining. Trees were using its light. Palm trees and cypresses and oaks. Gian Franco had found his lawyer's number and telephoned him from his parked car. Milli was thinking hard about calling Irene. She had money on the plastic card and was confused now about where to go. Susan was standing in front of the Caffos and crying. Charlotte was dead. In the house itself, the sun reached only through windows, that in their way, were gnomons. They were slits to let in what could not be sustained or felt for hours on end, the sunlight. The light coming in through the shutters filled the sandbox, and poured over for a few minutes the picturesque toy trees and owl. Ramada was walking towards Bori and the sun scalded his face, and indicated his direction. Not that its blinding power had a meaning, not that anything was being measured. It fell on him and made him hurry, even though he felt faint. And the sun fell on Virgil, a reader of sun, a reader like the cypresses and the wild oaks in the forests of Bucharest, readers of rays, like Toscanelli and Galileo, and Melandri who tried with utmost humility to find one more detail in an infinite cosmos. The sunlight fell on Virgil who felt an opaqueness drop from his eyes. There was no trace left of the morning's travail. He had swallowed the last dead cell and uncovered his new skin.

The sun and the ray, Melandri said. One is unknowable and the other belongs to human understanding and invention. Here comes the light. Watch its speed as it strikes the brass line, the meridian that took money from the Catholic coffers to conceive, the summer solstice declared, because it is waited for on a line embedded in the cathedral. The meridian, like all experiments, defines one fluid glimpse of a reality, defined by the experiment itself.

Luigi is dialing Maria Grazia again.

Piero sits and, as he closes his eyes, he thinks that suffering, too, is illusion.

Your honor, Guidice Pingello, the plump prostitute says, I hope my story helps.

Down under the soil in Susan Notingham's yard, the skeleton, whose name was once Cocolichi, lies flat next to a linen papoose.

Aki watches a tear blot his name as he finishes his letter with no address.

Irene is lying in the dark.

In the study, twenty unopened tapes hold a voice that made itself cheerful whenever it could.

Signor and Signora Caffo have quietly closed the gate.

Sunlight is breaking into seven colors in Maria Grazia's prism.

Carlo has just taken Marina back into his arms.

And that long sensitive finger touching the convent's bell. It's Milli's. She presses the brass button hard. She's holding Farina in her other arm. She won't lift it until someone opens the door.

Once. Now. Arvon. Virgil. The gardener. Emmanuel who is standing at Susan's door.

Doors. The Arno. Horses that the police ride. The horses in Cocolichi's tomb. Oil. Thomas Simpson's daughter's horse. Oil. Oil in the rivers. Oil and the banks. Cypress. The sandbox. Pears. Maria Grazia's guppies who mourn. The orange dome with its nine spheres. The cell. The phone. Vaclav Slovecki's empty bed. Luigi's parents' bed. Identity as passport. As place. As story. As stars.

Melandri felt fine calling for applause. Here the ray is, just on time, since time is something we invented. Here it, or is it she or he, here the sunlight has come and is striking the meridian. Now people, applaud the ray's information, applaud Toscanelli and Ximenes, those proud Florentine minds, applaud all that transpired to make us understand that the earth is spinning and is not at the center of this universe we are still exploring. Applaud the light and the sun in the cathedral. Here it is, the round image of the gnomon having reached the floor. Ladies and Gentlemen. The ray has arrived with learning that lifted darkness. Applaud summer. It's official. Applaud Florence and its history.

AUTHOR'S NOTE

I wish to thank Jeffrey Miller, the publisher of Cadmus Editions, for having said "yes" to my unsolicited manuscript, *Toscanelli's Ray*. The odds for an independent publishing house to flourish are special and call for people who are willing to take risks. Believing in a mission to enlarge the collective imagination through the books that they publish, they open ways crucial to keeping culture authentic.

Jeffrey Miller decided to set *Toscanelli's Ray* in a typeface called "Arno." The electronic font draws upon early Italian humanistic ones. Named for the river in the city in which the novel takes place, its glints are beautifully suited for mixing past and present. Colleen Dwire, who composed the book, contributed greatly to the lively feel of the pages. Thanks, too, to John Taylor-Convery for his superb finishing touch.

I am grateful for two separate stays at Yaddo during which I wrote parts of this novel. Many readers looked over drafts and gave supportive pushes: these include Kathleen Cambor, the late Shirley Jeffrey, John Peck, Martha Haynes, Susan Tiberghien, Jonathan Galassi, Vassili Serebriakov, Clare Menozzi, Paolo Menozzi, Gail Hochman, Anna Podesta, Lois Clegg, Lisa Wilde, Alex Wilde and Susan Schulman, my agent.

My dear friend, Elizabeth Pauncz, who has lived in Florence for more than forty years, is the primary reason that I know Florence well. We watched the solstice ceremony in Santa Maria del Fiore in 1997, when the meridian in the floor of the church was uncovered and the gnomon, first set ninety meters up in a southern part of the cupola lantern by Paolo Toscanelli in the fifteenth century, was used in a ceremony marking the cathedral's seven hundred years.

Sunlight, having reached the gnomon, took the form of a disc. It captured us all, seemingly gliding on air currents, a bobbing circle of light descending along the walls for an hour until it touched the cathedral floor. It fluttered and whirled and, for brief golden minutes, matched perfectly the larger marble circle in the meridian embedded in the floor of the Chapel of the Cross. The novel found its genesis in that bobbing circle of light.

I visited the observatory in Arcetri, the Archives in Florence, the Mugnone River; at each stop my story grew. The image each of us invents about a city as venerable and beloved as Florence was gradually challenged by the stressed, contemporary city, flooded by tourists. When I wandered down along the Mugnone, and discovered, under the bridge, an African woman asleep, with a little girl playing alongside her in the grass, I met Milli. She awoke, startled and shaking her fists. I glimpsed wide-eyed obedient Farina, who looked the other way.

Farina is the character that most captured my imagination. But the real child, whom I stumbled across near the river, concerns me more. Her destiny played through the lives and perceptions of all my characters. The book is pure fiction. Everything is an invention in an imagined space, drawn with the colors of actual events. Nevertheless, like Saint Exupery's rose, it matters if Farina is safe.

ACKNOWLEDGEMENTS AND CREDITS

One of photographer Franco Furoncoli's most sought-after books is a study of light in the Parma Cathedral over a period of 365 days. He and his son Francesco are responsible for the cover photograph of Brunelleschi's dome and the sun. It took them a day of climbing on bridges and cars to find the place from which to shoot.

David Battistella, a Canadian filmmaker and writer, generously offered his scintillating photos of the solstice ceremony and the Duomo. His special angles on the city are part of a larger exploration for his film on Brunelleschi.

Piero's essay on trees contains some material from the two volume book, *The Monumental Trees of Italy*. A review of books about cosmological issues in Church science published by Ingrid D. Rowland in the "New York Review of Books," February 22, 2001 was a brilliant and useful summary of many things dealt with in my pages. The text from Peter Grimes was taken from that essay.

Luigi's concluding thought on the women in his life echoes Anna Akhmatova's line about her relationship to her husband, Nicolai Gumilev.

Here are suggestions for further reading:

Lucciole nere, Iyamu Kennedy, Pino Nicotri, le prostitute nigeriane si raccontano, Kaos editioni, Milano, 1997

Mai piu' Schiave, Slaves no more, Anna Pozzi, Federazione Stampa Missionaria Italiana, EMI della Coop. SERMIS, Bologna, 2008

Etruscologia, Massimo Pallottino, Hoepli, Milano, seventh edition, 1984

Teresa of Avila, The progress of a soul, Cathleen Medwick, Doubleday, New York, 1999

The Sun in the Church, J.L. Heilbron, Harvard University Press, Cambridge, Massachusetts, London, England, fourth printing 2001

The Homeric Hymn to Demeter, Translation, Commentary, and Interpretive Essays, Helene P. Foley, Editor, Princeton University Press, Princeton, New Jersey, third edition, 1999

A Short History of the Italian Peoples, J.P. Trevelyn, George Allen and Unwin Ltd, London, fourth edition, 1956

Dante's Inferno, Italian text with English translation, John D. Sinclair, Oxford University Press, Oxford, reprint, 1969

Il "Gioco della Sabbia" nella Pratica Analitica, a cura di Francesco Montecchi, FrancoAngeli, Milano, 1997

Sandplay Therapy, Treatment of Psychpathologies, edited by Eva Pattis Zoja, Daimon Verlag, 2004

Mitologia Degli Alberi, Jacques Brosse, Supersaggi, Rizzoli, Milano, 1989

Gli alberi monumentali d'Italia, Edizione Abete, Roma, 1989, text, Alfonso Alessandrini, Federico Fazzud, Stanislao Nievo, Mario Rigoni Stern, Lucio Bortolotti

Nigeria since Independence, Crippled Giant, Eghosa E. Osaghae, Indiana University Press, Bloomington and Indianapolis, 1998

This House has Fallen, Midnight in Nigeria, Karl Maier, Public Affairs, NYC, NY, 2000

The Famished Road, Ben Okri, Anchor Books, Random House, New York, 1991

Home and Exile, Chinua Achebe, Oxford University Press, Oxford, 2000

Fortune is a River, Leonardo Da Vinci and Niccolo' Machiavelli's Magnificent Dream to Change the Course of Florentine History, Roger D. Masters, Plume, Penguin, New York, 1999

Florence, A Delicate Case, David Leavitt, Bloomsbury, New York and London, 2002

A Firenze Ai Tempi di Dante, Pierre Antonetti, translated from the French, in series La Vita Quotidiana, Rizzoli, 1998

The Dark Heart of Italy, Tobias Jones, Faber and Faber, London, 2003

ABOUT THE AUTHOR

Wallis Wilde-Menozzi grew up in Wisconsin and resides in Parma, Italy where she has participated in Italian life for more than thirty years. Her memoir, *Mother Tongue: An American Life in Italy* was published by North Point Press to critical acclaim. *The Other Side of the Tiber, Reflections on Time in Italy*, Farrar, Straus and Giroux ("a rare and mesmerizing book . . ." Rosanna Warren) was released on the same day as *Toscanelli's Ray*. A collection of her prize-winning essays appeared in Italian in 2011: *L'oceano è dentro di noi*, Moretti e Vitalli. A founding member of the international Ledig Rowohlt Writers Residence in Lavigny, Switzerland, Wilde-Menozzi has been characterized as a "cauldron of a mind."

This
first
edition of
W a l l i s
Wilde-Menozzi's *Toscanelli's*
Ray has been printed for Cadmus
Editions by McNaughton & Gunn in
February 2013. Composed and set in Robert
Slimbach's Arno, a typeface named for the river
which runs through Florence, this face draws its
inspiration from 15th and 16th century early
humanistic typefaces such as Venetian and Aldine.
Book design by Colleen Dwire and Jeffrey Miller.